FA C PREMIERSHIP

POCKET ANNUAL 1993-94

Editor Bruce Smith

Phil Heady

1st Year of Publication

Cover photograph: Eric Cantona (Manchester United) attempts to beat his
cross City rival Keith Curle in the FA Premier League derby game.

ISBN: 1-898351-01-5

Typeset by Bruce Smith Books Ltd

Printed and bound in Great Britain

Words on Sport
Bruce Smith Books Limited
PO Box 382
St. Albans
Herts, AL2 3JD

CONTENTS

Acknowledgments

Many thanks to all those people who have contributed in one way or another to this first FA Carling Premiership Annual. Phil Heady in particular for his efforts in producing the Players A-Z which was no mean task along with the various other statistics that he compiled. Sue Thearle for the various club reviews and checking through various aspects of the publication.

In house thanks go to Late-Late Crew of Peter Fitzpatrick, Martin Ritchie, Dave Tavener, Tanuja Warnsewak, Flo Naughton and Mark Webb.

Review of 1992-93 Season

There's something strangely ironic that, having waited and failed to win the Football League Division One Championship for 26 years, Manchester United should win the first FA Premier League title. In the end United finished very strongly recording seven successive wins to achieve a ten point margin over the team that looked as though they might snatch it from them, Aston Villa.

The turning point for United came in their home encounter with Arsenal on 24th March. The Highbury side dominated the game for large periods and a second half volley from Paul Merson rattled the crossbar late in the game. Had that gone in then United would have had just 2 points from 12 with confidence draining. As it was they survived and wins over long-time rivals Norwich City, Sheffield Wednesday, Coventry City, Chelsea, Crystal Palace, Blackburn Rovers and Wimbledon ensured the championship trophy was presented at the end of a most memorable night against Blackburn Rovers.

Despite Villa's challenge it was unfashionable Norwich City who were in the driving seat for long periods of the season. As 1992 entered its last month the Canaries had established an eight point lead over Blackburn Rovers,

FA Premier League Final Table 1992-93

	P	W	D	L	F	A	Pts
MANCHESTER UNITED	42	24	12	6	67	31	84
Aston Villa	42	21	11	10	57	40	74
Norwich City	42	21	9	12	61	65	72
Blackburn Rovers	42	20	11	11	68	46	71
Queens Park Rangers	42	17	12	13	63	55	63
Liverpool	42	16	11	15	62	55	59
Sheffield Wednesday	42	15	14	13	55	51	59
Tottenham Hotspur	42	16	11	15	60	66	59
Manchester City	42	15	12	15	56	51	57
Arsenal	42	15	11	16	40	38	56
Chelsea	42	14	14	14	51	54	56
Wimbledon	42	14	12	16	56	55	54
Everton	42	15	8	19	53	55	53
Sheffield United	42	14	10	18	54	53	52
Coventry City	42	13	13	16	52	57	52
Ipswich Town	42	12	16	14	50	55	52
Leeds United	42	12	15	15	57	62	51
Southampton	42	13	11	18	54	61	50
Oldham Athletic	42	13	10	19	63	74	49
Crystal Palace	42	11	16	15	48	61	49
Middlesbrough	42	11	11	20	54	75	44
Nottingham Forest	42	10	10	22	41	62	40

Aston Villa and Chelsea with Manchester United 12 points behind in seventh place. As the season ended the first month of the new year Norwich remained in top spot. However the interim period was to prove disastrous having taken just nine points from a possible 27 and failing to score in five successive games.

Aston Villa took over the mantle as main contender and for long periods Atkinson's side looked the more likely winners especially after going top of the pile on 13th February with a 1-0 win at Chelsea. But, as with Norwich in the previous months, the goals began to dry up. Dean Saunders – who proved to be such a sensational buy from Liverpool – found the back of the net only twice in their last 15 games of the season. And when they lost 3-0 at Blackburn towards the end of April their challenge was all but gone.

Without doubt the driving force behind United's triumph was Paul Ince whose performances led him to the England captaincy in the close season tour of the USA. Ince, a £1.5 million signing from West Ham United in September 1989 was just one of a range of expensive imports totalling over £19 million.

How the Champions were Bought:

Player	From	Fee	Date
Brian McClair	Celtic	£850,000	Jun 87
Viv Anderson	Arsenal	£250,000	Jul 87
Steve Bruce	Norwich	£825,000	Dec 87
Lee Sharpe	Torquay	£180,000	May 88
Jim Leighton	Aberdeen	£750,000	May 88
Mark Hughes	Barcelona	£1,800,000	Jun 88
Mal Donaghy	Luton	£650,000	Oct 88
Ralph Milne	Bristol City	£170,000	Nov 88
Giuliano Maiorana	Histon	£30,000	Nov 88
Mike Phelan	Norwich	£750,000	Jun 89
Neil Webb	Nottm Forest	£1,000,000	Jun 89
Brian Carey	Cork	£100,000	Jul 89
Gary Pallister	Middlesbrough	£2,300,000,	Aug 89
Danny Wallace	Southampton	£1,200,000	Sep 89
Paul Ince	West Ham	£1,500,000	Sep 89
Les Sealey	Luton	Free	Jun 90
Dennis Irwin	Oldham	£625,000	Jun 90
Neil Whitworth	Wigan	£150,000	Jun 90
Andrei Kanchelskis	Donetsk	£850,000	Apr 91
Peter Schmeichel	Brondby	£550,000	Jul 91
Paul Parker	QPR	£2,000,000	Aug 91
Dion Dublin	Cambridge	£1,000,000	Aug 92
Pat McGibbon	Portadown	£100,000	Aug 92
Eric Cantona	Leeds	£1,200,000	Nov 92
Les Sealey	Aston Villa	Free	Jan 93
	Total	£19,130,000	

Blackburn Rovers effectively fell out of contention on Boxing Day when Alan Shearer was injured after scoring twice against Leeds United. Despite hitting Norwich City for seven to record the largest score, 7-1, of the season in the Premier League, they failed to find the net in their next four matches.

At the start of the season Arsenal were clear favourites to take the first FA Premier League title – they failed miserably but found suitable compensation in becoming the first club ever to win both domestic cup competitions. Their total of 40 league goals was less than relegated Nottingham Forest. Despite failing to score in 19 of their matches they did top the table in early November following six straight wins.

Another side to disappoint were Liverpool – finishing sixth thanks to a last day 6-2 thrashing of Tottenham Hotspur who perhaps had their minds more on the Boardroom tussles than those on the pitch.

The sales of Des Walker and Darren Wassall in the close season were never plugged by Brian Clough and this caused concern among many pundits as the season started for Nottingham Forest. But a 1-0 win over Liverpool in front of the Sky Sports cameras on the opening day of the season seemed to calm the nerves. However, the scorer of that winner Teddy Sheringham, was soon on his way to Tottenham and as the goals dried up they were soon conceded and in the end Forest's good football was never enough to keep them in the top sphere. They were joined by Crystal Palace who had a disastrous 1993 and Middlesbrough, who despite a late rally paid for earlier defeats.

Arsenal and Sheffield Wednesday contested both the Wembley finals. In both cases they were won for the Gunners by most unlikely heroes. Steve Morrow – an Irish International – was on hand to snap up a poor clearance by Carlton Palmer to clinch the Coca-Cola Cup only to have his FA Cup Final place painfully taken from him by skipper Tony Adams who in his celebrations dropped Morrow on his shoulder breaking it in the process. In the FA Cup Final Andy Linighan – often taunted by the Arsenal supporters – rose to meet a Paul Merson corner seconds from the end of extra time in the reply to make it a Gunners Cup double.

Huge disappointment for the Hillsborough club who sacrificed the good football that had taken them to Wembley and provided them with one of their best league campaigns for many a year. Seeking safety first for the FA Cup Final they moved their top scorer, Paul Warhurst, back to the defence which he had exploded from as a re-vamped centre forward and used the running power of Palmer to shackle Merson.

The new 1993-94 season starts with sponsorship and a new name – the FA Carling Premiership. Manchester United move into the Champions' Cup, Arsenal the Cup-Winners' Cup, Villa the UEFA cup joined by Norwich City in their first ever European venture.

European Review

In Europe FA Premier League teams struggled to make any real progress and the wounds opened by an enforced exile are still there to be seen – despite Manchester United's Cup-Winners' Cup triumph of 1991. For many parts the three competitions will doubtless be remembered as much for what happened off the field as on it. Marseille won the Champions' Cup but the French bribery scandal looks set to run and run long after the final itself has receded into distant memory, the progress of the British teams was to be much admired.

Without doubt the tie of the first round was Leeds United's epic against Stuttgart. Making their first appearance in European competition for 17 years, Leeds lost the first leg in Germany 3-0 and looked certain to exit the competition despite a valiant 4-1 fightback in the second leg at Elland Road.

But, remarkably, the Germans were found to have fielded an illegal foreign player and UEFA ordered the match to be replayed in Barcelona on a Friday night, after Leeds had been awarded a 3-0 home result. Happily for English football, justice was seen to be done when substitute Carl Shutt gave his side a well-deserved victory with a late winner, after the irrepressible Gordon Strachan had put Leeds in front.

However, the Yorkshire side's joy was short-lived. The second round draw threw up the intriguing prospect of a Championship of Britain, the English champions against Scottish champions Rangers, who eventually ran out relatively easy winners.

Gary McAllister struck the first blow in this epic contest, scoring an unbelievable 25-yard drive after just two minutes of the first leg. But on a wet and windy night at Ibrox, Rangers fought their way back into contention thanks to a goal from poacher extraordinaire Ally McCoist and an own goal from Leeds keeper John Lukic, who inexplicably punched the ball into his own net direct from a corner.

Regrettably Leeds did not fare much better in the second leg. Mark Hateley produced a spectacular 30-yard volley again after just two minutes of the contest, and McCoist added a second before Leeds could reply with a late consolation from Eric Cantona.

A 2-0 FA Cup victory had given Liverpool the opportunity to emulate the achievement of rivals Manchester United in the Cup-Winners' Cup by lifting the trophy that had previously been won by Merseyside neighbours Everton in 1985.

Graeme Souness's side kicked off their campaign against Cypriot Cup holders Apollon Limassol at Anfield. An early goal from Paul Stewart set the crowd's nerves at ease and another Stewart strike, plus a four-goal blast from Ian Rush, who surpassed Roger Hunt's European goal-scoring record in the process, clinched an impressive first-leg advantage of 6-1.

Limassol's task was not made any easier by the somewhat harsh dismissal of midfielder Marios Charalambous, and their resolve had all but disappeared by the time Liverpool travelled to Cyprus for the second leg and conjured a 2-1 victory, courtesy of goals from Rush, inevitably, and Don Hutchison.

In the second round Liverpool were in all sorts of trouble after a calamitous first leg trip to Spartak Moscow. Like Manchester United before them in the UEFA Cup, whose downfall was precipitated by a miserable excursion to Moscow, Liverpool soon found themselves facing an uphill battle.

The main cause of their downfall was a disastrous defence which eventually conceded four goals, two of which were the direct result of catastrophic errors of judgement by goalkeeper Bruce Grobbelaar, who was eventually sent off for a professional foul. Goals from Mark Wright and Steve McManaman briefly offered the Merseysiders hope of a 2-2 draw, but with Grobbelaar's 82nd minute dismissal, Spartak added two more goals and the tie was effectively relinquished.

Graeme Souness's reaction after the game cost him a UEFA touchline ban for allegedly abusing the referee and, two weeks later, in front of 38,000 Liverpool fans at Anfield, the vulnerability of the Liverpool defence was cruelly exposed once more as the home side crashed to an embarrassing 2-0 defeat to leave the contest, the fourth English side to fail to get further than the second round of any of the competitions.

FA Premier League clubs entered the UEFA Cup full of confidence. Manchester United, winners of the Rumbelows Cup, had emerged from a traumatic season when they had narrowly failed to clinch their first league title for 25 years, with a powerful young squad well-equipped for European competition.

But their high hopes for a repeat of the success they enjoyed in 1991 in the Cup-Winners' competition were not to be. A goalless draw at home to Torpedo Moscow left United facing a tricky away leg in the Russian capital. Needing to score, the United attack failed to breach the Moscow rearguard, and despite extra-time, the only way of deciding the tie was the inevitable and odious penalty shoot-out, where Alex Ferguson's side capitulated 4-3.

Meanwhile Sheffield Wednesday, English football's other representatives in the competition, were continuing to develop as future title contenders under the watchful gaze of manager Trevor Francis. Wednesday it was who made the most impressive start, producing the highest score of the first round with an 8-1 demolition of Spora Luxembourg, with Paul Warhurst showing all the predatory instincts he demonstrated later in the season to collect a brace of goals. However, he narrowly escaped death when he swallowed his tongue. But the young striker/defender recovered in time to play in the second leg and notch another goal as Wednesday recorded a 10-2 aggregate victory.

Wednesday's next opponents in the competition produced a disastrous result. German Bundesliga side Kaiserslautern triumphed 3-1 at home and to make matters worse, England ace David Hirst was sent off in a bad-tempered encounter. A 2-2 draw at Hillsborough spelt the end for Wednesday and European participation for Premier League clubs.

FA Carling Premiership Pre-Season Odds

As supplied by William Hills before the start of the season:

7-4	Manchester United
5-1	Arsenal
7-1	Blackburn Rovers
	Liverpool
8-1	Aston Villa
16-1	Newcastle United
	Sheffield Wednesday
20-1	Leeds United
33-1	Manchester City
	Tottenham Hotspur
40-1	Chelsea
	Everton
	Norwich City
	Queens Park Rangers
66-1	West Ham United
100-1	Sheffield United
	Wimbledon
125-1	Ipswich Town
150-1	Coventry City
	Southampton
200-1	Oldham Athletic
	Swindon Town

FINAL TABLES 1992-93

FA Premier League

	P	W	D	L	F	A	W	D	L	F	A	Pts
			HOME						AWAY			
Manchester United	42	14	5	2	39	14	10	7	4	28	17	84
Aston Villa	42	13	5	3	36	16	8	6	7	21	24	74
Norwich City	42	13	6	2	31	19	8	3	10	30	46	72
Blackburn Rovers	42	13	4	4	38	18	7	7	7	30	28	71
Queens Park Rangers	42	11	5	5	41	32	6	7	8	22	23	63
Liverpool	42	13	4	4	41	18	3	7	11	21	37	59
Sheffield Wednesday	42	9	8	4	34	36	6	9	6	21	25	59
Tottenham Hotspur	42	11	5	5	40	25	5	6	10	20	41	59
Manchester City	42	7	8	6	30	25	8	4	9	26	26	57
Arsenal	42	8	6	7	24	20	7	5	9	15	18	56
Chelsea	42	9	7	5	29	22	5	7	9	22	32	56
Wimbledon	42	9	4	8	32	32	5	8	8	24	32	54
Everton	42	7	6	8	25	26	8	2	11	27	28	53
Sheffield United	42	10	6	5	33	19	4	4	13	21	34	52
Coventry City	42	7	4	10	29	28	6	9	6	23	29	52
Ipswich Town	42	8	9	4	29	22	4	7	10	21	33	52
Leeds United	42	12	8	1	40	17	0	7	14	17	45	51
Southampton	42	10	6	5	30	21	3	5	13	24	40	50
Oldham Athletic	42	10	6	5	43	30	4	3	14	20	44	49
Crystal Palace	42	6	9	6	27	25	5	7	9	21	36	49
Middlesbrough	42	8	5	8	33	27	3	6	12	21	48	44
Nottingham Forest	42	6	4	11	17	25	4	6	11	24	27	40

Barclays League Division 1

	P	W	D	L	F	A	W	D	L	F	A	Pts
			HOME						AWAY			
Newcastle United	46	16	6	1	58	15	13	3	7	34	23	96
West Ham United	46	16	5	2	50	17	10	5	8	31	24	88
Portsmouth	46	19	2	2	48	9	7	8	8	32	37	88
Tranmere Rovers	46	15	4	4	48	24	8	6	9	24	32	79
Swindon Town	46	15	3	5	41	23	6	8	9	33	36	76
Leicester City	46	14	5	4	43	24	8	5	10	28	40	76
Millwall	46	14	6	3	46	21	4	10	9	19	32	70
Derby County	46	11	2	10	40	33	8	7	8	28	24	66
Grimsby Town	46	12	6	5	33	25	7	1	15	25	32	64
Peterborough United	46	7	11	5	30	26	9	3	11	25	37	62
Wolverhampton Wanderers	46	11	6	6	37	26	5	7	11	29	39	61
Charlton	46	10	8	5	28	19	6	5	12	21	29	61
Barnsley	46	12	4	7	29	19	5	5	13	27	41	60

	P	W	D	L	F	A	W	D	L	F	A	Pts
Oxford United	46	8	7	8	29	21	6	7	19	24	35	56
Bristol City	46	10	7	6	29	25	4	7	12	20	42	56
Watford	46	8	7	8	26	30	6	6	11	30	41	55
Notts County	46	10	7	6	33	21	2	9	12	22	49	52
Southend United	46	9	8	6	33	22	4	5	14	21	42	52
Birmingham City	35	10	4	9	30	32	3	8	12	20	40	51
Luton Town	46	6	13	4	26	26	4	8	11	22	36	51
Sunderland	46	9	6	8	34	28	4	5	14	16	36	50
Brentford	46	7	6	10	28	30	6	4	13	24	41	49
Cambridge United	46	8	6	9	29	32	3	10	10	19	27	49
Bristol City	46	6	6	11	20	42	4	5	14	25	45	41

Barclays League Division 2

		HOME					AWAY					
	P	W	D	L	F	A	W	D	L	F	A	Pts
Stoke City	46	17	4	2	41	13	10	8	5	32	21	93
Bolton Wanderers	46	18	2	3	48	14	9	7	7	32	27	90
Port Vale	46	14	7	2	44	17	12	4	7	35	27	89
West Bromich Albion	46	17	3	3	56	22	8	7	8	32	32	85
Swansea City	36	12	7	4	28	17	8	6	9	27	30	73
Stockport County	46	11	11	1	47	18	8	4	11	34	39	72
Leyton Orient	46	16	4	3	49	20	5	5	13	20	33	72
Reading	46	14	4	5	44	20	4	11	8	22	31	69
Brighton & Hove Albion	46	13	4	6	36	24	7	4	11	27	35	69
Rotherham United	46	9	7	7	30	27	8	7	8	30	33	65
Fulham	46	9	9	5	28	22	7	8	8	29	33	65
Burnley	46	11	6	6	38	28	5	6	12	21	38	80
Plymouth Argyll	46	11	6	6	38	28	4	8	12	21	36	60
Huddersfield Town	46	10	6	7	30	22	7	3	13	24	39	60
Hartlepool United	46	8	6	9	19	23	6	6	11	23	37	54
Bournemouth	46	7	10	6	28	24	5	7	11	17	28	53
Blackpool	46	9	9	5	40	30	3	6	14	23	45	51
Exeter City	46	5	8	10	26	30	6	9	8	28	39	40
Hull	46	9	5	9	28	26	4	6	13	18	43	50
Preston North End	46	8	5	10	41	47	5	3	15	24	47	47
Mansfield Town	46	7	8	8	34	34	4	3	16	18	46	44
Wigan Athletic	46	6	6	11	26	34	5	5	14	17	38	41
Chester City	46	6	2	15	30	47	2	3	18	19	55	29

Barclays League Division 3

		HOME					AWAY					
	P	W	D	L	F	A	W	D	L	F	A	Pts
Cardiff City	42	13	7	1	42	20	12	1	8	35	27	83
Wrexham	42	14	3	4	48	26	9	8	4	27	26	80
Barnet	42	16	4	1	45	19	7	6	8	21	29	79
York City	42	13	6	2	41	15	8	6	7	31	30	75
Walsall	42	11	6	4	42	31	11	1	9	34	30	73

Crewe Alexandra	42	13	3	5	47	23	8	4	9	28	33	70
Bury	42	10	7	4	36	19	8	2	11	27	36	63
Lincoln City	42	10	6	5	31	20	8	3	10	26	33	63
Shrewsbury Town	42	11	3	7	36	30	6	8	7	21	22	62
Colchester United	42	13	3	5	38	26	5	2	14	29	50	59
Rochdale	42	10	3	8	38	29	6	7	8	32	41	58
Chesterfield	42	11	3	7	32	28	4	8	9	27	35	56
Scarborough	42	7	7	7	32	30	8	2	11	34	41	54
Scunthorpe	42	8	7	6	38	25	6	5	10	19	29	54
Darlington	42	5	6	10	23	31	7	8	6	25	22	50
Doncaster Rovers	42	6	5	10	22	28	5	9	7	20	29	47
Hereford United	42	7	3	5	31	27	3	6	12	16	33	45
Carlisle	42	7	4	9	29	27	4	6	11	22	38	44
Torquay United	42	6	6	11	18	26	6	3	12	27	41	43
Northampton Town	42	6	5	10	19	28	5	3	13	29	46	41
Gillingham	42	9	0	8	32	28	0	9	12	16	36	40
HalifaxTown	42	3	6	13	20	35	6	4	11	25	33	36

FA Premier League Promotions and Relegations

1992-93	Promoted	Newcastle United	FLD1 Champions
		West Ham United	FLD1 Runners-up
		Swindon Town	FLD1 Play-off winners
	Relegated	Crystal Palace	20th
		Middlesbrough	21st
		Nottingham Forest	22nd

FA PREMIER LEAGUE

	Arsenal	Aston Villa	Blackburn R	Chelsea	Coventry City	Crystal Palace	Everton	Ipswich Town	Leeds United	Liverpool	Man City
Arsenal	•	0-1	0-1	2-1	3-0	3-0	2-0	0-0	0-0	0-1	1-0
Aston Villa	1-0	•	0-0	1-3	0-0	3-0	2-1	2-0	1-1	4-2	3-1
Blackburn Rovers	1-0	3-0	•	2-0	2-5	1-2	2-3	3-1	3-1	4-1	1-0
Chelsea	1-0	0-1	0-0	•	2-1	3-1	0-1	2-1	1-0	0-0	2-4
Coventry City	0-2	3-0	0-2	1-2	•	2-2	0-2	2-2	3-3	5-1	2-3
Crystal Palace	1-2	1-0	3-3	1-1	2-2	•	1-0	3-1	1-0	1-1	0-0
Everton	0-0	1-1	2-1	1-1	0-0	0-2	•	3-0	2-0	2-1	2-3
Ipswich Town	1-2	1-1	2-1	1-1	0-0	2-2	2-0	•	4-2	2-2	3-1
Leeds United	3-0	1-1	5-2	1-1	2-2	0-0	1-0	1-0	•	2-2	1-1
Liverpool	0-2	1-2	2-1	2-1	4-0	5-0	2-0	0-0	2-0	•	1-1
Manchester City	0-0	1-1	1-3	3-0	1-0	1-0	1-0	4-2	4-0	1-1	•
Manchester United	1-0	1-1	0-0	3-0	5-0	1-0	0-2	0-1	2-0	2-2	2-1
Middlesbrough	1-1	2-3	3-2	0-0	0-2	0-1	1-2	2-2	4-1	1-2	2-0
Norwich City	1-1	1-0	0-0	2-1	1-1	4-2	1-1	0-1	2-2	1-0	2-1
Nottingham Forest	0-1	1-1	1-3	3-0	1-0	1-1	1-0	0-1	1-1	1-0	0-2
Oldham Athletic	0-0	1-1	0-1	2-1	1-1	1-1	1-0	4-2	2-2	3-2	1-1
QPR	0-0	2-1	0-3	1-1	2-0	1-3	4-2	0-0	2-1	1-1	1-1
Sheffield United	1-1	0-2	1-3	4-2	1-1	0-1	1-0	3-0	2-1	1-0	0-3
Sheffield Wednesday	1-0	1-2	0-0	3-3	1-2	2-1	3-1	4-3	1-1	2-1	1-1
Southampton	2-0	2-0	1-1	1-0	2-2	1-0	0-0	0-2	1-1	2-0	0-1
Tottenham Hotspur	1-0	0-0	1-2	1-2	0-2	2-2	2-1	0-2	4-0	2-0	3-1
Wimbledon	3-2	2-3	1-1	0-0	1-2	4-0	1-3	0-1	1-0	2-0	0-1

RESULTS 1992-93

	Man United	Middlesbrough	Norwich City	Nottingham F	Oldham Ath	QPR	Sheffield Utd	Sheffield Wed	Southampton	Tottenham Hot	Wimbledon
Arsenal	0-1	1-1	2-4	1-1	2-0	0-0	1-1	2-1	4-3	1-3	0-1
Aston Villa	1-0	5-1	2-3	2-1	0-1	2-0	3-1	2-0	1-1	0-0	1-0
Blackburn Rovers	1-1	7-1	7-1	4-1	2-0	1-0	1-0	1-0	0-0	0-2	0-0
Chelsea	1-1	4-0	2-3	0-0	1-1	1-0	1-2	0-2	1-1	1-1	4-2
Coventry City	0-1	2-1	1-1	0-1	3-0	0-1	1-3	0-1	2-0	1-0	0-2
Crystal Palace	0-2	4-1	1-2	1-1	2-2	1-1	2-0	1-1	1-2	1-3	2-0
Everton	0-2	2-2	0-1	3-0	2-2	3-5	2-0	1-1	2-1	1-2	0-0
Ipswich Town	2-1	0-1	3-1	2-1	1-2	1-1	0-0	0-1	0-0	1-1	2-1
Leeds United	0-0	3-0	0-0	1-4	2-0	1-1	3-1	3-1	2-1	5-0	2-1
Liverpool	1-2	4-1	4-1	0-0	1-0	1-0	2-1	1-0	1-1	6-2	2-3
Manchester City	1-1	0-1	3-1	2-2	3-3	1-1	2-0	1-2	1-0	1-0	1-1
Manchester United	•	3-0	3-3	2-0	3-0	0-0	2-1	2-1	2-1	4-1	0-1
Middlesbrough	1-1	•	3-3	1-2	2-1	0-1	2-0	1-0	2-1	3-0	2-0
Norwich City	1-3	1-1	•	3-1	1-0	1-0	2-1	1-0	1-0	0-0	2-1
Nottingham Forest	0-2	1-0	0-3	•	2-0	1-0	0-2	1-1	1-2	2-1	1-1
Oldham Athletic	1-0	4-1	2-3	5-3	•	2-2	3-2	1-1	4-3	2-1	6-2
QPR	1-3	3-3	3-1	4-3	3-2	•	3-2	3-1	3-1	4-1	1-2
Sheffield United	2-1	2-0	1-1	0-0	2-0	1-2	•	1-1	2-0	6-0	2-2
Sheffield Wednesday	3-3	2-3	1-0	0-0	2-1	0-2	1-1	•	5-2	2-0	1-1
Southampton	0-1	2-1	3-0	1-2	1-0	1-2	3-2	1-2	•	0-0	2-2
Tottenham Hotspur	1-1	2-2	5-1	2-1	4-1	3-1	2-0	0-2	4-2	•	1-1
Wimbledon	1-2	2-0	3-0	1-0	5-2	1-2	2-0	1-1	1-2	1-1	•

FA PREMIER LEAGUE

	Arsenal	Aston Villa	Blackburn R	Chelsea	Coventry City	Crystal Palace	Everton	Ipswich Town	Leeds United	Liverpool	Man City
Arsenal	•	27,125	28,643	27,780	27,693	25,225	28,052	26,198	21,061	27,580	21,504
Aston Villa	35,170	•	30,398	19,125	38,543	17,120	32,913	25,395	29,151	37,863	33,108
Blackburn Rovers	16,424	15,127	•	14,780	15,215	14,163	16,180	14,071	19,910	15,028	19,433
Chelsea	17,725	20,081	19,575	•	14,816	17,141	12,739	16,702	24,345	20,981	15,939
Coventry City	15,419	24,135	14,496	15,553	•	11,833	11,273	11,281	19,571	19,847	14,556
Crystal Palace	20,734	22,270	17,086	12,610	12,248	•	13,227	18,881	14,462	18,688	14,005
Everton	19,140	22,373	18,105	17,419	17,627	18,083	•	15,243	21,034	35,827	20,247
Ipswich Town	20,403	16,977	21,227	17,912	16,677	17,302	18,377	•	21,449	20,432	17,005
Leeds United	30,516	27,815	31,791	28,135	27,890	27,545	28,199	28,848	•	30,021	30,840
Liverpool	34,961	40,826	43,668	34,199	33,328	36,380	44,619	36,680	34,992	•	43,037
Manchester City	25,041	23,525	29,122	22,420	20,092	21,167	25,180	20,680	27,255	28,098	•
Manchester United	37,301	36,163	40,447	40,139	36,025	29,736	31,901	31,704	31,296	33,243	35,408
Middlesbrough	16,627	20,905	20,096	15,599	14,008	21,123	12,729	14,255	18,649	22,463	15,369
Norwich City	14,820	19,528	15,821	13,564	13,613	13,543	12,650	20,032	18,613	20,610	16,386
Nottingham Forest	17,553	26,742	20,467	23,249	19,420	20,603	20,941	21,411	25,148	20,038	25,956
Oldham Athletic	12,311	13,457	13,742	11,762	11,254	11,063	13,013	11,150	13,848	15,381	14,903
QPR	20,861	18,904	10,677	15,806	12,453	14,571	14,802	12,806	19,326	21,056	13,003
Sheffield United	19,105	18,773	18,186	24,850	15,625	18,857	16,266	16,758	20,562	20,632	18,231
Sheffield Wednesday	36,668	29,964	31,044	26,338	22,874	24,979	23,645	24,270	26,855	26,459	27,169
Southampton	17,286	19,087	16,626	15,135	12,306	13,397	16,911	15,428	16,229	17,216	16,730
Tottenham Hotspur	33,709	32,852	23,097	31,540	24,388	22,328	26,503	23,738	32,040	32,917	27,247
Wimbledon	12,906	6,849	6,117	14,687	3,759	12,275	3,039	4,954	6,704	11,294	4,714

ATTENDANCES 1992-93

	Man United	Middlesbrough	Norwich City	Nottingham F	Oldham Ath	QPR	Sheffield Utd	Sheffield Wed	Southampton	Tottenham Hot	Wimbledon
Arsenal	29,790	23,197	24,030	19,024	20,796	18,817	23,818	23,389	24,149	26,393	18,253
Aston Villa	39,063	19,977	28,837	29,015	37,247	20,140	20,266	38,024	17,894	37,727	34,496
Blackburn Rovers	20,305	14,041	16,312	19,563	18,383	15,850	16,057	14,956	13,556	17,305	14,504
Chelsea	34,496	13,043	16,880	19,760	20,699	22,910	13,763	16,261	18,344	25,157	13,168
Coventry City	24,410	12,345	16,425	15,254	11,657	13,437	13,016	13,192	10,455	15,293	10,515
Crystal Palace	30,115	15,123	12,033	15,330	11,224	14,705	12,361	14,005	13,829	20,937	16,825
Everton	30,004	24,338	20,292	21,398	18,076	19,026	15,122	27,686	14,023	16,056	18,223
Ipswich Town	22,007	14,809	21,174	22,002	15,469	17,426	15,675	16,283	15,890	20,043	14,053
Leeds United	34,166	30,344	30,242	29,448	16,129	31,408	29,706	29,770	26,071	28,061	25,774
Liverpool	44,374	30,974	36,318	40,463	36,129	30,370	33,003	35,785	30,024	43,385	29,574
Manchester City	37,136	25,244	23,182	22,571	27,288	24,471	27,455	23,619	20,089	25,496	19,524
Manchester United	•	36,251	34,688	36,085	33,497	33,287	36,156	40,102	13,920	35,648	32,622
Middlesbrough	24,172	•	15,155	15,639	12,290	15,616	15,184	18,414	12,452	14,472	14,524
Norwich City	20,582	14,499	•	14,104	•	16,009	14,874	•	19,942	19,413	14,161
Nottingham Forest	24,862	25,959	20,799	•	21,240	22,436	26,752	19,694	•	25,682	19,326
Oldham Athletic	17,106	12,401	11,018	11,632	•	10,946	14,794	12,312	14,597	11,735	11,606
QPR	20,142	12,272	13,892	16,782	11,804	•	10,932	12,177	10,925	19,845	12,270
Sheffield United	28,070	15,184	15,583	19,152	14,628	16,366	•	30,039	15,842	19,845	15,463
Sheffield Wednesday	37,708	23,360	22,360	29,623	24,485	23,164	33,694	•	26,184	24,895	20,918
Southampton	15,623	13,002	12,969	18,005	10,827	14,125	13,814	17,426	•	19,654	11,221
Tottenham Hotspur	33,296	24,735	31,425	32,118	26,663	32,341	21,322	25,702	20,098	•	24,473
Wimbledon	30,115	5,821	10,875	9,358	3,386	6,771	3,979	5,740	4,534	8,628	•

FA PREMIER LEAGUE RECORDS 1992-93

Top Scorers All Competitions

Player	Club	L	F	C	O	Tot
Ian WRIGHT	Arsenal	15	10	5	0	30
Teddy SHERINGHAM	Tottenham Hotspur	21	4	3	0	28
Les FERDINAND	QPR	20	2	2	0	24
Ian RUSH	Liverpool	14	1	1	6	22
Alan SHEARER	Blackburn Rovers	16	0	6	0	22
Mike NEWELL	Blackburn Rovers	13	3	5	0	21
Mark BRIGHT	Sheffield Wednesday	11	3	6	0	20
Brian DEANE	Sheffield United	15	3	2	0	20
Lee CHAPMAN	Leeds United	15	1	2	1	19
Dean HOLDSWORTH	Wimbledon	19	0	0	0	19
David WHITE	Manchester City	16	3	0	0	19
Mathew LE TISSIER	Southampton	15	1	2	0	18
Paul WARHURST	Sheffield Wednesday	6	5	4	3	18
Chris KIWOMYA	Ipswich Town	10	1	6	0	17
Mick QUINN	Coventry City	17	0	0	0	17
Dean SAUNDERS	Aston Villa	13	2	2	0	17
David HIRST	Sheffield Wednesday	11	1	3	1	16
Mike HUGHES	Manchester United	15	0	1	0	16
Mark ROBINS	Norwich City	15	0	1	0	16
Paul WILKINSON	Middlesbrough	15	0	1	0	16
Chris ARMSTRONG	Crystal Palace	15	0	0	0	15
Mike SHERON	Manchester City	11	3	0	0	14
Dalian ATKINSON	Aston Villa	11	0	2	0	13
Tony COTTEE	Everton	12	0	1	0	13
Ian OLNEY	Oldham Athletic	12	1	0	0	13
Nigel CLOUGH	Nottingham Forest	10	1	1	0	12
Iain DOWIE	Southampton	11	0	1	0	12
Gary SPEED	Leeds United	7	3	1	1	12

L=Premier League, F=FA Cup, C=Coca-Cola Cup, O=other (European etc)

FA Premier League Top Scorers

Player	Club	Goals	All-time total
Teddy SHERINGHAM	Tottenham Hotspur	22	22
	Including 1 for Nottingham Forest		
Les FERDINAND	QPR	20	21
Dean HOLDSWORTH	Wimbledon	19	19
Mick QUINN	Coventry City	17	17
Alan SHEARER	Blackburn Rovers	16	16

David WHITE	Manchester City	16	16
Chris ARMSTRONG	Crystal Palace	15	15
Eric CANTONA	Manchester United	15	15
Including 6 for Leeds United			
Lee CHAPMAN	Leeds United	15	15
Brian DEANE	Sheffield United	15	15
Mark HUGHES	Manchester United	15	15
Mathew LE TISSIER	Southampton	15	15
Mark ROBINS	Norwich City	15	15
Paul WILKINSON	Middlesbrough	15	15
Ian WRIGHT	Arsenal	15	15
Ian RUSH	Liverpool	14	14
Dean SAUNDERS	Aston Villa	14	14
Including 1 for Liverpool			
Mike NEWELL	Blackburn Rovers	13	13
Mark BRIGHT	Sheffield Wednesday	12	12
Including 1 for Crystal Palace			
Tony COTTEE	Everton	12	12
Ian OLNEY	Oldham Athletic	12	12
Dalian ATKINSON	Aston Villa	11	11
Iain DOWIE	Southampton	11	11
David HIRST	Sheffield Wednesday	11	11
Mike SHERON	Manchester City	11	11
Mark WALTERS	Liverpool	11	11
Peter BEARDSLEY	Everton	10	10
Nigel CLOUGH	Nottingham Forest	10	10
Chris KIWOMYA	Ipswich Town	10	10

FA Premier League Top Scorers by Club

Club	*Scorers*
Arsenal	Wright 15, Merson 6, Campbell 4
Aston Villa	Saunders 13, Atkinson 11, Parker 9
Blackburn Rovers	Shearer 16, Newell 13, Ripley 7
Chelsea	Harford 9, Stuart 9, Spencer 7
Coventry City	Quinn 17, J Williams 8, Ndlovu 7
Crystal Palace	Armstrong 15, McGoldrick 8, Young 6
Everton	Cottee 12, Beardsley 10, Barlow 5
Ipswich Town	Kiwomya 10, Dozzell 7, Wark 6
Leeds United	Chapman 15, Speed 7, Wallace 7
Liverpool	Rush 14, Walters 11, Hutchison 7
Manchester City	White 16, Sheron 11, Quinn 9
Manchester United	Hughes 15, Cantona 9, Giggs 9, McClair 9
Middlesbrough	Wilkinson 15, Hendrie 9, Falconer 5, Wright 5
Norwich City	Robins 15, Phillips 9, Sutton 8
Nottingham Forest	Clough 10, Bannister 8, Keane 6
Oldham Athletic	Olney 12, Adams 9, Sharp 7
Queens Park Rangers	Ferdinand 20, Allen 10, Sinton 7

Sheffield United	Deane 15, Littlejohn 8, Whitehouse 5
Sheffield Wednesday	Bright 11, Hirst 11, Bart-Williams 6, Warhurst 6
Southampton	Le Tissier 15, Dowie 11, Banger 6
Tottenham Hotspur	Sheringham 21, Anderton 6, Barmby 6
Wimbledon	Holdsworth 19, Fashanu 6, Clark 5

FA Premier League Hat-tricks

Player	Match	Date
Eric Cantona	LEEDS UNITED v Tottenham Hotspur	25/08/92
Mark Robins	Oldham Athletic v NORWICH CITY	09/11/92
John Hendrie	MIDDLESBROUGH v Blackburn Rovers	05/12/92
Andy Sinton	QPR v Everton	28/12/92
Brian Deane	SHEFFIELD UNITED v Ipswich Town	16/01/93
Teddy Sheringham	TOTTENHAM HOTSPUR v Leeds United	20/02/93
Gordon Strachan	LEEDS UNITED v Blackburn Rovers	10/04/93
Les Ferdinand	QPR v Nottingham Forest	10/04/93
Les Ferdinand	QPR v Everton	12/04/93
Chris Bart-Williams	SHEFFIELD WEDNESDAY v Southampton	12/04/93
Chris Sutton	NORWICH CITY v Leeds United	14/04/93
Mark Walters	LIVERPOOL v Coventry City	17/04/93
Mathew Le Tissier	Oldham Athletic v SOUTHAMPTON	08/05/93
Rod Wallace	Coventry City v LEEDS UNITED	05/05/93

ATTENDANCES

Attendance Summaries by Club

	Home		Away	
Club	Total	Ave	Total	Ave
Arsenal	512,517	24,403	474,680	22,604
Aston Villa	621,472	29,594	473,478	22,547
Blackburn Rovers	341,163	16,246	442,034	21,049
Chelsea	394,525	18,787	442,602	21,076
Coventry City	313,963	14,951	409,854	19,517
Crystal Palace	330,698	15,748	408,434	19,449
Everton	429,342	20,445	423,159	20,150
Ipswich Town	382,692	18,223	410,485	19,547
Leeds United	614,244	29,250	462,500	22,024
Liverpool	777,089	37,004	495,674	23,604
Manchester City	518,655	24,698	444,790	21,180
Manchester United	738,202	35,152	597,542	28,454
Middlesbrough	351,209	16,724	412,421	19,639
Norwich City	339,238	16,154	435,489	20,738
Nottingham Forest	460,107	21,910	456,326	21,730

Oldham Athletic	270,031	12,859	423,039	20,145
Queens Park Rangers	315,306	15,015	419,621	19,982
Sheffield United	394,826	18,801	411,743	19,607
Sheffield Wednesday	572,525	27,263	448,943	21,378
Southampton	323,017	15,382	379,075	18,051
Tottenham Hotspur	582,532	27,740	472,479	22,499
Wimbledon	176,505	8,405	391,493	18,643
Total	9,759,808	21,125		

Top Attendances by Number

Club	Posn	Total	Ave
Liverpool	6th	777,089	37,004
Manchester United	1st	738,202	35,152
Aston Villa	2nd	621,472	29,594
Leeds United	17th	614,244	29,250
Tottenham Hotspur	8th	582,532	27,740
Sheffield Wednesday	7th	572,525	27,263
Manchester City	9th	518,655	24,698
Arsenal	10th	512,467	24,403
Nottingham Forest	22nd	460,123	21,910
Everton	13th	429,342	20,445
Sheffield United	14th	394,826	18,801
Chelsea	11th	394,525	18,787
Ipswich Town	16th	382,692	18,223
Middlesbrough	21st	351,209	16,724
Blackburn Rovers	4th	341,163	16,246
Norwich City	3rd	339,238	16,154
Crystal Palace	20th	330,698	15,748
Southampton	18th	323,017	15,382
Queens Park Rangers	5th	315,306	15,015
Coventry City	15th	313,963	14,951
Oldham Athletic	19th	270,032	12,859
Wimbledon	12th	176,505	8,405

SCORES

Highest Aggregate Scores

8	Blackburn Rovers v Norwich City	7-1
	Liverpool v Tottenham Hotspur	6-2
	Oldham Athletic v Wimbledon	6-2
	Oldham Athletic v Nottingham Forest	5-3
	Everton v QPR	3-5

Biggest Home Wins

7-1	Blackburn Rovers v Norwich City	02/10/92
6-0	Sheffield United v Tottenham Hotspur	02/03/93

Biggest Away Wins

2-5	Manchester City v Everton	08/05/93
2-5	Blackburn Rovers v Coventry City	26/01/93

Highest Score Draws

3-3	Coventry City v Leeds United	08/05/93
	Crystal Palace v Blackburn Rovers	15/08/92
	Middlesbrough v Norwich City	08/05/93
	Sheffield Wednesday v Manchester United	26/12/92

Score Frequencies 1992-93

Score	Total No.	Score	Total No.
0-0	37	4-3	4
1-0	51	5-3	1
2-0	33	0-1	36
3-0	19	0-2	21
4-0	5	0-3	4
5-0	2	1-2	29
6-0	1	1-3	11
2-1	42	1-4	1
3-1	19	2-3	10
4-1	10	2-4	2
5-1	3	2-5	2
7-1	1	3-5	1
3-2	8	1-1	66
4-2	9	2-2	19
5-2	3	3-3	7
6-2	2	**Total**	**462**

TRANSFERS of £500,000+

Transfers involving FA Premier League Clubs

Fee	Player	From	To
£3,750,000	Roy Keane	Nottingham Forest	Manchester United
£2,900,000	Brian Deane	Sheffield United	Leeds United
£2,700,000	Des Walker	Sampdoria	Sheffield United
£2,500,000	Neil Ruddock	Tottenham Hotspur	Liverpool

£2,500,000	Terry Phelan	Wimbledon	Manchester City
£2,275,000	Nigel Clough	Nottingham Forest	Liverpool
£2,100,000	Andy Townsend	Chelsea	Aston Villa
£2,100,000	Teddy Sheringham	Nottingham Forest	TottenhamHotspur
£2,100,000	Robert Fleck	Norwich City	Chelsea
£2,000,000	Martin Keown	Everton	Arsenal
£1,750,000	Andy Cole	Bristol City	Newcaslte United
£1,500,000	Kevin Galacher	Coventry City	Blackburn Rovers
£1,400,000	Peter Beardsley	Everton	Newcastle
£1,250,000	Gavin Peacock	Newcastle United	Chelsea
£1,200,000	Guy Whittingham	Portsmouth Argyl	Aston Villa
£1,200,000	Eric Cantona	Leeds United	Manchester United
£1,000,000	Eddie McGoldrick	Crystal Palace	Arsenal
£1,000,000	Roy Waqerle	Blackburn Rovers	Coventry City
£1,000,000	David James	Watford	Liverpool
£1,000,000	Chris Armstrong	Millwall	Crystal Palace
£900,000	Andy Payton	Middlesbrough	Celtic
£800,000	Patrik Andersen	Malmo	Blackburn Rovers
£800,000	Neil Webb	Manchester United	Nottingham Forest
£800,000	Mark Robins	Manchester United	Norwich City
£750,000	Gordon	Rangers	West Ham United
£750,000	Neil Ruddock	Southampton	Tottenham Hotspur
£750,000	Ken Monkou	Chelsea	Southampton
£750,000	Perry Groves	Arsenal	Southampton
£720,000	Dean Holdsworth	Brentford	Wimbledon
£600,000	Kare Ingebrigtsen	Rosenborg	Manchester City
£600,000	Stig Inge Bjornbye	Rosenborg	Liverpool
£575,000	Barry Horne	Southampton	Everton
£525,000	Webster	Charlton	West Ham United
£500,000	Pearce	Coventry City	Sheffield W
£500,000	Groenendijk	Ajax	Manchester City
£500,000	Fjortoft	Rapid Vienna	Swindon Town
£500,000	David Kerslake	Swindon Town	Leeds United
£500,000	Alf Inge Haaland	Bryne	Nottingham Forest
£500,000	Craig Hignett	Crewe Alexandra	Middlesbrough

BOOKINGS & DISMISSALS

Players Sent Off

Player	Match	Date
Niall QUINN	Middlesborough v MANCHESTER CITY	19/08/92
Micky ADAMS	Queens Park Rangers v SOUTHAMPTON	19/08/92
Andy THORN	CRYSTAL PALACE v Tottenham Hotspur	22/08/92
Neil RUDDOCK	TOTTENHAM HOTSPUR v Crystal Palace	22/08/92
Simon TRACEY †	Tottenham Hotspur v SHEFFIELD UNITED	02/09/92
Vinnie JONES	WIMBLEDON v Blackburn	19/09/92
Tony DOBSON	Wimbledon v BLACKBURN ROVERS	19/09/92
Mike NEWELL	Wimbledon BLACKBURN ROVERS	19/09/92
Craig FOREST †	IPSWICH TOWN v Sheffield United	26/09/92
Lee SINNOT	Chelsea v CRYSTAL PALACE	07/11/92
Carl BRADSHAW	SHEFFIELD UNITED v Coventry City	28/11/92
Jamie REDKNAPP	LIVERPOOL v Coventry City	19/12/92
Brian McALLISTER	Wimbledon v Crystal Palace	26/12/92
Neville SOUTHALL †	Queens Park Rangers v EVERTON	28/12/92
Paul RIDEOUT	Queens Park Rangers v EVERTON	28/12/92
Terry HURLOCK	Middlesborough v SOUTHAMPTON	26/01/93
Willie FALCONER	MIDDLESBOROUGH v Southampton	26/01/93
Nigel WINTERBURN	ARSENAL v Liverpool	31/01/93
Nevill SOUTHALL †	Sheffield Wednesday v EVERTON	06/02/93
Francis BENALI	Tottenham Hotspur v SOUTHAMPTON	07/02/93
Frank SINCLAIR	CHELSEA v Blackburen Rovers	21/02/93
Nigel WORTHINGTON	SHEFFIELD WEDNESDAY v Liverpool	27/02/93
Tim SHERWOOD	Everton v BLACKBURN ROVERS	03/03/93
Chris ARMSTRONG	Sheffield United v CRYSTAL PALACE	20/02/92
Tony CASCARINO	Leeds United v CHELSEA	24/03/93
John FASHANU	Sheffield Wednesday v WIMBLEDON	24/03/93
Gerald DOBBS	Oldham Athletic v WIMBLEDON	03/04/93
Gary CHARLES	NOTTINGHAM FOREST v Blackburn Rovers	07/04/93
Alan KERNAGHAN	MIDDLESBROUGH v Everton	10/04/93
Glyn HODGES	Sheffield Wednesday v Sheffield United	21/04/93
David JAMES †	Norwich City LIVERPOOL	01/05/93
Brian McALLISTER	Tottenham Hotspur v Wimbledon	01/05/93
Don HUTCHINSON	Oldham Athletic v LIVERPOOL	05/05/93
Chris WHYTE	Coventry City LEEDS UNITED	08/05/93

† *Goalkeeper*

Mick QUINN of Coventry City was sent off against Manchester United on the 12/4/93). However, following video evidence Quinn's dismissal was removed from the record books.

24

Players Sent Off by Club

	Y	R	Player(s)
Arsenal	37	1	Winterburn
Aston Villa	24	0	
Blackburn Rovers	40	3	Dobson, Newell, Sherwood
Crystal Palace		3	Thorn, Armstrong, Sinnot
Chelsea	45	2	Sinclair, Cascarino
Coventry City	34	0	
Everton	29	3	Southall (x2), Rideout
Ipswich Town	34	1	Forest
Leeds United	41	1	Whyte
Liverpool	35	3	Redknapp, James, Hutchinson
Manchester City	44	1	Quinn
Manchester United	33	0	
Middlesbrough		2	Falconer, Kernaghan
Norwich City	23	0	
Nottingham Forest		1	Charles
Oldham Athletic	39	0	
QPR	35	0	
Sheffield United	56	3	Tracey, Bradshaw, Hodges
Sheffield Wednesday	32	1	Worthington
Southampton	55	3	Adams, Hurlock, Benali
Tottenham Hotspur	39	1	Ruddock
Wimbledon	50	5	Jones, Fashanu, McAllister (*2), Dobbs

Referees by Number of Bookings Issued

Y	R	Referee	Players Sent Off
58	2	Ray LEWIS	Brian McAllister (twice!)
43		Mike REED	
40	4	Philip DON	Andy Thorn, Neil Ruddock, Carl Bradshaw, Jamie Redknapp
36	1	David ELLERAY	David James
33	2	Ron GROVES	Craig Forrest, Lee Sinnott,
29		Keren BARRATT	
28	2	John MARTIN	Chris Armstrong, Gerald Dobbs
27		Alf BUKSE	
27	2	Gerald ASHBY	Neville Southall, Paul Rideout
23		Jim BORRETT	
23	1	Vic CALLOW	Nigel Worthington
22	1	Steve LODGE	Niall Quinn
22	3	Martin BODENHAM	Vinnie Jones, Tony Dobson, Mike Newell

22		Mike PECK	
21	1	Paul DURKIN	Don Hutchinson
20		Roger MILFORD	
20		Keith HACKET	
19	2	Ken REDFERN	Francis Benali, Glyn Hodges
19	3	Peter FOKES	Terry Hurlock, Willie Falconer, Tim Sherwood
18		Robbie HART	
17	1	Tony WARD	Gary Charles
16	1	Keith COOPER	Nigel Winterburn
16		Keith BURGE	
15	1	David ALLISON	Frank Sinclair
15		Roger DILKES	
14		Brian HILL	
14		Dermot GALLAGHER	
13		Allan GUNN	
13	1	Ray BIGGER	Micky Adams
11		Joe WORRALL	
10		John KEY	
10		Rodger GIFFORD	
9		Alan WILKIE	Tony Cascarino
6		Philip WRIGHT	
6		Mike PECK	
6		Bob NIXON	
6		Howard KING	
4	2	John LLOYD	Gerald Dobbs, Alan Kernaghan
3	2	Kelvin MORTON	Neville Southall, Chris Whyte
3	1	Ian MITCHELL	Simon Tracey
3		Bob HAMER	

PRIZE MONEY

Position	Club	Prize Money
1st	Manchester United	£815,210
2nd	Aston Villa	£778,155
3rd	Norwich City	£741,100
4th	Blackburn Rovers	£704,045
5th	Queens Park Rangers	£666,990
6th	Liverpool	£629,975
7th	Sheffield Wednesday	£592.880
8th	Tottenham Hotspur	£555,825

9th	Manchester City	£518,770
10th	Arsenal	£481,715
11th	Chelsea	£444,660
12th	Wimbledon	£407,605
13th	Everton	£370,550
14th	Sheffield United	£333,495
15th	Coventry City	£296,440
16th	Ipswich Town	£259,385
17th	Leeds United	£222,330
18th	Southampton	£185,275
19th	Oldham Athletic	£148,220
20th	Crystal Palace	£111,165
21st	Middlesbrough	£74,110
22nd	Nottingham Forest	£37,055

Football League: In the First Division of the Football League Newcastle United received £50,000 in prize money and West Ham United, the runners-up, received £25,000.

THE MANAGERS

FAPL Managers by Club

Club	Manager	Arrived
Arsenal	George Graham	May '86
Aston Villa	Ron Atkinson	June '91
Blackburn Rovers	Kenny Dalglish	October '91
Chelsea	Glenn Hoddle	June '93
Coventry City	Bobby Gould	May '92
Everton	Howard Kendall	November '90
Ipswich Town	Mick McGiven	July '92
Leeds United	Howard Wilkinson	October '88
Liverpool	Graeme Souness	April '91
Manchester City	Peter Reid	November '90
Manchester United	Alex Ferguson	November '86
Newcastle United	Kevin Keegan	February '92
Norwich City	Mike Walker	June '92
Oldham Athletic	Joe Royle	July '82
Queens Park Rangers	Gerry Francis	May '91
Sheffield United	Dave Bassett	January '88
Sheffield Wednesday	Trevor Francis	June '91
Southampton	Ian Branfoot	June '91

Swindon Town	John Gorman	June '93
Tottenham Hotspur	Osvaldo Ardiles	June '93
West Ham United	Billy Bonds	February '90
Wimbledon	Joe Kinnear	January '91

Managers by Length of Tenure

Club	Manager	Arrived
Oldham Athletic	Joe Royle	July '82
Arsenal	George Graham	May '86
Manchester United	Alex Ferguson	November '86
Sheffield United	Dave Bassett	January '88
Leeds United	Howard Wilkinson	October '88
West Ham United	Billy Bonds	February '90
Manchester City	Peter Reid	November '90
Everton	Howard Kendall	November '90
Wimbledon	Joe Kinnear	January '91
Liverpool	Graeme Souness	April '91
Queens Park Rangers	Gerry Francis	May '91
Aston Villa	Ron Atkinson	June '91
Sheffield Wednesday	Trevor Francis	June '91
Southampton	Ian Branfoot	June '91
Blackburn Rovers	Kenny Dalglish	October '91
Newcastle United	Kevin Keegan	February '92
Coventry City	Bobby Gould	May '92
Norwich City	Mike Walker	June '92
Ipswich Town	Mick McGiven	July '92
Swindon Town	John Gorman	June '93
Tottenham Hotspur	Osvaldo Ardiles	June '93
Chelsea	Glenn Hoddle	June '93

FA PREMIER LEAGUE ALL-TIME RECORDS

All-Time Record FAPL Attendances by Club

Club	Att	Opponents	Date
Arsenal	29,740	Manchester United	28/11/92
Aston Villa	39,063	Manchester United	07/11/92
Blackburn Rovers	20,305	Manchester United	24/10/92
Chelsea	34,496	Manchester United	19/12/92
Coventry City	24,410	Manchester United	12/04/93
Crystal Palace	30,115	Manchester United	21/04/93
Everton	35,827	Liverpool	07/12/92
Ipswich Town	22,007	Manchester United	30/01/93
Leeds United	34,166	Manchester United	08/02/93
Liverpool	44,619	Everton	20/03/93
Manchester City	37,136	Manchester United	20/03/93
Manchester United	40,693	Blackburn Rovers	03/05/93
Middlesborough	24,172	Manchester United	03/10/92
Norwich City	20,610	Liverpool	01/05/93
Nottingham Forest	26,752	Sheffield United	01/05/93
Oldham Athletic	17,106	Manchester United	09/03/93
Queens Park Rangers	21,056	Liverpool	23/11/92
Sheffield United	30,039	Sheffield Wednesday	08/11/92
Sheffield Wednesday	38,668	Sheffield United	13/03/93
Southampton	19,654	Tottenham Hotspur	15/08/92
Tottenham Hotspur	33,709	Arsenal	12/12/92
Wimbledon	30,115	Manchester United	08/05/93

All-Time Top 10 FAPL Attendances

Psn	Att	Match	Date
1	44,619	Liverpool v Everton	20/03/93
2	44,374	Liverpool v Manchester United	06/03/93
3	43,668	Liverpool v Blackburn Rovers	13/12/92
4	43,385	Liverpool v Tottenham Hotspur	08/05/93
5	43,073	Liverpool v Manchester City	28/12/92
6	40,826	Liverpool v Aston Villa	09/01/93
7	40,463	Liverpool v Nottingham Forest	06/02/93
8	40,447	Manchester United v Blackburn Rovers	03/05/93
9	40,139	Manchester United v Chelsea	17/04/93
10	40,102	Manchester United v Sheffield Wednesday	10/04/93

All-time FAPL Lowest Attendances by Club

Club	Att	Opponents	Date
Arsenal	18,253	Wimbledon	10/02/93
Aston Villa	17,120	Crystal Palace	05/09/92
Blackburn Rovers	14,041	Middlesbrough	20/03/93
Chelsea	13,043	Middlesbrough	03/04/93
Coventry City	10,455	Southampton	03/04/93
Crystal Palace	11,224	Oldham Athletic	12/09/92
Everton	15,122	Sheffield United	04/05/93
Ipswich Town	14,053	Wimbledon	12/09/92
Leeds United	25,774	Wimbledon	15/08/92
Liverpool	29,574	Wimbledon	26/09/92
Manchester City	19,524	Wimbledon	21/04/93
Manchester United	29,736	Crystal Palace	02/09/92
Middlesbrough	12,290	Oldham Athletic	22/03/93
Norwich City	12,452	Southampton	05/09/92
Nottingham Forest	17,553	Arsenal	17/10/92
Oldham Athletic	11,018	Norwich City	09/11/92
Queens Park Rangers	10,667	Blackburn Rovers	24/03/93
Sheffield United	14,628	Oldham Athletic	22/02/93
Sheffield Wednesday	20,918	Wimbledon	24/03/92
Southampton	10,827	Oldham Athletic	31/10/92
Tottenham Hotspur	20,098	Southampton	07/02/93
Wimbledon	3,039	Everton	26/01/93

All Time Lowest FAPL Attendances

Psn	Att	Match	Date
1	3,039	Wimbledon v Everton	26/01/93
2	3,386	Wimbledon v Oldham Athletic	12/12/92
3	3,759	Wimbledon v Coventry City	22/08/92
4	3,979	Wimbledon v Sheffield United	20/02/93
5	4,534	Wimbledon v Southampton	06/03/93
6	4,714	Wimbledon v Manchester City	01/09/92
7	4,954	Wimbledon v Ipswich Town	18/08/92
8	5,740	Wimbledon v Sheffield Wednesday	28/11/92
9	5,821	Wimbledon v Middlesbrough	09/03/93
10	6,117	Wimbledon v Blackburn Rovers	19/09/92

All-Time Biggest Home Wins

7-1	Blackburn Rovers v Norwich City	02/10/92
6-0	Sheffield United v Tottenham Hotspur	02/03/93

All-Time Biggest Away Wins

2-5	Manchester City v Everton	08/05/93
2-5	Blackburn Rovers v Coventry City	26/01/93

All-Time Highest Score Draws

3-3	Coventry City v Leeds United	08/05/93
	Crystal Palace v Blackburn Rovers	15/08/92
	Middlesbrough v Norwich City	08/05/93
	Sheffield Wednesday v Manchester United	26/12/92

General Records

Most Goals Scored in a Season:	Blackburn Rovers	68	1992-93	†
Fewest Goals Scored in a Season:	Arsenal	40	1992-93	†
Most Goals Conceded in a Season	Middlesbrough	75	1992-93	†
Fewest Goals Conceded in a Season:	Manchester United	31	1992-93	†
Most Points in a Season:	Manchester United	84	1992-93	†
Fewest Points in a Season:	Nottingham Forest	40	1992-93	†
Most Wins in a Season:	Manchester United	24	1992-93	†
Fewest Wins in a Season:	Nottingham Forest	10	1992-93	†
Fewest Defeats in a Season:	Manchester United	6	1992-93	†
Most Defeats in a Season:	Nottingham Forest	22	1992-93	†
Most Draws in a Season:	Crystal Palace	16	1992-93	†
	Ipswich Town	16	1992-93	†

Sequences

Consecutive Wins:	7	Manchester United	1992-93	†
		Sheffield Wednesday	1992-93	†
Consecutive Draws:	5	Ipswich Town	1992-93	†
		Manchester United	1992-93	†
		Sheffield Wednesday	1992-93	†
Consecutive Defeats:	6	Nottingham Forest	1992-93	†
Matches Without Defeat:	11	Manchester United	1992-93	†
Matches Without Victory:	13	Ipswich Town	1992-93	†

† 42 games

FA CHALLENGE CUP
1992-93

Third Round – 2nd January 1993

Aston Villa	v	Bristol Rovers	1-1	27,040
Blackburn Rovers	v	AFC Bournemouth	3-1	13,773
Bolton Wanderers	v	Liverpool	2-2	21,502
Brentford	v	Grimsby Town	0-2	6,880
Brighton & Hove Albion	v	Portsmouth	1-0	17,581
Cambridge United	v	Sheffield Wed	1-2	7,754
Crewe Alexandra	v	Marine	3-1	4,036
Derby County	v	Stockport County	2-1	17,960
Gillingham	v	Huddersfield Town	0-0	5,413
Hartlepool United	v	Crystal Palace	1-0	6,721
Ipswich Town	v	Plymouth Argyle	3-1	12,803
Leeds United	v	Charlton Athletic	1-1	22,088
Leicester City	v	Barnsley	2-2	19,137
Luton Town	v	Bristol City	2-0	6,094
Manchester City	v	Reading	1-1	20,523
Manchester United	v	Bury	2-0	30,668
Marlow	v	Tottenham Hotspur	1-5	26,636
(at Tottenham Hotspur)				
Middlesbrough	v	Chelsea	2-1	16,776
Newcastle United	v	Port Vale	4-0	29,926
Northampton Town	v	Rotherham United	0-1	7,256
Norwich City	v	Coventry City	1-0	15,301
Nottingham Forest	v	Southampton	2-1	13,592
Notts County	v	Sunderland	0-2	8,522
Oldham Athletic	v	Tranmere Rovers	2-2	13,389
Queens Park Rangers	v	Swindon Town	3-0	12,106
Sheffield United	v	Burnley	2-2	23,041
Southend United	v	Millwall	1-0	8,028
Swansea City	v	Oxford United	1-1	6,985
Watford	v	Wolverhampton Wanderers	1-4	12,363
West Bromwich Albion	v	West Ham United	0-2	25,896
Wimbledon	v	Everton	0-0	7,818
Yeovil Town	v	Arsenal	1-3	8,612

Third Round Replays

Bristol Rovers	v	Aston Villa	0-3	8,880

Barnsley	v	Leicester City	† 1-1	15,238

(Barnsley won 5-4 on penalties)

Burnley	v	Sheffield United	2-4	19,061
Charlton Athletic	v	Leeds United	1-3	8,337
Everton v	v	Wimbledon	1-2	15,293
Huddersfield Town	v	Gillingham	2-1	5,144
Liverpool	v	Bolton Wanderers	0-2	34,790
Oxford United	v	Swansea City	† 2-2	4,707

(Swansea City won 5-4 on penalties)

Reading	v	Manchester City	0-4	12,065
Tranmere Rovers	v	Oldham Athletic	3-0	12,525

Fourth Round – 23rd January 1993

Arsenal	v	Leeds United	2-2	26,516
Aston Villa	v	Wimbledon	1-1	21,088
Barnsley	v	West Ham United	4-1	13,716
Crewe Alexandra	v	Blackburn Rovers	0-3	7,054
Huddersfield Town	v	Southend United	1-2	7,961
Luton Town	v	Derby County	1-5	9,170
Manchester United	v	Brighton & Hove Albion	1-0	33,610
Norwich City	v	Tottenham Hotspur	0-2	15,003
Nottingham Forest	v	Middlesbrough	1-1	22,296
Queens Park Rangers	v	Manchester City	1-2	18,652
Rotherham United	v	Newcastle United	1-1	13,405
Sheffield United	v	Hartlepool United	1-0	20,074
Sheffield Wednesday	v	Sunderland	1-0	33,422
Swansea City	v	Grimsby Town	0-0	8,307
Tranmere Rovers	v	Ipswich Town	1-2	13,683
Wolverhampton Wand'rs	v	Bolton Wanderers	0-2	19,120

Fourth Round Replays

Grimsby Town	v	Swansea City	2-0	8,452
Leeds United	v	Arsenal	† 2-3	26,449
Middlesbrough	v	Nottingham Forest	0-3	20,519
Newcastle United	v	Rotherham United	2-0	28,966
Wimbledon	v	Aston Villa	† 0-0	8,048

(Wimbledon won 6-5 on penalties)

Fifth Round – 13th February 1993

Arsenal	v	Nottingham Forest	2-0	27,591
Blackburn Rovers	v	Newcastle United	1-0	19,972
Derby County	v	Bolton Wanderers	3-1	20,289
Ipswich Town	v	Grimsby Town	4-0	17,530
Manchester City	v	Barnsley	2-0	32,807

Sheffield United	v	Manchester Utd	3-1	27,150
Sheffield Wednesday	v	Southend United	2-1	26,446
Tottenham Hotspur	v	Wimbledon	3-2	26,594

Sixth Round – 6th March 1993

Blackburn Rovers	v	Sheffield United	0-0	15,107
Derby County	v	Sheffield Wednesday	3-3	22,511
Ipswich Town	v	Arsenal	2-4	22,054
Manchester City	v	Tottenham Hotspur	2-4	34,050

Sixth Round Replays

| Sheffield United | v | Blackburn Rovers | † 2-2 | 23,920 |

(Sheffield United won 5-3 on penalties)

| Sheffield Wednesday | v | Derby County | 1-0 | 32,033 |

Semi Finals

| Sheffield Wednesday | v | Sheffield United | † 2-1 | 75,364 |

(Wembley Stadium, 3rd April 93)

| Arsenal | v | Tottenham Hotspurs | 1-0 | 76,263 |

(Wembley Stadium, 4th April 93)

Final – 15th May 1993 at Wembley Stadium

| Arsenal | v | Sheffield Wednesday | † 1-1 | 79,347 |
| Wright | | Hirst | | |

Arsenal: Seaman, Dixon, Winterburn, Davis, Linighan, Adams, Jensen, Wright (O'Leary), Campbell, Merson, Parlour (Smith).
Sheffield Wednesday: Woods, Nilsson, Worthington, Palmer, Anderson (Hyde), Warhurst, Harkes, Waddle (Bart-Williams), Hirst, Bright, Sheridan.

Final Replay – 20th May 1993 at Wembley Stadium

| Arsenal | v | Sheffield Wednesday | † 2-1 | 62,267 |
| Wright, Linighan | | Waddle | | |

Arsenal: Seaman, Dixon, Winterburn, Davis, Linighan, Adams, Jensen, Wright (O'Leary), Smith, Campbell, Merson.
Sheffield Wednesday: Woods, Nilsson (Bart-Williams), Worthington, Harkes, Palmer, Warhurst, Wilson (Hyde), Waddle, Hirst, Bright, Sheridan.
† *after extra time*

FA CHALLENGE CUP
FINALS 1872-1993

Year	Winners	Runners-up	Score
1872	The Wanderers	Royal Engineers	1-0
1873	The Wanderers	Oxford University	2-0
1874	Oxford University	Royal Engineers	2-0
1875	Royal Engineers	Old Etonians	1-1
	Royal Engineers	Old Etonians	2-0
1876	The Wanderers	Old Etonians	1-1 †
	The Wanderers	Old Etonians	3-0
1877	The Wanderers	Oxford University	2-1 †
1878	The Wanderers*	Royal Engineers	3-1
1879	Old Etonians	Clapham Rovers	1-0
1880	Clapham Rovers	Oxford University	1-0
1881	Old Carthusians	Old Etonians	3-0
1882	Old Etonians	Blackburn Rovers	1-0
1883	Blackburn Olympic	Old Etonians	2-1 †
1884	Blackburn Rovers	Queen's Park, Glasgow	2-1
1885	Blackburn Rovers	Queen's Park, Glasgow	2-0
1886	Blackburn Rovers**	West Bromwich Albion	0-0
	Blackburn Rovers**	West Bromwich Albion	2-0
1887	Aston Villa	West Bromwich Albion	2-0
1888	West Bromwich Albion	Preston North End	2-1
1889	Preston North End	Wolverhampton Wanderers	3-0
1890	Blackburn Rovers	Sheffield Wednesday	6-1
1891	Blackburn Rovers	Notts County	3-1
1892	West Bromwich Albion	Aston Villa	3-0
1893	Wolverhampton Wanderers	Everton	1-0
1894	Notts County	Bolton Wanderers	4-1
1895	Aston Villa	West Bromwich Albion	1-0
1896	Sheffield Wednesday	Wolverhampton Wanderers	2-1
1897	Aston Villa	Everton	3-2
1898	Nottingham Forest	Derby County	3-1
1899	Sheffield United	Derby County	4-1
1900	Bury	Southampton	4-0
1901	Tottenham Hotspur	Sheffield United	2-2
	Tottenham Hotspur	Sheffield United	3-1

Year	Winners	Runners-up	Score
1902	Sheffield United	Southampton	1-1
	Sheffield United	Southampton	2-1
1903	Bury	Derby County	6-0
1904	Manchester City	Bolton Wanderers	1-0
1905	Aston Villa	Newcastle United	2-0
1906	Everton	Newcastle United	1-0
1907	Sheffield Wednesday	Everton	2-1
1908	Wolverhampton Wanderers	Newcastle United	3-1
1909	Manchester United	Bristol City	1-0
1910	Newcastle United	Barnsley	1-1
	Newcastle United	Barnsley	2-0
1911	Bradford City	Newcastle United	0-0
	Bradford City	Newcastle United	1-0
1912	Barnsley	West Bromwich Albion	0-0 †
	Barnsley	West Bromwich Albion	1-0
1913	Aston Villa	Sunderland	1-0
1914	Burnley	Liverpool	1-0
1915	Sheffield United	Chelsea	3-0
1920	Aston Villa	Huddersfield Town	1-0 †
1921	Tottenham Hotspur	Wolverhampton Wanderers	1-0
1922	Huddersfield Town	Preston North End	1-0
1923	Bolton Wanderers	West Ham United	2-0
1924	Newcastle United	Aston Villa	2-0
1925	Sheffield United	Cardiff City	1-0
1926	Bolton Wanderers	Manchester City	1-0
1927	Cardiff City	Arsenal	1-0
1928	Blackburn Rovers	Huddersfield Town	3-1
1929	Bolton Wanderers	Portsmouth	2-0
1930	Arsenal	Huddersfield Town	2-0
1931	West Bromwich Albion	Birmingham	2-1
1932	Newcastle United	Arsenal	2-1
1933	Everton	Manchester City	3-0
1934	Manchester City	Portsmouth	2-1
1935	Sheffield Wednesday	West Bromwich Albion	4-2
1936	Arsenal	Sheffield United	1-0
1937	Sunderland	Preston North End	3-1
1938	Preston North End	Huddersfield Town	1-0 †
1939	Portsmouth	Wolverhampton Wanderers	4-1
1946	Derby County	Charlton Athletic	4-1 †

Year	Winners	Runners-up	Score
1947	Charlton Athletic	Burnley	1-0 †
1948	Manchester United	Blackpool	4-2
1949	Wolverhampton Wanderers	Leicester City	3-1
1950	Arsenal	Liverpool	2-0
1951	Newcastle United	Blackpool	2-0
1952	Newcastle United	Arsenal	1-0
1953	Blackpool	Bolton Wanderers	4-3
1954	West Bromwich Albion	Preston North End	3-2
1955	Newcastle United	Manchester City	3-1
1956	Manchester City	Birmingham City	3-1
1957	Aston Villa	Manchester United	2-1
1958	Bolton Wanderers	Manchester United	2-0
1959	Nottingham Forest	Luton Town	2-1
1960	Wolverhampton Wanderers	Blackburn Rovers	3-0
1961	Tottenham Hotspur	Leicester City	2-0
1962	Tottenham Hotspur	Burnley	3-1
1963	Manchester United	Leicester City	3-1
1964	West Ham United	Preston North End	3-2
1965	Liverpool	Leeds United	2-1 †
1966	Everton	Sheffield Wednesday	3-2
1967	Tottenham Hotspur	Chelsea	2-1
1968	West Bromwich Albion	Everton	1-0 †
1969	Manchester City	Leicester City	1-0
1970	Chelsea	Leeds United	2-2 †
	Chelsea	Leeds United	2-1 †
1971	Arsenal	Liverpool	2-1 †
1972	Leeds United	Arsenal	1-0
1973	Sunderland	Leeds United	1-0
1974	Liverpool	Newcastle United	3-0
1975	West Ham United	Fulham	2-0
1976	Southampton	Manchester United	1-0
1977	Manchester United	Liverpool	2-1
1978	Ipswich Town	Arsenal	1-0
1979	Arsenal	Manchester United	3-2
1980	West Ham United	Arsenal	1-0
1981	Tottenham Hotspur	Manchester City	1-1 †
	Tottenham Hotspur	Manchester City	3-2
1982	Tottenham Hotspur	Queens Park Rangers	1-1 †
	Tottenham Hotspur	Queens Park Rangers	1-0

Year	Winners	Runners-up	Score
1983	Manchester United	Brighton & Hove Albion	2-2
	Manchester United	Brighton & Hove Albion	4-0
1984	Everton	Watford	2-0
1985	Manchester United	Everton	1-0 †
1986	Liverpool	Everton	3-1
1987	Coventry City	Tottenham Hotspur	3-2 †
1988	Wimbledon	Liverpool	1-0
1989	Liverpool	Everton	3-2 †
1990	Manchester United	Crystal Palace	3-3 †
	Manchester United	Crystal Palace	1-0
1991	Tottenham Hotspur	Nottingham Forest	2-1 †
1992	Liverpool	Sunderland	2-0
1993	Arsenal	Sheffield Wednesday	1-1 †
	Arsenal	Sheffield Wednesday	2-1 †

Final Venues

1872	Kennington Oval
1873	Lillie Bridge
1874-92	Kennington Oval
1893	Fallowfield, Manchester
1894	Everton
1912	Replay at Bramall Lane
1886	Replay at Derby
1895-1914	Crystal Palace
1915	Old Trafford, Manchester
1920-22	Stamford Bridge
1923–1993	Wembley

Replay Venues

1901	Bolton
1910	Everton
1911	Old Trafford
1970	Old Trafford
1981	Wembley
1982	Wembley
1983	Wembley
1990	Wembley
1993	Wembley

* *Trophy won outright by The Wanderers, but restored to the FA*
** *Special trophy awarded for a third consecutive win*

FA CHALLENGE CUP
WINS BY CLUB

Tottenham Hotspur	1901, 1921, 1961, 1962, 1967, 1981, 1982, 1991
Aston Villa	1887, 1895, 1897, 1905, 1913, 1920, 1957
Manchester United	1909, 1948, 1963, 1977, 1983, 1985, 1990
Blackburn Rovers	1884, 1885, 1886, 1890, 1891, 1928
Newcastle United	1910, 1924, 1932, 1951, 1952, 1955
Arsenal	1930, 1936, 1950, 1971, 1979, 1993
Liverpool	1965, 1974, 1986, 1989, 1992
The Wanderers	1872, 1873, 1876, 1877, 1878
West Bromwich Albion	1888, 1892, 1931, 1954, 1968
Bolton	1923, 1926, 1929, 1958
Everton	1894, 1906, 1933, 1966
Manchester City	1904, 1934, 1956, 1969
Sheffield United	1899, 1902, 1915, 1925
Wolverhampton Wanderers	1893, 1908, 1949, 1960
Sheffield Wednesday	1896, 1907, 1935
West Ham United	1964, 1975, 1980
Bury	1900, 1903
Nottingham Forrest	1898, 1959
Old Etonians	1879, 1882
Preston North End	1889, 1938
Sunderland	1937, 1973

Club	Year	Club	Year
Barnsley	1912	Leeds United	1972
Blackburn Olympic	1883	Notts County	1894
Blackpool	1953	Old Carthusians	1881
Bradford City	1911	Oxford University	1874
Burnley	1914	Portsmouth	1939
Cardiff City	1927	Royal Engineers	1875
Charlton Athletic	1947	Southampton	1976
Chelsea	1970	Wimbledon	1988
Clapham Rangers	1880		
Coventry City	1987		
Derby County	1946		
Huddersfield Town	1922		
Ipswich Town	1978		

FA CHARITY SHIELD WINNERS 1908-91

Year	Match	Score
1908	Manchester United v Queens Park Rangers *after 1-1 draw*	4-0
1909	Newcastle United v Northampton Town	2-0
1910	Brighton & Hove Albion v Aston Villa	1-0
1911	Manchester United v Swindon Town	8-4
1912	Blackburn Rovers v Queens Park Rangers	2-1
1913	Professionals v Amateurs	7-2
1919	WBA v Tottenham Hotspur	2-0
1920	Tottenham Hotspur v Burnley	2-0
1921	Huddersfield Town v Liverpool	1-0
1922	Not Played	
1923	Professionals v Amateurs	2-0
1924	Professionals v Amateurs	3-1
1925	Amateurs v Professionals	6-1
1926	Amateurs v Professionals	6-3
1927	Cardiff City v Corinthians	2-1
1928	Everton v Blackburn Rovers	2-1
1929	Professionals v Amateurs	3-0
1930	Arsenal v Sheffield Wednesday	2-1
1931	Arsenal v West Bromwich Albion	1-0
1932	Everton v Newcastle United	5-3
1933	Arsenal v Everton	3-0
1934	Arsenal v Manchester City	4-0
1935	Sheffield Wednesday v Arsenal	1-0
1936	Sunderland v Arsenal	2-1
1937	Manchester City v Sunderland	2-0
1938	Arsenal v Preston North End	2-1
1948	Arsenal v Manchester United	4-3
1949	Portsmouth v Wolverhampton Wanderes	† 1-1
1950	World Cup Team v Canadian Touring Team	4-2
1951	Tottenham Hotspur v Newcastle United	2-1
1952	Manchester United v Newcastle United	4-2
1953	Arsenal v Blackpool	† 3-1
1954	Wolverhampton Wanderers v West Bromwich Albion	† 4-4
1955	Chelsea v Newcastle United	3-0
1956	Manchester United v Manchester City	1-0

1957	Manchester United v Aston Villa	4-0
1958	Bolton Wanderers v Wolverhampton Wanderers	4-1
1959	Wolverhampton Wanderers v Nottingham Forest	3-1
1960	Burnley v Wolverhampton Wanderers	† 2-2
1961	Tottenham Hotspur v FA XI	3-2
1962	Tottenham Hotspur v Ipswich Town	5-1
1963	Everton v Manchester United	4-0
1964	Liverpool v West Ham United	† 2-2
1965	Manchester United v Liverpool	† 2-2
1966	Liverpool v Everton	1-0
1967	Manchester United v Tottenham Hotspur	† 3-3
1968	Manchester City v West Bromwich Albion	6-1
1969	Leeds United v Manchester City	2-1
1970	Everton v Chelsea	2-1
1971	Leicester City v Liverpool	1-0
1972	Manchester City v Aston Villa	1-0
1973	Burnley v Manchester City	1-0
1974	Liverpool v Leeds United	1-1
	Liverpool won on penalties	
1975	Derby County v West Ham United	2-0
1976	Liverpool v Southampton	1-0
1977	Liverpool v Manchester United	† 0-0
1978	Nottingham Forest v Ipswich Town	5-0
1979	Liverpool v Arsenal	3-1
1980	Liverpool v West Ham United	1-0
1981	Aston Villa v Tottenham Hotspur	† 2-2
1982	Liverpool v Tottenham Hotspur	1-0
1983	Manchester United v Liverpool	2-0
1984	Everton v Liverpool	1-0
1985	Everton v Manchester United	2-0
1986	Everton v Liverpool	† 1-1
1987	Everton v Coventry City	1-0
1988	Liverpool v Wimbledon	2-1
1989	Liverpool v Arsenal	1-0
1990	Liverpool v Manchester United	† 1-1
1991	Arsenal v Tottenham Hotspur	† 0-0
1992	Leeds United v Manchester United	4-3
1993	Manchester United v Arsenal	1-1
	Manchester United won on penalties	

† *Each club retained Shield for six months*

FOOTBALL LEAGUE
COCA-COLA CUP 1992-93

First Round – two legs

			1st Leg	2nd Leg	Agg
Preston North End	v	Stoke City	2-1	0-4	2-5
Exeter City	v	Birmingham City	0-1	0-4	0-5
Hereford United	v	Torquay United	2-5	2-0	4-5
Sunderland	v	Huddersfield Town	2-3	1-0	3-3
Carlisle United	v	Burnley	4-1	1-1	5-2
Darlington	v	Scunthorpe	1-1	0-2	1-3
Tranmere Rovers	v	Blackpool	3-0	0-4	3-4
Shrewsbury Town	v	Wigan Athletic	1-2	1-0	2-2
Oxford United	v	Swansea City	3-0	0-1	3-1
Colchester United	v	Brighton & Hove Alb	1-1	0-1	1-2
Halifax Town	v	Hartlepool United	1-2	2-3	3-5
Peterborough	v	Barnet	4-0	2-2	6-2
Wrexham	v	Bury	1-1	3-4	4-5
Grimsby Town	v	Barnsley	1-1	1-1	2-2
Crewe Alexandra	v	Rochdale	4-1	2-1	6-2
Chester City	v	Stockport County	3-2	2-1	5-3
Fulham	v	Brentford	0-2	0-2	0-4
Leyton Orient	v	Millwall	2-2	0-3	2-5
Scarborough	v	Bradford City	3-0	5-3	8-3
West Bromwich Alb	v	Plymouth Argyle	1-0	0-2	1-2
Gillingham	v	Northampton Town	2-1	2-0	4-1
Doncaster Rovers	v	Lincoln City	0-3	1-1	1-4
Cardiff City	v	Bristol City	1-0	1-5	2-5
Chesterfield	v	York City	2-0	0-0	2-0
Walsall	v	Bournemouth	1-1	1-0	2-1
Newcastle United	v	Mansfield Town	2-1	0-0	2-1
Bolton Wanderers	v	Port Vale	2-1	1-1	3-1
Hull City	v	Rotherham United	2-2	0-1	2-3

Second Round – two legs

			1st Leg	2nd Leg	Agg
Cambridge United	v	Stoke City	2-2	2-1	4-3
Notts County	v	Wolverhampton Wand	3-2	1-1	4-3
Oldham Athletic	v	Exeter City	1-0	0-0	1-0
Swindon Town	v	Torquay United	6-0	3-2	9-2
Blackburn Rovers	v	Huddersfield Town	1-1	4-3	5-4
Norwich City	v	Carlisle United	2-2	2-0	4-2
Watford	v	Reading	2-2	2-0	4-2
Leeds United	v	Scunthorpe United	4-0	2-2	4-2
Portsmouth	v	Blackpool	4-0	2-0	6-0
Ipswich Town	v	Wigan Athletic	2-2	4-0	6-2
Aston Villa	v	Oxford United	2-1	2-1	4-2
Manchester United	v	Brighton & Hove Alb	1-1	1-0	2-1
Sheffield Wedneseday	v	Hartlepool United	3-0	2-2	5-2
Leicester City	v	Peterborough	2-0	1-2	3-2
Bury	v	Charlton Athletic	0-0	1-0	1-0
Queens Park Rangers	v	Grimsby Town	2-1	1-2	3-3
Crewe Alexandra	v	West Ham United	0-0	2-0	2-0
Nottingham Forest	v	Stockport County	3-2	2-1	5-3
Manchester City	v	Bristol Rovers	0-0	2-1	2-1
Tottenham Hotspur	v	Brentford	3-1	4-2	7-3
Arsenal	v	Millwall	1-1	1-1	1-1
(Arsenal won on penalties)					
Derby County	v	Southend United	0-1	7-0	7-1
Scarborough	v	Coventry City	0-2	3-0	3-2
Plymouth Argyle	v	Luton Town	2-2	3-2	5-4
Southampton	v	Gillingham	0-0	3-0	3-0
Crystal Palace	v	Lincoln City	3-1	1-1	4-2
Sheffield United	v	Bristol City	1-2	4-1	5-3
Liverpool	v	Chesterfield	4-4	4-1	8-5
Chelsea	v	Walsall	3-0	1-0	4-0
Newcastle	v	Middlesbrough	0-0	3-1	3-1
Wimbledon	v	Bolton Wanderers	3-1	0-1	3-2
Everton	v	Rotherham United	0-1	3-0	3-1

Third Round

				Replay
Cambridge United	v	Notts County	3-2	
Oldham Athletic	v	Swindon Town	1-0	

Blackburn Rovers	v	Norwich City	2-0	
Watford	v	Leeds United	2-1	
Portsmouth	v	Ipswich Town	0-1	
Aston Villa	v	Manchester United	1-0	
Sheffield Wednesday	v	Leicester City	7-1	
Bury	v	Quens Park Rangers	0-2	
Crewe Alexandra	v	Nottingham Forest	0-1	
Manchester City	v	Tottenham Hotspur	0-1	
Arsenal	v	Derby County	1-1	2-1
Scarborough	v	Plymouth Argyle	3-3	2-1
Southampton	v	Crystal Palace	0-2	
Sheffield United	v	Liverpool	0-0	0-3
Chelsea	v	Newcastle United	2-1	
Wimbledon	v	Everton	0-0	0-1

Fourth Round

				Replay
Cambridge	v	Oldham Athletic	1-0	
Blackburn Rovers	v	Watford	6-1	
Ipswich Town	v	Aston Villa	2-2	1-0
Sheffield Wednesday	v	Queens Park Rangers	4-0	
Nottingham Forest	v	Tottenham Hotspur	2-0	
Arsenal	v	Scarborough	1-0	
Crystal Palace	v	Liverpool	1-1	2-1
Chelsea	v	Everton	2-2	1-0

Fifth Round

				Replay
Cambridge United	v	Blackburn Rovers	2-3	
Ipswich Town	v	Sheffield Wednesday	1-1	0-1
Nottingham Forest	v	Arsenal	0-2	
Crystal Palace	v	Chelsea	3-1	

Semi-Finals – two legs

			1st leg	*2nd leg*	*Agg*
Blackburn Rovers	v	Sheffield Wednesday	2-4	1-2	3-6
Arsenal	v	Crystal Palace	3-1	2-0	5-1

Final – 18th April 1993 at Wembley Stadium

Arsenal	v	Sheffield Wednesday	2-1	74,007
Merson, Morrow		Hawkes		

Arsenal: Seaman, O'Leary, Winterburn, Palour, Adams, Linighan, Morrow, Merson, Wright, Campbell, Davis.

Sheffield Wednesday: Woods, Nilsson, King (Hyde), Palmer, Anderson, Harkes, Wilson (Hirst), Waddle, Warhurst, Bright, Sheridan.

FOOTBALL LEAGUE
CUP FINALS 1961-1993

Year	Winners	Runners-up	1st	2nd	Agg
1961	Aston Villa	Rotherham United	0-2†	3-0	3-2
1962	Norwich City	Rochdale	3-0	1-0	4-0
1963	Birmingham City	Aston Villa	3-1	0-0	3-1
1964	Leicester City	Stoke City	1-1	3-2	4-3
1965	Chelsea	Leicester City	3-2	0-0	3-2
1966	West Bromwich Albion	West Ham United	1-2	4-1	5-3
1967	Queens Park Rangers	West Bromwich Albion	3-2		
1968	Leeds United	Arsenal	1-0		
1969	Swindon Town	Arsenal	† 3-1		
1970	Manchester City	West Bromwich Albion	2-1		
1971	Tottenham Hotspur	Aston Villa	† 2-0		
1972	Stoke City	Chelsea	2-1		
1973	Tottenham Hotspur	Norwich City	1-0		
1974	Wolverhampton W.	Manchester City	2-1		
1975	Aston Villa	Norwich City	1-0		
1976	Manchester City	Newcastle United	2-1		
1977	Aston Villa	Everton	† 3-2		
	after 0-0 draw and 1-1 draw aet				
1978	Nottingham Forest	Liverpool	1-0		
	after 0-0 draw aet				
1979	Nottingham Forest	Southampton	3-2		
1980	Wolverhampton W.	Nottingham	1-0		
1981	Liverpool	West Ham United	2-1		
	after 1-1 draw aet				

Milk Cup

Year	Winners	Runners-up	1st	2nd	Agg
1982	Liverpool	Tottenham Hotspur	† 3-1		
1983	Liverpool	Manchester United	† 2-1		
1984	Liverpool	Everton	1-0		
	after 0-0 draw aet				
1985	Norwich City	Sunderland	1-0		
1986	Oxford United	Queens Park Rangers	3-0		

Littlewoods Cup

1987	Arsenal	Liverpool	2-1
1988	Luton Town	Arsenal	3-2
1989	Nottingham Forest	Luton Town	3-1
1990	Nottingham Forest	Oldham Athletic	1-0

Rumbelows League Cup

| 1991 | Sheffield Wednesday | Manchester United | 1-0 |
| 1992 | Manchester United | Nottingham Forest | 1-0 |

Coca Cola Cup

| 1993 | Arsenal | Sheffield Wednesday | 2-1 |

FOOTBALL LEAGUE CUP WINS BY CLUB

Liverpool	1981, 1982, 1983, 1984
Nottingham Forest	1978, 1979, 1989, 1990
Aston Villa	1961, 1975, 1977
Arsenal	1987, 1993
Manchester City	1970, 1976
Tottenham Hotspur	1971, 1973
Norwich City	1962, 1985
Wolverhampton Wanderers	1974, 1980
Birmingham City	1963
Leicester City	1964
Chelsea	1965
WBA	1966
QPR	1967
Leeds United	1968
Swindon Town	1969
Stoke City	1972
Oxford United	1986
Luton Town	1988
Sheffield Wednesday	1991
Manchester United	1992

FA PREMIER LEAGUE CLUBS IN EUROPE 92-93

Champions' Cup

1st Round

Stuttgart
Walter (62, 68), Buck (82)
| **Leeds United** | **3-0** | 38,000 |

Leeds United
Speed (18), McAllister (38), Cantona (66), Chapman (80)
| **Stuttgart** Buck (33) | **4-1** | 20,457 |

Stuttgart win on away goals but replay ordered as
Stuttgart field an ineligible player

Leeds United
Strachan (34), Shutt (76)
| **Stuttgart** Golke (40) | **2-1** | 10,000 |

Leeds win 6-5 on aggregate. Replay Nou Camp, Barcelona

2nd Round

Rangers
Lukic (21 o.g.), McCoist (37)
| **Leeds United** McAllister (1) | **2-1** | 44,000 |

Leeds United
Cantona (85)
| **Rangers** Hateley (3), McCoist (59) | **1-2** | 25,118 |

Rangers win 4-2 on aggregate

Cup-Winners' Cup

1st Round

Liverpool
Stewart (4, 38), Rush (40, 50, 55, 74)
| **Apollon** Spoljaric (83 pen) | **6-1** | 12,769 |

Apollon
Spoljaric (60)
| **Liverpool** Rush (62), Hutchison (68) | **1-2** | 12,000 |

Liverpool win 8-2 on aggregate

2nd Round

Spartak Moscow
Pisarev (10), Karpin (68, 82 pen), Ledyakhov (89)
| **Liverpool** Wright (67), McManaman (78) | **4-2** | 55,000 |

Liverpool
| **Spartak Moscow** Radchenko (63), Piatnitski (89) | **0-2** | 37,993 |

Spartak win 6-2 on aggregate

48

UEFA Cup

1st Round

Manchester United   **Torpedo Moscow**   **0-0**   **19,998**

Torpedo Moscow   **Manchester United**   **0-0**   **11,357**

Aggregate 0-0, Torpedo win 4-3 on pens after extra time

Sheffield Wednesday   **Spora Luxembourg**   **8-1**   **19,792**
Waddle (9), Anderson (23, 29),   Cruz (11)
Warhurst (31, 77), Bart Williams (60, 81),
Worthington (65)

Spora Luxembourg   **Sheffield Wednesday**   **1-2**   **3,500**
Cruz (20)   Watson (18), Warhurst (36)

Sheffield Wednesday win 10-2 on aggregate

2nd Round

Kaiserslautern   **Sheffield Wednesday**   **3-1**   **20,802**
Funkel (5 pen), Marin (55),   Hirst (5)
Witeczek (57)

Sheffield Wednesday   **Kaiserslautern**   **2-2**   **27,597**
D. Wilson (27), Sheridan (64)   Witeczek (62), Zeyer (76)

Kaiserslautern win 5-3 on aggregate

Scorers by Club

Leeds United – Champions Cup
2:   Cantona, McAllister
1:   Chapman, Shutt, Strachan, Speed

Liverpool – Cup Winners' Cup
5:   Rush
2:   Stewart
1:   Hutchison, McManaman, Wright

Sheffield Wednesday – UEFA Cup
3:   Warhurst
2:   Anderson, Bart-Williams
1:   Hirst, Sheridan, Waddle, Watson, Wilson D, Worthington

European Cup Draws 1993-94

Champions' Cup Preliminary Round

To be played over two legs with the first named clubs at home in the first-leg. Matches to be played on August 17-18 and August 31 or September 1.

Avenir Beggen (Lux)	v	Rosenborg BK (Nor)
Cwmbran Town (Wal)	v	Cork City (Rep. Ire)
Ekranas Panevezys (Lith)	v	Floriana (Mal)
HJK Helsinki (Fin)	v	Norma Tallinn (Est)
Iberya (Dynamo) Tbilisi (Geo)	v	Linfield (N. Ire)
Omonia Nicosia (Cyp)	v	FC Aarau (Swi)
Partizani Tirana (Alb)	v	IA Akranes (Ice)
Skonto Riga (Lat)	v	Olimpija Ljubljana (Slove)
Tofta B68 (Fae)	v	Croatia Zagreb (Cro)
Zimbru Kishinev (Mold)	v	Beitar Jerusalem (Isr)

Champions' Cup 1st Round

To be played over two legs with the first named clubs at home in the first-leg.
Matches to be played on September 14-15 and September 28-29.

AIK Stockholm (Swe)	v	Sparta Prague (Czech)
Avenir Beggen (Lux) or Rosenborg BK (Nor)	v	Austria Vienna (Aus)
Dynamo Kiev (Ukr)	v	Barcelona (Esp)
FC Porto (Por)	v	Ekranas Panevezys (Lith) or Floriana (Mal)
Galatasaray (Tur)	v	Cwmbran Town (Wal) or Cork City (Rep. Ire)
HJK Helsinki (Fin) or Norma Tallinn (Est)	v	RSC Anderlecht (Bel)
Honved Kipest (Hun)	v	**MANCHESTER UNITED**
Iberya Tbilisi (Geo) or Linfield (N. Ire)	v	FC Copenhagen (Den)
Lech Poznan (Pol)	v	Zimbru Kishinev (Mold) or Beitar Jerusalem (Isr)
Marseille (Fra)	v	AEK Athens (Gre)
Omonia Nicosia (Cyp) or FC Aarau (Swi)	v	Milan (Ita)
Partizani Tirana (Alb) or IA Akranes (Ice)	v	Feyenoord (Hol)
Rangers (Sco)	v	Levski Sofia (Bul)
Skonto Riga (Lat) or Olimpija Ljubljana (Slove)	v	Spartak Moscow (Rus)
Steaua Bucharest (Rom)	v	Tofta B68 (Fae) or Croatia Zagreb (Cro)
Werder Bremen (Ger)	v	Dinamo Minsk (Biel)

Cup-Winners' Cup Preliminary Round

To be played over two legs with the first named clubs at home in the first-leg.
Matches to be played on August 17-18 and August 31 or September 1.

Bangor (N. Ire)	v	Apoel Nicosia (Cyp)
Belzers (Liech)	v	Albpetrol (Alb)
FC Lugano (Swi)	v	Neman Grodno (Biel)

Karpaty Lvov (Ukr)	v	Shelbourne (Rep. Ire)
Maccabi Haifa (Isr)	v	Dudelange (Lux)
Nikol Tallinn (Est)	v	Lillestrom SK (Nor)
OB Odense (Den)	v	Publikum Celje (Slova)
RAF Jelgava (Lat)	v	Havnar HB (Fae)
Sliema Wanderers (Mal)	v	Degerfors IF (Swe)
Valur (Ice)	v	MyPa (Fin)
VSZ Kosice (Slove)	v	Zhalgiris Vilnius (Lith)

Cup-Winners' Cup 1st Round

To be played over two legs with the first named clubs at home in the first-leg.
Matches to be played on September 14-15 and September 28-29.

Bangor (N. Ire) or Apoel Nicosia (Cyp)	v	Paris Saint-Germain (Fra)
Bayer Leverkusen (Ger)	v	Zbrojovka Brno (Czech)
Benfica (Por)	v	GKS Katowice (Pol)
Besiktas (Tur)	v	VSZ Kosice (Slove) or Zhalgiris Vilnius (Lith)
CSKA Sofia (Bul)	v	Belzers (Liech) or Albpetrol (Alb)
FC Tirol-Innsbruck (Aus)	v	Ferencvaros (Hun)
Hajduk Split (Cro)	v	Ajax (Hol)
Nikol Tallinn (Est) or Lillestrom SK (Nor)	v	Torino (Ita)
OB Odense (Den) or Publikum Celje (Slova)	v	**ARSENAL**
Panathinaikos (Gre)	v	Karpaty Lvov (Ukr) or Shelbourne (Rep. Ire)
Real Madrid (Esp)	v	FC Lugano (Swi) or Neman Grodno (Biel)
Sliema Wanderers (Mal) or Degerfors IF (Swe)	v	Parma (Ita)
Standard Liege (Bel)	v	Cardiff City (Wal)
Torpedo Moscow (Rus)	v	Dudelange (Lux) or Maccabi Haifa (Isr)
Universitatea Craiova (Rom)	v	RAF Jelgava (Lat) or Havnar HB (Fae)
Valur (Ice) or MyPa (Fin)	v	Aberdeen (Sco)

UEFA Cup 1st Round

To be played over two legs with the first named clubs at home in the first-leg.
Matches to be played on September 14-15 and September 28-29.

AaB Aalborg (Den)	v	Deportivo La Coruna (Esp)
Admira Wacker (Aus)	v	Dnepr Dnepropetrovsk (Ukr)
Bohemians (Rep. Ire)	v	Bordeaux (Fra)
Borussia Dortmund (Ger)	v	Spartak Vladikavkaz (Rus)
Botev Plovdiv (Bul)	v	Olympiakos (Gre)
Brondby (Den)	v	Dundee United (Sco)
Crusaders (N. Ire)	v	Servette (Swi)
Dinamo Bucharest (Rom)	v	Cagliari (Ita)
Dinamo Moscow (Rus)	v	Eintracht Frankfurt (Ger)
FC Nantes (Fra)	v	Valencia (Esp)
FC Twente (Hol)	v	Bayern Munich (Ger)
Gloria Bistrita (Rom)	v	Maribor Branik (Slova)
Heart of Midlothian (Sco)	v	Atletico Madrid (Esp)
IFK Norrkoping (Swe)	v	KV Mechelen (Bel)
Internazionale (Ita)	v	Rapid Bucharest (Rom)
Juventus (Ita)	v	Lokomotiv Moscow (Rus)
Karlsruhe SC (Ger)	v	PSV Eindhoven (Hol)
Kocaelispor Kulubu (Tur)	v	Sporting Lisbon (Por)
KR Reykjavik (Ice)	v	MTK Budapest (Hun)
Kuusysi Lahti (Fin)	v	KSV Waregem (Bel)
Lazio (Ita)	v	Lokomotiv Plovdiv (Bul)
NORWICH CITY	v	Vitesse Arnhem (Hol)
Osters IF (Swe)	v	Kongsvinger IL (Nor)
Royal Antwerp (Bel)	v	Maritimo (Por)
Slavia Prague (Czech)	v	OFI Crete (Gre)
Slovan Bratislava (Slova)	v	**ASTON VILLA**
SV Casino Salzburg (Aus)	v	Dac Dunjaska Streda (Slova)
Tenerife (Esp)	v	Monaco (Fra)
Trabzonspor (Tur)	v	Valletta (Mal)
US Luxembourg (Lux)	v	Boavista FC (Por)
Vac FC Samsung (Hun)	v	Apollon Limassol (Cyp)
Young Boys Berne (Swit)	v	Celtic (Sco)

Player	Birthplace	From	To	Fee
Patrik Andersson	Borgeby, Sweden	Malmo	Blackburn	£600,000
Stefan Beixlich	Berlin	Bergmann Borsig	Aston Villa	£100,000
Gudni Bergsson	Reyjkavik	Valur	Tottenham	£350,000
Stig Inge Bjornbye	Rosenborg, Norway	Rosenborg	Liverpool	£600,000
Mark Bosnich	Sydney	Sydney Croatia	Aston Villa	Free
Vlado Bozinoski	Ohrid Msstonie	Sporting Lisbon	Ipswich	£100,000
Matthias Breitkreuz	Crivitz, Germany	Bergmann Borsig	Aston Villa	£100,000
Alex Bunbury	British Guyana	Supra, Canada	West Ham	£200,000
Eric Cantona	Paris	Leeds	Man Utd	£1,200,000
Aleksey Cherednik	Dnepr, Georgia	Dnepr	Southampton	£150,000
Bruce Grobbelaar,	Zimbabwe	Vancouver	Liverpool	£250,000
Bontcho Guentchev	Tchoxhavo Bsigsris	Sporting Lisbon	Ipswich	£250,000
Gunnar Halle	Oslo	Lillestrom	Oldham	£250,000
John Jensen	Copenhagen	Brondby	Arsenal	£1,100,000
Erland Johnson	Fredrikstad, Norway	Bayern Munich	Chelsea	£300,000
Andrei Kanchelskis	Ukraine	Donetsk	Man Utd	£650,000
Jason Kearton	Ipswich, Australia	Brisbane Lions	Everton	Free
Dimitri Kharin	Moscow	CSKA Moscow	Chelsea	£200,000
Born Kristensen	Malling, Denmark	Aarhus	Newcastle	£250,000
Dariusz Kubicki	Warsaw	Legia Warsaw	Aston Villa	£200,000
Anders Limpar	Sweden	Cremonese	Arsenal	£1,000,000
Pal Lydersen	Kristisnsand, Norway	Start	Arsenal	£500,000
Ludek Miklosko	Ostrava, Czech	Banik Ostrava	West Ham	£300,000
Jan Molby	Kolding, Denmark	Ajax	Liverpool	£576,000
Ken Monkou	Suriname	Chelsea	Southampton	£750,000

54

FA PREMIER LEAGUE

Player	Birthplace	From	To	Fee
Peter Ndlovu	Zimbabwe	Highlanders	Coventry	£10,000
Roland Nilsson	Helsingborg, Sweden	Gothenberg	Sheff Wed	£375,000
Torben Picchnik	Copenhagen	Copenhagen	Liverpool	£500,000
Predrag Radosavljevic	Belgrade	St Louis	Everton	£100,000
Ronny Rosenthal	Haifa, Israel	Standard Liege	Liverpool	£1,000,000
Peter Schmeichal	Gladsake, Denmark	Brondby	Man Utd	£550,000
Hans Segers	Eindhoven	Nottingham For	Wimbledon	£125,000
Pavel Smicek	Ostrava	Banik Ostrava	Newcastle	£300,000
Jan Stejskal	Brunn, Czech	Sparta Prague	QPR	£600,000
Erik Thorstvedt	Stavanger, Norway	Gothenberg	Tottenham	£400,000
Michel Vonk	Alkmaar, Holland	SVV Dordrecht	Man City	£400,000
Robert Warzycha	Warsaw	Gornik Zabrze	Everton	Unknown
Roy Wegerle	South Africa	QPR	Blackburn	£1,000,000
Dwight Yorke	Canaan, Tobago	Signal Hill	Aston Villa	£120,000

55

ENGLAND 1992-93

Santander, September 9th – friendly
SPAIN   **ENGLAND**   **1-0**   **22,000**
Fonesca 11
England: Woods, Dixon (Bardsley 46, Palmer 63), Pearce, Walker, Wright, Ince, White (Merson 79), Platt, Shearer, Sinton (Deane 79), Clough

Wembley, October 14th – World Cup European Qualifying Group 2
ENGLAND   **NORWAY**   **1-1**   **51,441**
Platt 55   Rekdal 76
England: Woods, Dixon (Palmer 89), Walker, Adams, Pearce, Batty, Ince, Platt, Gascoigne, Wright (Merson 69), Shearer

Wembley, November 16th – World Cup European Qualifying Group 2
ENGLAND   **TURKEY**   **4-0**   **42,984**
Gascoigne 16, 61,
Shearer 28, Pearce 60
England: Woods, Dixon, Pearce, Palmer, Walker, Adams, Platt, Gascoigne, Shearer, I Wright, Ince

Wembley, February 17th – World Cup European Qualifying Group 2
ENGLAND   **SAN MARINO**   **6-0**   **51,154**
Platt 13, 24, 67, 83,
Palmer 78, Ferdinand 86
England: Woods, Dixon, Walker, Adams, Dorigo, Gascoigne, Batty, Platt, Palmer, Ferdinand, Barnes

Izmir, May 31st – World Cup European Qualifying Group 2
TURKEY   **ENGLAND**   **0-2**   **60,000**
Platt 6, Gascoigne 44
England: Woods, Dixon (Clough 46), Sinton, Palmer, Walker, Adams, Platt, Gascoigne, Barnes, Wright, (Sharpe 84), Ince

Wembley, April 28th – World Cup European Qualifying Group 2

ENGLAND   **HOLLAND**   **2-2**   **73,163**

Barnes 2, Platt 23   Bergkamp 34, Van Vossen 85 (pen)

England: Woods, Dixon, Walker, Adams, Keown, Ince, Gascoigne (Merson 46), Palmer, Barnes, Platt, Ferdinand

Chorzow, May 29th – World Cup European Qualifying Group 2

POLAND   **ENGLAND**   **1-1**   **60,000**

Adamczuk 34,   Wright 84

England: Woods, Bardsley, Dorigo, Palmer (Wright 72), Walker, Adams, Platt, Gascoigne (Clough 79), Sheringham, Barnes, Ince

Oslo, June 2nd – World Cup European Qualifying Group 2

NORWAY   **ENGLAND**   **2-0**   **22,250**

Leonhardsen 42, Bohinen 48

England: Woods, Dixon, Pallister, Palmer, Walker (Clough 63), Adams, Platt, Gascoigne, Ferdinand, Sheringham (Wright 46), Sharpe

Foxboro, June 6th – US Cup

USA   **ENGLAND**   **2-0**   **37,652**

Dooley 42, Lalas 72

England: Woods, Dixon, Pallister, Palmer (Walker 61), Dorigo, Batty, Ince, Clough, Sharpe, Ferdinand (Wright 35), Barnes

Washington, June 9th – US Cup

ENGLAND   **BRAZIL**   **1-1**   **54,118**

Platt 47   Santos 76

England: Flowers, Barrett, Walker, Pallister, Dorigo, Sinton, Batty (Platt 46), Clough (Merson 82), Ince (Palmer 67), Sharpe, Wright

Chicago, June 19th – US Cup

ENGLAND   **GERMANY**   **1-2**   **62,126**

Platt 31   Effenberg 26, Klinsmann 55

England: Martyn, Barrett, Pallister, (Keown 53), Walker, Platt, Ince, Clough (Wright 70), Sinton, Merson, Barnes, Sharpe (Winterburn 46)

England Record 92-93

	P	W	D	L	F	A
	11	3	4	4	18	12

Appearance and Goalscorers Summary 1992-93

Player	Club	Apps	Sub	Goals
Tony ADAMS	Arsenal	3	0	0
David BARDSLEY	QPR	1	1	0
John BARNES	Liverpool	6	0	1
Earl BARRETT	Aston Villa	2	0	0
David BATTY	Leeds United	4	0	0
Nigel CLOUGH	Nottingham Forest	4	3	0
Brian DEANE	Sheffield United	0	1	0
Lee DIXON	Arsenal	8	0	0
Tony DORIGO	Leeds United	4	0	0
Les FERDINAND	QPR	4	0	1
Tim FLOWERS	Southampton	1	0	0
Paul GASCOIGNE	Lazio	7	0	3
Paul INCE	Manchester United	9	0	0
Martin KEOWN	Arsenal	1	1	0
Nigel MARTYN	Crystal Palace	1	0	0
Paul MERSON	Arsenal	1	4	0
Gary PALLISTER	Manchester United	4	0	0
Carlton PALMER	Sheffield Wednesday	7	3	1
Stuart PEARCE	Nottingham Forest	3	0	1
David PLATT	Juventus	9	1	9
Lee SHARPE	Manchester United	4	1	0
Alan SHEARER	Blackburn Rovers	3	0	1
Teddy SHERINGHAM	Tottenham Hotspur	2	0	0
Andy SINTON	QPR	4	0	0
Des WALKER	Sampdoria	10	1	0
David WHITE	Manchester City	1	0	0
Nigel WINTERBURN	Arsenal	1	0	0
Chris WOODS	Sheffield Wednesday	9	0	0
Ian WRIGHT	Arsenal	5	4	1

1992-93 APPEARANCE CHART

	Spain	Norway	Turkey	San Marino	Turkey	Holland	Poland	Norway	United States	Brazil	Germany
Adams	–	•	•	•	•	•	•	•	•	•	•
Bardsley	46	–	–	–	–	•	–	–	–	–	–
Barnes	–	•	–	•	•	•	•	–	•	•	•
Barrett	–	–	–	–	–	–	–	–	•	•	•
Batty	–	•	•	•	•	•	•	•	•	•	•
Clough	•	–	–	–	46	–	79	63	•	•	•
Deane	79	–	–	–	–	–	–	–	–	–	–
Dixon	•	•	•	•	•	•	•	•	•	–	–
Dorigo	–	–	–	•	–	–	–	–	–	–	–
Ferdinand	–	–	–	–	–	–	–	•	•	–	–
Flowers	–	–	•	–	•	–	–	–	–	•	–
Gascoigne	–	•	•	•	•	•	•	•	•	–	–
Ince	•	•	•	•	•	•	•	•	•	•	–
Keown	–	–	–	–	–	•	–	–	–	–	53
Martyn	–	–	–	–	–	–	–	–	–	–	•
Merson	79	69	–	–	–	46	–	–	–	82	•
Pallister	–	–	–	–	–	–	–	•	•	•	•
Palmer	63	89	•	•	•	•	•	•	•	67	–
Pearce	•	•	•	•	•	•	•	•	–	–	–
Platt	•	•	•	•	•	•	•	•	•	46	•
Sharpe	–	•	•	–	84	–	•	•	•	•	•
Shearer	•	•	•	•	–	–	–	–	–	–	–
Sheringham	–	–	–	–	–	–	•	–	–	•	•
Sinton	–	–	–	–	–	•	–	–	–	•	•
Walker	•	•	•	•	•	•	•	•	61	•	•
White	•	–	–	–	–	–	–	–	–	–	–
Winterburn	–	–	–	–	–	–	–	–	–	–	•
Woods	–	–	–	–	–	•	•	•	•	–	•
Wright, I	•	•	•	•	•	–	72	46	35	•	70

• Started match. – No appearance. A number indicates an appearance as substitute, the number relating the minute the player entered the match.

FA CARLING PREMIERSHIP CLUB DIRECTORY 1993-94

ARSENAL

Formed as Dial Square, a workshop in Woolwich Arsenal with a sundial over the entrance, in October 1886, becoming Royal Arsenal, the 'Royal' possibly from a local public house, later the same year. Turned professional and became Woolwich Arsenal in 1891. Selected for an expanded Football League Division Two in 1893, the first southern team to join.

Moved from the Manor Ground, Plumstead south-east London, to Highbury, north London, in 1913 changing name again at the same time. Elected from fifth in Division Two to the expanded First Division for the 1919-20 season and never relegated. Premier League founder members 1992.

Ground: Arsenal Stadium, Highbury, London N5.
Phone: 071-226 0304   **Nickname:** Gunners
Colours: Red/White sleeves, White, Red
Change: Yellow, Navy Blue, Yellow
Capacity: 28,000   **Pitch:** 110 yds x 71 ydS
Directions: *From North:* M1, J2 follow sign for City. After Holloway Rd station (c 6 miles) take third left into Drayton Park. Then right into Aubert Park after ¾ mile and 2nd left into Avenell Rd. *From South:* Signs for Bank of England then Angel from London Bridge. Right at traffic lights towards Highbury roundabout. Follow Holloway Rd then third right into Drayton Pk, thereafter as above. *From West:* A40(M) to A501 ring road. Left at Angel to Highbury roundabout, then as above.
Rail: Drayton Park/Finsbury Park   **Tube** (Piccadilly line): Arsenal

Chairman: P.D. Hill-Wood   **Vice-Chairman:** D. Dein
Managing Director: K.J. Friar   **Secretary:** K.J. Friar
Manager: George Graham   **Assistant/Coach:** Stewart Houston
Physio: Gary Lewin

Record FAPL Win: 3-0 v Coventry, 7/11/92 *and* 3-0 v Crystal Palace, 8/5/93
Record FAPL Defeat: 0-3 v Leeds United, 21/11/92
Record FL Win: 12-0 v Loughborough T, Division 2, 12th March, 1900
Record FL Defeat: 0-8 v Loughborough T, Division 2, 12th December, 1896
Record Cup Win: 11-1 v Darwen, FA Cup, 3rd round, 9th January, 1932
Record Fee Received: £1.5m from Liverpool for Michael Thomas, 11/1991
Record Fee Paid: £2.5m to Crystal Palace for Ian Wright, 9/1991
Most FAPL Appearances: 39: David Seaman 1992-93
Most FL Appearances: David O'Leary, 547, 1975-92
Record Attendance (all-time): 73,295 v Sunderland, Division 1, 9/3/35
Record Attendance (FAPL): 29,740 v Manchester United, 28/11/92
Highest Scorer in FAPL Season: Ian Wright, 30, 92-93

Most FAPL Goals in season: 40, 1992-93
Most FAPL Points in season: 56, 1992-93
Most Capped Player: Kenny Sansom, 77 (86), England

Close Season Transfers
In: Eddie McGoldrick (Crystal Palace, £1m)
Out: Steve Clements (Hereford United, Free), David O'Leary (Leeds United, Free), Nicky Rust (Brighton & HA, Free), Jason Brissett (Peterborough, non-contract), Colin Pates (Brighton & HA, Trial)

Season 1992-93
Biggest Home Win: 3-0 v Coventry *and* 3-0 v Crystal Palace
Biggest Home Defeat: 2-4 v Norwich City
Biggest Away Win: 2-0 v Coventry City *and* 2-0 v Liverpool
Biggest Away Defeat: 0-3 v Leeds United
Biggest Home Attendance: 29,740 v Manchester United, 28/11/92
Smallest Home Attendance: 18,253 v Wimbledon, 10/2/93
Average Attendance: 24,403 (-23.50%)
Last Season: *FAPL:* 10th *FA Cup:* Winners *Coca-Cola Cup:* Winners
Leading Scorer: Wright (30)

League History: 1893 Elected to Division 2; 1904-13 Division 1; 1913-19 Division 2; 1919-92 Division 1; 1992 – FA Premier League.
Honours: Football League: Division 1 – Champions 1930-31, 1932-33, 1933-34, 1934-35, 1937-38, 1947-48, 1952-53, 1970-71, 1988-89, 1990-91; Runners-up 1925-26, 1931-32, 1972-73; Division 2 – Runners-up 1903-04. FA Cup: Winners 1929-30, 1935-36, 1949-50, 1970-71, 1978-79, 1992-93; Runners-up 1926-27, 1931-32, 1951-52, 1971-72, 1977-78, 1979-80. Football League Cup: Winners 1986-87, 1992-93; Runners-up 1967-68, 1968-69, 1987-88. League-Cup Double Performed: 1970-71. Cup-Cup Double Performed: 1992-93
European Competitions: European Cup: 1971-72, 1991-92; European Cup-Winners' Cup: 1979-80 (runners-up); European Fairs Cup: 1963-64, 1969-70 (winners), 1970-71; UEFA Cup: 1978-79, 1981-82, 1982-83.
Managers (and Secretary-managers): Sam Hollis 1894-97, Tom Mitchell 1897-98, George Elcoat 1898-99, Harry Bradshaw 1899-1904, Phil Kelso 1904-08, George Morrell 1908-15, Leslie Knighton 1919-25, Herbert Chapman 1925-34, George Allison 1934-47, Tom Whittaker 1947-56, Jack Crayston 1956-58, George Swindin 1958-62, Billy Wright 1962-66, Bertie Mee 1966-76, Terry Neill 1976-83, Don Howe 1984-86, George Graham May, 1986-.

5-Year League Record

	Div.	P	W	D	L	F	A	Pts	Pos	FAC	FLC
88-89	1	83	22	10	6	73	36	76	1	3	3
89-90	1	38	18	8	12	54	38	62	4	4	4
90-91	1	38	24	13	1	74	18	83*	1	SF	4
91-92	1	42	19	15	8	81	46	72	4	3	3
92-93	PL	42	15	11	16	40	38	56	10	W	W

*2 points deducted

Summary of Appearances and Goals 1992-93

	Apps	Sub	Goals		Apps	Sub	Goals
Tony Adams	33	2	0	Pål Lyderson	7	1	0
Steve Bould	24		1	Scott Marshall	2		0
Kevin Campbell	32	5	4	Gavin McGowan	0	2	0
Jimmy Carter	11	5	2	Paul Merson	32	1	6
Paul Davis	6		0	Alan Miller	3	1	0
Paul Dickov	1	2	2	Steve Morrow	13	3	0
Lee Dixon	29		0	David O'Leary	6	5	0
Mark Flatts	6	4	0	Ray Parfour	16	5	1
Perry Groves	0	1	0	Colin Pates	2	5	0
Neil Heaney	3	2	0	David Seaman	39		0
David Hillier	27	3	1	Ian Selley	9		0
John Jensen	29	3	0	Alan Smith	27	4	3
Martin Keown	15	1	0	Nigel Winterburn	29		1
Anders Limpar	12	11	2	Ian Wright	30	1	15
Andy Linighan	19	2	2				

FA Premier League Squad Numbers 1993-94

No.	Player	No.	Player	No.	Player
1	Seaman	10	Merson	19	Carter
2	Dixon	11	McGoldrick	20	Lydersen
3	Winterburn	12	Bould	21	Morrow
4	Davis	13	Miller	22	Selley
5	Linighan	14	Keown	23	Parlour
6	Adams	15	Limper	24	Flatts
7	Campbell	16	*	25	Heaney
8	Wright	17	Jensen	26	Will
9	Smith	18	Hillier		

Arsenal's Cups of Joy

The burden of expectancy again proved to be too much for the hot pre-season favourites to bear, as the Gunners produced their most disappointing league placing so far under manager George Graham, a mediocre 12th spot.

But even more difficult to accept for Arsenal fans was the manner in which the Gunners appeared to lose interest in the title. Having garnered only eleven points from their first nine games, George Graham's side rallied slightly, only to effectively surrender any credible hopes of winning the title with a miserable run of two months without a win from mid November to mid January, the worst slump at the club for five years.

To make matters worse, all this was achieved under a black disciplinary cloud with the Gunners easily collecting more bookings than any other Premier League side, and England striker Ian Wright getting into more trouble at Lancaster Gate, incurring a three-match ban following an incident during a bad-tempered North London derby at White Hart Lane in December.

But if there was to be a saving grace about the season at Highbury, it was surely Arsenal's form in the cup competitions. Their momentous progress towards two Wembley Cup Finals began in earnest in January with a 3-1 demolition of non-league Yeovil Town in the third round of the FA Cup. Further victories over Leeds (courtesy of a replay), Nottingham Forest and then Ipswich in an epic 4-2 win at Portman Road, set up the prospect of a mouth-watering semi-final against the old enemy Tottenham.

Spurs had of course disposed of the Gunners 3-1 at the same stage of the competition in a thrilling match in 1991, but on this occasion it was a Tony Adams header that avenged the disappointment of two seasons before.

Important goals by defenders were to become something of a fashion for Arsenal as the season progressed. Stephen Morrow popped up with his first goal for the club in April to help Arsenal to a 2-1 Coca-Cola victory over Sheffield Wednesday. Tragically Morrow suffered a freak accident as he participated in the post-match celebrations and a badly broken elbow meant he would miss the FA Cup Final again against Wednesday in May.

But as the young Irishman watched from the stands, after having been afforded the precedent of receiving his Coca-Cola Cup medal before the FA Cup Final, Arsenal struggled to a 1-1 draw after extra-time. Wright it was inevitably who provided the only Gunners' strike of the game, exposing a chronic lack of goals from other players during the season.

When Arsenal went into the lead against The Owls in the replay, once more thanks to Wright, and again surrendered their advantage when Chris Waddle replied, it seemed that the Gunners might miss out on a unique double. But with only seconds left in extra-time, defender Andy Linighan, a £1 million misfit since his move to Highbury in 1990, crept up to score a header from a corner to complete an amazing season for Arsenal.

ASTON VILLA

Founded in 1874 by cricketers from the Aston Wesleyan Chapel, Lozells, who played on Aston Park, moving to a field in Wellington Road, Perry Barr in 1876. Prominent nationally, the club was a founder member of the Football League in 1888.

The landlord at Perry Barr made such demands that the club sought its own ground and eventually moved back to Aston occupying the Aston Lower Grounds, which had already been used for some big games. Not known as Villa Park until some time later, the ground first saw League football in 1897. Premier League founder members 1992.

Ground: Villa Park, Trinity Rd, Birmingham, B6 6HE
Phone: 021-327 2299　　　　　　　　**Nickname:** The Villains
Colours: Claret/Blue, White, Blue/Claret
Change Colours: White, Black, White
Capacity: 40,312　　　　　　**Pitch:** 115 yds x 75 yds
Directions: M6 J6, follow signs for Birminham NE. 3rd exit at roundabout then right into Ashton Hall Rd after $1/2$ mile.
Rail: Witton

President: H.J. Musgrove　　　　**Chairman:** H.D. Ellis
Secretary: Steven Stride
Manager: Ron Atkinson　　　　　**Assistant:** Jim Barron
First Team Coach: Dave Sexton　　**Physio:** Jim Walker

Record FAPL Win: 5-1 v Middlesbrough, 7/1/93
Record FAPL Defeat: 0-3 v Blackburn Rovers, 21/4/93 *and*
　　　　　　　　　　0-3 v Coventry, 26/12/97
Record FL Win: 12-2 v Accrington S, Division 1, 12/3/1892
Record FL Defeat: 1-8 v Blackburn R, FA Cup, 3rd R, 16/2/1889
Record Cup Win: 13-0 v Wednesbury Old Ath, FA Cup, 1st R, 30/10/ 1886
Record Fee Received: £5.5m from Bari for David Platt, 8/1991
Record Fee Paid: £1.7m to Oldham Athletic for Earl Barrett, 2/1992
Most FAPL Appearances: 42: Earl Barrett, Paul McGrath, Kevin Richardson, Steve Staunton. 1992-93
Most FL Appearances: Charlie Aitken, 561, 1961-76
Record Attendance (all-time): 76,588 v Derby Co, FA Cup 6th R, 2/2/1946
Record Attendance (FAPL): 39,063 v Manchester United, 7/11/92
Highest Scorer in FAPL season: 17: Dean Saunders, 1992-93
Most FAPL Goals in season: 57, 1992-93
Most FAPL Points in season: 74, 1992-93

Most Capped Player: Peter McParland, 33 (34), Northern Ireland
Close Season Transfers
In: Andy Townsend (Chelsea, £2.1m), Guy Whittingham (Portsmouth, £1.2m including Blake), Gordon Cowans (Blackburn, Free)
Out: Martin Carruthers (Stoke, Tribunal fee), Cyrille Regis (Wolves, Free), Mark Blake (Portsmouth, Swap)

Season 1992-93
Biggest Home Win: 5-1 v Middlesbrough
Biggest Home Defeat: 1-3 v Chelsea
Biggest Away Win: 2-0 v Sheffield United
Biggest Away Defeat: 0-3 v Blackburn Rovers *and* 0-3 v Coventry City
Biggest Home Attendance: 39,063 v Manchester United, 7/11/92
Smallest Home Attendance: 17,120 v Crystal Palace, 5/9/92
Average Attendance: 29,642 (+ 19.46%)
Last Season: *PL:* 2nd *FA Cup:* 4th round *Coca-Cola Cup:* 4th round
Leading Scorer: Saunders (17)

League History: 1888 Founder Member of the League; 1936-38 Division 2; 1938-59 Division 1; 1959-60 Division 2; 1960-67 Division 1; 1967-70 Division 2; 1970-72 Division 3; 1972-75 Division 2; 1975-87 Division 1; 1987-88 Division 2; 1988-92 Division 1; 1992- FA Premier League
Honours: FA Premier League – Runners-up 1992-93; Football League: Division 1 – Champions 1893-94, 1895-96, 1896-97, 1898-99, 1899-1900, 1909-10, 1980-81; Runners-up 1888-89, 1902-03, 1907-08, 1910-11, 1912-13, 1913-14, 1930-31, 1932-33, 1989-90; Division 2 – Champions 1937-38, 1959-60; Runners-up 1974-75, 1987-88; Division 3 – Champions 1971-72. FA Cup: Winners 1887, 1895, 1897, 1905, 1913, 1920, 1957; Runners-up 1892, 1924. League-Cup Double Performed: 1896-97. Football League Cup: Winners 1961, 1975, 1977; Runners-up 1963, 1971
European Competitions: European Cup: 1981-82 (winners), 1982-83; UEFA Cup: 1975-76, 1977-78, 1983-84, 1990-91. World Cup Championship: 1982-83; European Super Cup: 1982-83 (winners)
Managers (and Secretary-managers): George Ramsay 1884-1926, W.J. Smith 1926-34, Jimmy McMullan 1934-35, Jimmy Hogan 1936-44, Alex Massie 1945-50, George Martin 1950-53, Eric Houghton 1953-58, Joe Mercer 1958-64, Dick Taylor 1965-67, Tommy Cummings 1967-68, Tommy Docherty 1968-70, Vic Crowe 1970-74, Ron Saunders 1974-82, Tony Barton 1982-84, Graham Turner 1984-86, Billy McNeill 1986-87, Graham Taylor 1987-90, Dr Jozef Venglos 1990-91, Ron Atkinson June 1991-.

5-Year League Record

	Div.	P	W	D	L	F	A	Pts	Pos	FAC	FLC
88-89	1	38	9	13	16	45	56	40	17	4	5
89-90	1	38	21	7	10	57	38	70	2	6	3
90-91	1	38	9	14	15	46	58	41	17	3	5
91-92	1	42	17	9	16	48	44	60	7	2	6
92-93	PL	42	21	11	10	57	40	74	2	4	4

Summary of Appearances and Goals 1992-93

	Apps	Sub	Goals		Apps	Sub	Goals
Dalian Atkinson	28		11	Ray Houghton	39		3
Earl Barrett	42		1	Frank McAvennie	0	3	0
Stefan Beinlich	1	6	0	Paul McGrath	42		4
Mark Blake	0	1	0	Garry Parker	37		9
Mark Bosnich	17		0	Cyrill Regis	7	6	1
Mathias Breitkreutz	2	1	0	Kevin Richardson	42		2
Martin Carruthers	0	1	0	Dean Saunders	35		13
Neil Cox	6	9	1	Bryan Small	10	4	0
Tony Daley	8	5	2	Nigel Spink	25		0
Ugo Ehlogo	1	3	0	Steve Staunton	42		2
Dave Farrell	1	1	0	Shaun Teale	39		1
Stephen Froggett	16	1	1	Dwight Yorke	22	5	6

FA Premier League Squad Numbers 1993-94

No.	Player	No.	Player	No.	Player
1	Spink	9	Saunders	17	Cox
2	Barrett	10	Atkinson	18	Yorke
3	Staunton	11	Daley	19	Beinlich
4	Teale	12	Froggart	20	Breitkreutz
5	McGrath	13	Bosnich	21	Farrell
6	Richardson	14	Townsend	22	Whittingham
7	Houghton	15	Cowans		
8	Parker	16	Ehiogu		

Villa Run Out of Steam

For so long the Villa Park faithful had visions of the first championship campaign since 1982, until the last but one week of the season brought an unexpected defeat at home to Oldham and the end of a dream.

But little can be taken away from the garrulous Ron Atkinson and his impressive side who provided such an impressive foil to title winners Manchester United. Having started the season as modest bets for a good year, 40-1 for the title at the bookies, Atkinson provided one of his many shrewd pieces of football business by concluding the £2.3 million signing of Welsh international striker Dean Saunders.

Saunders immediately linked up successfully with powerful Villa teammate Dalian Atkinson, whose season could well have ended with international recognition had he not been plagued with a series of niggling injuries.

After a modest start to the season, in which there had been little indication of what was to follow, Saunders' arrival in September provided the spark to a low-burning fuse which was finally to explode into a dramatic title campaign.

Saunders himself exploded into action when faced with the prospect of playing his old side Liverpool at the end of September at Villa Park. Saunders collected a superb brace of goals as Villa triumphed 4-2 and began to surge up the table.

By the start of November a 2-0 home victory over Queen's Park Rangers pushed Villa up to third and by Christmas Ron Atkinson's side had progressed smoothly into second position behind Norwich.

It was business as usual for Dean Saunders when he returned to Anfield in January to face his old side. Goals from Garry Parker and of course Saunders defeated Liverpool 2-1 and put Villa level on points at the top of the table with Manchester United, the race had really begun.

Two weeks later Villa led the table outright following a crushing 5-1 victory over Middlesbrough. Villa's championship pretensions continued, despite a disappointing Coca-Cola Cup performance and a disastrous fourth round FA Cup exit at the hands of Wimbledon at Selhurst Park.

A 1-0 defeat of Chelsea on fifth round FA Cup day took Villa two points clear of United, but despite a series of impressive results, Ron Atkinson's side were never able to truly pull away from Big Ron's old side.

Almost inevitably it was left to a tense run-in to decide the fate of the Championship, with United, who had fallen away so badly in the closing stages, producing the results when it mattered, and Villa, who disintegrated under pressure over the last 10 games, to hand the title to Old Trafford.

By the time that Villa faced Oldham on the last but one week of the season, the belief in Atkinson's team had all but disappeared and with Oldham battling hard to win points in their fight against relegation, Villa slipped to an embarrassing 1-0 defeat and surrendered the title to United.

But the new season brought fresh hope for the Villa faithful, with the impressive acquisition of Andy Townsend for £2.1 million from Chelsea and the nostalgic arrival at Villa park of former claret and blue favourite Gordon Cowans, who returned to the fold from Blackburn on a free transfer.

BLACKBURN ROVERS

Founded in 1875 by local school-leavers. Used several pitches, including Alexander Meadows, the East Lancashire Cricket Club ground, and became known nationally for their FA Cup exploits, eclipsing the record of Blackburn Olympic, the first club to take the trophy away from London. Three consecutive wins in the 1880s, when in the finals Queen's Park (twice) and West Bromwich Albion were beaten, brought recognition by way of a special shield awarded by the FA to commemorate the achievement.

Founder member of the Football League in 1888, the club settled at Ewood Park in 1890, purchasing the ground outright in 1893-94. Premier League founder member 1992.

Ground: Ewood Park, Blackburn, BB2 4JF
Phone: (0254) 55432   **Nickname:** Blue and Whites
Colours: Blue/White, White, Blue   **Change:** Black/Red, Black, Black/Red
Capacity: 19,947   **Pitch:** 115yds x 76yds
Directions: *From North, South & West:* M6 J31 follow signs for Blackburn then Bolton Rd. Turn left after 1½ miles into Kidder St. *From East:* A677 or A679 following signs for Bolton Rd, then as above.
Rail: Blackburn Central

Chairman: R.D. Coar BSC   **Vice-Chairman:** R.D. Coar BSC
Secretary: John W. Howarth FAAI
Manager: Kenny Dalglish MBE   **Assistant:** Ray Harford
Physio: M. Pettigrew

Record FAPL Win: 7-1 v Norwich City, 3/10/92
Record FAPL Defeat: 2-5 v Coventry City, 26/1/93 *and*
                 2-5 v Leeds United, 10/4/93
Record FL Win: 9-0 v Middlesbrough, Division 2, 6/11/1954
Record FL Defeat: 0-8 v Arsenal, Division 1, 25/2/1933
Record Cup Win: 11-0 v Rossendale, FA Cup 1st R, 13/10/1884
Record Fee Received: £600,000 from Man City for Colin Hendry, 11/1989
Record Fee Paid: £3.3m to Southampton for Alan Shearer, 7/1992
Most FAPL Appearances: 42: Bobby Mimms, 1992-93
Most FL Appearances: Derek Fazackerley, 596, 1970-86
Record Attendance (all-time): 61,783 v Bolton W, FA Cup 6th R, 2/3/1929
Record Attendance (FAPL): 20,305 v Manchester United, 24/10/92
Highest Scorer in FAPL Season: Shearer, 22, 92-93
Most FAPL Goals in season: 68, 1992-93
Most FAPL Points in season: 71, 1992-93

Most Capped Player: Bob Crompton, 41, England
Close Season Transfers
In: Andy Morrison (Plymouth, £150,000 + swap)
Out: Wayne Burnett (Plymouth, Swap), Gordon Cowans (Aston Villa, Free), Darren Collier (Darlington, small fee), Darren Donnelly (Chester, Free)

Season 1992-93
Biggest Home Win: 7-1 v Norwich City, 3/10/92
Biggest Home Defeat: 2-5 v Coventry City, 26/1/93
Biggest Away Win: 3-0 v Queens Park Rangers,
Biggest Away Defeat: 2-5 v Leeds United
Biggest Home Attendance: 20,305 v Manchester United, 24/10/92
Smallest Home Attendance: 14,401 v Middlesbrough, 20/3/93
Average Attendance: 16,248 (+ 22.28%)
Last Season: *PL:* 4th *FA Cup:* 6th round *Coca-Cola Cup:* semi-finals
Leading Scorer: Shearer (22)

League History: 1888 Founder member of the League; 1936-39 Division 2; 1946-48 Division 1; 1948-58 Division 2; 1958-66 Division 1; 1966-71 Division 2; 1971-75 Division 3; 1975-79 Division 2; 1979-80 Division 3; 1980-92 Division 2; 1992 – FA Premier League.
Honours: Football League: Division 1 – Champions 1911-12, 1913-14; Division 2 – Champions 1938-39; Runners-up 1957-58; Division 3 – Champions 1974-75; Runners-up 1979-1980. FA Cup : Winners 1884, 1885, 1886, 1890, 1891, 1928; Runners-up 1882, 1960. Football League Cup: Semi-final 1961-62. Full Members' Cup: Winners 1986-87.
Managers (and Secretary-managers): Thomas Mitchell 1884-96, J. Walmsley 1896-1903, R.B. Middleton 1903-25, Jack Carr 1922-26 (TM under Middleton to 1925), Bob Crompton 1926-31 (Hon. TM), Arthur Barritt 1931-36 (had been Secretary from 1927), Reg Taylor 1936-38, Bob Crompton 1938-41, Eddie Hapgood 1944-47, Will Scott 1947, Jack Burton 1947-49, Jackie Bestall 1949-53, Johnny Carey 1953-58, Dally Duncan 1958-60, Jack Marshall 1960-67, Eddie Quigley 1967-70, Johnny Carey 1970-71, Ken Furphy 1971-73, Gordon Lee 1974-75, Jim Smith 1975-78, Jim Iley 1978, John Pickering 1978-79, Howard Kendall 1979-81, Bobby Saxton 1981-86, Don Mackay 1987-91, Kenny Dalglish October 1991-.

5-Year League Record

	Div.	P	W	D	L	F	A	Pts	Pos	FAC	FLC
88-89	2	46	24	11	13	74	59	77	5	5	3
89-90	2	46	19	17	10	74	59	74	5	3	2
90-91	2	46	14	10	22	51	66	52	19	3	3
91-92	2	46	21	11	14	70	53	74	6	4	1
92-93	PL	42	20	11	11	68	46	71	4	6	SF

Summary of Appearances and Goals 1992-93

	Apps	Sub	Goals		Apps	Sub	Goals
Patrik Andersson	6	5	0	Nicky Marker	12	3	0
Mark Atkins	24	7	5	David May	34		1
Henning Berg	2	2	0	Bobby Mimms	42		0
Richard Brown	2		0	Kevin Moran	36		4
Gordon Cowans	23	1	1	Mike Newell	40		13
Tony Dobson	15	4	0	Chris Price	2	4	0
Kevin Gallacher	9		5	Stuart Ripley	38	2	7
Colin Hendry	41		1	Alan Shearer	21		16
Keith Hill	0	1	0	Tim Sherwood	38	1	3
Simon Ireland	0	1	0	Roy Wegerle	11	11	4
Graeme Le Saux	9		0	Jason Wilcox	31	2	4
Steve Livingstone	1	1	0	Alan Wright	24		0
Lee Makel	1						

FA Premier League Squad Numbers 1993-94

No.	Player	No.	Player	No.	Player
1	Mimms	9	Shearer	17	Andersson
2	May	10	Newell	18	Morrison
3	Wright	11	Wilcox	19	Ireland
4	Sherwood	12	Marker	20	Berg
5	Hendry	13	Dickens	21	Moran
6	Le Saux	14	Makel	22	Atkins
7	Ripley	15	Brown		
8	Gallacher	16	Dobson		

Shearer's Injury Crucial

From the very moment that Alan Shearer cracked two magnificent goals on the first day of the season at Crystal Palace, one sensed that the £3.6 million former Southampton striker would be nothing but a success at Ewood Park. Joining a side that had been forged out of proprietor Jack Walker's millions, Shearer formed an electric partnership with striker Mike Newell and in his absence Roy Wegerle.

Playing in a side which also included new £1.3 million signing Stuart Ripley, the Lancashire outfit wasted little time in making an impact on the title race. By the beginning of October they had triumphed in seven of their 11 games, led the table by a point and had the runaway top marksmen in Shearer who had found the net 13 times in 12 games.

On a pleasant Saturday afternoon at Ewood on October 5th, Blackburn provided conclusive proof, if ever it were needed, that they were a true force to be reckoned with, when they disposed of league leaders Norwich 7-1. Shearer scored two and made four others as the Rovers produced an emphatic triumph. Little it seemed could go wrong for Dalglish and his men, particularly with the electric form of Shearer. By the end of November, Rovers were joint second in the table, having been knocked off their perch by Norwich, but Shearer had taken his goal tally to 16.

In December Dalglish took his championship pretenders on an emotional return trip to Anfield. Dalglish's reception was warm and when Shearer collected his 20th goal of the season with a dipping volley, it appeared that Blackburn might slip away unnoticed with the points. But a crowd of 43,000 witnessed a rare Liverpool performance of true grit and determination and two goals from Mark Walters presented the points to the home side.

At Christmas Blackburn were again flirting tantalisingly with the title, moving into second slot with a 3-1 defeat of the previous season's fallen champions Leeds. Shearer again collected two more goals, his tally now standing at 22, when disaster struck. Shearer injured his knee during the Christmas programme and exacerbated the knock in a Coca-Cola Cup tie against Cambridge United. The injury was to prove far more serious than first feared and the England striker didn't appear for Rovers again.

His place in the side was taken by the perfectly capable Wegerle, but something about the team had disappeared with the absence of Shearer and their league form suffered accordingly. Suddenly matches that were being won started to turn into draws and defeats. Their FA Cup ambitions were ended in the fifth round by Sheffield United and their Coca-Cola Cup campaign ended at the semi-final stage when they were emphatically beaten by Sheffield Wednesday.

A late rally towards the end of the season meant that Blackburn never slipped out of contention for a place in Europe, although ultimately they were denied them by a Norwich side who had surprised all the experts with an outstanding campaign that left them an agonising point ahead of Rovers in third place.

Rovers fans may look back to their last game of the season when they were forced to face a buoyant Manchester United side at Old Trafford, celebrating their first title for 26 years and on an unstoppable high. Blackburn needed to win to have a hope of a place in Europe should Arsenal win both Cup competitions, and when they took the lead through new signing Kevin Gallacher, it seemed they might just spoil the party. When an obvious penalty appeal was turned down, the game swung United's way and Rovers fell to a 3-1 defeat and their European dream ended.

But manager Kenny Dalglish can be more than satisfied with the efforts of his side. Despite the continuing absence of the influential Shearer, which is a major worry, the addition of combative midfielder Graeme Le Saux from Chelsea at the tail end of last season, will add extra bite to the midfield, as will the presence of Gallacher up front. In fact so confident was Dalglish of his squad for the new campaign, that his only close season transfer activity was to release Gordon Cowans on a free transfer back to Aston Villa.

CHELSEA

Founded in 1905. The Mears brothers developed Stamford Bridge Athletic Ground, which they owned, into a football stadium for use for prestigious matches and, prospectively, nearby Fulham FC. But Fulham did not take up the chance so the Mears brothers established their own club, rejecting possible names such as 'London' and 'Kensington' in favour, eventually, of Chelsea.

Judging that the club would not be accepted into the Southern League, it sought membership of the Football League. This was gained at the first attempt and it started the 1906-07 season in Division Two. Premier League founder members 1992.

Ground: Stamford Bridge, London SW6
Phone: 071-385 5545   **Nickname:** The Blues
Colours: Royal Blue, Royal Blue, White
Change: White/Red, Black, Black
Capacity: 36,965 (28,000) covered   **Pitch:** 110 yds x 72 yds
Directions: *From North & East:* A1 or M1 to central London and Hyde Park corner. Follow signs for Guildford (A3) and then Knightsbridge (A4). After a mile turn left into Fulham Rd. *From South:* A219 Putney Bridge then follow signs for West End joining A308 and then into Fulham Rd. *From West:* M4 then A4 to central London. Follow A3220 to Westminster, after ³/₄ miles right at crossroads into Fulham Rd.
Rail/Tube (District line): Fulham Broadway

President: G.M. Thomson   **Chairman:** K.W. Bates
Company Secretary/Director: Yvonne Todd
Manager: Glenn Hoddle   **Assistant:** Peter Shreeves
First Team Coach: Don Howe   **Physio:** Bob Ward

Record FAPL Win: 4-0 v Middlesbrough, 3/4/93
Record FAPL Defeat: 0-3 v Manchester United, 17/4/93 *and*
                         0-3 v Nottingham Forest, 16/1/93
Record FL Win: 9-2 v Glossop N E, Division 2, 1/9/1906
Record FL Defeat: 1-8 v Wolverhampton W, Division 1, 26/9/1953
Record Cup Win: 13-0 v Jeunesse Hautcharage, ECWC, 1R 2L, 29/9/1971
Record Fee Received: £2.2m from Tottenham H for Gordon Durie, 7/1991
Record Fee Paid: £1.6m to Wimbledon for Dennis Wise, 7/1990
Most FAPL Appearances: 41: Andy Townsend, 1992-93
Most FL Appearances: Ron Harris, 655, 1962-80
Record Attendance (all-time): 82,905 v Arsenal, Div 1, 12/10/1935

Record Attendance (FAPL): 34,496 v Manchester United, 19/12/92
Highest Scorer in FAPL Season: Harford, 11, 92-93
Most FAPL Goals in Season: 51, 1992-93
Most FAPL Points in Season: 56, 1992-93
Most Capped Player: Ray Wilkins, 24 (84), England

Close Season Transfers
In: Gavin Peacock (Newcastle, £1.25m), Andy Dow (Dundee, Tribunal fee),
Glenn Hoddle (Swindon, £75,000)
Out: Andy Townsend (Aston Villa, £2.1m)

Season 1992-93
Biggest Home Win: 4-0 v Middlesbrough
Biggest Home Defeat: 2-4 v Manchester City
Biggest Away Win: 3-1 v Aston Villa
Biggest Away Defeat: 3-0 v Manchester United *and* 3-0 v Nottingham F.
Biggest Home Attendance: 34,496 v Manchester United
Smallest Home Attendance: 13, 043 v Middlesbrough
Average Attendance: 19,022 (+ 1.29%)
Last Season: *PL:* 11th *FA Cup:* 3rd round *Coca-Cola Cup:* 5th round
Leading Scorer: Harford (11)

League History: 1905 Elected to Division 2; 1907-10 Division 1; 1910-12
Division 2; 1912-24 Division 1; 1924-30 Division 2; 1930-62 Division 1;
1962-63 Division 2; 1963-75 Division 1; 1975-77 Division 2; 1977-79
Division 1; 1979-84 Division 2; 1984-88 Division 1; 1988-89 Division 2;
1989-92 Division 1; 1992- FA Premier League.
Honours: Football League: Division 1 – Champions 1954-55; Division 2 –
Champions 1983-84, 1988-89; runners-up 1906-7, 1911-12, 1929-30,1962-
63, 1976-77. FA Cup: Winners 1970; Runners-up 1914-15, 1966-67. Football
League Cup: Winners 1964-65; Runners-up 1971-72. Full Members' Cup:
Winners 1985-86. Zenith Data Systems Cup: Winners 1989-90.
European Competitions: European Cup-Winners' Cup: 1970-71 (winners),
1971-72. European Fairs Cup: 1958-60, 1965-66, 1968-69.
Managers (and Secretary-managers): John Tait Robertson 1905-07, David
Calderhead 1907-33, A. Leslie Knighton 1933-39, Billy Birrell 1939-52, Ted
Drake 1952-61, Tommy Docherty 1962-67, Dave Sexton 1967-74, Ron Stuart
1974-75, Eddie McCreadie 1975-77, Ken Shellito 1977-78, Danny
Blanchflower 1978-79, Geoff Hurst 1979-81, John Neal 1981-85 (Director to
1986), John Hollins 1985-88, Bobby Campbell 1988-91, Ian Porterfield June
1991-1993, Dave Webb 1993, Glenn Hoddle 1993-.

5-Year League Record

	Div.	P	W	D	L	F	A	Pts	Pos	FAC	FLC
88-89	2	46	29	12	5	96	50	99	1	3	2
89-90	1	38	16	12	10	58	50	60	5	4	2
90-91	1	38	13	10	15	58	69	49	11	3	SF
91-92	1	42	13	14	13	50	60	53	14	6	2
92-93	PL	42	14	14	14	51	54	56	11	3	4

Summary of Appearances and Goals 1992-93

Player	Apps	Sub	Goals	Player	Apps	Sub	Goals
Joe Allon	1	2	0	Dimitri Kharin	5		0
Darren Bernard	8	5	1	David Lee	23	2	0
Tony Barness	2		0	Graeme Le Saux	10	4	0
Dave Beasant	17		0	Steve Livingstone	0	1	0
Craig Burley	1	2	0	Damien Matthew	3	1	0
Tony Cascarino	8	1	2	Andy Myers	3		0
Steve Clarke	18	2	0	Eddie Newton	32	2	5
Mal Donaghy	39	1	2	Ian Pearce	0	1	0
Paul Elliott	7		0	Gerry Peyton	0	1	0
Robert Fleck	28	3	2	Neil Shipperley	2	1	1
Gareth Hall	36	1	2	Frank Sinclair	32		0
Mick Harford	27	1	9	Nigel Spackman	5		0
Kevin Hitchcock	20		0	John Spencer	13	10	7
David Hopkin	2	2	0	Graham Stuart	31	8	9
Erland Johnson	13		0	Andy Townsend	41		4
Vinny Jones	7		1	Dennis Wise	27		3

FA Premier League Squad Numbers 1993-94

No.	Player	No.	Player	No.	Player
	Colgan		Hall		Myers
	Hitchcock		Sinclair		Newton
	Kharine		Hopkin		Rowe
	Dow		Hoddle		Cascarino
	Barnard		Johnsen		Fleck
	Barness		Lee		Shipperley
	Clarke		Burley		Spencer
	Donaghy		Livingstone		Stuart
	Elliott		Damian		Wise
	Pearce		Peacock		

Note: No squad numbers given.

Managers the only Change

Little changes at Stamford and 12 months on and two managers later, Mr Bates and Co are still hunting an elusive trophy or dare one even suggest, a championship. Having made their customary start to the season – sluggish – the Blues tortured their long-suffering followers with a brief flirtation with the championship race. Despite the depressing injury to influential defender Paul Elliott, sustained in a league game at Liverpool in September and liable to keep him out until the beginning of 1994, the emergence of a string of much-talented young stars-in-the-making such as Graham Stuart, Frank Sinclair, Eddie Newton, Neil Shipperley and John Spencer, propelled Chelsea to an unbeaten run of 10 matches which stretched from the end of October until the beginning of January.

In that time Ian Porterfield's side galloped up to fourth spot in the table and offered increasing evidence of an improbable title challenge. Ten goals from veteran striker Mick Harford, filling the gap left by injured new signing Tony Cascarino and the disappointing form of £2 million arrival Robert Fleck, and the continuing good form of inspirational midfielder Andy Townsend, were the main impetus behind the Stamford Bridge revival, but sadly almost as soon as it had begun, it was over.

A relatively poor Christmas programme was initially Chelsea's undoing and before long a mini slump had turned into a disastrous one. Harford was forced out of action with a niggling injury and when he returned the goals had dried up. Suddenly the Blues went ten games without a win and by the end of February, with Chelsea out of the championship, and also out of the Coca-Cola and FA Cup competitions, their season effectively over, chairman Ken Bates had lost patience with manager Ian Porterfield. With relegation, previously not even a peripheral consideration, suddenly looming large, Mr Porterfield was dispatched and in came former Chelsea hero David Webb, on a three-month trial basis.

Mr Webb's task was a simple one, stop the rot and steer Chelsea to some sort of Premier League respectability. The initial results were encouraging, with home victories against Arsenal and Everton and an unbeaten sequence of seven matches almost immediately allayed relegation fears. But an indifferent run-in cost Chelsea a top ten finish and with a heavy defeat at Sheffield United on the last day of the season, the Blues were forced to settle for 11th spot.

Unsettled midfielder Graeme Le Saux, who had had his public differences with previous manager Ian Porterfield, was sold to Blackburn for £700,000 and David Webb, whose herculean efforts had undoubtedly saved the club from relegation, was told that his services, gratefully received, were no longer required.

His place at the helm was taken by former Tottenham and England midfielder Glenn Hoddle, who had made a storming success at Swindon by steering them to a Premier League place via the play-offs at the end of May, and his position was confirmed at the start of June. One of Hoddle's first jobs was to complete the £2.1 million transfer of Andy Townsend to Aston Villa and bring in Newcastle midfielder Gavin Peacock for £1 million.

The prospects of a good season were further lifted by an emphatic 4-0 defeat of London rivals Tottenham Hotspur to clinch the prestigious pre-season Makita Tournament. Not only the first victory for an English club for four years, but also Chelsea's first trophy for a staggering 22 years!

COVENTRY CITY

Founded as Singer's FC, cycle manufacturers, in 1883. Joined the Birmingham and District League in 1894; in 1898 changed name to Coventry City; and in 1905 moved to the Athletic Ground, Highfield Road. Elected to Division One of the Southern League in 1908, but relegated to the Second in 1914.

Joined the Wartime Midland Section of the Football League in 1918 and elected to an expanded Second Division of the Football League for 1919-20. Founder members of the Fourth Division in 1958. Promoted to Division One for the first time in 1967 and never relegated. Premier League founder members 1992.

Ground: Highfield Road Stadium, King Richard Street, Coventry, CV2 4FW
Phone: (0203) 223535   **Nickname:** Sky Blues
Colours: All Sky Blue   **Change Colours:** Yellow, Blue, Yellow
Capacity: 25,311   **Pitch:** 110 yds x 75 yds
Directions: *From North & West:* M6 J3, after 3½ miles turn left into Eagle St and straight on to Swan Lane. *From South & East:* M1 to M45 then A45 to Ryton-on-Dunsmore where 3rd exit at roundabout is A423. After 1 mile turn right into B4110. Left at T-junction then right into Swan Lane.
Rail: Coventry

Life President: Derrick H. Robbins   **Chairman:** P.D.H. Robins
Vice-chairman: B.A. Richardson   **Secretary:** Graham Hover
Manager: Bobby Gould   **Assistant:** Mike Kelly
Physio: George Dalton

Record FAPL Win: 5-1 v Liverpool, 19/12/92
Record FAPL Defeat: 0-5 v Manchester United, 28/12/92
Record FL Win: 9-0 v Bristol C, Division 3 (S), 28/4/1934
Record FL Defeat: 2-10 v Norwich C, Division 3 (S), 15/3/1930
Record Cup Win: 7-0 v Scunthorpe U, FA Cup, 1st round, 24/11/1934
Record Fee Received: £1.25m from Nottingham F for Ian Wallace, 7/1980
Record Fee Paid: £900,000 to Dundee U for Kevin Gallacher, 1/1990
Most FAPL Appearances: 39: Peter Atherton, 1992-93
Most FL Appearances: George Curtis, 486, 1956-70
Record Attendance (all-time): 51,455 v Wolves, Division 2, 29/4/1967
Record Attendance (FAPL): 24,410 v Manchester United
Highest Scorer in FAPL Season: 17: Quinn, 1992-93
Most FAPL Goals in Season: 62, 1992-93

Most FAPL Points in Season: 52, 1992-93
Most Capped Player: Dave Clements, 21 (48), N. Ireland and Ronnie Rees, 21 (39), Wales

Close Season Transfers
In: Mick Harford (Sunderland, £200,000), Steve Morgan (Plymouth, £110,000), Jason Smith (Tiverton, Free), Lee Hirst (Scarborough, Free)
Out: Andy Pearce (Sheffield Wednesday, £500,000), Terry Fleming (Northampton, Free), Peter Billing (Port Vale, £35,000) Craig Middleton (Cambridge, Free), Mickey Gynn (Carlisle, Trial)

Season 1992-93
Biggest Home Win: 5-1 v Liverpool
Biggest Home Defeat: 1-3 v Sheffield Wednesday
Biggest Away Win: 5-2 v Blackburn Rovers
Biggest Away Defeat: 0-5 v Manchester United
Biggest Home Attendance: 24,410 v Manchester United
Smallest Home Attendance: 10, 455 v Southampton
Average Attendance: 14,995 (+ 7.89%)
Last Season: *PL:* 15th *FA Cup:* 3rd round *Coca-Cola Cup:* 2nd round
Leading Scorer: Quinn (17)

League History: 1919 Elected to Division 2; 1925-26 Division 3 (N); 1926-36 Division 3 (S); 1936-52 Division 2; 1952-58 Division 3 (S); 1958-59 Division 4; 1959-64 Division 3; 1964-67 Division 2; 1967-92 Division 1; 1992 - FA Premier League.
Honours: Football League: Division 1 best season: 6th, 1969-70; Division 2 Champions 1966-67: Division 3 Champions 1963-64; Division 3 (S) Champions 1935-36; Runners-up 1933-34; Division 4 Runners-up 1958-59. FA Cup: Winners 1986-87. Football League Cup: best season: Semi-final 1980-81, 1989-90
European Competitions: European Fairs Cup: 1964-65
Managers (and Secretary-managers): H.R. Buckle 1909-10, Robert Wallace 1910-13, Frank Scott-Walford 1913-15, William Clayton 1917-19, H. Pollitt 1919-20, Albert Evans 1920-24, Jimmy Ker 1924-28, James McIntyre 1928-31, Harry Storer 1931-45, Dick Bayliss 1945-47, Billy Frith 1947-48, Harry Storer 1948-53, Jack Fairbrother 1953-54, Charlie Elliott 1954-55, Jesse Carver 1955-56, Harry Warren 1956-57, Billy Firth 1957-61, Jimmy Hill 1961-67, Noel Cantwell 1967-72, Bob Dennison 1972, Joe Mercer 1972-75, Gordon Milne 1972-81, Dave Sexton 1981-83, Bobby Gould 1983-84, Don Mackay 1985-86, George Curtis 1986-87 (became MD), John Sillett 1987-90, Terry Butcher 1990-92, Don Howe 1992, Bobby Gould July 1992-.

5-Year League Record

	Div.	P	W	D	L	F	A	Pts	Pos	FAC	FLC
88-89	1	38	14	13	11	47	42	55	7	3	3
89-90	1	38	14	7	17	39	59	49	12	3	SF
90-91	1	38	11	11	16	42	49	44	16	4	5
91-92	1	42	11	11	20	35	44	44	19	3	4
92-93	PL	42	13	13	16	52	57	52	15	3	2

Summary of Appearances and Goals 1992-93

	Apps	Sub	Goals		Apps	Sub	Goals
Peter Atherton	39		0	Craig Middleton	1		0
Phil Babb	27	7	0	Peter Ndlovu	27	5	7
Peter Billiag	3		0	Steve Ogrizevic	33		0
Willie Boland	0	1	0	Andy Pearce	21	3	1
Brian Borrows	36	2	2	Mick Quinn	26		17
David Busst	10	0	0	David Rennie	4		0
Terry Flemleg	8	3	0	Stewart Robson	14	1	0
Sean Flynn	4	3	0	Robert Rosario	28		4
Kevin Gallacher	19	1	6	Keith Rowland	0	2	0
Jonathan Gould	9		0	Kenny Sampson	21		0
Chris Greenman	1	1	0	Tony Sheridan	1		0
Micky Gynn	18	2	2	David Smith	6		1
Lee Hurst	35		2	John Williams	38	3	8
Leigh Jenkinson	2	3	0	Paul Williams	1	1	0
Lloyd McGrath	20	5	0	Roy Wegerle	5	1	0

FA Premier League Squad Numbers 1993-94

No.	Player	No.	Player	No.	Player
1	Ogrizovic	9	Harford	17	Wegerle
2	Borrows	10	Quinn	18	Flynn
3	Morgan	11	Robson	19	Sheridan
4	Atherton	12	Ndlovu	20	Babb
5	Hirst	13	Davies	21	Booty
6	Rennie	14	Busst	22	Jenkinson
7	Williams	15	*	23	Gould
8	Hurst	16	*		

Postal Delay

Not many people would have given Coventry City much chance of surviving the season in the Premier League. Bobby Gould's squad was regarded as too flimsy to provide a palpable challenge to the top sides in the division. But Mr Gould, whose previous experience included steering Wimbledon to unexpected FA Cup success in 1988, took great delight in proving the experts wrong with a sensational start to the campaign which saw the Sky Blues fifth after seven games.

The chief instigator behind this impressive form was striker John Williams, a former postman who had arrived cheaply from Swansea during the close season and who took great delight in using his pace to trouble Premier League defences.

A 2-0 win at Tottenham with both goals coming from Williams, highlighted his potential and gave Gould's side the confidence to approach every match as a possible win. With Steve Ogrizovic still providing a sizable presence in the Coventry goal and the midfield experience of Stewart Robson, Lloyd McGrath and the promising wing play of Peter Ndlovu, Coventry fans had plenty to smile about.

By October Coventry were third and looking every inch a significant Premier Division force, although this was to be the zenith of their achievements.

By Christmas the Sky Blues had slipped to eighth, but still had enough fuel in the tank to dispose of Liverpool 5-1 at Highfield Road. One of the chief protagonists that day was recent £250,000 signing Mick Quinn, a forward not known for his mobility or slender shape, but who was to contribute two goals that day and a further 12 before the season had ended.

Quinn linked up well with striker Kevin Gallacher and although the season was to end with Gallacher scoring goals for Blackburn after swapping places with Roy Wegerle, the Sky Blues can look forward to more of the same from Quinn and Wegerle next season.

A third round FA Cup defeat at the hands of Tottenham did little to stop the gloom that rather settled on Highfield Road after Christmas. The early season consistency had gone and the side struggled to get results. Striker Robert Rosario, whose goal contributions had been minimal, left to join a sinking ship at Nottingham Forest, and it was left to the illuminating form of Quinn to maintain the enthusiasm.

Coventry remained in the top ten right up until the closing stages of the season, when even the mercurial Quinn had a barren spell and the team slipped to a series of bad results.

But a finishing spot of 15th represented a qualified success for manager Gould, who had succeeded in staving off the threat of relegation.

In a bid to add even more bite to the attack for the new campaign, Gould completed the £200,000 of another wily old striker in swooping for Chelsea's Mick Harford, to link up with Quinn and Wegerle.

EVERTON

The cricket team of St. Domingo's Church turned to football around 1878. Playing in Stanley Park, in late 1879 changed name to Everton FC, the name of the district to the west of the park.

Moved to a field at Priory Road in 1882 and then, in 1884, moved to a site in Anfield Road. As one of the country's leading teams, became founder members of the Football League in 1888. Moved to Goodison Park, a field on the north side of Stanley Park, in 1892 following a dispute with the ground's landlord. Premier League founder members 1992.

Ground: Goodison Park, Liverpool, L4 4EL
Phone: 051-521 2020   **Club Nickname:** The Toffees
Colours: Royal Blue, White, Blue
Change: Salmon/Dark Blue, Salmon, Salmon
Capacity: 38,500 (35,235 seats)   **Pitch:** 112 yds x 78 yds
Directions: *From North:* M6 J8 take A58 to A580 and follow into Walton Hall Ave. *From South & East:* M6 J21A to M62, turn right into Queen's Drive then, after 4 miles, left into Walton Hall Ave. *From West:* M53 through Wallasey Tunnel, follow signs for Preston on A580. Walton Hall Ave is signposted.
Rail: Liverpool Lime Street

Chairman: Dr. D.M. Marsh
Chief Executive & Secretary: Jim Greenwood
Manager: Howard Kendall   **Assistant Manager:** Colin Harvey
First Team Coach: Jimmy Gabriel   **Physio:** Les Helm

Record FAPL Win: 5-2 v Manchester City, 8/5/93
Record FAPL Defeat: 3-5 v Queens Park Rangers, 12/4/93
Record FL Win: 9-1 v Manchester City, Division 1, 3/9/1906 *and*
             9-1 v Plymouth Argyle, Division 2, 27/12/1930
Record FL Defeat: 4-10 v Tottenham H, Division 1, 11/10/1958
Record Cup Win: 11-2 v Derby County, FA Cup, 1R, 18/1/1890
Record Fee Received: £2.75m from Barcelona for Gary Lineker, 7/1986
Record Fee Paid: £2m to West Ham United for Tony Cottee, 7/1988
Most FAPL Appearances: 40: Neville Southall, Dave Watson, 1992-93
Most FL Appearances: Ted Sagar, 465, 1929-53
Record Attendance (all-time): 78,299 v Liverpool, Division 1, 18/9/1948
Record Attendance (FAPL): 35,827 v Liverpool, 7/12/92
Highest Scorer in FAPL season: 13: Cottee, 1992-93

Most FAPL Goals in Season: 53, 1992-93
Most FAPL Points in Season: 53, 1992-93
Most Capped Player: Neville Southall, 61, Wales

Close Season Transfers
In: Alan McInally (Bayern Munich, Trial)
Out: Peter Beardsley (Newcastle, £1.4 m), Kenny Woods (Bury, Free),
Iain Jenkins (Chester, Free)

Season 1992-93
Biggest Home Win: 3-0 v Ipswich Town *and* 3-0 v Nottingham Forest
Biggest Home Defeat: 3-5 v Queens Park Rangers
Biggest Away Win: 5-2 v Manchester City
Biggest Away Defeat: 2-4 v Queens Park Rangers
Biggest Home Attendance: 35,827 v Liverpool
Smallest Home Attendance: 15,122 v Sheffield United
Average Attendance: 20,457 (-11.6%)
Last Season: *PL:* 13th *FA Cup:* 3rd round *Coca-Cola Cup:* 4th round
Leading Scorer: Cottee (13)

League History: 1888 Founder Member of the Football League; 1930-31
Division 2; 1931-51 Division 1; 1951-54 Division 2; 1954-92 Division 1;
1992-FA Premier League.
Honours: Football League: Division 1 – Champions 1890-91, 1914-15,
1927-28, 1931-32, 1938-39, 1962-63, 1969-70, 1984-85, 1986-87; Runners-
up 1889-90, 1894-95, 1901-02, 1904-05, 1908-09, 1911-12, 1985-86;
Division 2 Champions 1930-31; Runners-up 1953-54. FA Cup: Winners
1906, 1933, 1966, 1984; Runners-up 1893, 1897, 1907, 1968, 1985, 1986,
1989. Football League Cup: Runners-up 1976-77, 1983-84. League Super
Cup: Runners-up 1986. Simod Cup: Runners up 1989. Zenith Data Systems
Cup: Runners-up 1991.
European Competitions: European Cup: 1963-64, 1970-71. European Cup-
Winners' Cup: 1966-67, 1984-85 Winners). European Fairs Cup: 1962-63,
1964-65, 1965-66. UEFA Cup: 1975-76, 1978-79, 1979-80.
Managers (and Secretary-managers): W.E. Barclay 1888-89, Dick
Molyneux 1889-1901, William C. Cuff 1901-18, W.J. Sawyer 1918-19,
Thomas H. McIntosh 1919-35, Theo Kelly 1936-48, Cliff Britton 1948-56,
Ian Buchan 1956-58, Johnny Carey 1958-61, Harry Catterick 1961-73, Billy
Bingham 1973-77, Gordon Lee 1977-81, Howard Kendall 1981-87, Colin
Harvey 1987-90, Howard Kendall November 1990 -.

5-Year League Record

	Div.	P	W	D	L	F	A	Pts	Pos	FAC	FLC
88-89	1	38	14	12	12	50	35	54	8	F	4
89-90	1	38	17	8	13	57	46	59	6	5	4
90-91	1	38	13	12	13	50	46	51	9	6	3
91-92	1	42	13	14	15	52	51	53	12	4	4
92-93	PL	42	15	8	19	53	55	53	13	3	4

Summary of Appearances and Goals 1992-93

	Apps	Sub	Goals		Apps	Sub	Goals
Gary Ablett	40		0	Jason Kearton	2	3	0
Stuart Barlow	8	18	5	Billy Kenny	16	1	1
Peter Beagrie	11	11	3	Martin Keown	13		0
Peter Beardsley	39		10	Neil Moore	0	1	0
Tony Cottee	25	1	12	Pedrag Radosavijevic	13	11	3
John Ebbrell	24		1	Paul Rideout	17	7	3
Alan Harper	16	2	0	Kenny Sansom	6	1	1
Andy Hinchcliffe	25		1	Ian Snodin	19	1	1
Paul Holmes	4		0	Neville Southall	40		0
Barry Herne	34		1	David Unsworth	3		0
Matthew Jackson	25	2	3	Mark Ward	19		1
Iain Jenkins	1	0	0	Robert Warzycha	15	5	1
Mo Johnston	7	6	3	Dave Watson	40		1

FA Premier League Squad Numbers 1993-94

No.	Player	No.	Player	No.	Player
1	Southall	11	Beagrie	21	*
2	Jackson	12	Holmes	22	*
3	Hinchcliffe	13	Kearton	23	Doolan
4	Snodin	14	Ebbrell	24	Priest
5	Watson	15	Rideout	25	Moore
6	Ablett	16	Preki	26	Unsworth
7	Ward	17	Kenny	27	Powell
8	*	18	Johnston	28	Jones
9	Cottee	19	Barlow	29	Grant
10	Horne	20	Warzycha	30	Tait

Cloud Remains

For so long the shadow of Liverpool had cast a dark cloud over events at
Goodison Park as the Merseysiders struggled to make an impression on
footballing matters. The 1992-93 season was no exception, with Howard
Kendall under constant pressure to either win a trophy or tender his

resignation. As it turned-out neither happened as Everton struggled to find any consistency in the league, finishing a bitterly disappointing season in 13th spot.

In truth one of the major problems for the Toffees was scoring goals. Despite the continuing presence of the mercurial Peter Beardsley, the form of out-and-out strikers Paul Rideout, Maurice Johnston and Tony Cottee was initially very disappointing.

Rideout and Johnston, who was to end his season in the New Year when he sustained a broken wrist in a domestic accident, were eventually replaced by £2.3 million Tony Cottee who, back in favour with manager Howard Kendall and the Goodison crowd after an acrimonious November bust-up, plundered a hatful of goals in the closing stages of the season and secured his long-term future at the club.

The form of major summer signing Barry Horne, the Welsh international midfielder who arrived from Southampton for £675,000 in July, was one encouraging aspect of Everton's season, as was the emergence of promising youngsters Billy Kenny, Stuart Barlow and David Unsworth.

But the problems which dogged the Merseyside club for most of the season, really began to take shape. A disastrous early season showing sent the Toffees plummeting to the foot of the table and by the end of November and Cottee's public bust-up with his manager and teammates, the team were nestling uncomfortably one off the foot of the table, with only two wins from 14 games.

The dismal run continued through the remainder of November and December, and the New Year brought a depressing FA Cup defeat at home to Wimbledon, but also a slight improvement in league form.

By the time that Everton succumbed to a 1-0 home defeat to league leaders Norwich, some of the damage had been repaired by a rise in league status to mid-table mediocrity. But an alarming decline in results with four successive defeats in February sent Everton crashing back down into 18th position and relegation seemed a distinct possibility.

The departure of England defender Martin Keown to Arsenal for £2 million, did little to help the Goodison crisis and with only 4 wins in 14 home games, there seemed little way out of the mire.

But Kenny Sansom arriving on a free transfer to add his enormous experience to the host of young players breaking into the side, added impetus to a desperate campaign to escape the drop.

And the return to goal-scoring form of Tony Cottee provided the necessary momentum to propel the Toffees out of relegation danger and up to 13th place, and compensate for the Coca-Cola and FA Cup disappointments.

The close season brought no new players to Goodison although Kendall was constantly linked with a host of quality players who became available, but no new signings were completed.

IPSWICH TOWN

Originally founded in the 1880s, a strictly amateur set up and founder member of the AFA's Southern Amateur League in 1907. Four times League champions and seven times County Cup winners. In 1936 under the leadership of the Cobbold family a professional Ipswich Town was formed.

The new club used Portman Road, only recently occupied by the amateur side and the site of several sporting activities. After two Southern League campaigns and one championship, elected to Football League Division Three (South) in 1938. Football League Champions in 1963, the club's debut season in the top section. Premier League founder member 1992.

Ground: Portman Road, Ipswich, Suffolk, IP1 2DA
Phone: (0473) 219211   **Nickname:** Blues or Town
Colours: Blue/White, White, Blue   **Change:** Red/Black, Black, Red/Black
Capacity: 22,000   **Pitch:** 112 yds x 70 yds
Directions: Follow A45 and signs for Ipswich West. Through Post House traffic lights and turn right at second roundabout into West End Rd. Ground on left.
Rail: Ipswich

President: P.M. Cobbold   **Vice-Presidents:** J.M. Sangster
Chairman: J. Kerr MBE   **Secretary:** David C. Rose
Manager: John Lyall   **Assistant:** Charlie Woods
Team Manager: Mick McGiven   **Physio:** D. Bingham

Record FAPL Win: 4-2 v Leeds United
Record FAPL Defeat: 0-3 v Everton, 3/10/92 *and*
                 0-3 v Sheffield United, 16/1/93
Record FL Win: 7-0 v Portsmouth, Division 2, 7/11/64 *and*
                7-0 v West Bromwich Albion, Division 1, 11/1964
Record FL Defeat: 1-10 v Fulham, Division 1, 26/12/63
Record Cup Win: 10-0 v Floriana, European Cup, PrRd 25/9/62
Record Fee Received: £2m* Jason Dozzell (Tottenham) 08/93
Record Fee Paid: £650,000 Geraint Williams (Derby Co) 07/92
Most FAPL Appearances: 42: David Linighan 1992-93
Most FL Appearances: Mick Mills, 591, 1966-82
Record Attendance (all-time): 38,010 v Leeds Utd, FAC 6th R, 08/03/75

* *anticipated fee.*

Record Attendance (FAPL): 22,007 v Manchester United, 30/1/93
Highest Scorer in FAPL Season: Chris Kiwomya 10 in 38 apps, 1992-93
Most FAPL Goals in Season: 50, 1992-93
Most FAPL Points in Season: 52, 1992-93
Most Capped Player: Allan Hunter, 47 (53), Northern Ireland

Close Season Transfers
In: Paul Mason (Aberdeen, £400,000), Ian Marshall (Oldham Ath, £750,000)
Out: Jason Dozzell (Tottenham, to be decided)

Season 1992-93
Biggest Home Win: 4-2 v Leeds United
Biggest Home Defeat: 1-2 v Arsenal *and* 1-2 v Oldham Athletic
Biggest Away Win: 2-0 v Norwich City *and* 2-0 v Tottenham Hotspur
Biggest Away Defeat: 0-3 v Everton *and* 3-0 v Sheffield United
Biggest Home Attendance: 22,007 v Manchester United
Smallest Home Attendance: 14,053 v Wimbledon
Average Attendance: 18,185 (+ 27.38%)
Last Season: *PL:* 16th. *FA Cup:* 6th round. *Coca-Cola Cup:* 5th round
Leading Scorer: Kiwomya (17)

League History History: 1938 Elected to Division 3 (S); 1954-55 Division 2; 1955-57 Division 3 (S); 1957-61 Division 2; 1961-64 Division 1; 1964-68 Division 2; 1968-86 Division 1; 1986-92 Division 2; 1992- FA Premier League.

Honours: Football League: Division 1 – Champions 1961-62; Runners-up 1980-81, 1981-82; Division 2 – Champions 1960-61, 1967-68, 1991-92; Division 3 (S) – Champions 1953-54, 1956-57. FA Cup: Winners 1977-78. Football League Cup: best season: Semi-final 1981-82, 1984-85. Texaco Cup: 1972-73.

European Competitions: European Cup: 1962-63. European Cup-Winners' Cup: 1978-79. UEFA Cup: 1973-74, 1974-75, 1975-76, 1977-78, 1979-80, 1980-81 (winners), 1981-82, 1982-83.

Managers (and Secretary-managers): Mick O'Brien 1936-37, Scott Duncan 1937-55 (continued as secretary), Alf Ramsey 1955-63, Jackie Milburn 1963-64, Bill McGarry 1964-68, Bobby Robson 1969-82, Bobby Ferguson 1982-87, Johnny Duncan 1987-90, John Lyall, May 1990-July 1992, Mick McGiven July 1992-.

5-Year League Record

	Div.	P	W	D	L	F	A	Pts	Pos	FAC	FLC
88-89	2	46	22	7	17	71	61	73	8	3	4
89-90	2	46	19	12	15	67	66	69	9	4	2
90-91	2	46	13	18	15	60	68	57	14	3	3
91-92	2	46	24	12	10	70	50	84	1	5	2
92-93	PL	42	12	16	14	50	55	52	16	6	5

FA Premier League Appearances and Goals 1992-93

Player	Apps	Sub	Goals	Player	Apps	Sub	Goals
Clive Baker	30	1	0	Steve Palmer	4	3	0
Vlado Bozinoski	3	6	0	Glenn Pennyfather	2	2	0
Jason Dozzell	41		7	Andy Petterson	1		0
Craig Forrest	11		0	Mick Stockwell	38	1	4
Paul Goddard	19	6	3	Neil Thompson	31		3
David Gregory	1	2	1	John Wark	36	1	6
Bonicho Guentchev	19	2	3	Phil Whelan	28	4	0
Gavin Johnson	39	1	5	Steve Whitten	20	4	3
Chris Kiwomya	38		10	Geraint Williams	37		0
David Linighan	42		1	Frank Yallop	5	1	2
Simon Milton	7	5	2	Eddie Youds	10	6	0

FA Premier League Squad Numbers 1993-94

No.	Player	No.	Player	No.	Player
1	Forrest	11	Kiwomya	21	Bozinoski
2	Stockwell	12	Goddard	22	Durrant
3	N Thompson	13	Baker	23	Morgan
4	Mason	14	Whitton	24	Honeywood
5	Wark	15	Whelan	25	Tanner
6	Linighan	16	Youds	26	N Gregory
7	Williams	17	Milton	27	G Thompson
8	Johnson	18	Palmer	28	Cotterell
9	Guentchev	19	Yallop	29	Connell
10	*	20	D Gregory	30	Pirie

The Draw Specialists

Newly promoted Ipswich Town quickly established a reputation as the consistency side of the Premier League. Their reputation as draw specialists derived from a sequence of 16 draws out of 42 matches, a run which initially suggested that the East Anglian side might produce a push for a UEFA Cup spot. But a fall-off in form and an FA Cup quarter-final exit at the hands of Arsenal in front of their Portman Road fans, instigated a decline which saw Mick McGiven's side slide to an unrepresentative 16th position.

However, there was plenty to admire in a side fashioned by former West Ham darling John Lyall. The form of long-serving midfielder Jason Dozzell, a servant of nine years at Portman Road after making his debut at the tender age of 16, provided an impressive foil to the lightening quick skills of Chris Kiwomya up front and the improving Gavin Johnston in midfield.

At the back the evergreen John Wark, a veteran of the Bobby Robson era at Portman Road and more latterly an important member of an impressive Liverpool side, produced the experience required to cajole the very best out of a mainly young Ipswich side.

Ipswich's early autumn form suggested a season of consolidation with Paul Goddard and Kiwomya contributing mightily to a record of 10 draws in their first 16 games. By the time that Christmas arrived, Ipswich had risen to sixth in the table, having drawn 12 out 21 games and making emphatic strides in their first season back in the top flight.

At the start of the New Year, Mick McGiven clinched the signing of Bulgarian international Bontcho Guentchev from Sporting Lisbon, following a run-in with the Department of Employment about the little Bulgarian's registration. But Buentchev's arrival was to prove a popular addition to the Portman Road squad, with Bontcho providing eight goals before the end of the season, with some delightful continental touches on show.

By mid-February the East Anglians had risen to fifth, until a 2-0 defeat at Aston Villa highlighted their deficiencies with regard to winning top honours.

Suddenly the form that propelled Ipswich into the top six began to desert them. A quarter-final Coca-Cola Cup exit at the hands of Sheffield Wednesday precipitated a league slump with Ipswich clinching only 10 points from their last 15 games to slip worryingly down the table to a finishing position of 16th.

Manager McGiven must have been encouraged by what he saw and added to his squad in the summer by signing Aberdeen midfielder Paul Mason for £400,000. However the rebuilding process at Portman Road was hit by the £2 million sale of Jason Dozzell to Tottenham just before the start of the new season, although the money recouped from that sale was pledged towards buying new players.

LEEDS UNITED

Leeds City, founded in 1904, took over the Elland Road ground of the defunct Holbeck Club and in 1905 gained a Football League Division Two place. The club was, however, expelled in 1919 for disciplinary reasons associated with payments to players during the War. The club closed down.

Leeds United FC, a new professional club, emerged the same year and competed in the Midland League. The club was elected to Football League Division Two for season 1920-21, both clubs up for re-election failing. The club has subsequently never been out of the top two divisions. Premier League founder member 1992.

Ground: Elland Road, Leeds, LS11 0ES
Phone: (0532) 716037   **Nickname:** United
Colours: All White   **Change Colours:** All Yellow
Capacity: 30,900   **Pitch:** 117 yds x 76 yds
Directions: *From North & East:* A58, A61, A63 or A64 into city centre and then onto M621. Leave Motorway after 1½ miles onto A643 and Elland Rd. *From West:* take M62 to M621 then as above. *From South:* M1 then M621 then as above
Rail: Leeds City

President: The Right Hon. The Earl of Harewood LLD
Chairman: L. Silver OBE   **Vice-Chairman:** P.J. Gilman
Secretary: Nigel Pleasants
Manager: Howard Wilkinson   **Assistant:** Mike Hennigan
First Team Coaches: Peter Gunby, Paul Hart
Physio: Alan Sutton, Geoff Ladley

Record FAPL Win: 5-0 v Tottenham Hotspur, 25/8/92
Record FAPL Defeat: 0-4 v Manchester City, 7/11/92 *and*
                        0-4 v Tottenham Hotspur, 20/2/93
Record FL Win: 8-0 v Leicester City, Division 1, 7/4/1934
Record FL Defeat: 1-8 v Stoke City, Division 1, 27/8/1934
Record Cup Win: 10-0 v Lyn (Oslo), European Cup, 1R 1L, 17/9/1969
Record Fee Received: £825,000 from Everton for Ian Snodin, 1/1987
Record Fee Paid: £1.7m to Southampton for Rodney & Ray Wallace, 7/1991
Most FAPL Appearances: 39: John Lukic and Gary Speed, 1992-93
Most FL Appearances: Jack Charlton, 629, 1953-73
Record Attendance (all-time): 57,892 v Sunderland, FA Cup 5R (replay), 15/3/1967

Record Attendance (FAPL): 34,166 v Manchester United, 8/2/93
Highest Scorer in FAPL Season: Chapman, 15 (PL)
Most FAPL Goals in Season: 57, 1992-93
Most FAPL Points in Season: 51, 1992-93
Most Capped Player: Billy Bremner, 54, Scotland

Close Season Transfers
In: Brian Deane (Sheffield U, £2.9m.), Mark Humphries (Aberdeen, Free), David O'Leary (Arsenal, Free), Patrick Lennon (Montreal, Canada, Trial)
Out: Lee Chapman (Portsmouth, £25,000), Dylan Kerr (Reading, £75,000), Mervyn Day (Carlisle, Free), Damian Henderson (Scarborough, Free)

Season 1992-93
Biggest Home Win: 5-0 v Tottenham Hotspur
Biggest Home Defeat: 1-4 v Nottingham Forest
Biggest Away Win: No away games won!
Biggest Away Defeat: 4-0 v Manchester City *and* 4-0 v Tottenahm Hotspur
Biggest Home Attendance: 34,166 v Manchester United
Smallest Home Attendance: 25,774 v Wimbledon
Average Attendance: 28,834 (-2.08%)
Last Season: *PL:* 17th *FA Cup:* 4th round *Coca-Cola Cup:* 3rd round *European Cup:* 2nd round
Leading Scorer: Chapman (19)

League History: 1920 Elected to Division 2; 1924-27 Division 1; 1927-28 Division 2; 1928-31 Division 1; 1931-32 Division 2; 1932-47 Division 1; 1947-56 Division 2; 1956-60 Division 1; 1960-64 Division 2; 1964-82 Division 1; 1982-90 Division 2; 1990-92 Division 1; 1992- FA Premier League.
Honours: Football League: Division 1 – Champions 1968-69, 1973-74, 1991-92; Runners-up 1964-65, 1965-66, 1969-70, 1970-71, 1971-72; Division 2 – Champions 1923-24, 1963-64, 1989-90; Runners-up 1927-28, 1931-32, 1955-56. FA Cup: Winners 1972; Runners-up 1965, 1970, 1973. Football League Cup: Winners 1967-68.
European Competitions: European Cup: 1969-70, 1974-75 (runners-up), 1992-93. European Cup-Winners' Cup: 1972-73 (runners-up). European Fairs Cup: 1965-66, 1966-67 (runners-up), 1967-68 (winners), 1968-69, 1970-71 (winners). UEFA Cup: 1971-72, 1973-74, 1979-80.
Managers (and Secretary-managers): Dick Ray 1919-20, Arthur Fairclough 1920-27, Dick Ray 1927-35, Bill Hampson 1935-47, Willis Edwards 1947-48, Major Frank Buckley 1948-53, Raich Carter 1953-58, Bill Lambton 1958-59, Jack Taylor 1959-61, Don Revie 1961-74, Brian Clough 1974, Jimmy Armfield 1974-78, Jock Stein 1978, Jimmy Adamson 1978-80, Allan Clarke 1980-82, Eddie Gray 1982-85, Billy Bremner 1985-88, Howard Wilkinson October, 1988 -.

5-Year League Record

	Div.	P	W	D	L	F	A	Pts	Pos	FAC	FLC
88-89	2	46	17	16	13	59	50	67	10	4	3
89-90	2	46	24	13	9	79	52	85	1	3	2
90-91	1	38	19	7	12	65	47	64	4	4	SF
91-92	1	42	21	16	4	74	37	82	1	3	5
92-93	PL	42	12	15	15	57	62	51	17	4	3

Summary of Appearances and Goals 1992-93

	Apps	Sub	Goals		Apps	Sub	Goals
David Batty	30		1	David Rocastle	11	7	1
Mark Beeney	1		0	Scott Sellars	6	1	0
Robert Bowman	3	1	0	Kevin Sharp	4		0
Eric Cantona	12	1	6	Carl Shutt	6	9	0
Lee Chapman	36	4	14	Gary Speed	39		7
Mervyn Day	2		0	Mel Sterland	3		0
Tony Dorigo	33		1	Gordon Strachan	25	6	4
Chris Fairclough	29	1	3	Frank Strandli	5	5	2
Jamie Forrester	5	1	0	Mark Tinkler	5	2	0
Steve Hodge	9	14	2	Imre Varadi	2	2	1
Dylan Kerr	3	2	0	Ray Wallace	5	1	0
David Kerslake	8		0	Rod Wallace	31	1	7
John Lukic	39		0	David Wetherall	13		1
Gary McAllister	32		5	Noel Whelan	1		0
Jon Newsome	30	7	0	Chris Whyte	34		1

FA Premier League Squad Numbers 1993-94

No.	Player	No.	Player	No.	Player
	Lukic		Ray Wallace		Speed
	Dorigo		Wetherall		Strachan
	Kelly		Ford		Deane
	Sharp		Forrester		Tinkler
	O'Leary		Batty		Nicholls
	Fairclough		Rocastle		Rod Wallace
	Haddock		Hodge		Whelan
	Kerslake		O'Hara		Strandli
	Humphries		Petinger		Newsome.
	Newsome		Smithard		
	Sterland		McAllister		

Note: No squad numbers given

Championship Bogey Remains

As had happened the season before when Arsenal were defending champions, Leeds United found the strain of winning the title for a second successive season too much to bear. Howard Wilkinson's side never found the form which had proved so devastating just 12 months before, and their finishing position of a desperately disappointing 17th, belied a crisis which had grown in magnitude as the season had developed.

Matters were admittedly not helped by the baffling late November sale of terrace idol Eric Cantona to bitter rivals Manchester United for £1.5 million. Salt was poured into the festering wound when Cantona hit a rich vein of goalscoring which helped United secure their first title for 26 years.

But ultimately the chief problem lay not so much in their attack, in which Gary Speed proved once again his exceptional versatility, but in defence. The previous season's combination of Chris Whyte and Chris Fairclough, which had been the mainstay of Leeds' championship campaign in 92-93, began to leak goals regularly, and the introduction of David Wetherall and Jon Newsome failed to inject any stability. In midfield Gordon Strachan continued to roll back the years with the impressive assistance of David Batty and Gary McAllister, but there was strangely no place for £2 million summer signing from Arsenal David Rocastle, who spent much of a frustrating season on the bench.

Again, just like Arsenal the year before, Leeds' slump was precipitated by their performance in the European Cup. Having been offered a difficult draw in the first round against Stuttgart, Leeds crashed to a 3-0 defeat away in Germany in the first leg and faced a mountainous task to win by four clear goals at Elland Road.

To their credit they managed four goals, but conceded a vital away goal and seemed out of the competition. Then it became evident that Stuttgart had fielded an extra foreign player and as a result UEFA declared the match to be a 3-0 win for Leeds and ordered a replay in Barcelona. Leeds rose magnificently to the occasion and triumphed 2-1 thanks to goals from Gordon Strachan and substitute Carl Shutt. But their joy was short-lived; the second round draw threw up the prospect of a championship of Britain, their opponents were to be none other than Rangers.

The first leg at Ibrox started magnificently for Leeds with Gary McAllister scoring a wonderful 20-yard drive after just 60 seconds. But then Rangers equalised courtesy of a bizarre goalkeeping error by John Lukic and Ally McCoist added a second to make the first leg score 2-1. At Elland Road for the second leg the tie was effectively killed off by another early goal, this time in the second minute by Mark Hateley. Despite a fightback and a goal from Eric Cantona, McCoist added a second to give Rangers a 4-2 aggregate victory and leave Leeds deflated.

Their league form deteriorated and by Christmas all they effectively had left to fight for was a place in the FA Cup Final, and those hopes were dashed by Arsenal who beat them 3-2 in an epic fourth round replay at Elland Road in January.

But despite their dismal end to the season, and the fact that Leeds failed to win away from home all season, the 93-94 campaign looks likely to be boosted by the summer arrival of £2.7 million striker Brian Deane from Sheffield United, and the opening of their £5 million all-seater stadium.

LIVERPOOL

Following a dispute between Everton and its Anfield landlord a new club, Liverpool AFC was formed in 1892 by the landlord, former Everton committee-man John Houlding, with its headquarters at Anfield. An application for Football League membership was rejected without being put to the vote. Instead the team joined the Lancashire League and immediately won the championship.

After that one campaign, when the Liverpool Cup was won but there was early FACup elimination, Liverpool was selected to fill one of two vacancies in an expanded Football League Second Division in 1893. Premier League founder members 1992.

Ground: Anfield Road, Liverpool 4
Phone: 051-263 2361
Colours: All Red/White Trim
Capacity: 44,931

Nickname: Reds or Pool
Change: Racing Green/White Trim
Pitch: 110 yds x 75 yds

Directions: *From North:* M6 J8, follow A58 to Walton Hall Ave and pass Stanley Park then turn left into Anfield Rd. *From South & East:* to end of M62 and right into Queens Drive (A5058). Left after 3 miles into Utting Ave and right after another mile into Anfield Rd. *From West:* M53 through Wallasey Tunnel, follow signs for Preston then turn into Walton Hall Ave and right into Anfield Rd before Stanley Park.
Rail: Liverpool Lime Street

Chairman: D.R. Moores
Chief Executive/General Secretary: Peter Robinson
Manager: Graeme Souness

Vice-Chairman: S.T. Moss JP, DL

Coach: Ron Moran

Record FAPL Win: 5-0 v Crystal Palace, 28/11/92
Record FAPL Defeat: 1-5 v Coventry City, 19/12/92
Record FL Win: 10-1 v Rotherham T, Division 2, 18/2/1896
Record FL Defeat: 1-9 v Birmingham C, Division 2, 11/12/1954
Record Cup Win: 11-0 v Stromsgodset Drammen, ECWC 1R 1L, 17/9/1974
Record Fee Received: £3.2m from Juventus for Ian Rush, 6/1986
Record Fee Paid: £2.9m to Derby County for Dean Saunders, 7/1991
Most FAPL Appearances: 32: Steve Nicol and Mark Wright, 1992-93
Most FL Appearances: Ian Callaghan, 640, 1960-78
Record Attendance (all-time): 61,905 v Wolves, FA Cup 4R, 2/2/1952
Record Attendance (FAPL): 44,619 v Everton, 20/3/93
Highest Scorer in FAPL Season: Rush, 14, 92-93
Most FAPL Goals in Season: 62, 1992-93

Most FAPL Points in Season: 59, 1992-93
Most Capped Player: Emlyn Hughes, 59 (62), England.

Close Season Transfers
In: Neil Ruddock (Spurs, £2.5m), Nigel Clough (Nottingham Forest, £2.275m)
Out: Istvan Kozma (Ujpesti Te, Budapest, Unknown), Stuart Whittaker (Bolton, Free)

Season 1992-93
Biggest Home Win: 5-0 v Crystal Palace
Biggest Home Defeat: 0-2 v Arsenal
Biggest Away Win: 2-1 v Middlesbrough
Biggest Away Defeat: 1-5 v Coventry City
Biggest Home Attendance: 44,619 v Everton
Smallest Home Attendance: 29, 574 v Wimbledon
Average Attendance: 37,010 (+5.93%)
Last Season: *PL:* 6th *FA Cup:* 3rd round *Coca-Cola Cup:* 4th round
European Cup Winners' Cup: 2nd round
Leading Scorer: Rush (22)

League History: 1893 Elected to Division 2; 1894-95 Division 1; 1895-96 Division 2; 1896-1904 Division 1; 1904-05 Division 2; 1905-54 Division 1; 1954-62 Division 2; 1962-92 Division 1; 1992- FA Premier League.
Honours: Football League: Division 1 – Champions 1900-01, 1905-06, 1921-22, 1922-23, 1946-47, 1963-64, 1965-66, 1972-73, 1975-76, 1976-77, 1978-79, 1979-80, 1981-82, 1982-83, 1983-84, 1985-86, 1987-88, 1989-90 (Liverpool have a record number of 18 League Championship wins); Runners-up 1898-99, 1909-10, 1968-69, 1973-74, 1974-75, 1977-78, 1984-85, 1986-87, 1988-89, 1990-91; Division 2 – Champions 1893-94, 1895-96, 1904-05, 1961-62. FA Cup: Winners 1965, 1974, 1986, 1989, 1992; Runners-up 1914, 1950, 1971, 1977, 1988; Football League Cup: Winners 1981, 1982, 1983, 1984; Runners-up 1977-78, 1986-87 League Super Cup: Winners 1985-86.
European Competitions: European Cup: 1964-65, 1966-67, 1973-74,1976-77 (winners), 1977-78 (winners), 1978-79, 1979-80, 1980-81 (winners), 1981-82, 1982-83, 1983-84 (winners), 1984-85 (runners-up); European Cup-Winners' Cup: 1965-66 (runners-up), 1971-72, 1974-75, 1992-93; European Fairs Cup: 1967-68, 1968-69, 1969-70, 1970-71; UEFA Cup: 1972-73 (winners), 1975-76 (winners), 1991-92; Super Cup: 1977 (winners), 1978, 1984; World Club Championship: 1981 (runners-up).
Managers (and Secretary-managers):
W.E. Barclay 1892-96, Tom Watson 1896-1915, David Ashworth 1920-22, Matt McQueen 1923-28, George Patterson 1928-36 (continued as secretary),

George Kay 1936-51, Don Welsh 1951-56, Phil Taylor 1956-59, Bill Shankly 1959-74, Bob Paisley 1974-83, Joe Fagan 1983-85, Kenny Dalglish 1985-91, Graeme Souness April 1991-.

5-Year League Record

	Div.	P	W	D	L	F	A	Pts	Pos	FAC	FLC
88-89	1	38	22	10	6	65	28	76	2	W	4
89-90	1	38	23	10	5	78	37	79	1	SF	3
90-91	1	38	23	7	8	77	40	76	2	5	3
91-92	1	42	16	16	10	47	40	64	6	W	4
92-93	PL	42	16	11	15	62	55	59	6	3	4

Summary of Appearances and Goals 1992-93

	Apps	Sub	Goals		Apps	Sub	Goals
John Barnes	26	1	5	Steve Nicol	32		0
Stig Bjornebye	11		0	Torben Piechnik	15	1	0
David Burrows	29	1	2	Jamie Redknapp	27	2	2
Bruce Grobbelaar	5		0	Ronnis Rosenthal	16	11	6
Steve Harkness	9	1	1	Ian Rush	31	1	14
Mike Hooper	8	1	0	Dean Saunders	6		1
Don Hutchison	27	4	7	Paul Stewart	21	3	1
David James	29		0	Nicky Tanner	2	2	0
Rob Jones	30		0	Michael Thomas	6	2	1
Istvan Kozma	0	1	0	Ronnie Whelan	17		1
Mike Marsh	22	6	1	Mark Walters	26	8	11
Steve McManaman	27	4	4	Mark Wright	32	1	2
Jan Molby	8	2	3				

FA Premier League Squad Numbers 1993-94

No.	Player	No.	Player	No.	Player
1	Grobbelaar	10	Barnes	19	Piechnik
2	R Jones	11	Walters	20	Bjornbye
3	Burrows	12	Whelan	21	Marsh
4	Nicol	13	James	22	Harkness
5	Wright	14	Molby	23	*
6	Hutchison	15	Redknapp	24	Hooper
7	Clough	16	Thomas	25	Ruddock
8	Stewart	17	McManaman		
9	Rush	18	Rosenthal		

Turmoil Continues

After the traumas of the 1991-92 season, which had seen upheaval at Anfield, an FA Cup victory, heart-surgery for manager Graeme Souness and a growing displeasure amongst the Liverpool faithful about the way the team was been structured, there seemed little more that could go wrong for The Reds. But the 92-93 campaign will be remembered for yet more power-struggling behind the scenes and an FA Cup exit to rank with the most embarrassing of them all, as well as a mediocre league showing and another European disappointment.

Manager Souness again made his intentions clear with regard to moulding his very own distinctive side, when he announced the sale of striker Dean Saunders to Aston Villa for £2.7 million in September, little more than a year after the Welsh international had joined the club. Many observers were baffled by the sale, especially with the continuing long-term absence of England winger John Barnes, who had ruptured an Achilles tendon in June, prior to England's European Championship campaign and looked certain to be until Christmas.

New £1 million goalkeeper David James experienced a shaky start to his Anfield career, showing brilliance and immaturity as he struggled to assert himself in the first team. Bruce Grobbelaar and Mike Hooper were both used in goal as the number one jersey swapped hands on several occasions, and the Liverpool defence failed to show its former meanness and cohesion.

Consistency was again a major problem and was no better highlighted than by their Cup Winners' Cup campaign. Having secured an impressive 8-2 first round aggregate victory over Appollon Limassol. The Reds travelled to Moscow to face Spartak Moscow for the first leg of round two. Spartak opened the scoring, with a little help from Grobbelaar's more eccentric side, but Liverpool twice came from behind to level the score. However disaster struck with 10 minutes to go when Grobbelaar was dismissed for a reckless professional foul and with David Burrows in goal as an emergency keeper, Liverpool slumped to a 4-2 defeat.

To make matters worse, manager Souness was disciplined by UEFA for comments he made to the referee after the match and incurred another touchline ban and a fine. With Liverpool needing to win the second contest by two goals, their defensive frailties were cruelly exposed again before a live TV audience as Spartak produced an impressive professional performance to triumph 2-0 in front of 39,000 stunned fans at Anfield.

But worse was to come. With all but the most optimistic resigned to little more than a passing interest in the championship by Christmas, the defending FA Cup holders saw the cup as their best hope of a trophy. Having tumbled out of the Coca-Cola Cup at Crystal Palace only days after thrashing their London opponents 5-0 in the league, their third-round draw at Bolton appeared to offer every chance of a relatively easy passage through to the fourth round. But in a thrilling match at Burden Park, Liverpool had to come from 2-0 down to secure a replay, with Ian Rush scoring a late equaliser.

Surely at Anfield, with Liverpool only once failing to go beyond the third round in the previous 15 years, Bolton of the Second Division would offer little trouble? Instead a disbelieving Anfield was forced to endure a night they would never forget as Bruce Rioch, a former Scottish international teammate of Souness's, conjured an astonishing 2-0 victory with goals from John McGinlay and Andy Walker.

MANCHESTER CITY

Founded in 1880 as West Gorton AFC. Following ground difficulties, having lost the use of the Kirkmanshulme Cricket Ground, was relaunched as Gorton AFC in 1884. There were more ground problems before, in 1889, the Club moved to Hyde Road, adopted the title of Ardwick, and employed its first professional.

Joined the Football Alliance in 1891, finishing seventh, and was founder member of Football League Division Two in 1892. Ardwick too encountered difficulties and the club was restarted as Manchester City in 1894, retaining the Football League place. In 1923 the club moved to Maine Road. Premier League founder member 1992.

Ground: Maine Road, Moss Side, Manchester, M14 7WN
Phone: 061-226 1191/2   **Nickname:** Blues or The Citizens
Colours: Sky Blue, White, Sky Blue
Change: Purple/Candystripe, Purple, Purple
Capacity: 39,359   **Pitch:** 117 yds x 77 yds
Directions: *From North & West:* M61 to M63 J9. Follow signs into Manchester (A5103). Turn right after 3 miles into Claremont Rd. Turn right after 400 yards into Maine Rd. *From South:* M6 J19 to A556 joining M56. Leave at junction 3 following A5103 as above. *From East:* M62 J17 and follow signs for Manchester Airport (A56 and A57(M)). Then follow Birmingham signs to A5103. Left into Claremont Rd after 1 mile then right into Maine Rd.
Rail: Manchester Piccadilly

Chairman: P.J. Swales   **Vice-Chairman:** F. Pye
Secretary: J.B.Halford   **General Manager:** Jimmy Frizzell
Player-manager: Peter Reid   **Assistant:** Sam Ellis
First Team Coach: Tony Book   **Physio:** Eammon Salmon
Record FAPL Win: 4-0 v Leeds United, 7/11/92
Record FAPL Defeat: 2-5 v Everton, 8/5/93
Record FL Win: 10-1 v Huddersfield Town, Division 2, 7/11/1987
Record FL Defeat: 1-9 v Everton, Division 1, 3/9/1906
Record Cup Win: 10-1 v Swindon Town, FA Cup, 4R, 29/1/1930
Record Fee Received: £1.7m from Tottenham H. for Paul Stewart, 6/1988
Record Fee Paid: £2.5m to Wimbledon for Keith Curle, 8/1991
Most FAPL Appearances: 42: David White, 1992-93
Most FL Appearances: Alan Oakes, 565, 1959-76
Record Attendance (all-time): 84,569 v Stoke C, FA Cup 6R, 3/3/1934
British record for any game outside London or Glasgow

Record Attendance (FAPL): 37,136 v Manchester United
Highest Scorer in FAPL season: White, 16
Most FAPL Goals in Season: 56, 1992-93
Most FAPL Points in Season: 57, 1992-93
Most Capped Player: Colin Bell, 48, England

Close Season Transfers
In: Alphonse Groenendijk (Ajax, £500,000), David Crawley (Dundalk, £25,000)
Out: Kare Ingebrigtsen (Rosenborg, loan + £35,000), Ray Ranson (Reading, non-contract)

Season 1992-93
Biggest Home Win: 4-0 v Leeds United
Biggest Home Defeat: 2-5 v Everton
Biggest Away Win: 3-0 v Sheffield Wednesday
Biggest Away Defeat: 3-1 v Aston Villa *and* Ipswich Tn *and* Tottenham H.
Biggest Home Attendance: 37,136 v Manchester United
Smallest Home Attendance: 19, 524 v Wimbledon
Average Attendance: 24,460 (-10.11%)
Last Season: *PL:* 9th *FA Cup:* 6th round *Coca-Cola Cup:* 3rd round
Leading Scorer: White (19)

League History: 1892 Ardwick elected founder member of Division 2; 1894 Newly-formed Manchester C elected to Division 2; Division 1 1899-1902, 1903-09, 1910-26, 1928-38, 1947-50, 1951-63, 1966-83, 1985-87, 1989-92; Division 2 1902-03, 1909-10, 1926-28, 1938-47, 1950-51, 1963-66, 1983-85, 1987-89; 1992 – FA Premier League.
Honours: Football League: Division 1 – Champions 1936-37, 1967-68; Runners-up 1903-04, 1920-21, 1976-77; Division 2 – Champions 1898-99, 1902-03, 1909-10, 1927-28, 1946-47, 1965-66; Runners-up 1895-96, 1950-51, 1987-88. FA Cup: Winners 1970, 1976; Runners-up 1973-74.
European Competitions: European Cup: 1968-69. European Cup-Winners' Cup: 1969-70 (winners), 1970-71. UEFA Cup: 1972-73, 1976-77, 1977-78, 1978-79.
Managers (and Secretary-managers): Joshua Parlby 1893-95, Sam Omerod 1895-1902, Tom Maley 1902-06, Harry Newbould 1906-12, Ernest Magnall 1912-24, David Ashworth 1924-25, Peter Hodge 1926-32, Wilf Wild 1932-46 (continued as secretary to 1950), Sam Cowan 1946-47, John 'Jock' Thomson 1947-50, Leslie McDowall 1950-63, George Poyser 1963-65, Joe Mercer 1965-71 (continued as GM to 1972), Malcolm Allison 1972-73, Johnny Hart 1973, Ron Saunders 1973-74, Tony Brook 1974-79, Malcolm Allison 1979-80, John Bond 1980-83, John Benson 1983, Billy McNeill 1983-86, Jimmy Frizzell 1986-87 (continued as GM), Mel Machin 1987-89, Howard Kendall 1990, Peter Reid November, 1990-.

5-Year League Record

	Div.	P	W	D	L	F	A	Pts	Pos	FAC	FLC
88-89	2	46	23	13	10	77	53	82	2	4	4
89-90	1	38	12	12	14	43	52	48	14	3	4
90-91	1	38	17	11	10	64	53	62	5	5	3
91-92	1	42	20	10	12	61	48	70	5	3	4
92-93	PL	42	15	12	15	56	51	57	9	6	3

Summary of Appearances and Goals 1992-93

	Apps	Sub	Goals		Apps	Sub	Goals
David Brightwell	4	4	0	Martyn Margetson	1		0
Ian Brightwell	21		1	Adrian Mike	1	2	0
Tony Coton	40		0	Tery Phelan	37		1
Keith Curie	39		3	Mike Quigley	1	4	0
Andy Dibble	1	1	0	Niall Quinn	39		9
Gary Fillcroft	28	4	5	Ray Ranson	17		0
Andy Hill	23	1	1	Peter Reid	14	6	0
Rick Holdan	40	1	3	Mike Sheron	33	5	11
Kare Ingebrigtsen	2	5	0	Fitzroy Simpson	27	2	1
Dave Kerr	0	1	0	Michael Vonk	26		3
Paul Lake	2		0	David White	42		16
Steve McMahon	24	3	1				

FA Premier League Squad Numbers 1993-94

No.	Player	No.	Player	No.	Player
1	Coton	10	Flitcroft	19	Simpson
2	Hill	11	Holden	20	Groenendijk
3	Phelan	12	I Brightwell	21	Lomas
4	McMahon	13	Mergetson	22	Edghill
5	Curle	14	Lake	23	Kerr
6	Vonk	15	*	24	Mike
7	White	16	Reid	25	Dibble
8	Sheron	17	Quigley		
9	Quinn	18	D Brightwell		

Cross City Torment

Whilst their bitter rivals at Old Trafford were lifting their first championship for 26 years, it was business as usual for Manchester City fans with another season of under-achievement. A mediocre finish in the Premier League, which saw them in 9th place some 27 points behind champions United, was due largely to an injury crisis and a lack of experienced playing personnel.

City did flirt briefly with the dream of a FA Cup appearance, but their hopes were dashed when their quarter-final against Tottenham resulted in a 4-2 defeat and a pitch invasion which cost the club a large fine and a FA reprimand.

But despite all the doom and gloom, there were some bright spots. Midfielder Gary Flitcroft emerged from nowhere as one of the finds of the season. His powerful performances, coupled with a controlled aggression and enthusiasm in front of goal, made him an instant hit with the City fans and an automatic England U21 choice by the end of the season.

And on the transfer front, the departure of winger Michael Hughes to Strasbourg paved the way for the arrival of Rick Holden from Oldham, who formed a successful partnership with top scorer Niall Quinn. Keith Curle made a success of his £2.5 million transfer from Wimbledon, assuming the mantle of City skipper with great comfort.

And Michael Sheron vindicated manager Peter Reid's faith in his ability by contributing some important goals to the City cause throughout the season.

Indeed had winger David White been able to maintain his phenomenal early season strike-rate, some 11 goals in the first 15 matches which earned him an England call-up, then perhaps City's season may have turned out differently.

But he could not, and when the club was hit by long-term injuries to the unfortunate Paul Lake, who suffered a recurrence of a serious knee injury, David Brightwell, Andy Hill and Ian Brightwell, the season was effectively over in terms of honours.

The key to success this season appears to lie in strengthening the City squad, but no new players had been signed before the start of August. In fact City had turned down an Everton bid of £2 million for striker Niall Quinn.

MANCHESTER UNITED

Came into being in 1902 upon the bankruptcy of Newton Heath. Predecessors appear to have been formed in 1878 as Newton Heath (LYR) when workers at the Carriage and Wagon Department at the Lancashire and Yorkshire Railway formed a club. This soon outgrew railway competition.

Turned professional in 1885 and founder member of Football Alliance in 1889. In 1892 Alliance runners-up Newton Heath was elected to an enlarged Division One of the Football League. In 1902 the club became Manchester United and, in February 1910, moved from Bank Street, Clayton, to Old Trafford. Premier League founder member 1992.

Ground: Old Trafford, Manchester, M16 0RA
Phone: 061-872 1661   **Nickname:** Red Devils
Colours: Red, White, Black   **Change:** All Black
Capacity: 34,031   **Pitch:** 116yds x 76yds
Directions: *From North:* M63 J4 follow signs for Manchester (A5081). Right after 2½ miles into Warwick Rd. *From South:* M6 J19 follow A556 then A56 (Altrincham). From Altrincham follow signs for Manchester turning left into Warwick Rd after 6 miles. *From East:* M62 J17 then A56 to Manchester. Follow signs for South and then Chester. Turn right into Warwick Rd after two miles.

President: Sir Matt Busby CBE, KCSG
Vice-Presidents: J.A. Gibson, W.A. Young, J.G. Gulliver, R.L. Edwards
Chairman/Chief Executive: C.M. Edwards
Secretary: Kenneth Merrett.
Manager: Alex Ferguson   **Assistant:** Brian Kidd
First Team Coach: **Physio:** Jim McGregor

Record FAPL Win: 5-0 v Coventry City, 28/12/92
Record FAPL Defeat: 0-3 v Everton, 19/8/92
Record FL Win: 10-1 v Wolverhampton W, Division 2, 15/10/1892
Record FL Defeat: 0-7 v Blackburn R, Division 1, 10/4/1926 *and*
     0-7 v Aston Villa, Division 1, 27/12/1930 *and*
     0-7 v Wolves, Division 2, 26/12/1931
Record Cup Win: 10-0 v RSC Anderlecht, European Cup, PR 2L, 26/9/1956
Record Fee Received: £1.8m from Barcelona for Mark Hughes, 8/1986
Record Fee Paid: £2.3m to Middlesbrough for Gary Pallister, 8/1989
Most FAPL Appearances: 42: Steve Bruce and Peter Schmeichel 1992-93
Most FL Appearances: Bobby Charlton, 606, 1956-73

Record Attendance (all-time): 70,504 v Aston Villa, Division 1, 27/12/1920
Record Attendance (FAPL): 40,693 v Blackburn Rovers, 3/5/93
Highest Scorer in FAPL Season: Hughes, 15, 92-93
Most FAPL Goals in Season: 67, 1992-93
Most FAPL Points in Season: 84, 1992-93
Most Capped Player: Bobby Charlton, 106, England

Close Season Transfers
In: Roy Keane (Nottingham Forest, £3.75m.)
Out: Brian Carey (Leicester, tribunal fee), Russell Beardsmore (Bournemouth, Free), Raphael Burke (Bristol City, Free), George Switzer (Darlington, Free), Kiernan Toll (Stockport, Non-contract), Ian Wilkinson (Stockport, Non-contract)

Season 1992-93
Biggest Home Win: 5-0 v Coventry City
Biggest Home Defeat: 0-3 v Everton
Biggest Away Win: 3-1 v Norwich City *and* 3-1 v Queens Park Rangers
Biggest Away Defeat: 1-2 v Ipswich Town *and* 1-2 v Sheffield United
Biggest Home Attendance: 40,693 v Blackburn Rovers
Smallest Home Attendance: 29,736 v Crystal Palace
Average Attendance: 35,132 (-21.93%)
Last Season: *PL:* 1st *FA Cup:* 5th round *Coca-Cola Cup:* 3rd round. *UEFA Cup:* 1st round
Leading Scorer: Hughes (16)

League History: 1892 Newton Heath elected to Division 1; 1894-1906 Division 2; 1906-22 Division 1; 1922-25 Division 2; 1925-31 Division 1; 1931-36 Division 2; 1936-37 Division 1; 1937-38 Division 2; 1938-74 Division 1; 1974-75 Division 2; 1975-92 Division 1; 1992 – FA Premier League.
Honours: FA Premier League – Champions 1992-93; Football League: Division 1 – Champions 1907-8, 1910-11, 1951-52, 1955-56, 1956-57, 1964-65, 1966-67; Runners-up 1946-47, 1947-48, 1948-49, 1950-51, 1958-59, 1963-64, 1967-68, 1979-80, 1987-88, 1991-92. Division 2 – Champions 1935-36, 1974-75; Runners-up 1896-97, 1905-06, 1924-25, 1937-38. FA Cup: Winners 1909, 1948, 1963, 1977, 1983, 1985, 1990; Runners-up 1957, 1958, 1976, 1979. Football League Cup: Winners 1991-92; Runners-up 1982-83, 1990-91.
European Competitions: European Cup: 1956-57 (s-f), 1957-58 (s-f), 1965-66 (s-f), 1967-68 (winners), 1968-69 (s-f). European Cup-Winners' Cup: 1963-64, 1977-78, 1983-84, 1990-91 (winners), 1991-92. European Fairs Cup: 1964-65. UEFA Cup: 1976-77, 1980-81, 1982-83, 1984-85, 1992-93.

Managers (and Secretary-managers): Ernest Magnall 1900-12, John Robson 1914-21, John Chapman 1921-26, Clarence Hildrith 1926-27, Herbert Bamlett 1927-31, Walter Crickmer 1931-32, Scott Duncan 1932-37, Jimmy Porter 1938-44, Walter Crickmer 1944-45*, Matt Busby 1945-69 (continued as GM then Director), Wilf McGuinness 1969-70, Frank O'Farrell 1971-72, Tommy Docherty 1972-77, Dave Sexton 1977-81, Ron Atkinson 1981-86, Alex Ferguson November 1986-.

5-Year League Record

	Div.	P	W	D	L	F	A	Pts	Pos	FAC	FLC
88-89	1	38	13	12	13	45	35	51	11	6	3
89-90	1	38	13	9	16	46	47	48	13	W	3
90-91	1	38	16	12	10	58	45	59	6	5	F
91-92	1	42	21	15	6	63	33	78	2	4	W
92-93	PL	42	24	12	6	67	31	84	1	5	3

Summary of Appearances and Goals 1992-93

	Apps	Sub	Goals		Apps	Sub	Goals
Clayton Blackmore	12	2	0	Andrei Kanchelskis	14	12	3
Steve Bruce	42		5	Brian McClair	41	1	9
Nicky Butt	0	1	0	Gary Pallister	42		1
Eric Cantona	21	1	9	Paul Parker	31		1
Dion Dublin	3	4	1	Mike Phelan	5	6	0
Darren Ferguson	15		0	Bryan Robson	5	9	1
Ryan Giggs	40	1	9	Peter Schmeichel	42		0
Mark Hughes	41		15	Lee Sharpe	27		1
Paul Ince	41		6	Danny Wallace	0	2	0
Denis Irwin	40		5	Neil Webb	0	1	0

FA Premier League Squad Numbers 1993-94

No.	Player	No.	Player	No.	Player
1	Schmeichel	9	McClair	17	McKee
2	Parker	10	Hughes	18	Ferguson
3	Irwin	11	Giggs	19	*
4	Bruce	12	Robson	20	Dublin
5	Sharpe	13	Sealey	21	Martin
6	Pallister	14	Kanchelskis	22	Lawton
7	Cantona	15	Blackmore	23	Phelan
8	Ince	16	Keane		

What a Difference a Year Makes

At the end of 91-92, United fans were in despair at the prospect of being cheated in the run-in of a title which had seemed theirs. Leeds United's unlikely triumph had provoked more dark thoughts of the prospect of never winning the title again. It seemed that United would never have a better chance. But 12 months on the annals of Old Trafford are still reverberating with the talk of Alex Ferguson's young lions, who ended a barren run of 26 years without a championship, by romping to a 10-point margin of victory in the inaugural Premier League.

But all was not plain sailing for Alex Ferguson's men. Their start to the campaign was anything but emphatic and by the beginning of November, by which time the side had been dumped out of the Coca-Cola Cup and out of Europe, beaten on penalties in the first round by Torpedo Moscow, talk of crisis was once again rife at Old Trafford.

Goalscoring was identified as the cause of United's malaise. With new £1 million signing from Cambridge Dion Dublin sidelined for the rest of the season with a broken leg, they had managed just one goal a game for the previous 35 contests in 1992, and had not won in the Premier League since early September.

The solution and saviour came in the form of French international Eric Cantona, who stunned Leeds fans by accepting a £1.2 million transfer to United from the League champions and then steered the Lancashire side back on course for the title.

His goals, a total of 14 of them, galvanised the goalshy United attack into action, and Cantona became the first man to win championship medals in successive seasons at different clubs.

Suddenly Mark Hughes and Brian McClair began to find the net with unerring regularity and the precocious brilliance of Ryan Giggs proffered 12 more goals for the Old Trafford faithful to purr over.

Not even the brief setback of a FA Cup defeat at Sheffield United in the fourth round, could deter United who had a new resolution about them. They held their nerve in the closing stages of the season as they had failed to do a year before and in the end it was a defeat of rivals Aston Villa, who had pushed United hard all of the way since Christmas, which eventually handed the title to Alex Ferguson's men in the penultimate week of the season.

An unexpected 1-0 defeat at home to Oldham for Villa meant that United were in an unassailable position and when the Red Devils entertained Blackburn at home the following evening for their last home fixture of the season, there was a party atmosphere about Old Trafford. A thumping 3-1 victory followed by a 2-1 win at Wimbledon in their last game of the season, with the final goal coming from old timer Bryan Robson, at last a championship winner after 17 years in the game, capped a memorable season.

The £3.75m signing of Irish midfielder Roy Keane has added further quality to a formidable midfield line-up, and with the successful rehabilitation of Dublin, the squad looks ominously powerful.

NEWCASTLE UNITED

Formed 1882 as Newcastle East End on the amalgamation of Stanley and Rosewood. Founder members, as a professional club, of the Northern League in 1889. Moved from Chillington Road, Heaton in 1892 to take over the home of the defunct Newcastle West End, with several of those associated with the West End side joining the newcomers.

Applied for Football League Division One membership in 1892, failed and decided against a place in the new Second Division, staying in the Northern League. Later in 1892 changed name to Newcastle United. Elected to an expanded Football League Division Two in 1893.

Ground: St James' Park, Newcastle-upon-Tyne, NE1 4ST
Phone: 091-232 8361   **Nickname:** Magpies
Colours: Black/White, Black, Black   **Change:** All Blue
Capacity: 30,348   **Pitch:** 115 yds x 75 yds.
Directions: *From South:* Follow A1, A68 then A6127 to cross the Tyne. At roundabout, first exit into Moseley St. Left into Neville St, right at end for Clayton St. and then Newgate St. Left for Leaze Park Rd. *From West:* A69 towards city centre. Left into Clayton Street for Newgate St, left again for Leaze Park Rd. *From North:* A1 then follow signs for Hexham until Percy St. Right into Leaze Park Rd. *Rail:* Newcastle Central (½ mile).

President: T.L. Bennett
Chairman: Sir John Hall   **Vice-Chairman:** W.F. Shepherd
General Manager/Secretary: R. Cushing
Manager: Kevin Keegan   **Assistant:** Terry McDermott
Coaches: Derek Fazackerley and Colin Suggett   **Physio:** Derek Wright

Record FAPL Win: –
Record FAPL Defeat: –
Record FL Win: 13-0 v Newport Co, Division 2, 5/10/1946
Record FL Defeat: 0-9 v Burton Wanderers, Division 2, 15/4/1895
Record Cup Win: 9-0 v Southport (at Hillsborough) FA Cup 4R, 1/2/1932
Record Fee Received: £2m from Tottenham H for Paul Gascoigne, 7/1988
Record Fee Paid: £850,000 to Wimbledon for Dave Beasant, 6/1988 and £850,000 to Wimbledon for Andy Thorn, 8/1988
Most FAPL Appearances:
Most FL Appearances: Jim Lawrence, 432, 1904-22
Record Attendance (all-time): 68,386 v Chelsea, Division 1, 3/9/1930
Record Attendance (FAPL): –

Highest Scorer in FAPL Season: –
Most FAPL Goals in Season: –
Most FAPL Points in Season: –
Most Capped Player: Alf McMichael, 40, Northern Ireland

Close Season Transfers
In: Peter Beardsley (Everton, £1.4m), Alex Mathie (Morton, £285,000), Nicky Papavasiliou (OFI, Crete, £120,000)
Out: Gavin Peacock (Chelsea, £1.25m), David Kelly (Wolves, £750,000), Andy Hunt (WBA, £100,000), Mark Stimson (Portsmouth, £100,000), Alan Thompson (Bolton, tribunal fee), Kevin Sheedy (Blackpool, Free), John Watson (Scunthorpe, Free)

Season 1992-93
Biggest Home Win: 7-1 v Leicester City
Biggest Home Defeat: 0-1 v Grimsby Town
Biggest Away Win: 3-0 v Tranmere Rovers *and* 3-0 v Cambridge United
Biggest Away Defeat: 2-4 v Oxford United
Biggest Home Attendance: 30,364 v Sunderland
Smallest Home Attendance: 26,089 v Millwall
Average Attendance: 29,048 (+ 37.32%)
Last Season: *Div 1:* 1st *FA Cup:* 5th round *Coca-Cola Cup:* 3rd round
Leading Scorer: Kelly (28)

League History: 1893 Elected to Division 2; 1898-1934 Division 1; 1934-48 Division 2; 1948-61 Division 1; 1961-65 Division 2; 1965-78 Division 1; 1978-84 Division 2; 1984-89 Division 1; 1989-92 Division 2; 1992-1993 Division 1; 1993- FA Premier League.
Honours: Football League: Division 1 – Champions 1904-05, 1906-07, 1908-09, 1926-27, 1992-93; Division 2 – Champions 1964-65; Runners-up 1897-98, 1947-48. FA Cup: Winners 1910, 1924, 1932, 1951, 1952, 1955; Runners-up 1905, 1906, 1908, 1911, 1974. Football League Cup: Runners-up 1975-76. Texaco Cup: Winners 1973-74, 1974-75.
European Competitions: European Fairs Cup: 1968-69 Winners, 1969-70, 1970-71.
Managers (and Secretary-managers): Frank Watt 1895-1932 (secretary until 1932), Andy Cunningham 1930-35, Tom Mather 1935-39, Stan Seymour 1939-47 (hon manager), George Martin 1947-50, Stan Seymour 1950-54 (hon manager), Duggie Livingstone, 1954-56, Stan Seymour (Non manager) 1956-58, Charlie Mitten 1958-61, Norman Smith 1961-62, Joe Harvey 1962-75, Gordon Lee 1975-77, Richard Dinnis 1977, Bill McGarry 1977-80, Arthur Cox 1980-84, Jack Charlton 1984, Willie McFaul 1985-88, Jim Smith 1988-91, Ossie Ardiles 1991-92, Kevin Keegan 1992-.

5-Year League Record

	Div.	P	W	D	L	F	A	Pts	Pos	FAC	FLC
88-89	1	38	7	10	21	32	63	31	20	3	2
89-90	2	46	22	14	10	78	55	80	3	5	3
90-91	2	46	14	17	15	49	56	59	11	4	2
91-92	2	46	13	13	20	66	84	52	20	3	3
92-93	1	46	29	4	8	85	37	93	1	5	3

Summary of Appearances and Goals 1992-93

Player	Apps	Sub	Goals	Player	Apps	Sub	Goals
John Beresford	42		1	Gavin Peacock	29	4	12
Paul Bracewell	19	12	2	Mick Quinn	4	8	2
Kevin Brock	4	7	1	Ray Ranson	3	1	0
Franz Carr	8	7	2	Mark Robinson	2	10	0
Lee Clark	46		10	Kevin Scott	45		2
Andy Cole	11	1	12	Scott Sellars	13		2
Brian Kilcline	7	30	0	Kevin Sheedy	23	2	3
Steve Howey	41	2		Pavel Srnicek	32		0
David Kelly	45		24	Mark Stimson	1	3	0
Bjorn Kristensen	0	1	0	Alan Thompson	1	1	0
Robert Lee	36		10	Barry Venison	44		0
Alan Neilson	2	4	0	Steve Watson	1	1	0
Liam O'Brien	33		6	Tommy Wright	14		0

FA Premier League Squad Numbers 1993-94

No.	Player	No.	Player	No.	Player
1	Srnicek	11	Sellars	21	Thompson
2	Venison	12	Robinson	22	R Appleby
3	Beresford	13	Wright	23	McDonough
4	Bracewell	14	Mathie	24	M Appleby
5	Scott	15	Kilcline	25	Murray
6	Howey	16	O'Brien	26	Elliott
7	Lee	17	Papavasiliou	27	Cormack
8	Beardsley	18	Brock	28	Roche
9	Cole	19	Watson		
10	Clark	20	Nielson		

Fog Lifted on Tyne

As a player Kevin Keegan had been an influential figure at the Tyneside club helping steer them from the then Second Division into the First. His return to Newcastle United in February of 1992 as manager was a popular move in the north-east and much was expected of the team at the start of the 1992-93 season. No-one was disappointed as Newcastle set off on their best ever start to a season collecting eleven straight wins before finally losing at home to Grimsby as October drew to a close.

By this stage the club were already being labelled as Division One champions' a notion that was hard to dispel as they reached the New Year comfortably ahead of the chasing pack. The inevitable run of bad form that followed included a 2-0 defeat at Portsmouth who were, by that stage, closing fast. But the Magpies' nerves held steady and their performances picked up as the end of the season approached. They finished their season as they had started running out winners of the Football League with five straight victories to collect the trophy that, the year before had been awarded to Leeds United.

It was not just winning the Football League championship which put the smile back on Tyneside faces, though, it was the manner in which it was done with convincing displays of quality football that had the pundits predicting good times ahead for the club in the FA Premier League. This view was strengthened when Keegan added to his squad before the March transfer deadline with Andy Cole, Scott Sellars and Mark Robinson coming to St. James Park.

NORWICH CITY

Formed following a June 1902 public meeting organised by two local schoolteachers which agreed the desirability of a Norwich City Football Club. Started in the Norwich & Suffolk League. Turned professional and elected to the Southern League in 1905. Moved from Newmarket Road to The Nest, Rosary Road in 1908.

Founder members of Football League Divison Three with other Southern Leaguers in 1920, this becoming Divison Three (South) in 1921. Moved to Carrow Road, the home of Boulton & Paul Sports Club in 1935. Founder members of Division Three on the end of regionalisation in 1958. Premier League founder members 1992.

Ground: Carrow Road, Norwich, NR1 1JE
Phone: (0603) 612131   **Nickname:** The Canaries
Colours: Yellow, Green, Yellow   **Change:** All White
Capacity: 20,319   **Pitch:** 114yds x 74 yds
Directions: *From North:* A140 to ring road and follow signs for Yarmouth A47. Turn right at T junction after 3½ miles then left after ½ mile into Carrow Rd. *From South & West:* A11/A140 onto ring road. Follow signs for Yarmouith A47 etc. *From East:* A47 into Norwich then left onto ring road.

President: G.C. Watling   **Chairman:** Robert T. Chase JP
Vice-Chairman: J.A. Jones   **Secretary:** A.R.W. Neville
Manager: Mike Walker   **Assistant:** John Deehan
First Team Coach: **Physio:** Tim Sheppard MCSP, SRP

Record FAPL Win: 4-2 v Arsenal, 15/8/92 *and*
    4-2 v Crystal Palace, 27/11/93 *and*
    4-2 v Leeds United, 12/4/93
Record FAPL Defeat: 1-7 v Blackburn Rovers, 3/10/92
Record FL Win: 10-2 v Coventry C, Division 3 (S), 15/3/1930
Record FL Defeat: 2-10 v Swindon T, Southern League, 5/9/1908
Record Cup Win: 8-0 v Sutton U, FA Cup, 4R, 28/1/1989
Record Fee Received: £1.2m from Arsenal for Andy Linighan, 6/1990 *and*
    from Chelsea for Andy Townsend, 6/1990
Record Fee Paid: £925,000 to Port Vale for Darren Beckford, 6/1991
Most FAPL Appearances: 42: Mark Bowen, Bryan Gunn, David Phillips 1992-93
Most FL Appearances: Ron Ashman, 592, 1947-64
Record Attendance (all-time): 43,984 v Leicester C, FA Cup 6R, 30/3/1963

Record Attendance (FAPL): 20,610 v Liverpool, 1/5/93
Highest Scorer in FAPL Season: Robins, 15, 92-93
Most FAPL Goals in Season: 61, 1992-93
Most FAPL Points in Season: 72, 1992-93
Most Capped Player: Martin O'Neill, 18 (64), Northern Ireland

Close Season Transfers
In: Spencer Prior (Southend, £200,000)
Out: Jason Minnett (Exeter, Free), Glyn Roberts (Rotherham, Free)

Season 1992-93
Biggest Home Win: 4-2 v Crystal Palace *and* 4-2 v Leeds United
Biggest Home Defeat: 1-3 v Manchester United
Biggest Away Win: 4-2 v Arsenal
Biggest Away Defeat: 1-7 v Blackburn Rovers
Biggest Home Attendance: 20,610 v Liverpool
Smallest Home Attendance: 12,452 v Southampton
Average Attendance: 16,250 (+17.3%)
Last Season: *PL:* 3rd *FA Cup:* 4th round *Coca-Cola Cup:* 3rd round
Leading Scorer: Robins (16)

League History: 1920 Original Member of Division 3; 1921 Division 3 (S);
1934-39 Division 2; 1946-58 Division 3 (S); 1958-60 Division 3; 1960-72
Division 2; 1972-74 Division 1; 1974-75 Division 2; 1975-81 Division 1;
1981-82 Division 2; 1982-85 Division 1; 1985-86 Division 2; 1986-92
Division 1; 1992 – FA Premier League.
Honours: Football League: Division 1 best season: 4th, 1988-89; Division 2
– Champions 1971-72,1985-86. Division 3 (S) – Champions 1933-34;
Division 3 – Runners-up 1959-60. FA Cup: Semi-finals 1959, 1989, 1992.
Football League Cup: Winners 1962, 1985; Runners-up 1973, 1975.
Managers (and Secretary-managers):
John Bowman 1905-07, James McEwen 1907-08, Arthur Turner 1909-10,
Bert Stansfield 1910-15, Major Frank Buckley 1919-20, Charles O'Hagan
1920-21, Albert Gosnell 1921-26, Bert Stansfield 1926, Cecil Potter 1926-29,
James Kerr 1929-33, Tom Parker 1933-37, Bob Young 1937-39, Jimmy
Jewell 1939, Bob Young 1939-45, Cyril Spiers 1946-47, Duggie Lochhead
1945-50, Norman Low 1950-55, Tom Parker 1955-57, Archie Macaulay
1957-61, Willie Reid 1961-62, George Swindin 1962, Ron Ashman 1962-66,
Lol Morgan 1966-69, Ron Saunders 1969-73, John Bond 1973-80, Ken
Brown 1980-87, Dave Stringer December 1987-92, Mike Walker June 1992-.

5-Year League Record

	Div.	P	W	D	L	F	A	Pts	Pos	FAC	FLC
88-89	1	38	17	11	10	48	45	62	4	SF	3
89-90	1	38	13	14	11	44	42	53	10	4	3
90-91	1	38	13	6	19	41	64	45	15	6	3
91-92	1	42	11	12	19	47	63	45	18	SF	5
92-93	PL	42	21	9	12	61	65	72	3	4	3

Summary of Appearances and Goals 1992-93

	Apps	Sub	Goals		Apps	Sub	Goals
Darren Beckford	7	1	1	Jason Minett	0	1	0
Mark Bowen	42		1	Rob Newman	16	2	2
Ian Butterworth	26		1	David Phillips	42		9
Ian Crook	32	2	3	John Polston	34		1
Ian Culverhouse	41		0	Lee Power	11	7	6
Efan Ekoku	1	3	3	Mark Robins	34	3	15
Ruel Fox	32	2	4	David Smith	5	1	0
Jeremy Goss	25		1	Daryl Sutch	14	8	2
Bryan Gunn	42		0	Chris Sutton	32	6	8
Andy Johnson	1	1	1	Colin Woodthorpe	5	2	0
Gary Megson	20	3	1				

FA Premier League Squad Numbers 1993-94

No.	Player	No.	Player	No.	Player
1	Gunn	10	Polston	19	Johnson
2	Bowen	11	Goss	20	Eadie
3	Newman	12	Robins	21	Smith
4	Crook	13	Walton	22	Sutton
5	Culverhouse	14	Fox	23	Brace
6	Phillips	15	Sutch	24	Marshall
7	Ekoku	16	Power	25	Cureton
8	Woodthorpe	17	Butterworth	26	Akinbiyi
9	Megson	18	Ullathorne	27	Prior

Goals the Key

East Anglian football had rarely seen anything like it. A new manager in Mike Walker who had produced a side leading the Premier League for prolonged spells against all the odds and flying in the face of the predictions of the soccer pundits. The Premier League was indeed the launch of a new era for football.

It all started for Norwich on the first day of the season. Trailing 2-0 to Arsenal at Highbury at half-time, the Canaries hit back with four second-half goals to triumph 4-2 and post their intent for the season.

One of the chief protagonists behind this astonishing performance was former Manchester United striker Mark Robins. Discarded by Old Trafford, Robins was to make a name for himself at Carrow Road during the season for his impressive marksmanship and ability to bring others into the game.

After just nine games the Canaries led the division by four clear points and although a 7-1 thrashing at Blackburn at the beginning of October brought the Carrow Road fans down to earth with a crashing bump, the expected decline, which many predicted following this defeat, never materialised.

Such was the emphatic manner of Norwich's performances that they could afford to leave £925,000 signing Darren Beckford on the bench and rely on the guile and skill of Robins and rookie Chris Sutton up front.

Ian Crook, promising newcomer Daryl Sutch, Jeremy Goss and Ruel Fox provided a powerful midfield combination and the defence was shored up by the ever-present Ian Butterworth and John Polston, with the reliable Bryan Gunn in goal.

Not only did Norwich lead the table for virtually all of the first half of the season, but they did so with enormous style, playing some delightful passing football that earned them many new fans.

By the beginning of December the gap at the top of the Premier League had widened to a yawning eight points, as Norwich beat Wimbledon 2-1 and their immediate rivals faltered.

But that was to prove the peak of Norwich's Premier League challenge. Although they were a persistent thorn in the side of many sides last season, they were unable to sustain a challenge which at one stage looked likely to send them so far ahead of the chasing pack, they would not be caught.

In the early days of January, they were finally caught by both Manchester United and Aston Villa, who were to go on and eventually contest the championship between themselves.

To add insult to injury, the Canaries FA Cup interests were put to the sword by Tottenham in front of their own fans in a delightful fourth round tie, but Norwich were certainly never disgraced and thoroughly deserved their finishing position of third, 12 points behind United and two behind Villa, a placing that was to earn them a UEFA Cup spot when Arsenal clinched both cup competitions.

On the transfer front, the mid-season departure of Darren Beckford heralded the arrival of highly-rated striker Efan Ekoko from Bournemouth and during the summer the only signing was £200,000 centre-half Spencer Prior from Southend.

OLDHAM ATHLETIC

Founded in 1897 as Pine Villa by the licensee of the Featherstall & Junction Hotel and played in the Oldham Junior League. In 1899 at a meeting at the Black Cow, Chadderton, the club became Oldham Athletic; it moved to the defunct Oldham County FC's ground; and joined the Manchester Alliance.

Changed to the Manchester League in 1900 and the Lancashire Combination in 1904. Moved to Boundary Park in 1906. Initially rejected by the Football League in 1907, an unexpected vacancy arose and Oldham started 1907-08 in Division Two. Founder member of Division Four 1958 and of the Premier League in 1992.

Ground: Boundary Park, Oldham
Phone: 061-624 4972   **Nickname:** The Latics
Colours: All Blue with Red piping   **Change:** Red/White, White, White
Capacity: 16,839 (seats 11,295, standing 5,544)   **Pitch:** 110 yds x 74 yds
Directions: M62 J20 then A627(M) to A664. 1st exit off roundabout onto Broadway then 1st right into Hilbre Ave and car park.
Rail: Oldham Werneth

President: R. Schofield   **Chairman/Chief Executive:** I.H. Stott
Secretary: Terry Cale
Manager: Joe Royle   **Commercial Manager:** Alan Hardy
Coach: Willie Donachie   **Physio:** Ian Liversedge

Record FAPL Win: 6-2 v Wimbledon, 3/4/93
Record FAPL Defeat: 2-5 v Wimbledon, 12/12/92
Record FL Win: 11-0 v Southport, Division 4, 26/12/1962
Record FL Defeat: 4-13 v Tranmere R, Division 3 (N), 26/12/1935
Record Cup Win: 10-1 v Lytham, FA Cup, 1R, 28/11/1925
Record Fee Received: £1.7m from Aston Villa for Earl Barrett, 2/1992
Record Fee Paid: £700,000 to Aston Villa for Ian Olney, 6/1992
Most FAPL Appearances: 42: Mike Milligan, 1992-93
Most FL Appearances: Ian Wood, 525, 1966-80
Record Attendance (all-time): 47,671 v Sheffield W, FA Cup 4R, 25/1/1930
Record Attendance (FAPL): 17,106 v Manchester United, 9/3/93
Highest Scorer in FAPL Season: Olney, 12, 92-93
Most FAPL Goals in Season: 63, 1992-93
Most FAPL Points in Season: 49, 1992-93
Most Capped Player: Albert Gray, 9 (24), Wales

Close Season Transfers
In: –
Out: John Keeley (Colchester, Free), Ian Marshall (Ipswich Town, £750,000)

Season 1992-93
Biggest Home Win: 6-2 v Tottenham Hotspur
Biggest Home Defeat: 2-3 v Norwich City
Biggest Away Win: 3-2 v Middlesbrough
Biggest Away Defeat: 2-5 v Wimbledon
Biggest Home Attendance: 17,100 v Manchester United
Smallest Home Attendance: 11,018 v Norwich City
Average Attendance: 12,907 (-14.37%)
Last Season: *PL:* 19th *FA Cup:* 3rd round *Coca-Cola Cup:* 4th round
Leading Scorer: Olney (13)

League History: 1907 Elected to Division 2; 1910-23 Division 1; 1923-25
Division2; 1935-53 Division 3(N); 1953-54 Division2; 1954- 58 Division 3
(N); 1958-63 Division 4; 1963-69 Division 3; 1969-71 Division 4; 1971-74
Division 3; 1974-91 Division 2; 1991-92 Division 1; 1992- FA Premier
League.
Honours: Football League: Division 1 – Runners-up 1914-15; Division 2 –
Champions 1990-91; Runners-up 1909-10; Division 3 (N) – Champions
1952-53. F A Cup: Semi-Final 1913, 1990. Football League Cup: Runners-up
1990.
European Competitions: European Cup: European Cup-Winners' Cup:
European Fairs Cup: 1964-65. UEFA Cup:
Managers (and Secretary-managers): David Ashworth 1906-14, Herbert
Bamlett 1914-21, Charlie Roberts 1921-22, David Ashworth 1923-24, Bob
Mellor 1924-27, Andy Wilson 1927-32, Jimmy McMullan 1933-34, Bob
Mellor 1934-45, (continued as secretary to 1953), Frank Womack 1945-47,
Billy Wootton 1947-50, George Hardwick 1950-56, Ted Goodier 1956-58,
Norman Dodgin 1958-60, Jack Rowley 1960-63, Les McDowall 1963-65,
Gordon Hurst 1965-66, Jimmy McIlroy 1966-68,Jack Rowley 1968-69,
Jimmy Frizzell 1970-82, Joe Royle July 1982-.

5-Year League Record

	Div.	P	W	D	L	F	A	Pts	Pos	FAC	FLC
88-89	2	46	11	21	14	75	72	54	16	3	3
89-90	2	46	19	14	13	70	57	71	8	SF	F
90-91	2	46	25	13	8	83	53	88	1	4	3
91-92	1	42	14	9	19	63	67	51	17	3	4
92-93	PL	42	13	10	19	63	74	49	19	3	4

Summary of Appearances and Goals 1992-93

	Apps	Sub	Goals		Apps	Sub	Goals
Neil Adams	26	6	9	John Kelley	1		0
Andy Barlow	6		0	Neil McDonald	2	2	0
Darren Beckford	6	1	3	Ian Marshall	26	1	2
Paul Bernard	32	1	4	Mike Milligan	42		3
Mark Brennan	14		3	Paul Mouldon	1	3	0
Craig Fleming	23	1	0	Ian Olney	32	2	12
Paul Gerrard	25		0	Roger Palmer	5	12	0
Gunnar Halle	41		5	Neil Pointon	34		0
Jon Hallworth	16		0	Steve Redmond	28	3	0
Orpheo Keizerweerd	0	1	0	Andy Ritchie	10	2	3
Nick Henry	32		6	Graeme Sharp	20	1	7
Richard Jobson	40		2	Neil Tolson	0	3	0

FA Premier League Squad Numbers 1993-94

No.	Player	No.	Player	No.	Player
1	Gerrard	9	Olney	17	Beckford
2	Fleming	10	Milligan	18	McDonald
3	Pointon	11	Bernard	19	Palmer
4	Henry	12	Adams	20	Brennan
5	Jobson	13	Hallworth	21	Tolson
6	Redmond	14	Sharp	22	Makin
7	Halle	15	Barlow		
8	Ritchie	16	Marshall		

Latics Latent Delight

Oldham fans must have given up all hope of their side standing a chance of surviving the inevitable – relegation from the Premier League – with six weeks of the season to go.

The Latics were firmly ensconced at the foot of the table a point adrift of Nottingham Forest and another behind Middlesbrough.

With an unenviable run-in of matches including home fixtures against leaders Manchester United and Liverpool and away at Aston Villa, there appeared little prospect of a seeing Joe Royle's side playing Premier League football next season.

But an unbelievable recovery suddenly began to take shape. A 3-2 defeat of Liverpool on a cold, unwelcoming evening at Boundary Park, unexpectedly offered a glimmer of hope that had previously seemed impossible.

As the goals continued to flow at the Lancashire ground at both ends, as they had all season, Oldham again pulled off the impossible, clinching a 1-0 victory over Manchester United to add to their growing confidence and throw a spanner albeit temporarily into the Championship race.

Then as the run-in threw up the prospect of Oldham having to win their last matches, away at Aston Villa, who were still very much in the title race, and at home to Southampton, to have even a chance of survival, there were still few but the most ardent Latics fans, who would predict that there was a chance of survival.

But on the penultimate weekend of the season, as the nation held its breath, especially United fans, who knew that an Oldham win would hand them the title, a Nicky Henry goal at Villa Park provided the Oldham bandwagon with unexpected momentum and presented United with their first title for 26 years.

Their battle for a place in the Premier League was set to go right to the wire, with a home game against Southampton requiring a conclusive victory in the hope that Crystal Palace would fail to get any type of result against London rivals Arsenal.

In a bizarre afternoon of footballing action, Joe Royle's side plundered an astonishing 5-3 victory over the Saints as Palace, who required only a draw to stay in the Premier League, dived to a disastrous 2-0 defeat at Highbury.

Oldham had survived, tied level on points with Palace, but remained in the Premier League by virtue of a superior goal difference, thanks to the efforts over the season of Ian Olney, their £700,000 summer signing from Aston Villa, Ian Marshall, and the sporadic contribution of popular striker Andy Ritchie, who had missed a number of games with a severe back injury.

The form of Norwegian right-back Gunner Halle was again encouraging and defender Richard Jobson was rewarded for some consistent performances with a succession of call-ups to the England squad, although he never managed to make the breakthrough into the full international side.

QUEENS PARK RANGERS

Founded in 1885 as St. Jude's Institute. Changed name to Queens Park Rangers in 1887; joined the London League in 1896; and turned professional in 1898. Moved to the Southern League, 1899, and were twice champions.

Lead a nomadic existence in West London but in 1917 took over the home of the amateurs Shepherds Bush, Loftus Road, where, apart from a couple of seasons at White City, it has stayed. Founder members of Football League Division Three in 1920 (this becoming Division Three (South) the following season); of Division Three at the end of regionalisation in 1958; and of the Premier League, 1992.

Ground: South Africa Road, W12 7PA
Phone: 081-743 0262   **Nickname:** Rangers or R's
Colours: Blue/White Hoops, White, White
Change: Red/Black Hoops, Black, Black
Capacity: 23,480 (23,000 covered)   **Pitch:** 112 yds x 72 yds
Directions: *From North:* M1 to north circular A406 towards Neasden. Turn left onto A404 follow signs for Hammersmith past White City Stadium then right into South Africa Rd. *From South:* A3 across Putney Bridge and signs for Hammersmith. Folow A219 to Shepherds Bush and join A4020 towards Acton. Turn right after ¼ mile into Loftus Rd. *From East:* From A40(M) towards M41 roundabout. Take 3rd exit at roundabout to A4020 then as above. *From West:* M4 to Chiswick then A315 and A402 to Shepherd's Bush joining A4020 (then as above).
Rail: Shepherds Bush   **Tube** (Central Line): White City

Chairman/Chief Executive: R.C. Thompson
Secretary: Miss S.F. Marson
Manager: Gerry Francis   **Assistant/Coach:** Frank Sibley
Physio: Brian Morris

Record FAPL Win: 4-1 v Tottenham Hotspur, 3/10/92
Record FAPL Defeat: 0-3 v Blackburn Rovers, 28/11/92
Record FL Win: 9-2 v Tranmere R, Division 3, 3/12/1960
Record FL Defeat: 1-8 v Mansfield Town, Division 3, 15/3/1965 *and*
                                1-8 v Manchester United, Division 1, 19/3/1969
Record Cup Win: 8-1 v Bristol Rovers (away), FA Cup, 1R, 27/11/1937 *and*
                                8-1 v Crewe Alexander, Milk Cup, 1R, 3/10/1983
Record Fee Received: £1.3m from Arsenal for David Seaman, 5/1990

Record Fee Paid: £1m to Luton Town for Roy Wegerle, 12/1989
Most FAPL Appearances: 40: David Bardsley, 1992-93
Most FL Appearances: Tony Ingham, 519, 1950-63
Record Attendance (all-time): 35,353 v Leeds U, Division 1 on 27/4/1974
Record Attendance (FAPL): 21,056 v Liverpool
Highest Scorer in FAPL Season: 20: Les Ferdinand, 1992-93
Most FAPL Goals in Season: 63, 1992-93
Most FAPL Points in Season: 63, 1992-93
Most Capped Player: Don Givens, 26 (56), Eire

Close Season Transfers
In: Martin Spanring (Fortuna Dusseldorf, Trial)
Out: Garry Thompson (Cardiff, Trial)

Season 1992-93
Biggest Home Win: 4-1 v Tottenham Hotspur
Biggest Home Defeat: 0-3 v Blackburn Rovers
Biggest Away Win: 3-5 v Everton
Biggest Away Defeat: 0-2 v Aston Villa
Biggest Home Attendance: 21,056 v Liverpool
Smallest Home Attendance: 10,667 v Blackburn Rovers
Average Attendance: 15,000 (+ 10.22%)
Last Season: *PL:* 5th *FA Cup:* 4th round *Coca-Cola Cup:* 4th round
Leading Scorer: Ferdinand (24)

League History: 1920 Original Member of Divison 3; 1921 Division 3 (S);
1948-52 Division 2; 1952-58 Division 3 (S); 1958-67 Division 3; 1967-68
Division 2; 1968-69 Division 1; 1969-73 Division 2; 1973-79 Division 1;
1979-83 Division 2; 1983-92 Division 1; 1992 – FA Premier League.
Honours: Football League: Division 1 – Runners-up 1975-76; Division 2 –
Champions 1982-83; Runners-up 1967-68, 1972-73; Division 3 (S) –
Champions 1947-48; Runners-up 1946-47; Division 3 – Champions 1966-67.
FA Cup: Runners-up 1982. Football League Cup: Winners 1966-67; Runners-
up 1985-86. (In 1966-67 won Division 3 and Football League Cup.)
European Competitions: UEFA Cup: 1976-77, 1984-85.
Managers (and Secretary-managers): James Cowan 1906-13, James Howie
1913-20, Ted Liddell 1920-24, Will Wood 1924-25 (had been secretary since
1903), Bob Hewison 1925-30, John Bowman 1930-31, Archie Mitchell 1931-
33, Mick O'Brien 1933-35, Billy Birrell 1935-39, Ted Vizard 1939-44, Dave
Mangnall 1944-52, Jack Taylor 1952-59, Alec Stock 1959-65 (GM to 1968),
Jimmy Andrews 1965, Bill Dodgin Jnr 1968, Tommy Docherty 1968, Les
Allen 1969-70, Gordon Jago 1971-74, Dave Sexton 1974-77, Frank Sibley
1977-78, Steve Burtenshaw 1978-79, Tommy Docherty 1979-80, Terry
Venables 1980-84, Gordon Jago 1984, Alan Mullery 1984, Frank Sibley

1984-85, Jim Smith 1985-88, Trevor Francis 1988-90, Don Howe 1990-91, Gerry Francis June 1991-.

5-Year League Record

	Div.	P	W	D	L	F	A	Pts	Pos	FAC	FLC
88-89	1	38	14	11	13	43	37	53	9	3	5
89-90	1	38	13	11	14	45	44	50	11	6	3
90-91	1	38	12	10	16	44	53	46	12	3	4
91-92	1	42	12	18	12	48	47	54	11	3	3
92-93	PL	42	17	12	13	63	55	63	5	4	4

Summary of Appearances and Goals 1992-93

	Apps	Sub	Goals		Apps	Sub	Goals
Bradley Allen	21	4	10	Mike Meaker	3		0
Dennis Bailey	13	2	1	Darren Peacock	35	3	2
David Bardsley	40		3	Gary Penrice	10	4	6
Simon Barker	21	4	1	Karl Ready	2	1	0
Rufus Brevett	14	1	0	Tony Roberts	28		0
Justin Channing	2		1	Andy Sinton	36		7
Maurice Doyle	5		0	Jan Stejskal	14	1	0
Les Ferdinand	37		20	Garry Thompson	0	4	0
Ian Holloway	23	1	2	Devon White	3	4	2
Andrew Impey	39	1	2	Ray Wilkins	27		2
Danny Maddix	9	5	0	Clive Wilson	41		3
Alan McDonald	39		0				

FA Premier League Squad Numbers 1993-94

No.	Player	No.	Player	No.	Player
1	Roberts	9	Ferdinand	17	Bailey
2	Bardsley	10	Allen	18	Ready
3	Wilson	11	Sinton	19	White
4	Wilkins	12	Penrice	20	Doyle
5	Peacock	13	Stejskal	21	Witter
6	McDonald	14	Barker	22	Meaker
7	Impey	15	Brevett		
8	Holloway	16	Maddix		

Ranger Rovers

The unassuming West London club defied the odds and most of the pundits to earn the coveted award of best club in London, with an impressive string of results which propelled Gerry Francis's precocious young side to fifth in the table. Francis now faces a battle to keep his top stars at Loftus Road, especially the mercurial talents of England star winger Andy Sinton and striker Les Ferdinand, both the subject of intense transfer speculation.

The emergence of Ferdinand in particular was a revelation for the Rangers fans, with a series of powerful forward performances which earned the former Hayes player an England call-up and a goal against San Marino.

But perhaps more impressive about Rangers' rise was the development of a crop of young players such as Bradley Allen, the brother of Clive and cousin to Martin and Paul, who wasted little time in demonstrating the same predatory skills which seem to be a family trait. Andrew Impey and Welsh keeper Tony Roberts staked regular first-time places, with the ageless Ray Wilkins providing all the guile and movement from midfield.

Ironically at times, one of Rangers' key problems was scoring goals, with Ferdinand being deprived of a regular striking partner for much of the season with injuries to Gary Penrice and Dennis Bailey keeping both out of the side for long intervals.

Unfortunately Rangers' FA cup aspirations were ended by a 4-1 defeat at Manchester City in the fourth round following a replay, but the West London side continued to turn it on in the league.

Consistency was the main target for manager Francis, but a place in Europe was a tantalising possibility until a disastrous run of injuries, one of the worst in the club's history, robbed Rangers of a UEFA Cup berth.

Despite a mediocre run of results at home, with too many games drawn rather than won, Rangers will be encouraged by their ability to win regularly away from Loftus Road, and with the possible addition of one or two players during the close season to strengthen their depleted squad, the Hoopers could be a reasonable outside bet for some kind of honour this season.

SHEFFIELD UNITED

Founded 1889 as a professional club to fulfil the needs of those in charge at Bramhall Lane Cricket Club, including those associated with Sheffield United Cricket Club. The club failed in its application to join the Football Alliance in that competition's first season and played in the Midland League, moving to the Northern for 1891-92.

Failed too in its application for a place in Football League Division One in 1892, but joined the League instead as a founder member of Division Two. Played in all four divisions of the Football League and was a founder member of the Premier League in 1992.

Ground: Bramall Lane Ground, Sheffield, S2 4SU
Phone: (0742) 738955   **Nickname:** The Blades
Colours: Red/White, White, White
Change: Navy with Purple/Green stripe, Navy Blue, Navy Blue
Capacity: 32,000 (22,000 seats)   **Pitch:** 110 yds x 72 yds
Directions: *From North:* M1 J34 follow A6109 towards Sheffield. Left after 3½ miles then 4th exit from roundabout into Sheaf St. At 2nd roundabout take 5th exit into St Mary's Lane then left after ½ mile into Bramall Lane. *From South & East:* M1 junction 31 or 33 onto A57. Third exit from roundabout into Sheaf St. *From West:* A57 into Sheffield then 4th exit at roundabout into Upper Hanover St. Third exit at second roundabout leads into Bramall Lane.
Rail: Sheffield Midland

President: R. Wragg M.INST. BM   **Chairman:** D. Dooley
Secretary: D. Capper AFA
Manager: Dave Bassett   **Assistant Manager/Physio:** Derek French
First Team Coach: Geoff Taylor

Record FAPL Win: 6-0 v Tottenham Hotspur, 2/3/93
Record FAPL Defeat: 1-3 v Aston Villa, 27/1/93 *and*
          1-3 v Leeds United, 17/10/92
Record FL Win: 10-0 v Burslem Port Vale, Division 2, 10/12/1892
Record FL Defeat: 0-13 v Bolton Wanderers, FA Cup 2R, 1/2/1890
Record Cup Win: 5-0 v Newcastle U (away), FA Cup, 1R, 10/1/1914 *and*
          5-0 v Corinthians, FA Cup, 1R, 10/1/1925 *and*
          5-0 v Barrow, FA Cup, 3R, 7/1/1956
Record Fee Received: £400,000 from Leeds United for Alex Sabella, 5/1980
Record Fee Paid: £650,000 to Leeds United for Vinny Jones, 9/1990
Most FAPL Appearances: 41: Brian Deane, 1992-93

Most FL Appearances: Joe Shaw, 629, 1948-66
Record Attendance (all-time): 68,287 v Leeds U, FA Cup 5R, 15/2/1936
Record Attendance (FAPL): 30,039 v Sheffield Wednesday, 8/11/92
Highest Scorer in FAPL Season: 15: Brian Deane, 1992-93
Most FAPL Goals in Season: 54, 1992-93
Most FAPL Points in Season: 52, 1992-93
Most Capped Player: Billy Gillespie, 25, Northern Ireland

Close Season Transfers
In: David Tuttle (Tottenham, £350,000), Jonas Wirmola (Sparvagens, Stockholm, £50,000), Ross Davison (Walton & Hersham, Nominal), Chris Kamara (Luton, Free)
Out: Brian Deane (Leeds, £2.9 m), Phil Kite (Cardiff, Free)

Season 1992-93
Biggest Home Win: 6-0 v Tottenham Hotspur
Biggest Home Defeat: 1-3 v Blackburn Rovers
Biggest Away Win: 2-0 v Everton *and* 2-0 v Nottingham Forest
Biggest Away Defeat: 3-1 v Aston Villa *and* 3-1 v Leeds United
Biggest Home Attendance: 30,039 v Sheffield Wednesday
Smallest Home Attendance: 14,628 v Oldham Athletic
Average Attendance: 18,987 (-12.92%)
Last Season: *PL:* 14th *FA Cup:* semi-final *Coca-Cola Cup:* 3rd round
Leading Scorer: Deane (20)

League History: 1892 Elected to Division 2; 1893-1934 Division 1; 1934-39 Division 2; 1946-49 Division 1; 1949-53 Division 2; 1953-56 Division 1; 1956-61 Division 2; 1961-68 Division 1; 1968-71 Division 2; 1971-76 Division 1; 1976-79 Division 2; 1979-81 Division 1; 1981-82 Division 4; 1982-84 Division 3; 1984-88 Division 2; 1988-89 Division 3; 1989-90 Division 2; 1990-92 Division 1; 1992 – FA Premier League.
Honours: Football League: Division 1 – Champions 1897-98; Runners-up 1896-97, 1899-1900; Division 2 – Champions 1952-53; Runners-up 1892-93, 1938-39, 1960-61, 1970-71, 1989-90; Division 4 – Champions 1981-82. FA Cup: Winners 1899, 1902, 1915, 1925; Runners-up 1901, 1936. Football League Cup: best season: 5th round, 1961-62, 1966-67, 1971-72.
Managers (and Secretary-managers): J.B. Wostinholm 1889-1899, John Nicholson 1899-1932, Ted Davison 1932-52, Reg Freeman 1952-55, Joe Mercer 1955-58, Johnny Harris 1959-68 (continued as GM to 1970), Arthur Rowley 1968-69, Johnny Harris (GM resumed TM duties)1969-73, Ken Furphy 1973-75, Jimmy Sirrel 1975-77, Harry Haslam 1978-81, Martin Peters 1981, Ian Porterfield 1981-86, Billy McEwan 1986-88, Dave Bassett January, 1988-.

5-Year League Record

	Div.	P	W	D	L	F	A	Pts	Pos	FAC	FLC
88-89	3	46	25	9	12	93	54	84	2	5	3
89-90	2	46	24	13	9	78	58	85	2	6	1
90-91	1	38	13	7	18	36	55	46	13	3	4
91-92	1	42	16	9	17	65	63	57	9	5	3
92-93	PL	42	14	10	18	54	53	52	14	SF	3

Summary of Appearances and Goals 1992-93

Name	Apps	Sub	Goals	Name	Apps	Sub	Goals
David Barnes	13		0	Jamie Hoyland	15	7	2
Paul Beesley	39		2	Chris Kamara	6	2	0
Carl Bradshaw	24	8	1	Alan Kelly	32	1	0
Ian Bryson	9	7	3	Mike Lake	6		0
Franz Carr	8		3	Adrian Littlejohn	18	9	8
Alan Cork	11	16	2	Alan McLeary	3		0
Tom Cowan	21		0	John Pemberton	19		0
Brian Deane	41		15	Paul Rogers	26	1	3
Kevin Gage	27		0	Andy Scott	1	1	1
John Gannon	26	1	1	Simon Tracey	10		0
Brian Gayle	31		2	Mitch Ward	22	4	0
Charlie Hartfield	12	5	0	Dane Whitehouse	14		5
Clyn Hodges	28	3	4				

FA Premier League Squad Numbers 1993-94

No.	Player	No.	Player	No.	Player
1	Kelly	10	Hodges	19	Bryson
2	Gage	11	Ward	20	Pemberton
3	Cowan	12	Reed	21	Cork
4	Gannon	13	Tracey	22	Scott
5	Gayle	14	*	23	Kamara
6	Barnes	15	Hartfield	#	Tuttle
7	Carr	16	Beesley	#	Wirmola
8	Rogers	17	Bradshaw		
9	Littlejohn	18	Whitehouse		

Blades Blunted in Cup Run

Not much for Blades fans to cheer again in 92-93, although Dave Bassett's side thoroughly deserved their place in the Premier League for '94, albeit claimed at some nail-biting expense late on in the season.

Undoubtedly the highlight of the season was the appearance at Wembley in the semi-final of the FA Cup, facing bitter rivals Sheffield Wednesday in an all-Sheffield affair.

Unfortunately the match did not go according to script and despite a goal out of nothing from that experienced old warhorse Alan Cork, a member of Wimbledon's 1988 FA Cup winning squad, goals from Mark Bright and Chris Waddle ensured that it was Wednesday and not United who enjoyed their day out in May.

But despite the bitter disappointment of missing out on a Wembley final, Bassett's team can take enormous satisfaction from their fifth round dismissal of Manchester United in front of a packed Brammall Lane in February.

After Ryan Giggs had given the visitors the lead with a touch of precocious class, Jamie Hoyland had provided a scrambled equaliser and then Glyn Hodges, another old Wimbledon disciple of Bassett's, had produced an exquisite winner to give the Blades the advantage and ultimately the victory, after Steve Bruce had missed a late penalty opportunity.

Certainly a victory to build on and savour for a United side who again struggled to provide the consistency required to make a serious challenge for anything other than a relegation berth.

The presence of striker Brian Deane, whose goal-scoring skills were again recognised by his presence in Graham Taylor's England squad albeit as a squad member, were the difference between relegation and another season in the top flight, although in the early season the gangly striker was unable to find the target regularly.

Deane's close season departure to Yorkshire rivals Leeds for just under £3 million is a blow for the Blades, who will struggle to find a replacement for the powerful front man. Wimbledon's John Fashanu is one possibility or perhaps Liverpool's Ronnie Rosenthal, but Bassett will certainly have to go out and buy.

One player who will start the new season at Brammall Lane is former Spurs defender David Tuttle.

Tuttle moved north to the Blades for £350,000 in August, as cover for club skipper Brian Gayle who will miss the start of the new campaign with a troublesome knee injury.

Bassett and his men will certainly be looking for a better start to the 93-94 campaign than last year. By Christmas they were firmly entrenched in the relegation placings with only 21 points from 21 games, but showed great character and commitment to haul themselves free of the bottom three by late spring and be almost assured of safety by the final two weeks of the season.

On the last day of the campaign, they made completely sure of survival with a thumping 4-0 defeat of Chelsea and eventually finished in 14th spot, some three places above fallen champions Leeds, although on a sad note, the end of the season corresponded with the untimely death of 26-year-old goalkeeper Mel Rees, who tragically lost his battle against cancer.

SHEFFIELD WEDNESDAY

Founded in 1867 by members of the Wednesday Cricket Club and played at Highfield before moving to Myrtle Road. Were first holders of the Sheffield FACup. The club played at Sheaf House then Endcliff and became professionals in 1886. In 1887 moved to Olive Grove.

Refused admission to the Football League, the club was founder member, and first champions, of the Football Alliance in 1889. In 1892 most Alliance clubs became founder members of Football League Division Two, but Wednesday was elected to an enlarged top division. The club moved to Hillsborough in 1899. Founder member of the Premier League 1992.

Ground: Hillsborough, Sheffield, S6 1SW
Phone: (0742) 343122 **Nickname:** The Owls
Colours: Blue/White, Blue, Blue **Change:** All Black with Yellow/Grey trim
Capacity: 41,237 **Pitch:** 115 yds x 75 yds
Directions: *From North:* M1 J34 then A6109 to Sheffield. At roundabout after 1½ miles take 3rd exit then turn left after 3 miles into Herries Rd. *From South & East:* M1 junction 31 or 33 to A57. At roundabout take Prince of Wales Rd exit. A further 6 miles then turn left into Herries Rd South. *From West:* A57 to A6101 then turn left after 4 miles at T junction into Penistone Road.
Rail: Sheffield Midland

Chairman: D.G. Richards **Vice-chairman:** K.T. Addy
Secretary: G.H. Mackrell FCCA
Manager: Trevor Francis **Assistant:** Richie Barker
First Team Coach: **Physio:** A. Smith

Record FAPL Win: 5-2 v Southampton, 12/4/93
Record FAPL Defeat: 0-3 v Manchester City, 5/9/92
Record FL Win: 9-1 v Birmingham, Division 1, 13/12/1930
Record FL Defeat: 0-10 v Aston Villa, Division 1, 5/10/1912
Record Cup Win: 12-0 v Halliwell, FA Cup, 1R, 17/1/1891
Record Fee Received: £1.75m from Real Sociedad for D. Atkinson, 7/1990
Record Fee Paid: £1.2m to Rangers for Chris Woods, 8/1991
Most FAPL Appearances: 40: Nigel Worthington, 1992-93
Most FL Appearances: Andy Wilson, 502, 1900-20
Record Attendance (all-time): 72,841 v Man City, FA Cup 5R, 17/2/1934
Record Attendance (FAPL): 58,668 v Sheffield United
Highest Scorer in FAPL Season: Hirst and Bright, both 11, both 92-93

Most FAPL Goals in Season: 55, 1992-93
Most FAPL Points in Season: 59, 1992-93
Most Capped Player: Nigel Worthington, 37, Northern Ireland

Close Season Transfers
In: Des Walker (Sampdoria, £2.7m), Andy Pearce (Coventry, £500,000)
Out: Danny Wilson (Barnsley, £200,000), Viv Anderson (Barnsley, Free),
Paul Robinson (Scarborough, Free)

Season 1992-93
Biggest Home Win: 5-2 v Southampton
Biggest Home Defeat: 0-3 v Manchester City
Biggest Away Win: 2-0 v Chelsea *and* 2-0 v Tottenham Hotspur
Biggest Away Defeat: 1-3 v Leeds United *and* 1-3 v Queens Park Rangers
Biggest Home Attendance: 38,668 v Sheffield United
Smallest Home Attendance: 20,918 v Wimbledon
Average Attendance: 27,254 (-7.86%)
Last Season: *PL:* 7th *FA Cup:* Runners-up *Coca-Cola Cup:* Runners-up
UEFA Cup: 2nd round
Leading Scorer: Bright (20)

League History: 1892 Elected to Division 1; 1899-1900 Division 2; 1900-20
Division 1; 1920-26 Division 2; 1926-37 Division 1; 1937-50 Division 2;
1950-51 Division 1; 1951-52 Division 2; 1952-55 Division 1; 1955-56
Division 2; 1956-58 Division 1; 1958-59 Division 2; 1959-70 Division 1;
1970-75 Division 2; 1975-80 Division 3; 1980-84 Division 2; 1984-90
Division 1; 1990-91 Division 2; 1991-92 Division1; 1992- FA Premier
League.
Honours: Football League: Division 1 – Champions 1902-03, 1903-04,
1928-29, 1929-30; Runners-up 1960-61; Division 2 – Champions 1899-1900,
1925-26, 1951-52, 1955-56, 1958-59; Runners-up 1949-50, 1983-84. FA
Cup: Winners 1896, 1907, 1935; Runners-up 1890, 1966, 1993. Football
League Cup: Winners 1990-91, Runners-up 1993.
European Competitions: European Fairs Cup: 1961-62, 1963-64. UEFA
Cup: 1992-93
Managers (and Secretary-managers): Arthur Dickinson 1891-1920. Robert
Brown 1920-33, Billy Walker 1933-37, Jimmy McMullan 1937-42, Eric
Taylor 1942-58 (continued as GM to 1974), Harry Catterick 1958-61, Vic
Buckingham 1961-64, Alan Brown 1964-68, Jack Marshall 1968-69, Danny
Williams 1969-71, Derek Dooley 1971-73, Steve Burtenshaw 1974-75, Len
Ashurst 1975-77, Jackie Charlton 1977-83, Howard Wilkinson 1983-88, Peter
Eustace 1988-89, Ron Atkinson 1989-91, Trevor Francis June 1991-.

5-Year League Record

	Div.	P	W	D	L	F	A	Pts	Pos	FAC	FLC
88-89	1	38	10	12	16	34	51	42	15	4	2
89-90	1	38	11	10	17	35	51	43	18	4	3
90-91	2	46	22	16	8	80	51	82	3	5	W
91-92	1	42	21	12	9	62	49	75	3	4	3
92-93	PL	42	15	14	13	55	51	59	7	F	F

Summary of Appearances and Goals 1992-93

	Apps	Sub	Goals		Apps	Sub	Goals
Viv Anderson	23	2	3	Kevin Pressman	3		0
Chris Bart-Williams	21	13	6	John Sheridan	25		3
Mark Bright	28	2	11	Peter Shirtliff	20		0
Trevor Francis	1	4	0	Simon Stewart	6		0
John Harkes	23	6	2	Chris Waddle	32	1	1
David Hirst	22		11	Paul Warhurst	25	4	6
Graham Hyde	14	6	1	Gordon Watson	4	7	1
Nigel Jemson	5	8	0	Julian Watts	2	1	0
Ryan Jones	9		0	Michael Williams	2	1	0
Phil King	11	1	1	Paul Williams	7		1
Roland Nilsson	32		1	Danny Wilson	22	5	2
Carlton Palmer	33	1	1	Chris Woods	39		0
Nigel Pearson	13	3	1	Nigel Worthington	40		1

FA Premier League Squad Numbers 1993-94

No.	Player	No.	Player	No.	Player
1	Woods	10	Bright	19	Jemson
2	Nilsson	11	Sheridan	20	Watson
3	Worthington	12	Pearce	21	Jones
4	Palmer	13	Pressman	22	Stewart
5	Pearson	14	Bart-Williams	23	Key
6	Shirtliff	15	Harkes	24	Watts
7	Warhurst	16	Hyde	25	Williams
8	Waddle	17	Walker		
9	Hirst	18	King		

Cups of Woe

Two cup final appearances and nothing but losers medals to show for their efforts and the promise of what might have been – football can indeed be a cruel mistress. Last season certainly started well enough for Wednesday with the shrewd acquisition of former England winger Chris Waddle from Marseilles for a cut-price £1 million.

Waddle's performances, which were to earn him the Football Writers Association *Footballer Of The Year* accolade, were to become the mainstay of an impressive assortment of individual feats of genius by Wednesday players during the season, especially the emergence of promising young midfielder Chris Bart-Williams and forward-cum-defender Paul Warhurst.

But the purchase of Crystal Palace striker Mark Bright for £1 million really gave the Wednesday attack a potency about it, especially the combination of Bright and England forward David Hirst.

A promising league start was improved still further by steady progress in the UEFA Cup. An emphatic first round defeat of Spora Luxembourg, in which Paul Warhurst was to suffer a swallowed tongue and collect three goals as an early indication of his obvious goalscoring potential, proffered great optimism for their second round tie against German side Kaiserslautern.

But a bad-tempered affair in Germany saw the unlikely dismissal of Hirst and a 3-1 reverse for the Yorkshire side which proved too great a deficit for them to retrieve. A 2-2 draw at Hillsborough went some way towards making amends and provided great encouragement for Wednesday's burgeoning cup pedigree.

The domestic competitions proved to be manager Trevor Francis's greatest tactical achievements. Wednesday galloped impressively through the early rounds of the Coca-Cola Cup and punished a lethargic Blackburn side with a 4-2 second leg victory in the semi-final, with Warhurst deputising admirably for the injured Hirst, which steered them to Wembley.

Indeed Warhurst managed an astonishing 11 goals in 11 consecutive games in his improvised role as striker in Hirst's absence, just failing to collect the club goalscoring record of 12 goals in 12 consecutive games.

In the final they were to face Arsenal, an occasion that was to offer a sense of deja-vu when the two sides met a month later in the FA Cup Final. On this occasion Wednesday stole the lead with a John Harkes drive after Warhurst had rattled the post in the fifth minute and it seemed a trophy was at last heading to Hillsborough again. But goals from Paul Merson and Stephen Morrow provided an unlikely Gunners victory.

In the FA Cup Final in May it was Arsenal who took the lead courtesy of Ian Wright, but Hirst replied for Wednesday and a replay was required. Wright again paved the way for an Arsenal victory with the opening gambit, but Waddle, who else, improvised a moment of genius to reply late in the second half. With the match heading for penalties, Andy Linighan planted a header through the despairing clutches of Chris Woods and Wednesday's European dreams were ended.

But with the new season's approach being greeted by the arrival of £2 million defender Des Walker from Sampdoria and the return to fitness of striker David Hirst and broken-leg victim Nigel Pearson, Wednesday's encouraging finish in 7th position, shows every sign of acting as a foundation for further progress this year.

SOUTHAMPTON

Formed 1885 by members of the St Mary's Young Men's Association, St Mary's FC. The church link was dropped, though the name retained, in 1893. In 1895 applied for a Southern League place, but was refused only to be invited to fill a subsequent vacancy. 'St. Mary's' was dropped after two seasons. Moved from the County Cricket Ground to the Dell in 1898.

Six times Southern League champions, Southampton were founder members of Football League Division Three in 1920 (this becoming Division Three (South) the following season); of Division Three at the end of regionalisation in 1958; and of the Premier League, 1992.

Ground: The Dell, Milton Road, Southampton, SO9 4XX
Phone: (0703) 220505　　**Nickname:** The Saints
Colours: Red/White, Black, Black
Change: Turquoise/Royal Blue, Turquoise, Royal Blue
Capacity: 21,900　　**Pitch:** 110 yds x 72 yds
Directions: *From North:* A33 into The Avenue then right into Northlands Rd. Right at the end into Archer's Rd. *From East:* M27 then A334 and signs for Southampton along A3024. Follow signs for the West into Commercial Rd, right into Hill Lane then first right into Milton Rd. *From West:* Take A35 then A3024 towards city centre. Left into Hill Lane and first right into Milton Rd.　　**Rail:** Southampton Central

President: J. Corbett　　**Chairman:** F.G. Askham FCA
Vice-chairman: K. St. J. Wiseman　　**Secretary:** Brian Truscott
Manager: Ian Branfoot　　**Assistant:** John Mortimore
First Team Coach: Lew Chatterley　　**Physio:** Don Taylor

Record FAPL Win: 3-0 v Norwich City, 10/2/93
Record FAPL Defeat: 2-5 v Sheffield Wednesday, 12/4/93
Record FL Win: 9-3 v Wolverhampton Wanderers, Division 2, 18/9/1965
Record FL Defeat: 0-8 v Tottenham Hotspur, Division 2, 28/3/1936 *and* 0-8 v Everton, Division 1, 20/11/1971
Record Cup Win: 7-1 v Ipswich Town, FA Cup, 3R, 7/1/1961
Record Fee Received: £1.7m from Leeds U for Rod & Ray Wallace, 7/1991
Record Fee Paid: £1m to Swindon Town for Alan McLoughlin, 12/1990
Most FAPL Appearances: 42: Tim Flowers, 1992-93
Most FL Appearances: Terry Paine, 713, 1956-74
Record Attendance (all-time): 31,044 v Man United, Division 1, 8/10/1969
Record Attendance (FAPL): 19,654 v Tottenham Hotspur, 15/8/92
Highest Scorer in FAPL Season: 15: Mathew Le Tissier, 1992-93

Most FAPL Goals in Season: 54, 1992-93
Most FAPL Points in Season: 50, 1992-93
Most Capped Player: Peter Shilton, 49 (125), England

Close Season Transfers
In: Simon Charlton (Huddersfield, £250,000), Colin Cramb, Paul McDonald (Hamilton, £150,000 combined)
Out: David Speedie (Leicester, Free)

Season 1992-93
Biggest Home Win: 3-0 v Norwich City
Biggest Home Defeat: 1-2 v Queens Park Rangers and Sheffield Wednesday
Biggest Away Win: 2-1 v Crystal Palace, Nottingham Forest & Wimbledon
Biggest Away Defeat: 2-5 v Sheffield Wednesday
Biggest Home Attendance: 19,654 v Tottenham Hotspur, 15/8/92
Smallest Home Attendance: 10,827 v Oldham Athletic, 31/10/92
Average Attendance: 15,382 (+ 0.6%)
Last Season: *PL:* 18th *FA Cup:* 3rd round *Coca-Cola Cup:* 3rd round
Leading Scorer: Le Tissier (18)

League History: 1920 Original Member of Division 3; 1921 Division 3 (S); 1922-53 Division 2; 1953-58 Division 3 (S); 1958-60 Division 3; 1960-66 Division 2; 1966-74 Division 1; 1974-78 Division 2; 1978-92 Division 1; 1992 – FA Premier League.
Honours: Football League: Division 1 – Runners-up 1983-84; Division 2 – Runners-up 1965-66, 1977-78; Division 3 (S) – Champions 1921-22; Runners-up 1920-21; Division 3 – Champions 1959-60. FA Cup: Winners 1975-76; Runners-up 1900, 1902. Football League Cup: Runners-up 1978-79.
European Competitions: European Cup-Winners' Cup: 1976-77. European Fairs Cup: 1969-70.-70. UEFA Cup: 1971-72, 1981-82, 1982-83, 1984-85. Zenith Data Systems Cup: Runners-up 1991-92.
Managers (and Secretary-managers): Cecil Knight 1894-95, Charles Robson 1895-97, E. Arnfield 1897-1911 (continued as secretary), George Swift 1911-12, E. Arnfield 1912-19, Jimmy McIntyre 1919-24, Arthur Chadwick 1925-31, George Kay 1931-36, George Cross 1936-37, Tom Parker 1937-43, J.R. Sarjantson stepped down from the board to act as secretary-manager 1943-47 with the next two listed being team managers during this period), Arthur Dominy 1943-46, Bill Dodgin Snr 1946-49, Sid Cann 1949-51, George Roughton 1952-55, Ted Bates 1955-73, Lawrie McMenemy 1973-85, Chris Nicholl 1985-91, Ian Branfoot June 1991-.

5-Year League Record

	Div.	P	W	D	L	F	A	Pts	Pos	FAC	FLC
88-89	1	38	10	15	13	52	66	45	13	3	5
89-90	1	38	15	10	13	71	63	55	7	5	5
90-91	1	38	12	9	17	58	69	45	14	5	5
91-92	1	42	14	10	18	39	55	52	16	6	4
92-93	PL	42	13	11	18	54	61	50	18	3	3

Summary of Appearances and Goals 1992-93

	Apps	Sub	Goals		Apps	Sub	Goals
Mick Adams	38		4	Terry Hurlock	30		0
Peter Allen	0	1	0	Jeff Kenna	27	2	2
Nicky Banger	0	16	6	Matthew Le Tissier	40		15
Neal Bartlett	0	1	0	Dave Lee	0	1	0
Francis Benali	31	2	0	Neil Maddison	33	4	4
Mattew Bound	1	2	0	Ken Monkou	33		1
Glenn Cockerill	21	2	0	Paul Moody	2	1	0
Kerry Dixon	8	1	2	Kevin Moore	18		2
Jason Dodd	27	3	1	Lee Powell	0	2	0
Iain Dowlie	34	2	11	David Speedie	11		0
Tim Flowers	42		0	Tom Widdrington	11	1	0
Perry Groves	13	2	2	Steve Wood	4		0
Richard Hall	28		4				

FA Premier League Squad Numbers 1993-94

No.	Player	No.	Player	No.	Player
1	Flowers	9	Dowie	17	Moore
2	Kenna	10	Maddison	18	Wood
3	Adams	11	Benali	19	McDonald
4	Hurlock	12	Gray	20	Moody
5	Hall	13	Andrews	21	Widdrington
6	Monkou	14	Charlton	22	Bound
7	Le Tissier	15	Dodd		
8	Cockerill	16	Banger		

No Change at Southampton

The departure of England striker Alan Shearer for £3.4 million to Blackburn Rovers would have been a blow to any club. But to Southampton, who had carefully nurtured his progress from promising youngster to international star, the effects of losing a player of his status were potentially disastrous.

Having concerned themselves largely with an on-going battle against relegation for several successive seasons, the writing appeared to be on the wall for the Saints and manager Ian Branfoot early in the season as they slumped into the relegation zone.

Poor form and the disappointing efforts of new signings Perry Groves (£750,000), Kerry Dixon (£400,000) and David Speedie (£250,000), did little to aid the Southampton cause and it wasn't long before the dreaded chorus of 'Branfoot out' was struck up from the terraces.

Players were quickly farmed out to clubs on loan, as Southampton's defensive crises, exacerbated by the departure of Neil Ruddock to Tottenham and only partially relieved by the arrival of Kenneth Monkou from Chelsea, continued to cause hearts at the Dell to flutter.

To make matters worse, the Saints turned into sinners on the pitch, collecting the highest number of Premier League bookings, a whopping 55, with five dismissals, a disciplinary record which earned them a £25,000 suspended fine from the FA before the start of the new season.

But after Christmas a minor miracle occurred, with Southampton putting together a creditable run and then a significant string of results which lifted them out of immediate danger.

A 2-0 victory over championship pretenders Aston Villa at the beginning of February offered much needed relief, with goals from Iain Dowie and emerging striker Nicky Banger, one of the young successes of the season.

But despite a surge up the table, which took them to the brink of a top ten finish, a disappointing run late on, sent the side tumbling back into relegation territory, although their long-term place in the top flight was never seriously threatened.

The close season brought the inevitable departure of Speedie to Leicester on a free transfer, but the arrival of defender Simon Charlton from Huddersfield for £250,000, and strikers Colin Cramb and Paul McDonald from Hamilton for a combined fee of £150,000 provided renewed optimism about the campaign ahead.

SWINDON TOWN

Founded as Spartans around 1881 by cricketers from Swindon Spartans. Amalgamated with St Mark's Young Men's Friendly Society to become Swindon Town around 1883. First holders of the Wiltshire Senior Cup 1887. Founder member of the Southern League First Division 1894. Turned professional in 1895 and, having played on several sites, moved to the County Ground.

FA Cup semi-finalists in 1912 and Southern League champions 1914. Founder members of Football League Division Three in 1920 (this becoming Division Three (South) the following season) and of Division Three at the end of regionalisation in 1958. Denied promotion to the top division for disciplinary reasons 1991.

Ground: County Ground, Swindon, Wiltshire, SN1 2ED
Phone: (0793) 430430   **Nickname:** The Robins
Colours: All Red   **Change:** Yellow, Sky Blue, White
Capacity: 16,432   **Pitch:** 114yds x 72 yds
Directions: *From East & South:* M4 Junc 15 then A345. 4th exit at County roundabout into Shrivenham Rd. *From West:* M4 Junc 16 then A420. 1st exit at roundabout, follow Faringdon Rd to Fleet St, Milford St and Manchester Rd. Right at roundabout, then 1st exit at next (County) roundabout leads into Shrivenham Rd. *From North:* M4, A345, A361 or A420 to County rounabout, take Shrivenham Rd exit.
Rail: Swindon (½ mile)

President: C.J. Green   **Chairman:** R.v Hardman
Vice-chairman: J.M. Spearman   **Secretary:** Jon Pollard
Manager: John Gorman   **Assistant:** David Hay

First Team Coach: Andy Rowland   **Physio:** Kevin Morris
Record FAPL Win: –
Record FAPL Defeat: –
Record FL Win: 9-1 v Luton T, Division 3 (S), 28/8/1920
Record FL Defeat: 1-10 v Man City, FA Cup, 4R (replay), 25/1/1930
Record Cup Win: 10-1 v Farnham United Breweries (away), FA Cup, 1R (replay), 28/11/1925
Record Fee Received: £1m from Southampton for A. McLoughlin, 12/1990
Record Fee Paid: £250,000 to Huddersfield Tn for Duncan Shearer, 6/1988
Most FAPL Appearances: –
Most FL Appearances: John Trollope, 770, 1960-80
Record Attendance (all-time): 32,000 v Arsenal, FA Cup 3R, 15/1/1972

Record Attendance (FAPL): –
Highest Scorer in FAPL Season:
Most FAPL Goals in Season: –
Most FAPL Points in Season: –
Most Capped Player: Rod Thomas, 30 (50), Wales.

Close Season Transfers
In: Jan Aage Fjortoft (Rapid Vienna, £500,000), Adrian Whitbread (Leyton Orient, £500,000), Luc Nijholt (Motherwell, £175,000)
Out: Colin Calderwood (Tottenham, Tribunal fee), Glenn Hoddle (Chelsea, £75,000), David Mitchell (Altay Izmir, £20,000), Shaun Close (Barnet, Free), Brian Marwood (Barnet, Free)

Season 1992-93
Biggest Home Win: 5-1 v Notts County
Biggest Home Defeat: 2-4 v Derby County
Biggest Away Win: 4-0 v Watford
Biggest Away Defeat: 2-4 v Leicester City
Biggest Home Attendance: 17,574 v Newcastle United
Smallest Home Attendance: 5,759 v Grimsby Town
Average Attendance: 10,554 (+ 9.33%)
Last Season: *Div 1:* 5th *FA Cup:* 3rd round *Coca-Cola Cup:* 3rd round
Leading Scorer: Maskell (21)

League History: 1920 Original Member of Division 3; 1921-58 Division 3 (S); 1958-63 Division 3; 1963-65 Division 2; 1965-69 Division 3; 1969-74 Division 2; 1974-82 Division 3; 1982-86 Division 4; 1986-87 Division 3; 1987-92 Division 2; 1992-1993 Division 1; 1993- FA Premier League.
Honours: Football League: Division 2 best season; 4th, 1989-90; Division 3 – Runners-up 1962-63, 1968-69; Division 4 – Champions 1985-86 (with record 102 points). FA Cup: Semi-finals 1910, 1912. Football League Cup: Winners 1968-69. Anglo-Italian Cup: Winners 1970.
Managers (and Secretary-managers): Sam Allen 1902-33, Ted Vizard 1933-39, Neil Harris 1939-41, Louis Page 1945-53, Maurice Lindley 1953-55, Bert Head 1956-65, Danny Williams 1965-69, Fred Ford 1969-71, Dave Mackay 1971-72, Les Allen 1972-74, Danny Williams 1974-78, Bobby Smith 1978-80, John Trollope 1980-83, Ken Beamish 1983-84, Lou Macari 1984-89, Ossie Ardiles 1989-91, Glenn Hoddle 1991-1993, John Gorman June 1993-.

5-Year League Record

	Div.	P	W	D	L	F	A	Pts	Pos	FAC	FLC
88-89	2	46	20	16	10	68	53	76	6	4	2
89-90	2	46	20	14	12	79	59	74	4	3	4
90-91	2	46	12	14	20	65	73	50	21	4	3
91-92	2	46	18	15	13	69	55	69	8	5	4
92-93	1	46	21	13	12	74	59	76	5	3	3

Summary of Appearances and Goals 1992-93

Player	Apps	Sub	Goals	Player	Apps	Sub	Goals
Austin Berkley	0	1	0	Martin Ling	43	1	3
Paul Bodin	34	1	11	Marcus Phillips	0	1	0
Colin Calderwood	45		2	Ross McLaren	22	1	0
Shaun Close	1	19	0	Craig Maskell	32	1	18
Fraser Digby	30		0	Brian Marwood	6	5	1
Andy Gray	3		0	Dave Mitchell	37	5	12
Nicky Hammond	13		0	Eddie Murray	0	3	0
Chris Harmon	1	1	0	John Moncur	13	4	1
Micky Hazard	30	2	3	Nicky Summerbee	36	8	2
Glenn Hoddle	41	1	1	Shaun Taylor	46		10
Kevin Horlock	13	4	1	Adrian Viveash	5	5	0
Paul Hunt	3	6	0	Steve White	20	19	7
David Kerslake	30	1	1				

FA Premier League Squad Numbers 1993-94

No.	Player	No.	Player	No.	Player
1	Digby	9	Fjortoft	17	Hamon
2	Summerbee	10	Ling	18	Murray
3	Bodin	11	Maskell	19	Thomson
4	Hazard	12	White	20	O'Sullivan
5	Nijholt	13	*	21	Phillips
6	Taylor	14	Whitbread	22	Berkley
7	Moncur	15	Viveash	23	Hammond
8	MacLaren	16	Horlock	24	Middleton

Swindon Promoted *Again*

For several seasons Swindon Town have been playing the sort of intelligent attractive football that is normally equated with disaster in the lower divisions where a more direct *kick and run* approach is generally held to be the only effective way of competing. Few expected them to mount a serious challenge for the divisional title but under the stewardship of player-manager Glenn Hoddle they were always a force to be reckoned with.

They notched up some fine wins over Newcastle, West Ham and Portsmouth but never succeeded in maintaining their form for long stretches. In truth they never looked like taking one of the automatic promotion places but, with the sides finishing 3rd, 4th, 5th and 6th playing in a mini-cup series for the third available promotion place, they were always in with a shout. It didn't matter that they only gained two points from their last four games, fifth place was enough.

Their play-off "semi-final" pitched them against 1993's "best team on Merseyside", Tranmere Rovers. Swindon virtually made sure of their place in the final of the play-offs by scoring three goals in the first half with the first two goals coming in the first three minutes of their first, home, leg. Despite some spirited attacking by the Merseyside Minnows Swindon were not to be denied. The final matched them against Leicester City who had outfought a despondent Portsmouth side in their semi-final. A packed Wembley stadium could have been forgiven for thinking the tie was all over as Swindon went into a 3-0 lead after the interval. Leicester City had other ideas and, incredibly, they fought back to level the scores before a Swindon penalty finally swung the game the way of the Wiltshire club; 4-3 the final score.

TOTTENHAM HOTSPUR

Formed in 1882 by members of the schoolboys' Hotspur Cricket Club as Hotspur FC and had early Church connections. Added 'Tottenham' to distinguish club from others with similar names in 1885. Turned professional in 1895 and elected to the Southern League in 1896 having been rebuffed by the Football League.

Played at several places before moving to the site which became known as White Hart Lane in 1899. Joined the Football League Second Division 1908. Having failed to gain a place in the re-election voting, it secured a vacancy caused by a late resignation. Premier League founder members 1992.

Ground: 748 High Road, Tottenham, London, N17 0AP
Phone: 081-808 6666   **Nickname:** Spurs
Colours: White, Navy Blue, White   **Change:** All Yellow or all Sky Blue
Capacity: 32,786   **Pitch:** 110yds x 73 yds
Directions: A406 North Circular to Edmonton. At traffic lights follow signs for Tottenham along A1010 then Fore St for ground.
Rail: White Hart Lane (adjacent)
Tube: Seven Sisters (Victoria Line) or Manor House (Piccadilly Line).

Chairmen: Alan Sugar and A.G. Berry
Vice-presidents: F.P. Sinclair and N. Soloman
Secretary: Peter Barnes
Manager: Ossie Ardiles   **Assistant:** Steve Perryman MBE
First Team Coach: Doug Livermore
Physio: John Sheridan and Dave Butler

Record FAPL Win: 5-1 v Norwich City, 9/4/93
Record FAPL Defeat: 0-6 v Sheffield United, 2/3/93
Record FL Win: 9-0 v Bristol Rovers, Division 2, 22/10/1977
Record FL Defeat: 0-7 v Liverpool, Division 1, 2/9/1978
Record Cup Win: 13-2 v Crewe Alex, FA Cup, 4R (replay), 3/2/1960
Record Fee Received: £5.5m from Lazio for Paul Gascoigne, 5/1992
Record Fee Paid: £2.2m to Chelsea for Gordon Durie, 8/1991
Most FAPL Appearances: 38: Paul Allen and Neil Ruddock, 1992-93
Most FL Appearances: Steve Perryman, 655, 1969-86
Record Attendance (all-time): 75,038 v Sunderland, FA Cup 6R, 5/3/1938
Record Attendance (FAPL): 33,709 v Arsenal, 12/12/92
Highest Scorer in FAPL Season: Sheringham, 21, 92-93
Most FAPL Goals in Season: 60, 1992-93
Most FAPL Points in Season: 59, 1992-93

Most Capped Player: Pat Jennings, 74 (119), Northern Ireland

Close Season Transfers
In: Colin Calderwood (Swindon, Tribunal fee), Jason Dozell (Ipswich, to be decided)
Out: Neil Ruddock (Liverpool, £2.5 m.), Nayim (Real Zaragoza, £500,000), David Tuttle (Sheffield Utd, £350,000), Ian Hendon (Leyton Orient, £50,000)

Season 1992-93
Biggest Home Win: 5-1 v Norwich City
Biggest Home Defeat: 0-2 v Coventry, Ipswich Tn & Sheffield Wednesday
Biggest Away Win: 3-1 v Arsenal v Arsenal *and* 3-1 v Crystal Palace
Biggest Away Defeat: 0-6 v Sheffield United
Biggest Home Attendance: 33,709 v Arsenal
Smallest Home Attendance: 20,098 v Southampton
Average Attendance: 27,883 (+ 0.4%)
Last Season: *PL:* 8th *FA Cup:* semi-final *Coca-Cola Cup:* 4th round
Leading Scorer: Sheringham (28)

League History: 1908 Elected to Division 2; 1909-15 Division 1; 1919-20 Division 2; 1920-28 Division 1; 1928-33 Division 2; 1933-35 Division 1; 1935-50 Division 2; 1950-77 Division 1; 1977-78 Division 2; 1978-92 Division 1; 1992- FA Premier League.
Honours: Football League: Division 1 – Champions 1950-51, 1960-61; Runners-up 1921-22, 1951-52, 1956-57, 1962-63; Division 2 – Champions 1919-20, 1949-50; Runners-up 1908-09, 1932-33; Promoted 1977-78 (3rd). FA Cup: Winners 1901 (as non-League club), 1921, 1961, 1962, 1967, 1981, 1982, 1991 (8 wins stands as the record); Runners-up 1986-87. Football League Cup: Winners 1970-71, 1972-73; Runners-up 1981-82.
European Competitions: European Cup: 1961-62 European Cup-Winners' Cup: 1962-63 (winners), 1963-64, 1967-68, 1981-82 (runners-up), 1982-83, 1991-92. UEFA Cup: 1971-72 (winners), 1972-73, 1973-74 (runners-up), 1983-84 (winners), 1984-85.
Managers (and Secretary-managers): Frank Brettell 1898-99, John Cameron 1899-1906, Fred Kirkham 1907-08, Peter McWilliam 1912-27, Billy Minter 1927-29, Percy Smith 1930-35, Jack Tresadern 1935-38, Peter McWilliam 1938-42, Arthur Turner 1942-46, Joe Hulme 1946-49, Arthur Rowe 1949-55, Jimmy Anderson 1955-58, Bill Nicholson 1958-74, Terry Neill 1974-76, Keith Burkinshaw 1976-84, Peter Shreeves 1984-86, David Pleat 1986-87, Terry Venables 1987-91, Peter Shreeves 1991-92. Ossie Ardiles June 1993-.

5-Year League Record

	Div.	P	W	D	L	F	A	Pts	Pos	FAC	FLC
88-89	1	38	15	12	11	66	46	57	6	3	4
89-90	1	38	19	6	13	59	47	63	3	3	5
90-91	1	38	11	16	11	51	50	49	10	W	5
91-92	1	42	15	7	20	58	63	52	15	3	SF
92-93	PL	42	16	11	15	60	66	59	8	SF	4

Summary of Appearances and Goals 1992-93

	Apps	Sub	Goals		Apps	Sub	Goals
Paul Allen	38		3	Gary Mabbutt	29		2
Darren Anderton	32	2	6	David McDonald	2		0
Dean Austin	33	1	0	Paul Moran	0	3	0
Nick Barmby	17	5	6	Nayim	15	3	3
Gudni Bergsson	0	5	0	Stuart Nethercott	3	2	0
Suizeer Campbell	0	1	1	Neil Ruddock	38		3
Jason Cundy	13	2	1	Vinny Samways	34		0
Kevin Dearden	0	1	0	Steve Sedgley	20	2	3
Gordon Durie	17		3	Teddy Sheringham	38		21
Justin Edinburgh	31	1	0	Erik Thorstved	25	2	0
Terry Fenwick	3	2	0	Andy Turner	7	11	3
Andy Gray	9	8	1	David Tuttle	4	1	0
John Hendry	2	3	0	Pat Van den Hauwe	13	5	0
Danny Hill	2	2	0	Ian Walker	17		0
Lee Hodges	0	4	0	Kevin Watson	4	1	1
David Howells	18	2	1				

FA Premier League Squad Numbers 1993-94

No.	Player	No.	Player	No.	Player
1	Thorstvedt	11	Allen	21	Hill
2	Austin	12	Dozzell	22	Bergsson
3	Edinburgh	13	Walker	23	Campbell
4	Samways	14	Sedgley	24	Moran
5	Calderwood	15	Howells	25	Hendry
6	Mabbutt	16	*	26	*
7	Barmby	17	Turner	27	*
8	Durie	18	Cundy	28	*
9	Anderton	19	Watson	29	*
10	Sheringham	20	Caskey	30	Dearden

Courtroom Dramas Cast Shadow

Tottenham fans have become somewhat used to hitting the headlines in one way or another, as a club that has tended to court controversy rather than embrace success. But the prospects for Spurs fans were still swathed in gloom as the new season approached thanks to a painful and bitter court case between former manager Terry Venables and MD Alan Sugar, after Venables had been sacked from his post of Chief Executive in May.

On the management front Mr Sugar decided to try and woo disgruntled Spurs supporters by installing former Tottenham and Argentina favourite Ossie Ardiles as manager, the popular midfielder replacing the previous team of Ray Clemence who was sacked and Doug Livermore who remained at the club as a coach.

Not bad for a couple of month's close season work, but the feeling at White Hart Lane was certainly one of optimism at the close of the 1992-93 campaign. The introduction of new blood into a relatively inexperienced side had been a qualified success, with the North London side narrowly missing out on a trophy with an FA Cup semi-final defeat at the hands of rivals Arsenal.

Without doubt the success story of the season for Tottenham fans had been the blossoming partnership between September signing Teddy Sheringham, a £2.1 million capture from Nottingham Forest, and emerging young star Nick Barmby.

Sheringham helped himself to a total of 25 goals for the Spurs, effectively exorcising the lingering ghost of the now departed Gary Lineker in one fell swoop and rewarding himself with two England caps by the end of the summer and the accolade of top scorer in the inaugural Premier League.

But it was the form and potential of Barmby which really caught the imagination of the Tottenham fans. Following a sluggish start to the season, which saw the White Hart Lane side slide ignominiously towards the relegation zone, Messrs Clemence and Livermore rallied their squad and embarked upon a climb up the table which resulted in a well-deserved top six finish.

In what was always destined to be a season of consolidation and development for a predominantly inexperienced squad, the improvement in £1.75 million new boy Darren Anderton, already an England U21 regular, and Barmby, who became an intrinsic part of the England Youth side which clinched third place in the World Youth Cup in March, was very encouraging.

Despite the sale of fans' favourite Neil Ruddock to Liverpool for £2.5 million in July after just one effective season at White Hart Lane, Ardiles dipped into the transfer market to secure the signature of impressive Swindon centre-half Colin Calderwood.

With another former Spurs favourite Steve Perryman as his right-hand man, the future for Tottenham took on an air of quiet anticipation for the new season, as the White Hart Lane faithful plotted single-mindedly for an end to the domination of London football by neighbours Arsenal.

WEST HAM UNITED

Thames Ironworks founded 1895, to give recreation for the shipyard workers. Several different grounds were used as the club entered the London League (1896) and won the championship (1898). In 1899, having become professional, won the Southern League Second Division (London) and moved into Division One.

On becoming a limited liability company the name was changed to West Ham United. Moved from the Memorial Ground to a pitch in the Upton Park area, known originally as 'The Castle', in 1904. Elected to an expanded Football League Division Two for the 1919-20 season and never subsequently out of the top two divisions.

Ground: Boleyn Ground, Green Street, Upton Park, London E13
Phone: 081-472 2740   **Nickname:** The Hammers
Colours: Claret, White, White   **Change:** All Blue
Capacity: 22,503   **Pitch:** 112 yds x 72 yds
Directions: *From North & West:* North Circular to East Ham then Barking Rd for 1½ miles until traffic lights. Turn right into Green St. *From South:* Blackwall Tunnel then A13 to Canning Town. Then A124 to East Ham, Green St on left after 2 miles. *From East:* A13 then A117 and A124. Green St on right after ¾ miles.
Rail/Tube: Upton Park (¼ mile)

Chairman: T.W. Brown FCIS, ATII, FCCA   **Vice-Chairman:** M.W. Cearns
Secretary: T.M. Finn
Manager: Billy Bonds MBE   **Assistant:** Harry Redknapp
First Team Coach: Paul Hilton, Tony Carr
Physio: John Green BSC (Hons) MCSP, SRP

Record FAPL Win: –
Record FAPL Defeat: –
Record FL Win: 8-0 v Rotherham United, Division 2, 8/3/1958 *and*
               8-0 v Sunderland, Division 1, 19/10/1968
Record FL Defeat: 2-8 v Blackburn Rovers, Division 1, 26/12/1963
Record Cup Win: 10-0 v Bury, League Cup, 2R, 2L, 25/10/1983
Record Fee Received: £2m from Everton for Tony Cottee, 7/1988
Record Fee Paid: £1.25m to Celtic for Frank McAvennie, 3/1989
Most FAPL Appearances: –
Most FL Appearances: Billy Bonds, 663, 1967-88
Record Attendance (all-time): 42,322 v Tottenham H, Div 1, 17/10/1970

Record Attendance (FAPL): –
Highest Scorer in FAPL Season: –
Most FAPL Goals in Season: –
Most FAPL Points in Season: –
Most Capped Player: Bobby Moore, 108, England

Close Season Transfers
In: Dale Gordon (Glasgow Rangers, £750,000), Simon Webster (Charlton, £525,000), Keith Rowland (Bournemouth, £110,000), Paul Mitchell (Bournemouth, £40,000), Gerry Peyton (Brentford, Free), Paul Harding (Notts County, Trial)
Out: Kevin Keen (Wolves, £600,000), Steve Banks (Gillingham, Free)

Season 1992-93
Biggest Home Win: 6-0 v Sunderland
Biggest Home Defeat: 0-1 v Charlton Athletic *and* 0-1 v Swindon Town
Biggest Away Win: 5-1 v Bristol City
Biggest Away Defeat: 2-5 v Tranmere Rovers
Biggest Home Attendance: 27,399 v Cambridge United
Smallest Home Attendance: 10,326 v Sunderland
Average Attendance: 16,007 (-24.81%)
Last Season: *Div 1:* 2nd *FA Cup:* 4th round *Coca-Cola Cup:* 2nd round
Leading Scorer: Morley (22)

League History: 1919 Elected to Division 2; 1923-32 Division 1; 1932-58 Division 2; 1958-78 Division 1; 1978-81 Division 2; 1981-89 Divison 1; 1989-91 Division 2; 1991-1993 Division 1; 1993- FA Premier League.
Honours: Football League: Division 1 Runners-up 1992-93; Division 2 Champions 1957-58, 1980-81; Runners-up 1922-23, 1990-91. FA Cup: Winners 1964, 1975, 1980; Runners-up 1922-23. Football League Cup: Runners-up 1966, 1981.
European Competitions: European Cup-Winners' Cup: 1964-65 (winners), 1965-66, 1975-76 (runners-up), 1980-81.
Managers (and Secretary-managers): Syd King 1902-32, Charlie Paynter 1932-50, Ted Fenton 1950-61, Ron Greenwood 1961-74 (continued as GM to 1977), John Lyall 1974-89, Lou Macari 1989-90, Billy Bonds February 1990-

5-Year League Record

	Div.	P	W	D	L	F	A	Pts	Pos	FAC	FLC
88-89	1	38	10	8	20	37	62	38	19	6	SF
89-90	2	46	20	12	14	80	57	72	7	3	SF
90-91	2	46	24	15	7	60	34	87	2	SF	3
91-92	1	42	9	11	22	37	59	38	22	5	4
92-93	1	46	26	10	10	81	41	88	2	4	2

Summary of Appearances and Goals 1992-93

	Apps	Sub	Goals		Apps	Sub	Goals
Clive Allen	27		14	Steve Jones	4	2	2
Martin Allen	34		4	Kevin Keen	46		7
Ian Bishop	15	7	1	Alvin Martin	23		1
Tim Breacker	39		2	Ludek Miklosko	46		0
Kenny Brown	13	2	2	Trevor Morley	41		20
Alex Bunbury	2	2	0	George Parris	10	5	0
Peter Butler	39		0	Steve Potts	46		0
Simon Clarke	0	1	0	Mark Robson	41	3	8
Julian Dicks	34		11	Mike Small	5	4	0
Colin Foster	3	3	1	David Speedie	10		3
Tony Gale	21	2	1	Mitchell Thomas	3		0
Matt Holmes	5	11	1				

FA Premier League Squad Numbers 1993-94

No.	Player	No.	Player	No.	Player
	Miklosko		Bishop		Gordon
	Peyton		Butler		Small
	Breacker		Holmes		Basham
	Webster		Robson		Canham
	Brown		Rowland		Currie
	Dicks		Mitchell		Holland
	Foster		C Allen		Marquis
	Gale		Bunbury		Pratt
	A Martin		Jones		Whitmarsh
	Potts		D Martin		Williamson
	Thomas		Morley		
	M Allen		Rush		

Note: No squad numbers given.

Hammers Return

After a shaky start to their season West Ham came good in the New Year and battled for the First Division championship right up to the final few games. Playing the brand of attractive, passing football that has become a trademark of teams from Upton Park they were always in contention and even harboured hopes of landing the championship itself.

Unfortunately West Ham's strong finish was matched and indeed surpassed by Newcastle's own finish but in the end the Hammers were pleased to have grabbed the second available automatic promotion place saving themselves from the trauma of the play-off battles. They clinched that second place on goals scored from a hapless Portsmouth team who, for the second successive season, had failed at the very last having come so close. West Ham netted 81 Football League goals in total – a whole one goal more than their south coast rivals.

On a more sombre note the club were particularly saddened by the untimely death of Upton Park's favourite son, Bobby Moore. He had led the national side to the greatest moment of sporting triumph – the 1966 World Cup – as well as playing his part in several notable Hammers triumphs.

WIMBLEDON

Founded 1889 as Wimbledon Old Centrals, an old boys' side of the Central School playing on Wimbledon Common. Member of the Southern Suburban League, the name was changed to Wimbledon in 1905. Moved to Plough Lane in 1912. Athenian League member for two season before joining the Isthmian League in 1921.

FA Amateur Cup winners 1963 and seven times Isthmian League champions. Turned professional in 1965 joining the Southern League of which they were champions three times before being elected to Football League Division Four in 1977. Started ground sharing at Selhurst Park in 1991 and founder member of the Premier League 1992.

Ground: Selhurst Park, South Norwood, London E5
Phone: 081-771 2233   **Nickname:** The Dons
Colours: All Blue with Yellow trim   **Change:** All Red
Capacity: 29,949   **Pitch:** 110 yds x 74 yds
Directions: *From North:* M1/A1 to North Circular A406 and Chiswick. Follow South Circular A205 to Wandsworth then A3 and A214 towards Streatham and A23. Then left onto B273 for 1 mile and turn left at end into High St and Whitehorse Lane. *From South:* On A23 follow signs for Crystal Palace along B266 going through Thornton Heath into Whitehorse Lane. *From East:* A232 Croydon Rd to Shirley joining A215, Norwood Rd. Turn left after 2½ miles into Whitehorse Lane. *From West:* M4 to Chiswick then as above.
Rail: Selhurst, Norwood Junction or Thornton Heath.

President: Rt. Hon. Lord Michael Havers of Bury St. Edmunds.
Chairman: S.G. Reed   **Vice-Chairman:** J. Lelliott
Secretary: Steve Rooke
Manager: Joe Kinnear   **Assistant:** Terry Burton
First Team Coach: **Physio:** Steve Allen

Record FAPL Win: 4-0 v Crystal Palace, 9/4/1993
Record FAPL Defeat: 2-6 v Oldham Athletic, 3/4/1993
Record FL Win: 6-0 v Newport County, Division 3, 3/9/1983
Record FL Defeat: 0-8 v Everton, League Cup 2R, 29/8/1978
Record Cup Win: 7-2 v Windsor & Eton, FA Cup, 1R, 22111/1980
Record Fee Received: £2.5m from Man City for Keith Curle, 8/1991
Record Fee Paid: £775,000 to Port Vale for Robbie Earle, 7/1991
Most FAPL Appearances: 42: Robbie Earle, 1992-93
Most FL Appearances: Alan Cork, 430, 1977-92

Record Attendance (all-time): 18,000 v HMS Victory, FA Amateur Cup, 3R, 1934-35

Record Attendance (FAPL): 30,115 v Manchester United, 8/5/93

Record Scorer in FAPL Season: Holdsworth, 19, 92-93

Most FAPL Goals in Season: 56, 1992-93

Most FAPL Points in Season: 54, 1992-93

Most Capped Player: Glyn Hodges 5 (16), Wales

Close Season Transfers

In: Gary Blissett (Brentford, £350,000), Alan Kimble (Cambridge, £175,000)
Out: Steve Cotterill (Bournemouth, Tribunal fee), Carlton Fairweather (Carlisle, Trial)

Season 1992-93

Biggest Home Win: 4-0 v Crystal Palace

Biggest Home Defeat: 1-3 v Everton

Biggest Away Win: 2-0 v Coventry City

Biggest Away Defeat: 2-6 v Oldham Athletic

Biggest Home Attendance: 30,115 v Manchester United

Smallest Home Attendance: 3,039 v Everton

Average Attendance: 8,387 (+ 18.86%)

Last Season: *PL:* 12th *FA Cup:* 5th round *Coca-Cola Cup:* 3rd round

Leading Scorer: Holdsworth (19)

League History: 1977 Elected to Division 4; 1979-80 Division 3; 1980-81 Division 4; 1981-82 Division 3; 1982-83 Division 4; 1983-84 Division 3; 1984-86 Division 2; 1986-92 Division 1; 1992- FA Premier League.

Honours: Football League: Division 1 best season: 6th, 1986-87; Division 3 – Runners-up 1983-84; Division 4 – Champions 1982-83. FA Cup: Winners 1987-88. Football League Cup: best season: 4th round, 1979-80, 1983-84, 1988-89. League Group Cup: Runners-up 1981-82.

European Competitions:

Managers (and Secretary-managers): Les Henley 1955-71, Mike Everitt 1971-73, Dick Graham 1973-74, Allen Batsford 1974-78, Dario Gradi 1978-81, Dave Bassett 1981-87, Bobby Gould 1987-90, Ray Harford 1990-91, Peter Withe 1991, Joe Kinnear January, 1992-.

5-Year League Record

	Div.	P	W	D	L	F	A	Pts	Pos	FAC	FLC
88-89	1	38	14	9	15	50	46	51	12	6	4
89-90	1	38	13	16	9	47	40	55	8	3	4
90-91	1	38	14	14	10	53	46	56	7	4	2
91-92	1	42	13	14	15	53	53	53	13	3	2
92-93	PL	42	14	12	16	56	55	54	12	5	3

Summary of Appearances and Goals 1992-93

	Apps	Sub	Goals		Apps	Sub	Goals
Steve Anthrobus	4	1	0	Dean Holdsworth	34	2	19
Neal Ardley	24	2	4	Vinny Jones	27		1
Warren Barton	23		2	Roger Joseph	31	1	0
Greg Berry	2	1	0	Brian McAllister	28	1	0
Dean Blackwell	19	5	0	Paul McGee	1	2	0
Andy Clark	23	10	5	Alan McLeary	4		0
Steve Cotterill	4	3	3	Paul Miller	11	8	1
Gerry Dobbs	18	3	1	Aiden Newhouse	0	1	1
Robbie Earle	42	7		Lawrie Sanchez	23	4	4
Gary Elkins	17	1	0	John Scales	32		1
John Fashanu	27	2	6	Hans Segers	41		0
Peter Fear	2	2	0	Justin Sidnner	1		0
Scott Fitzgerald	18	2	0	Neil Sullivan	1		0
Terry Gibson	6	2	1	Steve Talboys	3	4	0

FA Premier League Squad Numbers 1993-94

No.	Player	No.	Player	No.	Player
1	Segers	13	*	25	Allen
2	Barton	14	Dobbs	26	Ardley
3	McAllister	15	Scales	27	Skinner
4	Jones	16	McGee	28	*
5	Blackwell	17	Joseph	29	Payne
6	Fitzgerald	18	Talboys	30	Thomas
7	Clarke	19	Castledine	31	Cable
8	Earle	20	Sanchez	32	Fairbairn
9	Fashanu	21	Perry	33	Elkins
10	Holdsworth	22	Newhouse	34	Berry
11	Miller	23	Sullivan	35	Kimble
12	Anthrobus	24	Fear	36	Blissett

Business as Usual

It was a case of business as usual for the team that everybody loves to hate as Wimbledon proved once again that you don't need a massive cheque book or million pound players to compete effectively in the Premier League.

The Dons embarrassed the pundits once more with a finishing position of 12th, just two points behind Arsenal and Chelsea, and a reputation of being irritatingly difficult to beat still intact.

The high point of the year for Wimbledon fans must surely have been the return of the prodigal son, Vinnie Jones, who returned in mid-season from Chelsea for a moderate fee. Almost as soon as he had returned, Jones was in trouble with the football authorities, for comments he made on a video called *Soccer's Hardmen*.

Jones incurred an enormous fine and was then banned, but before that things had been going even more atrociously for the Dons. By the middle of October, with 12 games of the season gone, Wimbledon were lodged firmly in the bottom three with a paltry 10 points, and only Crystal Palace and Nottingham Forest between them and the foot of the table.

But a brief revival began to take shape around the end of the year. A 5-2 defeat of Oldham in early December allowed the Dons to move out of the relegation zone for the first time since the season began, and their five-goal tally ended a miserable run of 10 games with only six goals scored.

Holdsworth's brace of goals in that match initiated a run of form that was to propel him into the race for the Premier League Golden Boot award, a title he finally had to surrender to Teddy Sheringham of Spurs, who managed four goals more than Holdsworth who collected 18.

Unfortunately the Dons' fightback didn't last long and it was Christmas when Joe Kinnear's side slipped into the bottom two and really began to look like relegation candidates.

With John Fashanu missing most of the early season through injury, there seemed little hope of escaping the inevitable slide into Division One. But with Fashanu's return in the New Year came a typically dogged third round FA Cup replay defeat of Everton at Goodison Park and a 0-0 draw in the league at Blackburn in which Fashanu was alleged to have deliberately broken Kevin Moran's nose. Business as usual you might say for the Dons.

A reasonable run of results in January lifted Wimbledon to seventh from bottom by the beginning of February, including a 1-0 home defeat of champions Leeds United.

By the end of the month, Wimbledon had extended their run to four successive wins without conceding a goal and 16 points out of a possible 21. Not bad for a side that were supposed to have been dead and buried at Christmas.

It was a run of form that was to continue for the Dons, propelling them successfully up the table to a finishing position of 12th and the promise of another season to irritate the big clubs in the top flight.

FA PREMIER LEAGUE CLUB
TRANSFERS 1992-93

AUGUST 1992

Player	From	To	Fee
Terry Phelan	Wimbledon	Manchester City	£2,500,000
Robert Fleck	Norwich City	Chelsea	£2,100,000
Teddy Sheringham	Nottingham Forest	TottenhamHotspur	£2,100,000
Chris Armstrong	Millwall	Crystal Palace	£1,000,000
Andy Payton	Middlesbrough	Celtic	£900,000
Mark Robins	Manchester United	Norwich City	£800,000
Perry Groves	Arsenal	Southampton	£750,000
Ken Monkou	Chelsea	Southampton	£750,000
Dean Holdsworth	Brentford	Wimbledon	£720,000
John Spencer	Rangers	Chelsea	£450,000
Mick Harford	Luton Town	Chelsea	£300,000
Greg Berry	Leyton Orient	Wimbledon	£250,000
Pat Nevin	Everton	Tranmere Rovers	£250,000
Colin Hill	Sheffield United	Leicester City	£200,000
Mal Donaghy	Manchester United	Chelsea	£150,000
Alan Kelly	Preston North End	Sheffield United	£150,000
Pat McGibbon	Portadown	Manchester United	£100,000
Derek Brazil	Manchester United	Cardiff City	£85,000
Clive Mendonca	Sheffield United	Grimsby Town	£85,000
Wayne Burnett	Leyton Orient	Blackburn Rovers	£80,000
Brian Croft	Chester City	Queens Park Rangers	£80,000
Bobby Davison	Leeds United	Leicester City	£50,000
Chris Wilder	Sheffield United	Rotherham United	£50,000
Adrian Pennock	Norwich City	Bournemouth	£35,000
Simon Garner	Blackburn Rovers	West Bromwich Albion	£30,000
Marlon Beresford	Sheffield United	Burnley	undecided
Vaughan Ryan	Wimbledon	Leyton Orient	swap
Chris Morris	Celtic	Middlesbrough	swap
DerekWhyte	Celtic	Middlesbrough	swap
Clive Baker	Coventry City	Ipswich Town	free
Jamie Morlee	Crystal Palace	Millwall	free
Kevin Ratcliffe	Everton	Dundee	free
Ian Savage	Southampton	Farnborough Town	free

Tribunal Hearings

David James	Watford	Liverpool	*£1,000,000
Neil Ruddock	Southampton	Tottenham Hotspur	**£750,000
Barry Horne	Southampton	Everton	£575,000

| Dean Austin | Southend United | Tottenham Hotspur | £375,000 |

*£125,000 after 50 games, a further £125,000 after 100 and £50,000 if he plays for England. ** Plus 20% of any profit*

SEPTEMBER 1992

Player	From	To	Fee
David Hopkin	Morton	Chelsea	£300,000
Nicky Marker	Plymouth Argyle	Blackburn Rovers	£260,000
Lee Richardson	Blackburn Rovers	Aberdeen	£152,000
Pedrag Radosavjevic	St Louis	Everton	£100,000

OCTOBER 1992

Player	From	To	Fee
Paul Blades	Norwich City	Wolverhampton W	£325,000
Simon Ireland	Huddersfield	Blackburn Rovers	£200,000
Paul Edwards	Coventry City	Wolverhampton W	£100,000
Peter Sheerin	Alloa	Southampton	£50,000

NOVEMBER 1992

Player	From	To	Fee
Eric Cantona	Leeds United	Manchester United	£1,200,000
Neil Webb	Manchester United	Nottingham Forest	£800,000
Stig Inge Bjornbye	Rosenborg	Liverpool	£600,000
Craig Hignett	Crewe Alexandra	Middlesbrough	£500,000
Alf Inge Haaland	Bryne	Nottingham Forest	£500,000
Andy Tilson	QPR	Bristol Rovers	£370,000
Joe Allon	Chelsea	Brentford	£275,000
Dimitri Kharin	CSKA Moscow	Chelsea	£200,000
Stan Collymore	Crystal Palace	Southend United	£150,000
Gray Waddock	QPR	Bristol Rovers	£100,000
Andy Scott	Sutton United	Sheffield United	£50,000
Robert Miller	Oldham Athletic	Hull	unknown
Michael Fox	Liverpool	Runcorn	free
Joe Mayo	Oldham Athletic	Stalybridge Celtic	free
Olisa Morah	Tottenham Hotspur	Swindon Town	free
Nicky Reid	Blackburn Rovers	WBA	free

DECEMBER 1992

Player	From	To	Fee
Patrik Andersen	Malmo	Blackburn Rovers	£800,000
Kare Ingebrigtsen	Rosenborg	Manchester City	£600,000
Henning Berg	Lillestrom	Blackburn Rovers	£400,000
Brad Friedel	Dallas	Nottingham Forest	£300,000
Bontcho Guentchev	Sporting Lisbon	Ipswich Town	£250,000
Mick Quinn	Newcastle United	Coventry City	£250,000
David Lee	Southampton	Bolton Wanderers	£200,000
Vlado Bozinoski	Sporting Lisbon	Ipswich Town	£100,000

Stan Collymore	Crystal Palace	Southend United	£100,000
Glen Livingstone	Aston Villa	York City	free
Michael Wallace	Manchester City	Stockport County	free

JANUARY 1993

Player	From	To	Fee
Frank Strandli	IK Start	Leeds United	£350,000
Justin Channing	QPR	Bristol Rovers	£250,000
Devon White	Cambridge City	QPR	£100,000
Chris Price	Blackburn Rovers	Portsmouth	£50,000
Craig McKernon	Arsenal	Kettering Town	Free
Les Sealey	Aston Villa	Manchester United	Free

FEBRUARY 1993

Player	From	To	Fee
Martin Keown	Everton	Arsenal	£2,000,000
Steve Agnew	Blackburn Rovers	Leicester City	£250,000
Nicos Papavassilou	OFI, Greece	Newcastle United	£130,000
Richard Lucas	Sheffield United	Preston North End	£40,000
Frankie Bennett	Halesowen Town	Southampton	£7,500
Alan Dickens	Chelsea	Brentford	Free
Kenny Samsom	Coventry City	Everton	Free
Stuart Munro	Blackburn Rovers	Bristol City	Free

MARCH 1993

Player	From	To	Fee
Andy Cole	Bristol City	Newcastle United	£1,750,000
Kevin Galacher	Coventry City	Blackburn Rovers	£1,500,000
Roy Wegerle	Blackburn Rovers	Coventry City	£1,000,000
Scott Sellars	Leeds United	Newcastle United	£700,000
Efan Ekoku	Bournemouth	Norwich City	£500,000
David Kerslake	Swindon Town	Leeds United	£500,000
Mark Robinson	Barnsley	Newcastle United	£450,000
Rob Rosario	Coventry City	Nottingham Forest	£400,000
Darren Beckford	Nowich City	Oldham Athletic	£300,000
Leigh Jenkinson	Hull	Coventry City	£300,000
Mick Harford	Chelsea	Sunderland	£250,000
George Parros	West Ham United	Birmingham City	£150,000
Bjorn Kristensen	Newcastle United	Portsmouth	£120,000
Paul Holmes	Birmingham City	Everton	£100,000
Glen Pennyfather	Ipswich Town	Bristol City	£80.000
Derek Allan	Ayr United	Southampton	£70.000
Michael Lake	Sheffield United	Wrexham	£60.000
David Smith	Coventry City	Birmingham City	Swap
David Rennie	Birmingham City	Coventry City	Swap
Graeme Le Saux	Chelsea	Blackburn Rovers	Swap
Steve Livingstone	Blackburn Rovers	Chelsea	Swap

Richard Crisp	Aston Villa	Scunthorpe United	Swap
Chris Greenman	Coventry City	Peterborough United	Free
Garry Payton	Everton	Brentford	Free
Kenny Sansom	Everton	Brentford	Free
Bernie Slaven	Middlesbrough	Port Vale	Free
Kioran Tool	Manchester United	Motherwell	Free
Imra Varadi	Leeds United	Rotherham United	Free
Brian Marwood	Sheffield United	Swindon Town	N/c

SUMMER 1993

Player	From	To	Fee
Roy Keane	Nottingham Forest	Manchester United	£3,750,000
Brian Deane	Sheffield United	Leeds United	£2,900,000
Des Walker	Sampdoria	Sheffield United	£2,700,000
Neil Ruddock	Tottenham Hotspur	Liverpool	£2,500,000
Nigel Clough	Nottingham Forest	Liverpool	£2,275,000
Andy Townsend	Chelsea	Aston Villa	£2,100,000
Peter Beardsley	Everton	Newcastle	£1,400,000
Gavin Peacock	Newcastle United	Chelsea	£1,250,000
Guy Whittingham	Portsmouth	Aston Villa	£1,200,000
Eddie McGoldrick	Crystal Palace	Arsenal	£1,000,000
Dale Gordon	Rangers	West Ham United	£750 000
Simon Webster	Charlton	West Ham United	£525,000
Jan-Aage Fjortoft	Rapid Vienna	Swindon Town	£500,000
Groenendijk	Ajax	Manchester City	£500,000
Andy Pearce	Coventry City	Sheffield Wednesday	£500,000
Paul Mason	Aberdeen	Ipswich Town	£400,000
Gary Blissett	Brentford	Wimbledon	£350,000
David Tuttle	Tottenham Hotspur	Sheffield United	£350,000
Mathie	Morton	Newcastle United	£285,000
Simon Charlton	Huddersfield Town	Southampton	£250,000
Mick Harford	Sunderland	Coventry City	£200,000
Spencer Prior	Southend United	Norwich City	£200,000
Alan Kimble	Cambridge United	Wimbledon	£175,000
Luc Nijholt	Motherwell	Swindon Town	£175,000
Andy Morrison	Plymouth Argyle	Blackburn Rovers	£150,000
Steve Morgan	Plymouth Argyle	Coventry City	£110,000
Keith Rowland	Bournemouth	West Ham United	£110,000
Jason Dozzell	Ipswich Town	Tottenham Hotspur	undecided
Colin Calderwood	Swindon Town	Tottenham Hotspur	tribunal
Andy Dow	Dundee	Chelsea	tribunal

N/c = non-contract player

PLAYER LOANS INVOLVING FA PREMIER LEAGUE CLUBS 1992-93

AUGUST 1992

Player	From	To
Paul Blades	Norwich City	Wolverhampton Wanderers
Stephen Cotterill	Wimbledon	Brighton & Hove Albion
Kevin Dearden	Tottenham Hotspur	Portsmouth
Paul Edwards	Coventry City	Wolverhampton Wanderers
Howard Gayle	Blackburn Rovers	Halifax Town
John Keeley	Oldham Athletic	Chester City
Chris Makin	Oldham Athletic	Wigan Athletic
Craig Skiner	Blackburn Rovers	Plymouth Argyle

SEPTEMBER 1992

Player	From	To
Alec Chamberlain	Luton Town	Chelsea
Micky Evans	Plymouth Argyle	Blackburn Rovers
Scott Houghton	Tottenham Hotspur	Cambridge United
Phil Kite	Sheffield United	Plymouth Argyle
Damian Matthew	Chelsea	Luton Town
Dave McDonald	Tottenham Hotspur	Bradford City
Paul Moran	Tottenham Hotspur	Cambridge United
Gerry Peyton	Everton	Brentford
Nick Reid	Blackburn Rovers	Bristol City
Steve Stone	Nottingham Forest	Stoke City
Andy Tillson	QPR	Grimsby Town

OCTOBER 1992

Player	From	To
Dave Beasant	Chelsea	Grimsby Town
Spencer Binks	Tottenham Hotspur	Nottingham Forest
Justin Channing	QPR	Bristol Rovers
Martin Curuthers	Aston Villa	Hull
Rob Dewhurst	Blackburn Rovers	Huddersfield Town
Robert Herera	QPR	Torquay United
Phil Kite	Shefield United	Rotherham United
Nick Limber	Manchester City	Peterborough United
Alan McLeary	Millwall	Wimbledon
Kevin Moore	Southampton	Bristol Rovers
Les Sealey	Aston Villa	Birmingham City

| David Speedie | Southampton | Birmingham City |
| Paul Williams | West Bromwich Albion | Coventry City |

NOVEMBER 1992

Player	*From*	*To*
Fraser Digby	Swindon Town	Manchester United
Ashely Fickling	Sheffield United	Darlington
David Johnson	Sheffield Wednesday	Hartlepool
Chris Kamara	Luton Town	Sheffield United
John Keeley	Oldham Athletic	Chester City
Phil Kite	Sheffield United	Crewe Alexandra
David Lee	Southampton	Bolton Wanderers
Glen Livingstone	Aston Villa	York City
George O'Hanlon	Leyton Orient	Swindon Town
Mick Quinn	Newcastle United	Coventry City
Ken Veysey	Oxford United	Sheffield United
Lee Willim	Aston Villa	Shewsbury Town

DECEMBER 1992

Player	*From*	*To*
Simon Clarke	West Ham United	Kettering Town
Alan Dickens	Chelsea	West Bromwich Albion
Andy Gray	Tottenham Hotspur	Swindon Town
Chris Hope	Nottingham Forest	Kettering Town
Scott Aaron Houghton	Tottenham Hotspur	Gillingham
Iain Jenkins	Everton	Bradford City
Richard Lucas	Sheffield United	Preston North End
Dean Martin	West Ham United	Colchester
Paul Moody	Southampton	Reading
Lee Power	Norwich City	Charlton Athletic
Mark Stimson	Newcastle United	Portsmouth
Julian Watts	Sheffield Wednesday	Shrewsbury Town
Michael Williams	Sheffield Wednesday	Halifax Town

JANUARY 1993

Player	*From*	*To*
Dave Beasant	Chelsea	Wolverhampton Wanderers
Franz Carr	Newcastle United	Sheffield United
Robert Dewhurst	Blackburn Rovers	Wycombe Wanderers
Peter Duffield	Sheffield United	Crewe Alexandra
Matt Dickins	Blackburn Rovers	Blackpool
Carlton Fairweather	Wimbledon	Slough Town
Dave Farrell	Aston Villa	Scunthorpe United
Phil Kite	Sheffield United	Crewe Alexandra
Henrick Larsen	Pisa	Aston Villa
Colin McKee	Manchester United	Bury

Paul Marquis	West Ham United	Dagenham & Redbridge
Gerry Peyton	Everton	Chelsea
Ray Ranson	Newcastle United	Manchester City
Mel Rees	Sheffield United	Chesterfield
Keith Rownland	Bournemouth	Coventry City
David Smith	Coventry City	Bournemouth
David Speedie	Southampton	West Bromwich Albion
Martin Thomas	Birmingham City	Aston Villa
David Tuttle	Tottenham Hotspur	Peterborough United
Imre Varadi	Leeds United	Oxford United
Adrian Viveash	Swindon Town	Reading
Ray Woods	Coventry City	Wigan Athletic

FEBRUARY 1993

Player	From	To
Peter Billing	Coventry City	Port Vale
Andy Dibble	Manchester City	Oldham Athletic
Kerry Dixon	Southampton	Luton Town
Lee Hodges	Tottenham Hotspur	Plymouth
Mathew Holland	West Ham United	Farnborough Town
Scott Houghton	Tottenham Hotspur	Charton Athletic
Nathan Peel	Sheffield United	Halifax Town
Glenn Pennyfather	Ipswich Town	Bristol City
Frank Talia	Blackburn Rovers	Hartlepool United
Paul Tisdale	Southampton	Northampton Town

MARCH 1993

Player	From	To
Steve Banks	West Ham United	Gillingham
Peter Beadle	Tottenham Hotspur	Bournemouth
Richard Crisp	Aston Villa	Scunthorpe United
Peter Duffield	Sheffield United	Stockport County
Bruce Grobbelaar	Liverpool	Stoke City
Ian Hendon	Tottenham Hotspur	Barnsley
Kevin Hitchcock	Chelsea	West Ham United
Andy Hunt	Newcastle United	West Bromwich Albion
Phil Kite	Sheffield United	Stockport
Jim Laighton	Dundee	Sheffield United
Dave McDonald	Tottenham Hotspur	Reading
Adrian Mike	Manchester City	Bury
Jason Minett	Norwich City	Exeter City
John Reed	Sheffield United	Darlington
Matthew Rush	West Ham United	Cambridge
David Speedie	Southampton	West Ham United
Danny Wallace	Manchester United	Millwall

The A-Z of
FA Premier League Players

ABLETT Gary

Everton

Full Name: ABLETT, Gary Ian — DOB: 19/11/65, Liverpool
FAPL Debut: Home v. Sheffield Wed 15/8/92 — Debut Goal: –

Previous Club Details

Clubs	Signed	Fee	Apps Lge	FLC	FAC	Goals Lge	FLC	FAC
Liverpool	11/83	–	103+6	10+1	16+2	1		
Derby County	1/85	Loan	3+3	–	–			
Hull City	9/86	Loan	5					
Everton	1/92	£750,000	17	–	1	1		

FA Premier Lge Record

92/93			40	6	2			

ADAMS Tony

Arsenal

Full Name: ADAMS, Anthony — DOB: 10/10/66, Romford
FAPL Debut: Home v. Norwich City 15/8/92 — Debut Goal: –
England International — Debut:

Previous Club Details

Clubs	Signed	Fee	Apps Lge	FLC	FAC	Goals Lge	FLC	FAC
Arsenal	1/84	–	248+1	33+1	18	20	2	1

FA Premier Lge Record

92/93			33+2	9	8			2

ADAMS Micky

Southampton

Full Name: ADAMS, Michael Richard — DOB: 8/11/61, Sheffield
FAPL Debut: Home v. Tottenham Hotspur 15/8/92
Debut Goal: Home v. Aston Villa 22/8/92

Previous Club Details

Clubs	Signed	Fee	Apps Lge	FLC	FAC	Goals Lge	FLC	FAC
Gillingham	11/79	–	85+7	5	6	5		
Coventry City	7/83	£75,000	85+5	9	7	9	1	
Leeds Utd	1/87	£110,000	72+1	4	6	2		1
Southampton	3/89	£250,000	86+1	12	6	3		

FA Premier Lge Record

92/93			38	3	1	4		

† denotes substitution

ADAMS Neil   Oldham Athletic

Full Name: ADAMS, Neil James   DOB: 23/11/65, Stoke
FAPL Debut: Home v. Nottingham Forest 22/8/92
Debut Goal: Home v. Nottingham Forest 22/8/92

Previous Club Details

Clubs	Signed	Fee	Lge	FLC	FAC	Lge	FLC	FAC
			Apps			Goals		
Stoke City	6/85	–	31+1	3	1	4		
Everton	6/86	£150,000	17+3	4+1	–		1	
Oldham Ath	1/89	Loan	9					
Oldham Ath	6/89	£100,000	60+24	7+1	8+2	14	1	2

FA Premier Lge Record

92/93			26+6	3+1	1	9		

ALLEN Bradley   Queens Park Rangers

Full Name: ALLEN, Bradley James   DOB: 13/9/71, Romford
FAPL Debut: Away v. Norwich † 17/10/92
Debut Goal: Away v. Norwich 17/10/92

Previous Club Details

Clubs	Signed	Fee	Lge	FLC	FAC	Lge	FLC	FAC
			Apps			Goals		
QPR	9/88	–	14+8	0+1	0+1	7		

FA Premier Lge Record

92/93			21+4	1+1	1	10	1	

ALLEN Clive   West Ham United

Name: Allen, Clive   DOB: 20/5/61, Stepney

Previous Club Details

Clubs	Signed	Fee	Lge	FLC	FAC	Lge	FLC	FAC
			Apps			Goals		
QPR	9/78		43+6	5	1	32	2	
Arsenal	6/80	£1.25m		9	2			
Crystal P	8/80	£1.25m	25	4		9	2	
QPR	5/81	£425,000	83+4	7	8	40	2	7
Tottenham H	8/84	£750,000	97+8	13+1	12+1	60	13	9
Bordeaux, Fra.	5/88	£1m						
Man. City	8/89	£1.1m	31+22	5+2	4+2	16	4	1
Chelsea	12/91	£250,000	15+1		4+1	7		2
West Ham	3/92	£250,000	29+2	2	1	16		1

ALLEN Martin   West Ham United

Full Name: ALLEN, Martin   DOB: 18/8/65 Reading

Previous Club Details

Clubs	Signed	Fee	Lge	FLC	FAC	Lge	FLC	FAC
			Apps			Goals		
QPR	6/83		128+8	15+3	9	16	1	1
West Ham	8/89	£660,000	114+18	12+1	7	16	4	2

ALLEN Paul — Tottenham Hotspur

Full Name: ALLEN, Paul Kevin
DOB: 28/8/62, Aveley
FAPL Debut: Away v. Southampton 15/8/92
Debut Goal: Home v. Everton 5/9/92

Previous Club Details

Clubs	Signed	Fee	Apps Lge	FLC	FAC	Goals Lge	FLC	FAC
West Ham	8/79	–	149+3	20+4	15+3	6	2	3
Tottenham H	6/85	£400,000	238+16	38+8	17+1	20	4	1

FA Premier Lge Record

92/93			38	4	5	3		

ALLEN Peter — Southampton

Full Name: ALLEN, Peter
DOB:
FAPL Debut: Home v. Manchester City † 1/5/93 Debut Goal:

Previous Club Details

Clubs	Signed	Fee	Apps Lge	FLC	FAC	Goals Lge	FLC	FAC
Southampton								

FA Premier Lge Record

92/93			0+1					

ANDERSSON Patrik — Blackburn Rovers

Name: ANDERSSON, Patrick
DOB: 18/8/71, Borgeby
FAPL Debut: Home v Wimbledon † 9/1/93 Debut Goal:

Previous Club Details

Clubs	Signed	Fee	Apps Lge	FLC	FAC	Goals Lge	FLC	FAC
Malmo, Swe								
Blackburn Rv	12/92	£800,000						

FA Premier Lge Record

92/93			6+5	2	1		1	

ANDERTON Darren — Tottenham Hotspur

Full Name: ANDERTON, Darren Robert
DOB: 3/3/72 Southampton
FAPL Debut: Away v. Southampton 15/8/92
Debut Goal: Home v. Southampton 7/2/93

Previous Club Details

Clubs	Signed	Fee	Apps Lge	FLC	FAC	Goals Lge	FLC	FAC
Portsmouth	2/90	–	53+9	3+2	7	7	1	5
Tottenham H	5/92	£1.75m						

FA Premier Lge Record

92/93			32+2	2	4+1	6	1	1

ANTHROBUS Steve — Wimbledon

Full Name: ANTHROBUS, Steven
DOB: 10/11/68, Lewisham
FAPL Debut: Home v. Coventry City 22/8/92 Debut Goal: –

FA Premier Lge Record

	92/93		4+1	1				

ARDLEY Neal — Wimbledon

Full Name: ARDLEY, Neal Christopher   DOB: 1/9/72, Epsom
FAPL Debut: Home v. Arsenal † 5/9/92
Debut Goal: Home v. Blackburn Rovers 19/9/92

Previous Club Details / *Apps* / *Goals*

Clubs	Signed	Fee	Lge	FLC	FAC	Lge	FLC	FAC
Wimbledon	7/91	–	8+1					

FA Premier Lge Record

	92/93		24+2	2	4	4	1	

ATHERTON Peter — Coventry City

Full Name: ATHERTON, Peter   DOB: 6/4/70, Orrell
FAPL Debut: Home v. Middlesbrough 15/8/92   Debut Goal: –

Previous Club Details / *Apps* / *Goals*

Clubs	Signed	Fee	Lge	FLC	FAC	Lge	FLC	FAC
Wigan Ath	2/88	–	145+4	8	7	1		
Coventry City	8/91	£300,000	35					

FA Premier Lge Record

	92/93		39	2	1			

ATKINS Mark — Blackburn Rovers

Full Name: ATKINS, Mark Nigel   DOB: 14/9/68, Doncaster
FAPL Debut: Away v. Crystal Palace 15/8/92
Debut Goal: Away v. Coventry City 29/8/92

Previous Club Details / *Apps* / *Goals*

Clubs	Signed	Fee	Lge	FLC	FAC	Lge	FLC	FAC
Scunthorpe Utd	7/86	–	45+5	3+1	5	2		
Blackburn Rv	6/88	£45,000	162+11	11	7	22	3	

FA Premier Lge Record

	92/93		23+6	5+2	2+2	5	1	

ATKINSON Dalian — Aston Villa

Full Name: ATKINSON, Dalian Robert   DOB: 21/3/68, Shrewsbury
FAPL Debut: Away v. Ipswich Town 15/8/92
Debut Goal: Away v. Ipswich Town 15/8/92

Previous Club Details / *Apps* / *Goals*

Clubs	Signed	Fee	Lge	FLC	FAC	Lge	FLC	FAC
Ipswich Town	6/85	–	49+11	5+1	–	18	3	

Clubs	Signed	Fee	Lge	FLC	FAC	Lge	FLC	FAC
Sheff Wed	7/87	£450,000	38	3	2	10	3	1
Real Sociedad	8/90	£1.7m						
Aston Villa	7/91	£1.6m	11+3	1	1	1		
FA Premier Lge Record								
92/93			28	4		11	2	

AUSTIN Dean   Tottenham Hotspur

Full Name: AUSTIN, Dean Barry   DOB: 26/4/70, Hemel Hemstead
FAPL Debut: Home v. Crystal Palace † 22/8/92   Debut Goal: –

Previous Club Details			Apps			Goals		
Clubs	Signed	Fee	Lge	FLC	FAC	Lge	FLC	FAC
Southend U	3/90	£12,000	96	4	2	2		
Tottenham H	5/92	£375,000						
FA Premier Lge Record								
92/93			33+1	2+1	5			

BABB Phil   Coventry City

Full Name: BABB, Phillip   DOB: 30/11/70, London
FAPL Debut: Home v. Middlesbrough † 15/8/92   Debut Goal:

Previous Club Details			Apps			Goals		
Clubs	Signed	Fee	Lge	FLC	FAC	Lge	FLC	FAC
Millwall	4/89							
Bradford City	8/90		73+7	5+1	3	14		
Coventry City	7/92							
FA Premier Lge Record								
92/93			27+7	2	1			

BAILEY Dennis   Queens Park Rangers

Full Name: BAILEY, Dennis Lincoln   DOB: 13/12/65, Lambeth
FAPL Debut: Away v. Manchester City 17/8/92
Debut Goal: Home v. Sheffield United 22/8/92

Previous Club Details			Apps			Goals		
Clubs	Signed	Fee	Lge	FLC	FAC	Lge	FLC	FAC
Crystal Palace	12/87	310,000	0+5			1		
Bristol Rv	2/89	Loan	17	–	–	9		
Birmingham C	8/89	£80,000	65+10	6	6	23	2	
Bristol Rv	3/91	Loan	6			1		
QPR	6/91	£175,000	19+5	3	1	9	2	
FA Premier Lge Record								
92/93			13+2	2	0+1	1	1	

BAKER Clive   Ipswich Town

Full Name: BAKER, Clive   DOB:
FAPL Debut: Home v. Sheffield United † 26/9/92   Debut Goal:

Previous Club Details			*Apps*			*Goals*		
Clubs	Signed	Fee	Lge	FLC	FAC	Lge	FLC	FAC
Ipswich Town								
FA Premier Lge Record								
	92/93		30+1	5	4			

BANGER Nicky   Southampton
Full Name: BANGER, Nicholas Lee   DOB: 25/4/71, Southampton
FAPL Debut: Home v. Middlesbrough † 29/8/92
Debut Goal: Home v. Middlesbrough 29/8/92

Previous Club Details			*Apps*			*Goals*		
Clubs	Signed	Fee	Lge	FLC	FAC	Lge	FLC	FAC
Southampton	4/89		0+10	1+1	–		3	
FA Premier Lge Record								
	92/93		10+16			6		

BARDSLEY David   Queens Park Rangers
Full Name: BARDSLEY, David John   DOB: 11/9/64, Manchester
FAPL Debut: Away v. Manchester City 17/8/92
Debut Goal: Home v. Southampton 19/8/92

Previous Club Details			*Apps*			*Goals*		
Clubs	Signed	Fee	Lge	FLC	FAC	Lge	FLC	FAC
Blackpool	9/82	–	45	2	2		1	
Watford	11/83	£150,000	97+3	6	13+1	7	1	1
Oxford Utd	9/87	£265,000	74	12	5	7		
QPR	9/89	£500,000	110	8	10	1	1	
FA Premier Lge Record								
	92/93		40	3	2	3		

BARKER Simon   Queens Park Rangers
Full Name: BARKER, Simon   DOB: 4/11/64, Farnworth
FAPL Debut: Home v. Sheffield United 22/8/92
Debut Goal: Home v. Sheffield United 22/8/92

Previous Club Details			*Apps*			*Goals*		
Clubs	Signed	Fee	Lge	FLC	FAC	Lge	FLC	FAC
Blackburn Rv	11/82	–	180+2	11	12	35	4	
QPR	7/88	£400,000	107+15	13+2	13+1	11	3	2
FA Premier Lge Record								
	92/93		21+4	1	2	1		

BARLOW Andy   Oldham Athletic
Full Name: BARLOW, Andrew, John   DOB: 24/11/65, Oldham
FAPL Debut: Away v. Chelsea 15/8/92   Debut Goal: –

Previous Club Details			*Apps*			*Goals*		
Clubs	Signed	Fee	Lge	FLC	FAC	Lge	FLC	FAC
Oldham Ath	7/84	–	234+13	20	17	5		
FA Premier Lge Record								
	92/93		6		2			

BARLOW Stuart   Everton

Full Name: BARLOW, Stuart   DOB: 16/7/68, Liverpool
FAPL Debut: Away v. Tottenham Hotspur † 5/9/92
Debut Goal: Away v. QPR 28/12/92

Previous Club Details			*Apps*			*Goals*		
Clubs	Signed	Fee	Lge	FLC	FAC	Lge	FLC	FAC
Everton	6/90	–	3+6					
Rotherham	1/92	Loan	–	–	–			
FA Premier Lge Record								
	92/93		8+18	1+3	1+1	5	1	

BARMBY Nicky   Tottenham Hotspur

Full Name: BARMBY, Nicholas Jonathan   DOB: 11/2/74, Hull
FAPL Debut: Away v. Sheffield Wednesday 27/9/92
Debut Goal: Home v. Middlesbrough 17/10/92

Previous Club Details			*Apps*			*Goals*		
Clubs	Signed	Fee	Lge	FLC	FAC	Lge	FLC	FAC
Tottenham H	2/91	–						
FA Premier Lge Record								
	92/93		17+5	2+1	3+1	6	3	

BARNARD Darren   Chelsea

Full Name: BARNARD, Darren Sean   DOB: 30/11/71, Germany
FAPL Debut: Away v. Coventry City 24/10/92
Debut Goal: Home v. Middlesbrough 3/4/93

Previous Club Details			*Apps*			*Goals*		
Clubs	Signed	Fee	Lge	FLC	FAC	Lge	FLC	FAC
Chelsea	7/90	£50,000	1+3					
FA Premier Lge Record								
	92/93		8+5	0+1		1		

BARNES David   Sheffield United

Full Name: BARNES, David   DOB: 16/11/61, Paddington

Previous Club Details			*Apps*			*Goals*		
Clubs	Signed	Fee	Lge	FLC	FAC	Lge	FLC	FAC
Coventry City	5/79	–	9		4			
Ipswich Town	5/82	—	16+1					
Wolves	10/84	£35,000	86+2	7	6	4		
Aldershot	8/87	£25,000	68+1	2	2+2	1		

Sheffield Utd	7/87	£50,000	67	4	11	1

FA Premier Lge Record
92/93

BARNES John
Liverpool

Full Name: BARNES, John DOB: 7/11/63, Jamaica, West Indies
FAPL Debut: Away v. QPR † 23/11/92
Debut Goal: Home v. Aston Villa 9/1/92

Previous Club Details			*Apps*			*Goals*		
Clubs	Signed	Fee	Lge	FLC	FAC	Lge	FLC	FAC
Watford	7/81	–	232+1	21	31	65	7	11
Liverpool	6/87	£900,000	152	10	32	62	2	14

FA Premier Lge Record
92/93			26+1	2	2	5		

BARNESS Tony
Chelsea

Full Name: BARNESS, Tony DOB: 25/2/73, Lewisham, London
FAPL Debut: Home v. Norwich City 12/9/92 Debut Goal:

Previous Club Details			*Apps*			*Goals*		
Clubs	Signed	Fee	Lge	FLC	FAC	Lge	FLC	FAC
Charlton	3/91		21+6	2	3	1		
Chelsea	9/92	£350,000						

FA Premier Lge Record
92/93			2					

BARRETT Earl
Aston Villa

Full Name: BARRETT, Earl Delisser DOB: 28/4/67, Rochdale
FAPL Debut: Away v. Ipswich Town 15/8/92
Debut Goal: Home v. Everton 20/2/93
England International

Previous Club Details			*Apps*			*Goals*		
Clubs	Signed	Fee	Lge	FLC	FAC	Lge	FLC	FAC
Man City	4/85	–	2+1	1	–			
Chester City	3/86	Loan	12					
Oldham Ath	11/87	£35,000	181+2	20	14	7	1	1
Aston Villa	2/92	£1.7m	13					

FA Premier Lge Record
92/93			42			1		

BARTLETT Neal
Southampton

Full Name: BARTLETT, Neil DOB: 7/4/75, Southampton
FAPL Debut: Home v. Manchester City † 1/5/93 Debut Goal:

Previous Club Details			*Apps*			*Goals*		
Clubs	Signed	Fee	Lge	FLC	FAC	Lge	FLC	FAC
Southampton								

BARTON Warren   Wimbledon

Full Name: BARTON, Warren Dean   DOB: 19/3/69, Stoke Newington
FAPL Debut: Away v. Leeds United 15/8/92
Debut Goal: Away v. Leeds United 15/8/92

Previous Club Details

Clubs	Signed	Fee	Apps Lge	FLC	FAC	Goals Lge	FLC	FAC
Maidstone U	7/87	£10,000	41+1	0+2	3			1
Wimbledon	6/90	£300,000	79	4	5	4		

FA Premier Lge Record

	92/93	23	4		2		

BART–WILLIAMS Chris   Sheffield Wednesday

Full Name: BART–WILLIAMS, Christopher Gerald
DOB: 16/6/74, Sierra Leone
FAPL Debut: Away v. Everton † 15/8/92
Debut Goal: Home v. Coventry City 2/9/92

Previous Club Details

Clubs	Signed	Fee	Apps Lge	FLC	FAC	Goals Lge	FLC	FAC
Leyton Orient	7/91	–	34+2	4	–	2		
Sheffield Wed	11/91	£275,000	12+3	–	1			1

FA Premier Lge Record

	92/93	21+13	3+4	1+3	6	1

BATTY David   Leeds United

Full Name: BATTY, David   DOB: 12/12/68, Leeds
FAPL Debut: Home v. Wimbledon 15/8/92
Debut Goal: Home v. Middlesbrough 30/1/93
England International

Previous Club Details

Clubs	Signed	Fee	Apps Lge	FLC	FAC	Goals Lge	FLC	FAC
Leeds United	7/87	–	163+9	15	9	3		

FA Premier Lge Record

	92/93	30	2	3	1	

BEAGRIE Peter   Everton

Full Name: BEAGRIE, Peter Sydney   DOB: 29/11/65, Middlesbrough
FAPL Debut: Home v. Sheffield Wednesday 15/8/92
Debut Goal: Home v. Coventry 17/10/92

Previous Club Details

Clubs	Signed	Fee	Apps Lge	FLC	FAC	Goals Lge	FLC	FAC
Middlesbrough	9/83	–	24+8	1	–	2		
Sheffield Wed	8/86	£35,000	81+3	5	5	11		

Club	Signed	Fee	Lge	FLC	FAC		Lge	FLC	FAC
Stoke City	6/88	£210,000	54	4	3	7			1
Everton	11/89	£750,000	48+50	1+1	5+2	5	2		
Sunderland	9/91	Loan	5	–	–				

FA Premier Lge Record

| | 92/93 | | 11+11 | 3+1 | | 3 | | | |

BEARDSLEY Peter Newcastle United

Full Name: BEARDSLEY, Peter Andrew   DOB: 18/1/61, Newcastle
FAPL Debut: Home v. Sheffield Wednesday 15/8/93
Debut Goal: Away v. Manchester United 19/8/93
England International

Previous Club Details			*Apps*			*Goals*		
Clubs	Signed	Fee	Lge	FLC	FAC	Lge	FLC	FAC
Carlisle Utd	8/79	–	93+11	6+1	15	2		7
Vancouver (US)	4/81	£275,000						
Man United	9/82	£300,000	1					
Vancouver (US)	9/83	–						
Newcastle Utd	9/83	£150,000	146+1	10	6	61		
Liverpool	7/87	£1.9m	120+11	13+1	22+3	46	1	11
Everton	8/91	£1m	42	4	2	15	3	1
Newcastle Utd	6/93	£1.4m						

FA Premier Lge Record

| Everton | 92/93 | | 39 | 4 | 2 | 10 | 3 | |

BEASANT Dave Chelsea

Full Name: BEASANT, David John   DOB: 20/3/59, Willesden
FAPL Debut: Home v. Oldham Athletic 15/8/92   Debut Goal: –
England International

Previous Club Details			*Apps*			*Goals*		
Clubs	Signed	Fee	Lge	FLC	FAC	Lge	FLC	FAC
Wimbledon	8/79	£1,000	340	21	27			
Newcastle U	6/88	£800,000	20	2	2			
Chelsea	1/89	£725,000	116	11	5			
Grimsby Tn	10/92	Loan	6					
Wolves	1/93	Loan	4	1				

FA Premier Lge Record

| | 92/93 | | 17 | | | | | |

BECKFORD Darren Oldham Athletic

Full Name: BECKFORD, Darren Richard   DOB: 12/5/67, Manchester
FAPL Debut: Home v. Middlesbrough † 31/10/92
Debut Goal: Away v. Aston Villa 28/11/92

Previous Club Details			*Apps*			*Goals*		
Clubs	Signed	Fee	Lge	FLC	FAC	Lge	FLC	FAC
Man United	8/84	–	7+4	0+1	–			

Bury	10/85	Loan	12			5		
Port Vale	3/87	£15,000	169+9	12	14	71	3	4
Norwich City	7/91	£925,000	25+5	3+2	2+1	7	3	
Oldham Ath	3/93	£300,000						

FA Premier Lge Record

| Norwich City | 92/93 | | 7+1 | | | 1 | | |
| Oldham Ath | 92/93 | | 6+1 | | | 3 | | |

BEENEY Mark　　　　　　　　　　　　　　Leeds United

Full Name: BEENEY, Mark　　　　　　DOB: 30/12/67, Tunbridge Wells
FAPL Debut: Away v. Coventry 8/5/93　　　Debut Goal:

Previous Club Details			Apps			Goals		
Clubs	Signed	Fee	Lge	FLC	FAC	Lge	FLC	FAC
Gillingham	8/86		2	1				
Maidstone	2/87		50	3	11			
Aldershot	3/90	Loan	7					
Brighton	391	£30,000	68+1	6	7			
Leeds Utd	4/93	£350,000						

FA Premier Lge Record

| | 92/93 | | 1 | | | | | |

BEESLEY Paul　　　　　　　　　　　　　Sheffield United

Full Name: BEESLEY, Paul　　　　　　　DOB: 21/7/65, Liverpool
FAPL Debut: Home v. Manchester United 15/8/92
Debut Goal: Home v. Wimbledon 25/8/93

Previous Club Details			Apps			Goals		
Clubs	Signed	Fee	Lge	FLC	FAC	Lge	FLC	FAC
Wigan Ath	9/84	–	153+2	13	6	3		
Leyton Orient	10/89	£175,000	32	–	1	1		1
Sheffield United	7/90	£300,000	75+2	6	4	3		

FA Premier Lge Record

| | 92/93 | | 39 | 4 | 4+2 | 2 | | 1 |

BEINLICH Stefan　　　　　　　　　　　　　Aston Villa

Full Name: BEINLICH, Stefan　　　　　　DOB: 13/1/72, Berlin, Germany
FAPL Debut: Away v. Coventry † 26/12/92　　Debut Goal: –

Previous Club Details			Apps			Goals		
Clubs	Signed	Fee	Lge	FLC	FAC	Lge	FLC	FAC
Bergmann B.								
Aston Villa	10/91	£100,000	0+2	–	–			

FA Premier Lge Record

| | 92/93 | | 1+6 | | | | | |

BENALI Francis   Southampton

Full Name: BENALI, Francis Vincent   DOB: 10/12/68, Southampton
FAPL Debut: Home v. Tottenham Hotspur 15/8/92   Debut Goal: –

Previous Club Details			*Apps*			*Goals*		
Clubs	Signed Fee		Lge	FLC	FAC	Lge	FLC	FAC
Southampton	12/86	–	54+14	7+4	11			

FA Premier Lge Record

| | 92/93 | | 31+2 | 1+2 | 1 | | | |

BERESFORD John   Newcastle United

Full Name: BERESFORD, John   DOB: 4/9/66 Sheffield

Previous Club Details			*Apps*			*Goals*		
Clubs	Signed Fee		Lge	FLC	FAC	Lge	FLC	FAC
Man City	9/83							
Barnsley	8/86		79+9	5+2	5	5	2	1
Portsmouth	3/89	£300,000	102+5	12	11	8	2	
Newcastle	6/92	£650,000	42	4	4			

BERG Henning   Blackburn Rovers

Name: BERG, Henning   DOB: 1/9/69, Eidsvell
FAPL Debut: Home v Crystal Palace † 2/2/93   Debut Goal:

Previous Club Details			*Apps*			*Goals*		
Clubs	Signed Fee		Lge	FLC	FAC	Lge	FLC	FAC
Lillestrom, Nor.								
Blackburn Rv	12/92	£400,000						

FA Premier Lge Record

| | 92/93 | | 2+2 | 2 | | | | |

BERGSSON Gudni   Tottenham Hotspur

Full Name: BERGSSON, Gudni   DOB: 21/7/65, Iceland
FAPL Debut: Home v. Nottingham Forest † 28/12/92   Debut Goal: –
Iceland International

Previous Club Details			*Apps*			*Goals*		
Clubs	Signed Fee		Lge	FLC	FAC	Lge	FLC	FAC
Tottenham H	12/88	£100,000	51+15	4+2	2+1	3		

FA Premier Lge Record

| | 92/93 | | 0+5 | 0+1 | | | | |

BERNARD Paul   Oldham Athletic

Full Name: BERNARD, Paul Robert James   DOB: 30/12/72, Edinburgh
FAPL Debut: Away v. Chelsea 15/8/92
Debut Goal: Home v. Nottingham Forest 22/8/92

Previous Club Details			*Apps*			*Goals*		
Clubs	Signed Fee		Lge	FLC	FAC	Lge	FLC	FAC
Oldham Ath	7/91	–	18+5	1+1	2	6		

BERRY Greg   Wimbledon

Full Name: BERRY, Gregory   DOB: 5/3/71, Grays
FAPL Debut: Home v. Ipswich Town 18/8/92   Debut Goal:

Previous Club Details			Apps			Goals		
Clubs	Signed	Fee	Lge	FLC	FAC	Lge	FLC	FAC
Leyton Orient	7/89		68+12	6	8+2	14	3	2
Wimbledon								

FA Premier Lge Record
    92/93   2+1   0+1

BJORNEBYE Stig   Liverpool

Full Name: BJORNEBYE, Stig Inge   DOB:
FAPL Debut: Away v. Coventry City 19/12/92   Debut Goal: –

Previous Club Details			Apps			Goals		
Clubs	Signed	Fee	Lge	FLC	FAC	Lge	FLC	FAC
Rosenborg (Nor)								
Liverpool	12/92	£600,000						

FA Premier Lge Record
    92/93   11   2

BISHOP Ian   West Ham United

Full Name: BISHOP, Ian   DOB: 29/5/65, Liverpool

Previous Club Details			Apps			Goals		
Clubs	Signed	Fee	Lge	FLC	FAC	Lge	FLC	FAC
Everton	6/83		0+1					
Crewe Alex	3/84	Loan	4					
Carlisle U	10/84	£15,000	131+1	8	5	14	1	1
Bournemouth	7/88	£35,000	44	4	5	2		
Man City	8/89	£465,000	18+1	4		2	1	
West Ham	12/89	Exchange	109+11	7	9+1	8		2

BLACKMORE Clayton   Manchester United

Full Name: BLACKMORE, Clayton Graham   DOB: 23/9/64, Neath
FAPL Debut: Away v. Sheffield Utd 15/8/93   Debut Goal: –
Welsh International

Previous Club Details			Apps			Goals		
Clubs	Signed	Fee	Lge	FLC	FAC	Lge	FLC	FAC
Man United	9/82	–	138+34	22+2	15+5	19	3	1

FA Premier Lge Record
    92/93   12+2   1   0+1

BLACKWELL Dean   Wimbledon

Full Name: BLACKWELL, Dean Robert   DOB: 15/12/69, Camden
FAPL Debut: Away v. Leeds United † 15/8/92   Debut Goal: –

Previous Club Details			*Apps*			*Goals*		
Clubs	Signed Fee		Lge	FLC	FAC	Lge	FLC	FAC
Wimbledon	7/88	–	32+10	2	3	1		
Plymouth Arg	3/90	Loan	5+2					
FA Premier Lge Record								
	92/93		19+5		4			

BLISSET Gary   Wimbledon

Name: BLISSET, Gary   DOB: 26/6/64, Manchester

Previous Club Details		*Apps*			*Goals*		
Clubs	Signed Fee	Lge	FLC	FAC	Lge	FLC	FAC
Crewe Alex	8/83	112+10	9	4	39	3	
Brentford	3/87	£60,000	220+13	16+3	14	79	9	7
Wimbledon	8/93	£350,000						

BODIN Paul   Swindon Town

Full Name: BODIN, Paul   DOB: 13/9/64 Cardiff
Welsh International

Previous Club Details		*Apps*			*Goals*		
Clubs	Signed Fee	Lge	FLC	FAC	Lge	FLC	FAC
Cardiff City	8/82						
Non-League							
Newport Cnty	1/88	£15,000	6			1	
Swindon Town	3/88	£30,000	87+6	12	6	9	
Crystal Palace	3/91	£550,000	8+1				
Newcastle Utd	12/91	Loan	6				
Swindon Town	1/92	£225,000	55+1	1	3	13	

BORROWS Brian   Coventry City

Full Name: BORROWS, Brian   DOB: 20/12/60, Liverpool
FAPL Debut: Away v. Sheffield Wednesday † 2/9/92
Debut Goal: Home v. Liverpool 19/12/92

Previous Club Details		*Apps*			*Goals*		
Clubs	Signed Fee	Lge	FLC	FAC	Lge	FLC	FAC
Everton	4/80	–	27	2	–		
Bolton Wan	3/83	£10,000	95	7	4		
Coventry City	6/85	£80,000	261+2	31	16	9		1
FA Premier Lge Record							
	92/93		36+2	2	1	2	1

BOSNICH Mark — Aston Villa

Full Name: BOSNICH, Mark John   DOB: 13/1/72, Sydney, Aus.
FAPL Debut: Away v. Sheffield Wednesday 5/12/92   Debut Goal:

Previous Club Details			*Apps*			*Goals*		
Clubs	Signed	Fee	Lge	FLC	FAC	Lge	FLC	FAC
Man United	6/89	–	3					
Sydney	8/91	–						
Croatia (Aust)								
Aston Villa	2/92	–	1					
FA Premier Lge Record								
	92/93		17		1			

BOULD Steve — Arsenal

Full Name: BOULD, Stephen Andrew   DOB: 16/11/62, Stoke
FAPL Debut: Home v. Norwich 15/8/92
Debut Goal: Home v. Norwich 15/8/92

Previous Club Details			*Apps*			*Goals*		
Clubs	Signed	Fee	Lge	FLC	FAC	Lge	FLC	FAC
Stoke City	11/80	–	179+4	13	10	6	1	
Torquay Utd	10/82	Loan	9	–	2			
Arsenal	6/89	£390,000	107+5	9	12	3		
FA Premier Lge Record								
	92/93		24	5	1	1		

BOUND Matthew — Southampton

Full Name: BOUND, Matthew Terence   DOB: 9/11/72, Melksham
FAPL Debut: Home v. Blackburn Rovers † 9/3/93   Debut Goal: –

Previous Club Details			*Apps*			*Goals*		
Clubs	Signed	Fee	Lge	FLC	FAC	Lge	FLC	FAC
Southampton	5/91		0+1					
FA Premier Lge Record								
	92/93		1+2					

BOWEN Mark — Norwich City

Full Name: BOWEN, Mark Rosslyn   DOB: 7/12/63, Neath
FAPL Debut: Away v. Arsenal 15/8/92
Debut Goal: Home v. QPR 17/10/92
Welsh International

Previous Club Details			*Apps*			*Goals*		
Clubs	Signed	Fee	Lge	FLC	FAC	Lge	FLC	FAC
Tottenham H	12/81	–	14+3	–	3	2		
Norwich City	7/87	£90,000	168+2	16	17	14	1	1
FA Premier Lge Record								
	92/93		42	3	2	1		

BOWMAN Robert — Leeds United

Full Name: BOWMAN, Robert
DOB:
FAPL Debut: Away v. Wimbledon † 6/2/93
Debut Goal:

Previous Club Details			Apps			Goals		
Clubs	Signed	Fee	Lge	FLC	FAC	Lge	FLC	FAC
Leeds Utd								

FA Premier Lge Record

92/93			3+1					

BOZINOSKI Valdo — Ipswich Town

Full Name: BOZINOSKI, Valdo
DOB: 30/3/64, Macedonia
FAPL Debut: Away v. Coventry City † 5/12/92
Debut Goal:

Previous Club Details			Apps			Goals		
Clubs	Signed	Fee	Lge	FLC	FAC	Lge	FLC	FAC
Sporting Lisbon	12/92	£100,000						
Ipswich Town								

FA Premier Lge Record

92/93			3+6	1+1	0+1			

BRACEWELL Paul — Newcastle United

Full Name: BRACEWELL, Paul
DOB: 19/7/62 Heswall, Cheshire

Previous Club Details			Apps			Goals		
Clubs	Signed	Fee	Lge	FLC	FAC	Lge	FLC	FAC
Stoke City	2/80		123+6	6	6	5	1	
Sunderland	7/83	£250,000	38	4	2	4		
Everton	5/84	£425,000	95	11	19+2	7	2	
Sunderland	9/89	£250 000	112+1	9	10	2		
Newcastle	6/92	£250, 000	19+12		2+2	2		

BRADSHAW Carl — Sheffield United

Full Name: BRADSHAW, Carl
DOB: 2/10/68, Sheffield
FAPL Debut: Home v. Manchester United 15/8/92
Debut Goal: Away v. Everton 4/5/93

Previous Club Details			Apps			Goals		
Clubs	Signed	Fee	Lge	FLC	FAC	Lge	FLC	FAC
Sheff Wed	8/86	–	16+16	2+2	6+1	4		3
Barnsley	8/86	Loan	6			1		
Man City	9/88	£50,000	1+4	–	0+1			
Sheffield Utd	9/89	£50,000	59+16	4+1	10	5	1	3

FA Premier Lge Record

92/93			24+8	4	1+1	1	1	

BREAKER Tim — West Ham United

Full Name: BREAKER, Tim
DOB: 2/7/65 Bicester

Previous Club Details		Apps			Goals		
Clubs	Signed Fee	Lge	FLC	FAC	Lge	FLC	FAC
Luton Tn	5/83	204+6	22+2	21	3		
West Ham	10/90 £600,000	95+2	6	14	5		

BREITKREUTZ Matthias Aston Villa

Full Name: BREITKREUTZ, Matthias
DOB: 12/5/71, Berlin, Germany
FAPL Debut: Away v. Manchester City † 19/12/92   Debut Goal: –

Previous Club Details		Apps			Goals		
Clubs	Signed Fee	Lge	FLC	FAC	Lge	FLC	FAC
Bergmann B.							
Aston Villa	10/91 £100,000	7+1					

FA Premier Lge Record

92/93		2+1	0+1	

BRENNAN Mark Oldham Athletic

Full Name: BRENNAN, Mark Robert   DOB: 4/10/65, Rossendale
FAPL Debut: Home v. Middlesbrough 28/11/92
Debut Goal: Away v.Wimbledon 12/12/92

Previous Club Details		Apps			Goals		
Clubs	Signed Fee	Lge	FLC	FAC	Lge	FLC	FAC
Ipswich Town	4/83 –	165+3	21+1	12	19	2	3
Middlesbrough	7/88 £375,000	61+4	6	4	6		
Man City	7/90 £500,000	25+4	4	1	6	1	
Oldham Ath	11/92						

FA Premier Lge Record

92/93		14	1	2	3

BREVETT Rufus Queens Park Rangers

Full Name: BREVETT, Rufus Emanuel   DOB: 24/9/69, Derby
FAPL Debut: Away v. Manchester Utd. 26/9/92   Debut Goal: –

Previous Club Details		Apps			Goals		
Clubs	Signed Fee	Lge	FLC	FAC	Lge	FLC	FAC
Doncaster Rv	6/88 –	106+3	5	4	3		
QPR	2/91 £250,000	16+1	1				

FA Premier Lge Record

92/93		14+1	1	1	

BRIGHT Mark Sheffield Wednesday

Full Name: BRIGHT, Mark Abraham   DOB: 6/6/62, Stoke
FAPL Debut: Home v. Blackburn Rovers 15/8/92
Debut Goal: Home v. Blackburn Rovers 15/8/92

Previous Club Details			Apps			Goals		
Clubs	Signed	Fee	Lge	FLC	FAC	Lge	FLC	FAC
Port Vale	10/81	–	18+11	1+1	0+1	10		1
Leicester City	7/84	£33,000	26+16	3+1	1	6		
Crystal Palace	11/86	£75,000	219+3	22	13+1	88	11	2
Sheffield Wed	9/92	£375,000						
FA Premier Lge Record								
Crystal Palace	92/93		5			1		
Sheffield Wed	09/92		28+2	7	6	11	6	3

BRIGHTWELL David — Manchester City

Full Name: BRIGHTWELL, David John   DOB: 7/1/71, Lutterworth
FAPL Debut: Away v. Coventry City † 21/11/92 Debut Goal: –

Previous Club Details			Apps			Goals		
Clubs	Signed	Fee	Lge	FLC	FAC	Lge	FLC	FAC
Man City	4/88	–	3+1					
Chester City	3/91	Loan	6					
FA Premier Lge Record								
	92/93		4+4	1+1				

BRIGHTWELL Ian — Manchester City

Full Name: BRIGHTWELL, Ian Robert   DOB: 9/4/68, Lutterworth
FAPL Debut: Home v. QPR 17/8/92
Debut Goal: Home v. Leeds United 7/11/92

Previous Club Details			Apps			Goals		
Clubs	Signed	Fee	Lge	FLC	FAC	Lge	FLC	FAC
Man City	5/85	–	148+28	10+2	8+4	15		1
FA Premier Lge Record								
	92/93		21	3	1	1		

BROCK Kevin — Newcastle United

Full Name: BROCK, Kevin   DOB: 9/9/62 Middleton Stoney, Oxon.

Previous Club Details			Apps			Goals		
Clubs	Signed	Fee	Lge	FLC	FAC	Lge	FLC	FAC
Oxford Utd	9/79		229+17	30+2	17+1	26	5	1
QPR	8/87	£260,000	38+2	6	4	2		1
Newcastle Utd	12/88	£300,000	135+14	7	11	14	1	1

BROWN Kenny — West Ham United

Full Name: BROWN, Kenny   DOB: 11/7/67 Barking

Previous Club Details			Apps			Goals		
Clubs	Signed	Fee	Lge	FLC	FAC	Lge	FLC	FAC
Norwich C	7/85		24+1					
Plymouth A	8/88		126	9	6	4		
West Ham	8/91	£175,000	38+4	1	5	5		

BROWN Richard
Blackburn Rovers
Full Name: BROWN, Richard Anthony   DOB: 13/1/67, Nottingham
FAPL Debut: Home v. Norwich City 3/10/92   Debut Goal: –

Previous Club Details

Clubs	Signed	Fee	Apps Lge	FLC	FAC	Goals Lge	FLC	FAC
Sheffield Wed	12/84	£10,000						
Blackburn Rv	9/90	£15,000	24+2	–	2			
Maidstone Utd	2/91	Loan	3					

FA Premier Lge Record

	92/93		2	1+1				

BRUCE Steve
Manchester United
Full Name: BRUCE, Stephen Roger   DOB: 31/12/60, Corbridge
FAPL Debut: Away v. Sheffield United 15/8/93
Debut Goal: Home v. Leeds United 6/9/93

Previous Club Details

Clubs	Signed	Fee	Apps Lge	FLC	FAC	Goals Lge	FLC	FAC
Gillingham	10/78	–	203+2	15	14	29	6	1
Norwich City	8/84	£125,000	141	20	9	14	5	1
Man United	12/87	£800,000	161	19	21	26	4	1

FA Premier Lge Record

	92/93		42	3	3	5		

BRYSON Ian
Sheffield United
Full Name: BRYSON, James Ian Cook   DOB: 26/11/62, Kilmarnock
FAPL Debut: Home v. Manchester United † 15/893
Debut Goal: Away v. Southampton 27/2/93

Previous Club Details

Clubs	Signed	Fee	Apps Lge	FLC	FAC	Goals Lge	FLC	FAC
Sheffield Utd	8/88	£40,000	129+10	10	15+3	33	1	4

FA Premier Lge Record

	92/93		9+7	1+2	3+1	3		

BUNBURY Alex
West Ham United
Full Name: BUNBURY, Alex   DOB: 18/6/67, British Guyana

Previous Club Details

Clubs	Signed	Fee	Apps Lge	FLC	FAC	Goals Lge	FLC	FAC
Supra, Canada								
West Ham	11/92	£200,000	2+2		0+1			

BURLEY Craig
Chelsea
Full Name: BURLEY, Craig William   DOB: 24/9/71, Irvine
FAPL Debut: Away v. Tottenham Hotspur 5/12/92   Debut Goal: –

Previous Club Details		Apps			Goals		
Clubs	Signed Fee	Lge	FLC	FAC	Lge	FLC	FAC
Chelsea	9/89 –	6+3					

FA Premier Lge Record

92/93		1+2	1				

BURROWS David   Liverpool

Full Name: BURROWS, David   DOB: 25/10/68, Dudley
FAPL Debut: Away v. Nottingham Forest 16/8/92
Debut Goal: Home v. Norwich City 25/10/92

Previous Club Details		Apps			Goals		
Clubs	Signed Fee	Lge	FLC	FAC	Lge	FLC	FAC
West Brom Alb	10/86 –	37+9	3+1	2	1		
Liverpool	10/88 £550,000	103+9	11	16+1	1		

FA Premier Lge Record

92/93		29+1	5		2		

BUSST David   Coventry City

Full Name: BUSST, David John   DOB: 30/6/67, Birmingham
FAPL Debut: Away v. Norwich City 16/1/93   Debut Goal: –

Previous Club Details		Apps			Goals		
Clubs	Signed Fee	Lge	FLC	FAC	Lge	FLC	FAC
Coventry City	1/92						

FA Premier Lge Record

92/93		10		0+1			

BUTLER Peter   West Ham United

Full Name: BUTLER, Peter   DOB: 26/8/66 Halifax

Previous Club Details		Apps			Goals		
Clubs	Signed Fee	Lge	FLC	FAC	Lge	FLC	FAC
Huddersfield Tn	8/84	0+5					
Cambridge Utd	1/86	14			1		
Bury	7/86	9+2	2	1		1	
Cambridge U	12/86	55	4	2	9		
Southend Utd	2/88	135+7	12	2	9	1	
Huddersfield Tn	3/92 Loan	7					
West Ham Utd	8/92 £170,000	38	2	2	2		

BUTT Nicky   Manchester United

Full Name: BUTT, Nicky   DOB: 21/1/75, Manchester
FAPL Debut: Home v. Oldham Athletic † 21/11/92   Debut Goal: –

Previous Club Details		Apps			Goals		
Clubs	Signed Fee	Lge	FLC	FAC	Lge	FLC	FAC
Manchester Utd							

FA Premier Lge Record

92/93		0+1					

BUTTERWORTH Ian   Norwich City

Full Name: BUTTERWORTH, Ian Stuart   DOB: 25/1/64, Crewe
FAPL Debut: Away v. Arsenal 15/8/92
Debut Goal: Away v. Liverpool 25/10/92

Previous Club Details			*Apps*			*Goals*		
Clubs	Signed	Fee	Lge	FLC	FAC	Lge	FLC	FAC
Coventry City	8/81	–	80+10	5	5+1	10		
Nottingham F	6/85	£250,000	26+1	6	1			
Norwich City	9/86	Loan	4					
Norwich City	12/86	£160,000	177+3	13+1	22		3	
FA Premier Lge Record								
	92/93		26	2	2		1	

CALDERWOOD Colin   Tottenham Hotspur

Full Name: Calderwood, Colin   DOB:20/1/65 Stranraer

Previous Club Details			*Apps*			*Goals*		
Clubs	Signed	Fee	Lge	FLC	FAC	Lge	FLC	FAC
Mansfield Tn	3/82	–	97+3	4	6	1		1
Swindon Tn	7/85	£30,000	328+2	35	17	20		1
Tottenham H	7/93	£1.25m						

CAMPBELL Kevin   Arsenal

Full Name: CAMPBELL, Kevin Joseph   DOB: 4/2/70, Lambeth
FAPL Debut: Home v. Norwich 15/8/92
Debut Goal: Home v. Norwich 15/8/92

Previous Club Details			*Apps*			*Goals*		
Clubs	Signed	Fee	Lge	FLC	FAC	Lge	FLC	FAC
Arsenal	2/88	–	45+23	2+4	5+2	24		
Leyton Orient	1/89	Loan	16			9		
Leicester City	11/89	Loan	11	–	–	5	–	–
FA Premier Lge Record								
	92/93		32+5	5+4	4+5	4	4	1

CAMPBELL Sol   Tottenham Hotspur

Full Name: CAMPBELL, Sulzeer   DOB: 18/9/74, Newham, London
FAPL Debut: Home v. Chelsea † 5/12/92   Debut Goal:

Previous Club Details			*Apps*			*Goals*		
Clubs	Signed	Fee	Lge	FLC	FAC	Lge	FLC	FAC
Tottenham Hotspur								
FA Premier Lge Record								
	92/93		0+1					

CANTONA Eric   Manchester United

Full Name: CANTONA, Eric   DOB: 24/5/66, Paris, France
FAPL Debut: Home v. Wimbledon 15/8/92

Debut Goal: Away v. Middlesbrough 22/8/92
French International

Previous Club Details			Apps			Goals		
Clubs	Signed	Fee	Lge	FLC	FAC	Lge	FLC	FAC
Nimes, France								

FA Premier Lge Record

	92/93							
Leeds United	2/92	£900,000	12+1	1		6		
Man Utd	11/92	£1.2m	21+1		1	9		

CARR Franz   Sheffield United
Full Name: CARR, Franz   DOB: 24/9/66, Preston
FAPL Debut: Away v. Coventry City 24/3/93
Debut Goal: Away v. Manchester United 6/2/93

Previous Club Details			Apps			Goals		
Clubs	Signed	Fee	Lge	FLC	FAC	Lge	FLC	FAC
Blackburn R	7/84							
Notts Forest	8/84	£100,000	122+9	16+2	4+2	17	5	
Sheffield Wed	12/89	Loan	9+3		2			
West Ham Utd	3/91	Loan	1+2					
Newcastle Utd	5/91	£250,000	20+4	2+2		3		
Sheffield Utd	4/93							

FA Premier Lge Record

	92/93		8					

CARTER Jimmy   Arsenal
Full Name: CARTER, James William Charles
DOB: 9/11/65, Hammersmith
FAPL Debut: Away v. Blackburn Rovers 18/8/92
Debut Goal: Home v. Southampton 20/3/93

Previous Club Details			Apps			Goals		
Clubs	Signed	Fee	Lge	FLC	FAC	Lge	FLC	FAC
Crystal Palce	11/83	–						
QPR	12/85	–						
Millwall	3/87	£15,000	99+11	3+1	6+1	11		2
Liverpool	1/91	£800,000	2+3	–	2			
Arsenal	10/91	£500,000	5+1	–	1			

FA Premier Lge Record

	92/93		11+5	1	1	2		1

CASCARINO Tony   Chelsea
Full Name: CASCARINO, Anthony Guy   DOB: 1/9/62, Orpington
FAPL Debut: Away v. Blackburn Rovers 21/2/93
Debut Goal: Home v. Tottenham Hotspur 20/3/93
Eire International

Previous Club Details			Apps			Goals		
Clubs	Signed	Fee	Lge	FLC	FAC	Lge	FLC	FAC
Gillingham	1/82	–	209+10			78		
Millwall	6/87	£200,000	105			42		
Aston Villa	3/90	£1.5m	43+3	20+1	17+1	11	1	
Celtic	7/91	£1,100,00						
Chelsea	2/92	£750,000	11	–	2	2		
FA Premier Lge Record								
	92/93		8+1				2	

CAWLEY David Manchester City

Name: CAWLEY, David   DOB:

Previous Club Details			Apps			Goals		
Clubs	Signed	Fee	Lge	FLC	FAC	Lge	FLC	FAC
Dundalk, Eire								
Man City	8/93	£25,000						

CHARLTON Simon Southampton

Name: CHARLTON, Simon   DOB: 25/10/71, Huddersfield

Previous Club Details			Apps			Goals		
Clubs	Signed	Fee	Lge	FLC	FAC	Lge	FLC	FAC
Huddersfield	7/89		121+3	9	10	1	1	
Southampton	8/93	£250,000						

CLARK Lee Newcastle United

Full Name: CLARKE, Lee   DOB: 27/10/72 Wallsend

Previous Club Details			Apps			Goals		
Clubs	Signed	Fee	Lge	FLC	FAC	Lge	FLC	FAC
Newcastle	11/89		84+10	8	6	17		

CLARKE Andy Wimbledon

Full Name: CLARKE, Andrew Weston   DOB: 22/7/67, Islington
FAPL Debut: Away v. Leeds United. 15/8/92
Debut Goal: Home v. Aston Villa 3/10/92

Previous Club Details			Apps			Goals		
Clubs	Signed	Fee	Lge	FLC	FAC	Lge	FLC	FAC
Non-League								
Wimbledon	2/91	£250,000	20+26	1+1	0+1	6	1	
FA Premier Lge Record								
	92/93		23+10	3	3	5		

CLARKE Simon West Ham United

Full Name: CLARKE, Simon   DOB: 23/9/71 Chelmsford

Previous Club Details			Apps			Goals		
Clubs	Signed	Fee	Lge	FLC	FAC	Lge	FLC	FAC
West Ham	3/90		0+3					

CLARKE Steve Chelsea

Full Name: CLARKE, Stephen DOB: 29/8/63, Saltcoats
FAPL Debut: Home v. Oldham Athletic 15/8/92 Debut Goal: –
Scottish International

Previous Club Details			Apps			Goals		
Clubs	Signed	Fee	Lge	FLC	FAC	Lge	FLC	FAC
Chelsea	1/87	£422,000	161+2	10	8	6	1	1
FA Premier Lge Record								
	92/93		18+2	1	1			

CLOUGH Nigel Liverpool

Full Name: CLOUGH, Nigel Howard DOB: 9/3/66, Sunderland
FAPL Debut: Home v. Liverpool 16/8/92
Debut Goal: Away v. Norwich City 31/8/93
English International

Previous Club Details			Apps			Goals		
Clubs	Signed	Fee	Lge	FLC	FAC	Lge	FLC	FAC
Nottingham F	9/84	–	265+4	41	24	91	21	5
Liverpool	8/93	£2.275m						
FA Premier Lge Record								
Nottingham F	92/93		42	5	4	10	1	1

COCKERILL Glenn Southampton

Full Name: COCKERILL, Glen DOB: 25/8/59, Grimsby
FAPL Debut: Home v. Tottenham H. 15/8/92 Debut Goal: –

Previous Club Details			Apps			Goals		
Clubs	Signed	Fee	Lge	FLC	FAC	Lge	FLC	FAC
Lincoln City	11/76	–	65+6	2	2	10		
Swindon Tn	12/79	£11,000	25+3	3		1		
Lincoln City	8/81	£40,000	114+1	16	7	25	1	
Sheffield Wed	3/84	£125,000	62	6	1	10	1	
Southampton	10/85	£225,000	239+11	32+1	19+2	32	5	2
FA Premier Lge Record								
	92/93		21+2	2	1			

COLE Andy Newcastle United

Full Name: COLE, Andrew DOB: 19/10/71, Nottingham

Previous Club Details			Apps			Goals		
Clubs	Signed	Fee	Lge	FLC	FAC	Lge	FLC	FAC
Arsenal	10/89		0+1					
Fulham	5/91	Loan						
Bristol City	3/92	£500,000	41			20		
Newcastle Utd	3/93	£1.75m	11+1			12		

CORK Alan
Sheffield United

Full Name: CORK, Alan Graham   DOB: 4/3/59, Derby
FAPL Debut: Home v. Manchester United 15/8/93
Debut Goal: Away v. QPR 2/8/93

Previous Club Details			*Apps*			*Goals*		
Clubs	Signed	Fee	Lge	FLC	FAC	Lge	FLC	FAC
Derby County	7/77	–						
Lincoln City	9/77	Loan	5					
Wimbledon	2/78	–	352+78	29+7	25+5	145	14	8
Sheffield Utd	3/92	–	7+1			2		

FA Premier Lge Record

92/93			11+16	2+1	4+1	2		1

COTON Tony
Manchester City

Full Name: COTON, Anthony Philip   DOB: 19/5/61, Tamworth
FAPL Debut: Home v. QPR 17/8/92   Debut Goal:

Previous Club Details			*Apps*			*Goals*		
Clubs	Signed	Fee	Lge	FLC	FAC	Lge	FLC	FAC
Birmingham C	10,78	–	94	10	10			
Watford	9/84	£300,000	233	18	32			
Man City	7/90	£1m	70	8	4			

FA Premier Lge Record

92/93			40	3	4			

COTTEE Tony
Everton

Full Name: COTTEE, Anthony   DOB: 11/7/65, West Ham
FAPL Debut: Away v. Blackburn Rovers 15/9/92
Debut Goal: Away v. Blackburn Rovers 15/9/92
English International

Previous Club Details			*Apps*			*Goals*		
Clubs	Signed	Fee	Lge	FLC	FAC	Lge	FLC	FAC
West Ham	9/82	–	203+9	19	24	92	14	11
Everton	8/88	£2.3m	97+19	12+3	13+6	44	6	4

FA Premier Lge Record

92/93			25+1	2+1		12	1	

COWAN Tom
Sheffield United

Full Name: COWAN, Thomas   DOB: 28/8/69, Bellshill
FAPL Debut: Home v. Wimbledon 25/8/92   Debut Goal:

Previous Club Details			*Apps*			*Goals*		
Clubs	Signed	Fee	Lge	FLC	FAC	Lge	FLC	FAC
Rangers								
Sheffield Utd	7/91	£350,000	20	2	1			

FA Premier Lge Record

92/93			21					

COWANS Gordon
Aston Villa

Full Name: COWANS, Gordon Sidney   DOB: 27/10/58, Cornforth
FAPL Debut: Home v. Oldham Athletic 26/9/92
Debut Goal: Home v. Norwich City 3/10/92
English International

Previous Club Details			Apps			Goals		
Clubs	Signed	Fee	Lge	FLC	FAC	Lge	FLC	FAC
Aston Villa	9/76	–	276+10	23+4	19+1	42	5	3
Bari (Italy)	7/85	£500,000						
Aston Villa	7/88	£250,000	114+3	15	9	7		
Blackburn Rv	11/91	£200,000	26		2	1		1
Aston Villa	8/93							
FA Premier Lge Record								
Blackburn Rv	92/93		23+1	4	3	1		

COX Neil
Aston Villa

Full Name: COX, Neil James   DOB: 8/10/71, Scunthorpe
FAPL Debut: Away v. Sheffield Wednesday 5/12/92
Debut Goal: Home v. Everton 20/2/93

Previous Club Details			Apps			Goals		
Clubs	Signed	Fee	Lge	FLC	FAC	Lge	FLC	FAC
ScunthorpeU	3/90	–	17	–	4	1		
Aston Villa	2/91	£400,000	4+3	–	–			
FA Premier Lge Record								
	92/93		6+9			1		

CRAMB Colin
Southampton

Name: CRAMB, Colin   DOB: 23/6/74, Lanark

Previous Club Details			Apps			Goals		
Clubs	Signed	Fee	Lge	FLC	FAC	Lge	FLC	FAC
Hamilton Acc								
Southampton	8/93	£150,000 (jt)						

CROOK Ian
Norwich City

Full Name: CROOK, Ian Stuart   DOB: 18/1/63, Romford
FAPL Debut: Home v. Everton † 22/8/92
Debut Goal: Home v. Nottingham Forest 31/8/92

Previous Club Details			Apps			Goals		
Clubs	Signed	Fee	Lge	FLC	FAC	Lge	FLC	FAC
Tottenham H	8/80	–	10+10	1	0+1	1		
Norwich City	6/86	£80,000	151+19	14+4	10+4	11	2	–
FA Premier Lge Record								
	92/93		32+2	3	1	3		

CULVERHOUSE Ian — Norwich City

Full Name: CULVERHOUSE, IAN Brett
DOB: 22/9/64, Bishops Stortford
FAPL Debut: Away v. Arsenal 15/8/92   Debut Goal: –

Previous Club Details

Clubs	Signed	Fee	Lge	FLC	FAC	Lge	FLC	FAC
			Apps			Goals		
Tottenham H	9/82	–	1+1					
Norwich City	10/85	£50,000	112+1	16	24			

FA Premier Lge Record

			Lge	FLC	FAC			
92/93			41	3	2			

CUNDY Jason — Tottenham Hotspur

Full Name: CUNDY, Jason Victor   DOB: 12/11/69, Wandsworth
FAPL Debut: Away v. Southampton 15/8/92
Debut Goal: Away v. Ipswich Town 30/8/92

Previous Club Details

Clubs	Signed	Fee	Lge	FLC	FAC	Lge	FLC	FAC
			Apps			Goals		
Chelsea	8/88	–	40+1	6	6	2		
Tottenham H	3/92	£750,000	10					

FA Premier Lge Record

			Lge	FLC	FAC			
92/93			13+2	2		1		

CURLE Keith — Manchester City

Full Name: CURLE, Keith   DOB: 14/11/63, Bristol
FAPL Debut: Home v. QPR 17/8/92
Debut Goal: Away v. Coventry 21/11/92

Previous Club Details

Clubs	Signed	Fee	Lge	FLC	FAC	Lge	FLC	FAC
			Apps			Goals		
Bristol Rv	11/81	–	21+11	3	1	4		
Torquay Utd	11/83	£5,000	16	–	1	5		1
Bristol City	3/84	£10,000	113+8	7+1	5	1		
Reading	10/87	£150,000	40	8	–			
Wimbledon	10/88	£500,000	91+2	7	5	3		
Man City	8/91	£2.5m	40	4	1	5		

FA Premier Lge Record

			Lge	FLC	FAC			
92/93			39	3	4	3		

DALEY Tony — Aston Villa

Full Name: DALEY, Anthony Mark   DOB: 18/10/67, Birmingham
FAPL Debut: Away v. Ipswich Town 15/8/92
Debut Goal: Away v. Arsenal 12/4/93

Previous Club Details

Clubs	Signed	Fee	Lge	FLC	FAC	Lge	FLC	FAC
			Apps			Goals		
Aston Villa	5/85	–	162+31	17+1	13+1	28	4	2

FA Premier Lge Record

			Lge	FLC	FAC			
92/93			8+5			2		

DAVIS Paul   Arsenal

Full Name: DAVIS, Paul Vincent   DOB: 9/12/61, Dulwich
FAPL Debut: Away v. Norwich 3/3/93   Debut Goal: –

Previous Club Details   *App*   *Goals*

Clubs	Signed	Fee	Lge	FLC	FAC	Lge	FLC	FAC
Arsenal	7/79	–	301+18	42+3	19+5	29	4	3

FA Premier Lge Record

	92/93		6	2	3			

DAVISON Ross   Sheffield United

Name: Davison, Ross   DOB:

Previous Club Details   *Apps*   *Goals*

Clubs	Signed	Fee	Lge	FLC	FAC	Lge	FLC	FAC
Sheffield U	8/93							

DEANE Brian   Leeds United

Full Name: DEANE, Brian Christopher   DOB: 7/2/68, Leeds
FAPL Debut: Home v. Manchester United 15/8/93
Debut Goal: Home v. Manchester United 15/8/93
English International

Previous Club Detais   *App*   *Goals*

Clubs	Signed	Fee	Lge	FLC	FAC	Lge	FLC	FAC
Doncaster R	12/85	–	59+7	3	2+1	12		1
Sheffield Utd	7/88	£30,000	156	12	18	68	9	8
Leeds Utd	7/93	£2.7m						

FA Premier Lge Record

Sheffield Utd	92/93		41	4	5+1	15	2	3

DEARDEN Kevin   Tottenham Hotspur

Full Name: DEARDEN, Kevin Charles   DOB: 8/3/70, Luton
FAPL Debut: Away v. Nottm. F. † 12/4/93   Debut Goal:

Previous Club Details   *App*   *Goals*

Clubs	Signed	Fee	Lge	FLC	FAC	Lge	FLC	FAC
Tottenham	7/88	–	1					
Cambridge Utd	3/89	Loan	15					
Hartlepool Utd	8/89	Loan	10					
Swindon Tn	3/90	Loan	1					
Peterboro Utd	8/90	Loan	7					
Hull City	1/91	Loan	3					
Rochdale	8/91	Loan	2					
Birmingham C	3/92	Loan	12					
Portsmouth	8/92	Loan						

FA Premier Lge Record

	92/93		0+1					

DIBBLE Andy   Manchester City

Full Name: DIBBLE, Andrew Gerald   DOB: 8/5/65, Cwmbran
FAPL Debut: Away v. QPR 6/2/93   Debut Goal:
Welsh International

Previous Club Details

Clubs	Signed	Fee	Apps Lge	FLC	FAC	Goals Lge	FLC	FAC
Cardiff City	8/82	–	62	4	4			
Luton Town	7/84	£125,000	30	4	1			
Sunderland	2/86	Loan	12					
Huddersfield T	2/87	Loan	5					
Man City	7/88	£240,000	74	6	5			
Middlesbrough	2/91	Loan	19	–	–			
Bolton Wnd	9/91	Loan	13	–	–			
West Brom A	2/92	Loan	9					
Oldham Ath	2/93	Loan						

FA Premier Lge Record

Man City	92/93		1+1					

DICKOV Paul   Arsenal

Full Name: DICKOV, Paul   DOB: 1/11/72, Livingston
FAPL Debut: Home v. Southampton † 20/3/93
Debut Goal: Home v. Crystal Palace 8/5/93

Previous Club Details

Clubs	Signed	Fee	Apps Lge	FLC	FAC	Goals Lge	FLC	FAC
Arsenal	12/90	–						

FA Premier Lge Record

	92/93		1+2			2		

DICKS Julian   West Ham United

Full Name: DICKS, Julian   DOB: 8/8/68, Bristol

Previous Club Details

Clubs	Signed	Fee	Apps Lge	FLC	FAC	Goals Lge	FLC	FAC
Birmingham C	4/86		83+6	5+1	5	1		
West Ham	3/88	£300,000	152	19	14	29	5	

DIGBY Fraser   Manchester United

Full Name: DIGBY, Fraser   DOB: 23/1/67, Sheffield

Previous Club Details

Clubs	Signed	Fee	Apps Lge	FLC	FAC	Goals Lge	FLC	FAC
Man Utd	4/85							
Oldham A	1/86	Loan						
Swindon Tn	12/86	£32,000	256	22	13			
Man Utd	11/92	Loan						

DIXON Kerry　　　　　　　　　　　　　　　　Southampton

Full Name:　DIXON, Derry Michael　　　　DOB: 24/7/61, Luton
FAPL Debut: Home v. Tottenham Hotspur 15/8/92
Debut Goal:　Away v. Liverpool 1/9/92
English International

Previous Club Details

Clubs	Signed	Fee	Lge	FLC	FAC	Lge	FLC	FAC
			Apps			*Goals*		
Tottenham H	7/78	–						
Reading	7/80	£20,000	110+6	6+1	2+1	51		
Chelsea	8/83	£175,000	331+4	40+1	19+2	147	24	8
Southampton								
Luton Town	2/93	Loan	16+1			3		

FA Premier Lge Record

92/93			8+1			2		

DIXON Lee　　　　　　　　　　　　　　　　　　　　Arsenal

Full Name:　DIXON, Lee Michael　　　　　　DOB: 17/3/64, Manchester
FAPL Debut: Home v. Norwich 15/8/92　　　　Debut Goal: –
English International

Previous Club Details

Clubs	Signed	Fee	Lge	FLC	FAC	Lge	FLC	FAC
			Apps			*Goals*		
Burnley	7/82	–	4	1				
Chester City	2/84	–	56+1	2	1	1		
Bury	7/85	–	45	4	8	6		1
Stoke City	7/86	£40,000	71	6	7	5		
Arsenal	1/88	£400,000	151+2	16	13	15		1

FA Premier Lge Record

92/93			29	7	8			

DOBBS Gerald　　　　　　　　　　　　　　　Wimbledon

Full Name:　DOBBS, Gerald Francis　　　　DOB: 24/1/71, Lambeth
FAPL Debut: Away v. Leeds United † 15/8/92
Debut Goal:　Home v. Sheffield United 20/2/93

Previous Club Details

Clubs	Signed	Fee	Lge	FLC	FAC	Lge	FLC	FAC
			Apps			*Goals*		
Wimbledon	7/89	–	2+2					

FA Premier Lge Record

92/93			16+3	2	1+1	1		1

DOBSON Tony　　　　　　　　　　　　　Blackburn Rovers

Full Name:　DOBSON, Anthony John　　　　DOB: 5/2/69, Coventry
FAPL Debut: Away v. Crystal Palace 15/8/92　Debut Goal:

Previous Club Details

Clubs	Signed	Fee	Lge	FLC	FAC	Lge	FLC	FAC
			Apps			*Goals*		
Coventry City	7/86	–	51+3	5+3	1	1		

Blackburn Rv   1/91   £300,000   21+1   2

FA Premier Lge Record
92/93   15+4   3   2

DODD Jason   Southampton
Full Name: DODD, Jason Robert   DOB: 2/11/70, Bath
FAPL Debut: Home v. Tottenham Hotspur 15/8/92
Debut Goal: Away v. Sheffield Wednesday 13/4/93

Previous Club Details			*Apps*			*Goals*		
Clubs	Signed	Fee	Lge	FLC	FAC	Lge	FLC	FAC
Southampton	3/89	£50,000	63+6	14+1	10			

FA Premier Lge Record
92/93   27+3   3   1   1

DONAGHY Mal   Chelsea
Full Name: DONAGHY, Malachy   DOB: 13/9/57, Belfast
FAPL Debut: Home v. Oldham Athletic 15/8/92
Debut Goal: Away v. Leeds United 24/3/93
Northern Ireland International

Previous Club Details			*Apps*			*Goals*		
Clubs	Signed	Fee	Lge	FLC	FAC	Lge	FLC	FAC
Luton Town	6/87	£20,000	410	34	36	2	3	
Man United	10/88	£650,000	76+12	9+5	10			
Luton Town	12/89	Loan	5					
Chelsea	8/92	£150,000						

FA Premier Lge Record
92/93   39+1   5   1   2

DORIGO Tony   Leeds United
Full Name: DORIGO, Anthony Robert
DOB: 31/1/65, Melbourne, Australia
FAPL Debut: Home v. Wimbledon 15/8/92
Debut Goal: Home v. Ipswich Town 27/2/93
English International

Previous Club Details			*Apps*			*Goals*		
Clubs	Signed	Fee	Lge	FLC	FAC	Lge	FLC	FAC
Aston Villa	7/83	–	106+5	14+1	7	1		
Chelsea	5/87	£475,000	146	14	4	11		
Leeds Utd	5/91	£1.3m	38	5	1	3		

FA Premier Lge Record
92/93   33   1   4   1

DOW Andy   Chelsea

Name: Dow, Andy   DOB: 07/02/73, Dundee
Previous Club Details   *Apps*   *Goals*
Clubs   Signed Fee   Lge FLC FAC   Lge FLC FAC
Dundee   11/90
Chelsea   8/93

DOWIE Iain   Southampton

Full Name: DOWIE, Iain   DOB: 9/1/65, Hatfield
FAPL Debut: Away v. QPR † 19/8/92
Debut Goal: Away v. Crystal Palace 26/9/92
Northern Ireland International
Previous Club Details   *Apps*   *Goals*
Clubs   Signed Fee   Lge FLC FAC   Lge FLC FAC
Luton Town   12/88 £30,000   53+13 3+1 1+2   15
Fulham   9/89   Loan   5   1
West Ham   3/91   £480,000   12   4
Southampton 9/91   £500,000   25+5 1+3 4+4   9
FA Premier Lge Record
             92/93   34+2 2   11

DOYLE Maurice   Queens Park Rangers

Full Name: DOYLE, Maurice   DOB: 17/10/69, Ellesmere Port
FAPL Debut: Away v. Ipswich Town 9/2/93   Debut Goal:
Previous Club Details   *Apps*   *Goals*
Clubs   Signed Fee   Lge FLC FAC   Lge FLC FAC
Crewe Alex   7/88   –   6+2   2
QPR   4/89   £120,000
Crewe Alex   1/91   Loan   6+1   2   2
FA Premier Lge Record
             92/93   5

DOZZELL Jason   Tottenham Hotspur

Full Name: DOZZELL, Jason Alvin Winans DOB: 9/12/67, Ipswich
FAPL Debut: Home v. Aston Villa 15/8/92
Debut Goal: Home v. Liverpool 25/8/92
Previous Club Details   *Apps*   *Goals*
Clubs   Signed Fee   Lge   FLC FAC   Lge FLC FAC
Ipswich Town 12/84 –   271+20 22+1 18   45 3   10
Tottenham H 8/93   Tribunal
FA Premier Lge Record
Ipswich Tn   92/93   41   7   4   7   2

DUBLIN Dion
Manchester United

Full Name: DUBLIN, Dion
DOB: 22/4/69, Leicester
FAPL Debut: Away v. Sheffield United † 15/8/92
Debut Goal: Away v. Southampton 24/8/92

Previous Club Details

Clubs	Signed	Fee	App Lge	FLC	FAC	Goals Lge	FLC	FAC
Norwich City								
Cambridge Utd	1/89		133+23	8+2	21	53	5	11
Manchester Utd	7/92	£1m						

FA Premier Lge Record

92/93			3+4			1		

DURIE Gordon
Tottenham Hotspur

Full Name: DURIE, Gordon Scott
DOB: 6/12/65, Paisley
FAPL Debut: Away v. Southampton 15/8/92
Debut Goal: Home v. Crystal Palace 22/8/92
Scottish International

Clubs Played at

Clubs	Signed	Fee	App Lge	FLC	FAC	Goals Lge	FLC	FAC
Chelsea	4/86	£380,000	115+8	10	6	51	5	1
Tottenham H	8/91	£2.2m	31	6	1	6	2	

FA Premier Lge Record

92/93			17	2	1	3	1	

EARLE Robbie
Wimbledon

Full Name: EARLE, Robert Gerald
DOB: 27/1/65, Newcastle-U-Lyme
FAPL Debut: Away v. Leeds United 15/8/92
Debut Goal: Home v. Arsenal 5/9/92

Previous Club Details

Clubs	Signed	Fee	Apps Lge	FLC	FAC	Goals Lge	FLC	FAC
Port Vale	7/82	–	284+10	21+2	20+1	77	4	4
Wimbledon	7/91	£775,000	40	2	2	44		

FA Premier Lge Record

92/93			42	4	5	7		1

EBBRELL John
Everton

Full Name: EBBRELL, John Deith
DOB: 1/10/69, Bromborough
FAPL Debut: Home v. Sheffield Wednesday 15/8/92
Debut Goal: Away v. Blackburn Rovers 15/9/92

Previous Club Details

Clubs	Signed	Fee	Apps Lge	FLC	FAC	Goals Lge	FLC	FAC
Everton	11/86	–	87+9	9	10	4	1	2

FA Premier Lge Record

92/93			24	2	2	1		

EDINBURGH Justin   Tottenham Hotspur

Full Name: EDINBURGH, Justin Charles   DOB: 18/12/69, Brentwood
FAPL Debut: Away v. Southampton 15/8/92 Debut Goal: –

Previous Club Details			Apps			Goals		
Clubs	Signed	Fee	Lge	FLC	FAC	Lge	FLC	FAC
Southend U	7/88	–	36+1	2+1	2			
Tottenham H	7/90	£150,000	36+3	6+2	5	1		
FA Premier Lge Record								
	92/93		31+1	3+1	5			

EHIOGU Ugo   Aston Villa

Full Name: EHIOGU, Ugochuku   DOB: 3/12/72, Hackney
FAPL Debut: Home v. Southampton † 22/8/92 Debut Goal: –

Previous Club Details			Apps			Goals		
Clubs	Signed	Fee	Lge	FLC	FAC	Lge	FLC	FAC
West Brom	7/89	–	0+2					
Aston Villa	7/91	£40,000	4+4	–	0+1			
FA Premier Lge Record								
	92/93		1+3	1				

EKOKO Efan   Norwich City

Full Name: EKOKO, Efan   DOB: 8/6/67, Manchester
FAPL Debut: Home v. Manchester United † 5/4/93
Debut Goal: Away v. Tottenham Hotspur 9/4/93

Previous Club Details			Apps			Goals		
Clubs	Signed	Fee	Lge	FLC	FAC	Lge	FLC	FAC
Bournemouth	5/90		53+19	0+2	5+2	20		1
Norwich City	3/93	£500,000						
FA Premier Lge Record								
	92/93		1+3			3		

ELKINS Gary   Wimbledon

Full Name: ELKINS, Gary   DOB: 4/5/66, Wallingford
FAPL Debut: Away v. Leeds Utd 15/8/92   Debut Goal:

Previous Club Details			Apps			Goals		
Clubs	Signed	Fee	Lge	FLC	FAC	Lge	FLC	FAC
Fulham	12/83	–	100+4	6	2+2	2		
Exeter City	12/89	Loan	5					
Wimbledon	8/90	£20,000	25+3	1		1		
FA Premier Lge Record								
	92/93		17+1	2	3			

ELLIOTT Paul   Chelsea

Full Name: ELLIOTT, Paul Marcellus   DOB: 18/3/64, Lewisham
FAPL Debut: Home v. Oldham Ath. 15/8/92 Debut Goal: –

Previous Club Details			Apps			Goals		
Clubs	Signed	Fee	Lge	FLC	FAC	Lge	FLC	FAC
Charton Ath	3/81	–	61+2	2	1	1		
Luton Town	3/83	£95,000	63+3	5	2	4		
Aston Villa	12/85	£400,000	56+1	7	4	7		
Pisa (Italy)	7/87	£400,000						
Celtic	6/89	£600,000						
Chelsea	7/91	£1.4m	35	2	5	3		
FA Premier Lge Record								
	92/93		7					

FAIRCLOUGH Chris Leeds United

Full Name: FAIRCLOUGH, Courtney Huw   DOB: 12/4/64, Nottingham
FAPL Debut: Home v. Wimbledon 15/8/92
Debut Goal: Home v. Coventry City 31/10/92

Previous Club Details			Apps			Goals		
Clubs	Signed	Fee	Lge	FLC	FAC	Lge	FLC	FAC
Nottingham F	10/81	–	102+5	9+1	6	1	1	
Tottenham H	6/87	£387,000	60	7	3	5		
Leeds Utd	3/89	£500,000	117+1	11+2	8	15	2	
FA Premier Lge Record								
	92/93		29+1	2	3+1	3		

FALCONER Willie Sheffield United

Name: FALCONER, Willie   DOB: 5/4/66, Aberdeen
FAPL Debut: Home v Coventry City 15/8/92
Debut Goal: Home v Sheffield United 5/9/92

Previous Club Details			Apps			Goals		
Clubs	Signed	Fee	Lge	FLC	FAC	Lge	FLC	FAC
Aberdeen								
Watford	6/88	£300,000	85+13	5	6	1		
Middlesbrough	8/91	£45,000	25	1+1				
Sheffield Utd	8/93							
FA Premier Lge Record								
Middlesbrough	92/93		22+6	1	3	5		2

FARRELL Dave Aston Villa

Full Name: FARRELL, David William   DOB: 11/11/71, Birmingham
FAPL Debut: Away v. Oldham Ath. † 24/10/92 Debut Goal:

Previous Club Details			Apps			Goals		
Clubs	Signed	Fee	Lge	FLC	FAC	Lge	FLC	FAC
Aston Villa	1/92	£45,000						
Scunthorpe	1/93	Loan	4+1			1		
FA Premier Lge Record								
	92/93		1+1					

FASHANU John   **Wimbledon**

Full Name: FASHANU, John   DOB: 18/9/62, Kensington
FAPL Debut: Home v. Manchester City 1/9/92
Debut Goal: Home v. Arsenal 5/9/93
English International

Previous Club Details			*Apps*			*Goals*		
Clubs	Signed	Fee	Lge	FFC	FAC	Lge	FLC	FAC
Norwich City	10/79	–	6+1			1		
Crystal Palace	8/83	Loan	1	1				
Lincoln City	9/83	–	31+5	2	2+1			
Millwall	11/84	£55,000	50	4	9	12	2	4
Wimbledon	3/86	£125,000	201+2	13+1	19	88	8	9
FA Premier Lge Record								
92/93			27+2	2+1	5	6	1	1

FEAR Peter   **Wimbledon**

Full Name: FEAR, Peter   DOB: 10/9/73, Sutton
FAPL Debut: Away v. Arsenal † 10/2/93   Debut Goal:

Previous Club Details			*Apps*			*Goals*		
Clubs	Signed	Fee	Lge	FLC	FAC	Lge	FLC	FAC
Wimbledon	6/92	–						
FA Premier Lge Record								
92/93			2+2					

FENWICK Terry   **Tottenham Hotspur**

Full Name: FENWICK, Terence   DOB: 17/11/59, Seaham
FAPL Debut: Away v. Southampton 15/8/92   Debut Goal: –
English International

Previous Club Details			*Apps*			*Goals*		
Clubs	Signed	Fee	Lge	FLC	FAC	Lge	FLC	FAC
Crystal Palace	12/76	–	62+8	4+1	7			1
QPR	12/80	£110,000	256	28+1	18	33	6	
Tottenham H	12/87	£550,000	87+1	14	7	38	2	6
Leicester City	10/90	Loan	8			1		
FA Premier Lge Record								
92/93			3+2					

FERDINAND Les   **Queens Park Rangers**

Full Name: FERDINAND, Leslie   DOB: 18/12/66, Acton
FAPL Debut: Away v. Manchester City 17/8/92
Debut Goal: Home v. Southampton 19/8/92
English International

Previous Club Details			*Apps*			*Goals*		
Clubs	Signed	Fee	Lge	FLC	FAC	Lge	FLC	FAC
Non-League								

QRP	4/87	£15,000	43+10	2+3	0+1	20	2	
Brentford	3/88	Loan	3					
Besiktas (Tur)	6/88	Loan						

FA Premier Lge Record

	92/93		37	3	2	20	2	2

FERGUSON Darren   **Manchester United**

Full Name: FERGUSON, Darren   DOB: 9/2/72, Glasgow
FAPL Debut: Away v. Sheffield Utd 15/8/93   Debut Goal: –

Previous Club Details			*Apps*			*Goals*		
Clubs	Signed	Fee	Lge	FLC	FAC	Lge	FLC	FAC
Man Utd	7/90	–	4+5					

FA Premier Lge Record

	92/93		15	1				

FITZGERALD Scott   **Wimbledon**

Full Name: FITZGERALD, Scott Brian   DOB: 13/8/69, Westminister
FAPL Debut: Away v. Leeds Utd 15/8/92   Debut Goal: –

Previous Club Details			*Apps*			*Goals*		
Clubs	Signed	Fee	Lge	FLC	FAC	Lge	FLC	FAC
Wimbledon	7/87	–	34+3	2	2	1		

FA Premier Lge Record

	92/93		18+2	2				

FJORTOFT Jan-Aage   **Swindon Town**

Name: FJORTOFT, Jan -Aage   DOB:

Previous Club Details			*Apps*			*Goals*		
Clubs	Signed	Fee	Lge	FLC	FAC	Lge	FLC	FAC
Rapid Vienna								
Swindon Town	8/93	£500,000						

FLATTS Mark   **Arsenal**

Full Name: FLATTS, Mark Michael   DOB: 14/10/72, Islington
FAPL Debut: Away v. Sheffield Utd † 19/9/92   Debut Goal:

Previous Club Details			*Apps*			*Goals*		
Clubs	Signed	Fee	Lge	FLC	FAC	Lge	FLC	FAC
Arsenal	12/90	–						

FA Premier Lge Record

	92/93		6+4	1				

FLECK Robert   **Chelsea**

Full Name: FLECK, Robert   DOB: 11/8/65, Glasgow
FAPL Debut: Home v. Oldham Athletic 15/8/92
Debut Goal: Away v. Aston Villa 2/9/92
Scottish International

Previous Club Details

Clubs	Signed	Fee	Apps Lge	FLC	FAC	Goals Lge	FLC	FAC
Rangers								
Norwich City	12/87	£580,000	130+13	13	13+2	39	11	11
Chelsea	8/92	£2.1m						

FA Premier Lge Record

92/93			28+3	6	1	2	1	

FLEMING Graig   Oldham Athletic

Full Name: FLEMING, Graig   DOB: 6/10/71, Halifax
FAPL Debut: Away v. Wimbledon † 12/12/92   Debut Goal: –

Previous Club Details

Clubs	Signed	Fee	Apps Lge	FLC	FAC	Goals Lge	FLC	FAC
Halifax Town	3/90	–	56+1	4	3			
Oldham Ath	8/91	£80,000	28+4	2+1	2	1		

FA Premier Lge Record

92/93			23+1	1	2			

FLITCROFT Gary   Manchester City

Full Name: FLITCROFT, Gary William   DOB: 6/12/72, Bolton
Debut Goal: Away v. Ipswich Town 12/12/92
FAPL Debut: Home v. Oldham Athletic † 29/8/92

Previous Club Details

Clubs	Signed	Fee	Apps Lge	FLC	FAC	Goals Lge	FLC	FAC
Man City	7/91	–						
Bury	3/92	Loan	12					

FA Premier Lge Record

92/93			28+4	1+1	5	5		1

FLOWERS Tim   Southampton

Full Name: FLOWERS, Timothy David   DOB: 3/2/67, Kenilworth
FAPL Debut: Home v. Tottenham H. 15/8/92   Debut Goal: –
English International

Previous Club Details

Clubs	Signed	Fee	Apps Lge	FLC	FAC	Goals Lge	FLC	FAC
Wolves	8/84	–	63	5	2			
Southampton	6/86	£70,000	136	21	15			
Swindon Town	3/87	Loan	2					
Swindon Town	11/87	Loan	5					

FA Premier Lge Record

92/93			42	3	1			

FLYNN Sean   Coventry City

Full Name: FLYNN, Sean Michael   DOB: 13/3/68, Birmingham
FAPL Debut: Home v. Middlesbrough † 15/8/92   Debut Goal: –

Previous Club Details   *Apps*   *Goals*

Clubs	Signed	Fee	Lge	FLC	FAC	Lge	FLC	FAC
Coventry City	12/91	£30,000	21+1			2		

FA Premier Lge Record

	92/93		4+3					

FORREST Craig   Ipswich Town

Full Name: FORREST, Craig Lorne   DOB: 20/9/67, Vancouver Canada
FAPL Debut: Home v. Aston Villa 15/8/92   Debut Goal:
Canadian International

Previous Club Details   *Apps*   *Goals*

Clubs	Signed	Fee	Lge	FLC	FAC	Lge	FLC	FAC
Ipswich Town	8/85	–	162	11	8			
Colchester Utd	3/88	Loan	11					

FA Premier Lge Record

	92/93		11	2				

FORRESTER Jamie   Leeds United

Full Name: FORRESTER, Jamie   DOB:
FAPL Debut: Away v. Nottingham Forest † 21/3/93   Debut Goal: –

Previous Club Details   *Apps*   *Goals*

Clubs	Signed	Fee	Lge	FLC	FAC	Lge	FLC	FAC
Auxerre (Fra)								
Leeds Utd		£120,000 (jt)						

FA Premier Lge Record

	92/93		5+5					

FOSTER Colin   West Ham United

Full Name: FOSTER, Colin   DOB:16/7/64 Chislehurst

Previous Club Details   *Apps*   *Goals*

Clubs	Signed	Fee	Lge	FLC	FAC	Lge	FLC	FAC
Leyton Ornt	2/82		173+1	12	19	10		5
Nottingham F	3/87		68+4	8	5	5	1	
West Ham	9/89	£750,000	83+5	5	9	4		1

FOX Ruel   Norwich City

Full Name: FOX, Ruel Adrian   DOB: 14/1/68, Ipswich
FAPL Debut: Away v. Arsenal 15/8/92
Debut Goal: Away v. Arsenal 15/8/92

Previous Club Details   *Apps*   *Goals*

Clubs	Signed	Fee	Lge	FLC	FAC	Lge	FLC	FAC
Norwich City	1/86	–	91+22	9+2	7+2	11	1	

FA Premier Lge Record

	92/93		32+2	0+1	2	4		

FRANCIS Trevor — Sheffield Wednesday

Full Name: FRANCIS, Trevor John
DOB: 19/4/54, Plymouth
FAPL Debut: Home v. Chelsea † 22/8/92
Debut Goal: –
English International

Previous Club Details			Apps			Goals		
Clubs	Signed	Fee	Lge	FLC	FAC	Lge	FLC	FAC
Birmingham C	5/71	–	278+2	18	19	118	3	6
Nottingham F	2/79	£1m	69+1	5	8	28		5
Man City	9/81	£1.2m	26	1	2	12		2
Sampdoria (Ita)	9/82	£800,000						
Atalanta (Ita)	7/86							
Rangers	9/7	£75,000						
QPR	3/88	–	30+2	8	1	12	3	
Sheffield Wed	2/90	–	28+42	5+2	2+1	5	3	1
FA Premier Lge Record								
	92/93		1+4					

FROGGATT Stephen — Aston Villa

Full Name: FROGGATT, Stephen Junior
DOB: 9/3/73, Lincoln
FAPL Debut: Away v. Ipswich Town 15/8/92
Debut Goal: Home v. Crystal Palace 5/9/92

Previous Club Details			Apps			Goals		
Clubs	Signed	Fee	Lge	FLC	FAC	Lge	FLC	FAC
Aston Villa	1/91	–	6+3		2+1			1
FA Premier Lge Record								
	92/93		16+1	2+1	1	1		

GAGE Kevin — Sheffield United

Full Name: GAGE, Kevin William
DOB: 21/4/64, Chiswick
FAPL Debut: Home v. Manchester United 15/8/92
Debut Goal: –

Previous Club Details			Apps			Goals		
Clubs	Signed	Fee	Lge	FLC	FAC	Lge	FLC	FAC
Wimbledon	1/82	–	135+33	7+2	8+3	15	1	1
Aston Villa	7/87	£100,000	113+2	13	9	8	3	1
Sheffield Utd	11/91	£150,000	22		2+2	1		
FA Premier Lge Record								
	92/93		27	3	5			

GALE Tony — West Ham United

Full Name: GALE, Tony
DOB: 19/11/59 Westminster

Previous Club Details			Apps			Goals		
Clubs	Signed	Fee	Lge	FLC	FAC	Lge	FLC	FAC
Fulham	8/77		277	22	16	19	2	
West Ham	7/84	£150,000	262+6	26+2	28	5	1	1

GALLACHER Kevin — Blackburn Rovers

Full Name: GALLACHER, Kevin William DOB: 23/11/66, Clydebank
FAPL Debut: Home v. Blackburn Rovers 29/8/92
Debut Goal: Away v. Oldham Athletic 5/9/92
Scottish International

Previous Club Details

Clubs	Signed	Fee	Apps Lge	FLC	FAC	Goals Lge	FLC	FAC
Coventry City	1/90		80	9	3	22	7	
Blackburn Rv	3/93	£1.6m						

FA Premier Lge Record

Coventry City	92/93		19+1	2	1	6		
Blackburn Rv			9			5		

GANNON John — Sheffield United

Full Name: GANNON, John Spencer DOB: 18/12/66, Wimbledon
FAPL Debut: Home v. Manchester United 15/8/92
Debut Goal: Home v. Oldham Athletic 22/2/93

Previous Club Details

Clubs	Signed	Fee	Apps Lge	FLC	FAC	Goals Lge	FLC	FAC
Wimbledon	12/84	–	13+3	1+1		2		
Crewe Alex	12/86	Loan	14+1					
Sheffield Utd	2/89	Loan	8+8			1		
Sheffield Utd	6/89	–	90+3	7	11	4		

FA Premier Lge Record

	92/93		26+1	4	2	1		

GAYLE Brian — Sheffield United

Full Name: GAYLE, Brian Wilbert DOB: 6/3/65, Kingston
FAPL Debut: Home v. Wimbledon 25/8/92
Debut Goal: Away v. Southampton 27/2/93

Previous Club Details

Clubs	Signed	Fee	Apps Lge	FLC	FAC	Goals Lge	FLC	FAC
Wimbledon	10/84	–	76+7	7	8	3	1	1
Man City	7/88	£325,000	55	8	2	3		
Ipswich Town	1/90	£330,000	58	3	0+1	4		
Sheffield Utd	9/91	£750,000	33	3	3	4		1

FA Premier Lge Record

	92/93		1	4	6	2		

GERRARD Paul — Oldham Athletic

Full Name: GERRARD, Paul William DOB: 22/1/73, Heywood
FAPL Debut: Away v. QPR 5/12/92 Debut Goal: –

Previous Club Details

Clubs	Signed	Fee	Apps Lge	FLC	FAC	Goals Lge	FLC	FAC
Oldham Ath	7/91	–						

FA Premier Lge Record

92/93	25	2

GIBSON Terry — Wimbledon

Full Name: GIBSON, Terence Bradley   DOB: 23/12/62, Walthamstow
FAPL Debut: Home v. Arsenal 5/9/92
Debut Goal: Home v. Tottenham Hotspur 25/10/92

Previous Club Details			*Apps*			*Goals*		
Clubs	Signed	Fee	Lge	FLC	FAC	Lge	FLC	FAC
Tottenham H	1/80	–	16+2	1	5	4	1	1
Coventry City	8/83	£100,000	97+1	7	6	43	3	5
Man Utd	1/86	£650,000	14+9	0+2	1+1	1		
Wimbledon	8/87	£200,000	74+4	10	10	20	6	3
Swindon Town	3/92	Loan	8+1			1		

FA Premier Lge Record

92/93	6+2	2		1	

GIGGS Ryan — Manchester United

Full Name: GIGGS, Ryan Joseph   DOB: 29/11/73, Cardiff
FAPL Debut: Away v. Sheffield United 15/8/92
Debut Goal: Away v. Nottingham Forest 29/8/92
Welsh International

Previous Club Details			*Apps*			*Goals*		
Clubs	Signed	Fee	Lge	FLC	FAC	Lge	FLC	FAC
Man United	12/90	–	23+7	6+2	1	4	3	

FA Premier Lge Record

92/93	40+1	2	2	9	2

GODDARD Paul — Ipswich Town

Full Name: GODDARD, Paul   DOB: 12/10/59, Harlington
FAPL Debut: Home v. Aston Villa 15/8/92
Debut Goal: Away v. Middlesbrough 1/9/92
English International

Previous Club Details			*Apps*			*Goals*		
Clubs	Signed	Fee	Lge	FLC	FAC	Lge	FLC	FAC
QPR	7/77	–	63+7	4+1		23		
West Ham	8/80	£800,000	159+11	26	10+1	54	12	3
Newcastle Utd	11/86	£415,000	61	3	6	19	1	3
Derby County	8/88	£425,000	49	7	1+1	15	2	
Millwall	12/89	£800,000	17+3		4+1	1		1
Ipswich Town	1/91	–	37+6	1	0+1	10		

FA Premier Lge Record

92/93	19+6	4	1+1	3	

GORDON Dale   West Ham United

Name: GORDON, Dale   DOB: 1/1/67, Gt. Yarmouth

Previous Club Details			*Apps*			*Goals*		
Clubs	Signed	Fee	Lge	FLC	FAC	Lge	FLC	FAC
Norwich City	1/84		194+12	21	19	31	3	6
Rangers								
West Ham Utd	8/93							

GOSS Jeremy   Norwich City

Full Name: GOSS, Jeremy   DOB: 11/5/65, Cyprus
FAPL Debut: Away v. Arsenal 15/8/92
Debut Goal: Home v. Crystal Palace 27/1/93
Welsh International

Previous Club Details			*Apps*			*Goals*		
Clubs	Signed	Fee	Lge	FLC	FAC	Lge	FLC	FAC
Norwich City	3/83	–	68+20	5	9+1	4	2	
FA Premier Lge Record								
	92/93		25	3	1+1	1	1	

GOULD Jonathon   Coventry City

Full Name: GOULD, Jonathon   DOB: 18/7/68 London
FAPL Debut: Home v. Liverpool 19/12/92   Debut Goal:

Previous Club Details			*Apps*			*Goals*		
Clubs	Signed	Fee	Lge	FLC	FAC	Lge	FLC	FAC
Coventry City								
FA Premier Lge Record								
	92/93		9					

GRAY Andy   Tottenham Hotspur

Full Name: GRAY, Andrew Arthur   DOB: 22/2/64, Lambeth
FAPL Debut: Away v. Southampton † 15/8/92
Debut Goal: Away v. Crystal Palace 30/1/93
English International

Previous Club Details			*Apps*			*Goals*		
Clubs	Signed	Fee	Lge	FLC	FAC	Lge	FLC	FAC
Crystal Palace	11/84	£2,000	91+7	91	3	27	2	
Aston Villa	11/87	£150,000	34+3	3	3+1	4	1	1
QPR	2/89	£425,000	11			2		
Crystal Palace	8/89	£500,000	87+3	15	11	12	4	2
Tottenham H	2/92	£900,000	14			1		
FA Premier Lge Record								
	92/93		9+8			1		

GREGORY David   Ipswich Town

Full Name: GREGORY, David Spencer   DOB: 23/1/70, Colchester
FAPL Debut: Home v. Crystal Palace † 24/10/92
Debut Goal: Away v. Crystal Palace 1/5/93

Previous Club Details			*Apps*			*Goals*		
Clubs	Signed	Fee	Lge	FLC	FAC	Lge	FLC	FAC
Ipswich Town	3/87	–	15+13	3+1	1	1		
FA Premier Lge Record								
	92/93		1+2	0+1		1		

GROBBELAAR Bruce   Liverpool

Full Name: GROBBELAAR, Bruce David
DOB: 16/10/57, Durban, South Africa
FAPL Debut: Home v. Wimbledon 26/9/92   Debut Goal: –
Zimbabwe International

Previous Club Details			*Apps*			*Goals*		
Clubs	Signed	Fee	Lge	FLC	FAC	Lge	FLC	FAC
Crewe Alex	21/79	–	24					
Vancouver (US)	5/80	–						
Liverpool	3/81	£250,000	406	63	60			
Stocke City	3/93	Loan	4					
FA Premier Lge Record								
	92/93		5	2				

GROENENDIJK Alphonse   Manchester City

Name: GROENENDIJK, Alphonse   DOB:

Previous Club Details			*Apps*			*Goals*		
Clubs	Signed	Fee	Lge	FLC	FAC	Lge	FLC	FAC
Ajax, Hol								
Man City	8/93	£500,000						

GROVES Perry   Southampton

Full Name: GROVES, Perry   DOB: 19/4/65, Bow
FAPL Debut: Away v. Blackburn Rovers † 18/8/92
Debut Goal: Home v. Leeds United 19/9/92

Previous Club Details			*Apps*			*Goals*		
Clubs	Signed	Fee	Lge	FLC	FAC	Lge	FLC	FAC
Colchester Utd	6/82	–	142+14	9+1	6	26	1	1
Arsenal	9/86	£50,000	91+64	18+8	11+6	21	5	1
Southampton	8/92	£750,000						
FA Premier Lge Record								
Arsenal	92/93		0+1					
Southampton			13+2	2	0+1	2		

GUENTHEV Bonitcho — Ipswich Town

Full Name: GUENTHEV, Bonitcho   DOB:
FAPL Debut: Home v. Manchester City 12/12/92
Debut Goal: Home v. Blackburn Rovers 28/12/92

Previous Club Details

Clubs	Signed	Fee	Apps Lge	FLC	FAC	Goals Lge	FLC	FAC
Sporting Lisbon								
Ipswich Town	12/92	£250,000						

FA Premier Lge Record

92/93			19+2	2	4	3 ·		3

GUNN Bryan — Norwich City

Full Name: GUNN, Bryan James   DOB: 22/12/63, Thurso
FAPL Debut: Away v. Arsenal 15/8/92   Debut Goal:
Scottish International

Previous Club Details

Clubs	Signed	Fee	Apps Lge	FLC	FAC	Goals Lge	FLC	FAC
Norwich City	10/86	£150,000	200	18	20			

FA Premier Lge Record

92/93			42	2	2			

HALL Gareth — Chelsea

Full Name: HALL, Gareth David   DOB: 20/3/69, Croydon
FAPL Debut: Home v. Oldham Athletic 15/8/92
Debut Goal: Home v. Ipswich Town 17/10/92
Welsh International

Previous Club Details

Clubs	Signed	Fee	Apps Lge	FLC	FAC	Goals Lge	FLC	FAC
Chelsea	5/86	–	71+12	7	6	1		

FA Premier Lge Record

92/93			36+1	4		2		

HALL Richard — Southampton

Full Name: HALL, Richard Anthony   DOB: 14/3/72, Ipswich
FAPL Debut: Home v. Tottenham Hotspur 15/8/92
Debut Goal: Away v. Oldham Athletic 31/10/92

Previous Club Details

Clubs	Signed	Fee	Apps Lge	FLC	FAC	Goals Lge	FLC	FAC
Scunthorpe	3/90	–	22	2	3	3		
Southampton	2/91	£200,000	21+6	4+1	5	2		2

FA Premier Lge Record

92/93			28	1	1	4		

HALLE Gunner   Oldham Athletic

Full Name: HALLE, Gunnar   DOB: 11/8/65, Oslo, Norway
FAPL Debut: Away v. Chelsea 15/8/92
Debut Goal: Home v. Oldham Athletic 22/8/92
Norwegian International

Previous Club Details			Apps			Goals		
Clubs	Signed	Fee	Lge	FLC	FAC	Lge	FLC	FAC
Oldham Ath	2/91	£280,000	27	1				
FA Premier Lge Record								
	92/93		41	1	2	5		

HALLWORTH Jon   Oldham Athletic

Full Name: HALLWORTH, Jonathan   DOB: 26/10/65, Stockport
FAPL Debut: Away v. Chelsea 15/8/92   Debut Goal: –

Previous Club Details			Apps			Goals		
Clubs	Signed	Fee	Lge	FLC	FAC	Lge	FLC	FAC
Ipswich Town	5/83	–	45	4	1			
Bristol Rovers	1/85	Loan	2					
Oldham Ath	2/89	£75,000	118	12	13			
FA Premier Lge Record								
	92/93		16	3				

HAMMOND Nicky   Swindon Town

Full Name: HAMMOND, Nicky   DOB: 7/9/67 Hornchurch

Previous Club Details			Apps			Goals		
Clubs	Signed	Fee	Lge	FLC	FAC	Lge	FLC	FAC
Arsenal	7/85							
Bristol Rovers	8/86	Loan	3					
Peterborough	9/86	Loan						
Aberdeen	2/87	Loan						
Swindon Tn	7/87		47	6	5			

HARDING Paul   West Ham United

Name: HARDING, Paul   DOB: 6/3/64, Mitcham

Previous Club Details			Apps			Goals		
Clubs	Signed	Fee	Lge	FLC	FAC	Lge	FLC	FAC
Barnet								
Notts County	9/90	£60,000	45+9	1	6	1		
West Ham U.	8/93							

HARFORD Mick   Coventry City

Full Name: HARFORD, Mick   DOB: 12/5/59, Sunderland
FAPL Debut: Home v. Oldham Athletic 15/8/92
Debut Goal: Home v. Oldham Athletic 15/8/92

Previous Club Details			*Apps*			*Goals*		
Clubs	Signed	Fee	Lge	FLC	FAC	Lge	FLC	FAC
Lincoln City	7/77		109+6	8	3	41	5	
Newcastle	12/80	£180,000	18+1			4		
Bristol City	8/81	£160,000	30	5	5	11	1	2
Birmingham	3/82	£100,000	92	10	7	25	6	2
Luton Town	12/84	£250,000	135+4	16	27	57	10	11
Derby County	1/90	£450,000	58	7	1	15	3	
Luton Town	9/91	£325,000	29	1		12		
Chelsea	8/92	£300,000						
Sunderland	3/93	£250,000	10+1			2		
Coventry City	7/93	£200,000						
FA Premier Lge Record								
Chelsea	92/93		27+1	5	1	9	2	

HARKES John   Sheffield Wednesday

Full Name: HARKES, John Andres   DOB: 8/3/67, New Jersey, USA
FAPL Debut: Home v. Nottingham Forrest † 19/8/92
Debut Goal: Away v. Chelsea 30/1/93
United States International

Previous Club Details			*Apps*			*Goals*		
Clubs	Signed	Fee	Lge	FLC	FAC	Lge	FLC	FAC
Sheffield Wed	10/90	£70,000	36+16	10	5+1	5	1	
FA Premier Lge Record								
	92/93		23+6	7	7	2	2	1

HARKNESS Steve   Liverpool

Full Name: HARKNESS, Steven   DOB: 27/8/71, Carlisle
FAPL Debut: Away v. Ipswich Town 25/8/92
Debut Goal: Home v. Tottenham Hotspur 8/5/93

Previous Club Details			*Apps*			*Goals*		
Clubs	Signed	Fee	Lge	FLC	FAC	Lge	FLC	FAC
Carlisle Utd	3/89	–	12+1					
Liverpool	7/89	£75,000	7+4	2+1	1			
FA Premier Lge Record								
	92/93		9+1			1		

HARPER Alan   Everton

Full Name: HARPER, Alan   DOB: 1/11/60, Liverpool
FAPL Debut: Away v. Manchester Utd 19/8/92   Debut Goal: –

Previous Club Details			*Apps*			*Goals*		
Clubs	Signed	Fee	Lge	FLC	FAC	Lge	FLC	FAC
Liverpool	4/78	–						
Everton	6/83	£100,000	103+24	17+2	10+8	4		1
Sheffield Wed	7/88	£275,000	32+3	1+1	1			

Man City	12/89	£150,000	46+4	3	6	1	1
Everton	8/91	£200,000	29+4	1+1	1		

FA Premier Lge Record

92/93	16+2	4	1+1		

HARTFIELD Charlie Sheffield United

Full Name: HARTFIELD, Charles   DOB: 4/9/71, Lambeth
FAPL Debut: Home v. Manchester United † 15/8/93   Debut Goal: –

Previous Club Details			*Apps*			*Goals*		
Clubs	Signed	Fee	Lge	FLC	FAC	Lge	FLC	FAC
Arsenal	9/89	–						
Sheffield Utd	8/91	–	6+1	1				

FA Premier Lge Record

92/93	12+5		3					

HAZARD Micky Swindon Town

Full Name: HOWEY, Stephen   DOB: 5/2/60 Sunderland

Previous Club Details			*Apps*			*Goals*		
Clubs	Signed	Fee	Lge	FLC	FAC	Lge	FLC	FAC
Tottenham H	2/78		73+18	11+3	7+3	13	5	2
Chealsea	9/85	£310,000	78+3	7+3	4+2	9	1	1
Portsmouth	1/90	£100,000	8			1		
Swindon Tn	9/90	£130,000	105+5	10	7	17	1	

HEANEY Neil Arsenal

Full Name: HEANEY, Neil Andrew   DOB: 3/11/71, Middlesbrough
FAPL Debut: Home v. Liverpool † 31/1/193   Debut Goal: –

Previous Club Details			*Apps*			*Goals*		
Clubs	Signed	Fee	Lge	FLC	FAC	Lge	FLC	FAC
Arsenal	11/89	–	0+1					
Hartlepool Utd	1/91	Loan	2+1					
Cambridge Utd	1/92	Loan	9+4		1	2		
Arsenal								

FA Premier Lge Record

92/93	3+2							

HENDRY Colin Blackburn Rovers

Full Name: HENDRY, Edward Colin James   DOB: 7/12/65, Keith
FAPL Debut: Away v. Crystal Palace 15/8/92
Debut Goal: Home v. Coventry City 26/1/93

Previous Club Details			*Apps*			*Goals*		
Clubs	Signed	Fee	Lge	FLC	FAC	Lge	FLC	FAC
Blackburn Rv	3/87	£30,000	99+3	4	3	22		
Man City	11/89	£700,000	57+6	4+1	5	5	1	2

Blackburn Rv	11/91	£700,000	24+4		0+1	4

FA Premier Lge Record

		92/93	41	7	4	1

HENRY John   Tottenham Hotspur

Full Name: HENDRY, John   DOB: 6/1/70, Glasgow
FAPL Debut: Home v. Manchester Utd † 19/9/92 Debut Goal: –

Previous Club Details			*Apps*			*Goals*		
Clubs	Signed	Fee	Lge	FLC	FAC	Lge	FLC	FAC
Tottenham H	7/90	£50,000	3+6	0+1		3		
Charlton Ath	2/92	Loan	1+4			1		

FA Premier Lge Record

		92/93	2+3				

HENRY Nick   Oldham Athletic

Full Name: HENRY, Nicholas Ian   DOB: 21/2/69, Liverpool
FAPL Debut: Away v. Chelsea 15/8/92
Debut Goal: Away v. Chelsea 15/8/92

Previous Club Details			*Apps*			*Goals*		
Clubs	Signed	Fee	Lge	FLC	FAC	Lge	FLC	FAC
Oldham Ath	6/87	–	142+7	16+3	14	10	2	

FA Premier Lge Record

		92/93	32	4	1	6	1

HILL Andy   Manchester City

Full Name: HILL, Andrew Rowland   DOB: 20/1/65, Maltby
FAPL Debut: Home v. QPR 17/8/92
Debut Goal: Home v. Leeds United 7/11/92

Previous Club Details			*Apps*			*Goals*		
Clubs	Signed	Fee	Lge	FLC	FAC	Lge	FLC	FAC
Man Utd	1/83	–						
Bury	7/84	–	264	22	12	10	1	
Man City	12/90	£200,000	43+1	5		5		

FA Premier Lge Record

		92/93	23+1	3	2+1	1

HILL Danny   Tottenham Hotspur

Full Name: HILL, Danny   DOB: 1/10/74, Edmonton, London
FAPL Debut: Away v. Chelsea † 23/3/92   Debut Goal: Away v.

Previous Club Details			*Apps*			*Goals*		
Clubs	Signed	Fee	Lge	FLC	FAC	Lge	FLC	FAC
Tottenham H								

FA Premier Lge Record

		92/93	2+2				

HILLIER David
Arsenal

Full Name: HILLIER, David   DOB: 18/12/69, Blackheath
FAPL Debut: Home v. Norwich 15/8/92
Debut Goal: Home v. Sheffield United 9/1/93

Previous Club Details			*Apps*			*Goals*		
Clubs	Signed	Fee	Lge	FLC	FAC	Lge	FLC	FAC
Arsenal	2/88	–	36+7	2	3+2	1		
FA Premier Lge Record								
	92/93		27+3	7+1	4+1	1		

HINCHCLIFFE Andy
Everton

Full Name: HINCHCLIFFE, Andrew   DOB: 5/2/69, Manchester
FAPL Debut: Home v. Sheffield Wednesday 15/8/92
Debut Goal: Home v. Nottingham Forest 13/3/93

Previous Club Details			*Apps*			*Goals*		
Clubs	Signed	Fee	Lge	FLC	FAC	Lge	FLC	FAC
Man City	6/86	–	107+5	11	12	8	1	1
Everton	7/90	£800,000	36+3	5	5	1		
FA Premier Lge Record								
	92/93		25	3+2		1		

HIRST David
Sheffield Wednesday

Full Name: HIRST, David Eric   DOB: 7/12/67, Cudworth
FAPL Debut: Away v. Everton 15/8/92
Debut Goal: Home v. Nottingham Forest 19/8/92
English International

Previous Club Details			*Apps*			*Goals*		
Clubs	Signed	Fee	Lge	FLC	FAC	Lge	FLC	FAC
Barnsley	11/85	–	26+2	1		9		
Sheffield Wed	8/86	£200,000	168+21	8+5	4+2	72	7	5
FA Premier Lge Record								
	92/93		22	3+2	3+2	11	3	1

HIRST Lee
Coventry City

Name: HIRST, Lee   DOB: 26/1/69, Sheffield

Previous Club Details			*Apps*			*Goals*		
Clubs	Signed	Fee	Lge	FLC	FAC	Lge	FLC	FAC
Scarborough	2/90		107+1	9	9	6	3	
Coventry City	8/93							

HITCHCOCK Kevin
Chelsea

Full Name: HITCHCOCK, Kevin Joseph   DOB: 5/10/62, Canning Town
FAPL Debut: Away v. Manchester C. 20/9/92   Debut Goal: –

Previous Club Details			Apps			Goals		
Clubs	Signed	Fee	Lge	FLC	FAC	Lge	FLC	FAC
Nottingham F	8/83	£15,000						
Mansfield Tn	2/84	Loan	14					
Mansfield Tn	6/84	£140,000	168	12	10			
Chelsea	3/88	£250,000	35	2	4			
Northampton T	12/90	Loan	17					
West Ham	3/93	Loan						
FA Premier Lge Record								
92/93			20	6	1			

HODDLE Glen
Chelsea
Full Name: HODDLE, Glen   DOB: 27/10/57 Hayes
International: England

Previous Club Details			Apps			Goals		
Clubs	Signed	Fee	Lge	FLC	FAC	Lge	FLC	FAC
Tottenham H	4/75		370+7	44	47+1	89	10	11
Monaco, Fra.	7/87	£800,000						
Swindon Tn	8/91		63+1	6	1	1	1	
Chelsea	6/93	£75,000						

HODGE Steve
Leeds United
Full Name: HODGE, Stephen Brian   DOB: 25/10/62, Nottingham
FAPL Debut: Home v. Wimbledon † 15/8/92
Debut Goal: Home v. Aston Villa 13/9/93

Previous Club Details			Apps			Goals		
Clubs	Signed	Fee	Lge	FLC	FAC	Lge	FLC	FAC
Nottingham F	10/80	–	122+1	10	6	30	2	
Aston Villa	8/85	£450,000	53	12	4	12	3	1
Tottenham H	12/86	£650,000	44+1	2	7	7		2
Nottingham F	8/88	£550,000	79+3	20+1	11+1	20	6	2
Leeds Utd	7/91	£900,000	12+11	3+2	1	7		
FA Premier Lge Record								
92/93			9+14	0+1		2		

HODGES Glyn
Sheffield United
Full Name: HODGES, Glyn Peter   DOB: 30/4/63, Streatham
FAPL Debut: Home v. Manchester United 15/8/92
Debut Goal: Home v. Wimbledon 25/8/92

Previous Club Details			Apps			Goals		
Clubs	Signed	Fee	Lge	FLC	FAC	Lge	FLC	FAC
Wimbledon	2/81	–	200+32	14+2	13+2	49	3	2
Newcastle Utd	7/87	£200,000	7					
Watford	10/87	£300,000	82+4	5	8	15	2	2
Crystal Palace	7/90	£410,000	5+2	2+2		1		

Sheffield Utd	1/91	£450,000	34+4		3+2	6		1
FA Premier Lge Record								
	92/93		28+3	2+1	7	4		2

HODGES Lee   Tottenham Hotspur

Full Name: HODGES, Lee Leslie   DOB: 4/9/73, Epping
FAPL Debut: Home v. Wimbledon 5/5/93   Debut Goal: –

Previous Club Details			Apps			Goals		
Clubs	Signed	Fee	Lge	FLC	FAC	Lge	FLC	FAC
Tottenham H	2/92	–						
Plymouth	2/93	Loan	6+1			2		
FA Premier Lge Record								
	92/93		0+4					

HOLDEN Rick   Manchester City

Full Name: HOLDEN, Richard William   DOB: 9/9/64, Skipton
FAPL Debut: Home v. QPR 17/8/92
Debut Goal: Home v. Nottingham Forest 3/10/92

Previous Club Details			Apps			Goals		
Clubs	Signed	Fee	Lge	FLC	FAC	Lge	FLC	FAC
Burnley	3/86	–	0+1					
Halifax Town	9/86	–	66+1	2	7	12		
Watford	3/88	£125,000	42	2	6	8		
Oldham Ath	8/89	£165,000	125+4	15+1	13	19	4	2
Man City								
FA Premier Lge Record								
	92/93		40+1	3	5	3	1	1

HOLDSWORTH Darren   Wimbledon

Full Name: HOLDSWORTH, Darren   DOB: 8/11/68, London
FAPL Debut: Away v. Leeds United 15/8/92
Debut Goal: Home v. Coventry City 22/8/92

Previous Club Details			Apps			Goals		
Clubs	Signed	Fee	Lge	FLC	FAC	Lge	FLC	FAC
Watford	11/86		2+14			3		
Carlisle Utd	2/88	Loan	4			1		
Port Vale	3/88	Loan	6			2		
Swansea City	8/88	Loan	4+1			1		
Brentford	10/88	Loan	2+5			1		
Brentford	9/89	£125,000	106+4	7+1	6	53	6	7
Wimbledon	7/92	£720,000						
FA Premier Lge Record								
	92/93		34+2	2+1	2+1	19		

HOLLOWAY Ian
Queens Park Rangers

Full Name: HOLLOWAY, Ian Scott
DOB: 12/3/63, Kingswood
FAPL Debut: Away v. Manchester City 17/8/92
Debut Goal: Home v. Tottenham Hotspur 3/10/92

Clubs	Signed	Fee	Apps Lge	FLC	FAC	Goals Lge	FLC	FAC
Previous Club Details								
Bristol Rovers	3/81		104+7	10	8	14	1	
Wimbledon	7/85	£35,000	19	3	1	2		
Brentford	3/86	£25,000	27+3	2	3	2		
Torquay Utd	1/87	Loan	5					
Bristol Rovers	8/87	£10,000	179	5		26		1
QPR	8/91	£230,000	34+6	3	1			
FA Premier Lge Record								
92/93			23+1	4	2	2		1

HOLMES Matt
West Ham United

Full Name: HOLMES, Matthew J.
DOB: 1/8/69, Luton

Clubs	Signed	Fee	Apps Lge	FLC	FAC	Goals Lge	FLC	FAC
Previous Club Details								
Bournemouth	9/88		105+9	7	8+2	8		
Cardiff City	3/89	Loan	0+1					
West Ham U	8/92	£40,000	6+11		1		1	

HOLMES Paul
Everton

Full Name: HOLMES, Paul
DOB: 18/2/68, Wortley
FAPL Debut: Home v. Ipswich Town 24/3/92
Debut Goal: –

Clubs	Signed	Fee	Apps Lge	FLC	FAC	Goals Lge	FLC	FAC
Previous Club Details								
Doncaster Rv	2/86		45+2		3+1	1		1
Torquay	8/88	£6,000	127+11	9	9+2	4		1
Birmingham C	6/92		12		1			
Everton	3/93	£100,000						
FA Premier Lge Record								
92/93			4					

HOOPER Mike
Liverpool

Full Name: HOOPER, Michael Dudley
DOB: 10/2/64, Bristol
FAPL Debut: Home v. Middlesbrough 7/11/92
Debut Goal:

Clubs	Signed	Fee	Apps Lge	FLC	FAC	Goals Lge	FLC	FAC
Previous Club Details								
Bristol City	1/84	–	1		1			
Wrexham	2/85		34	4				
Liverpool	10/85	£40,000	42	7	3			
Leicester City	9/90	Loan	14					
FA Premier Lge Record								
92/93			8+1	3	2			

HOPKIN David Chelsea

Full Name: HOPKIN, David   DOB: 21/8/70, Greenock
FAPL Debut: Away v. Liverpool 10/2/92   Debut Goal:

Previous Club Details

Clubs	Signed	Fee	Apps Lge	FLC	FAC	Goals Lge	FLC	FAC
Morton								
Chelsea	9/92	£300,000						

FA Premier Lge Record

92/93			2+2					

HORLOCK Kevin Swindon Town

Full Name: HORLOCK, Kevin   DOB: 1/11/72 Plumstead

Previous Club Details

Clubs	Signed	Fee	Apps Lge	FLC	FAC	Goals Lge	FLC	FAC
West Ham	7/91							
Swindon Tn	8/92	N/c	13+1	2	1	1		

HORNE Barry Everton

Full Name: HORNE, Barry   DOB: 18/5/62, St Asaph
FAPL Debut: Home v. Sheffield Wednesday 15/8/92
Debut Goal: Home v. Sheffield Wednesday 15/8/92

Previous Club Details

Clubs	Signed	Fee	Apps Lge	FLC	FAC	Goals Lge	FLC	FAC
Wrexham	6/84	–	136	10	7	17	1	2
Portsmouth	7/87	£60,000	66+4	3	6	7		
Southampton	3/89	£700,000	111+1	15+2	15	6	3	3
Everton	8/92	£695,000						

FA Premier Lge Record

92/93			34	5+1	0+1	1		

HOUGHTON Ray Aston Villa

Full Name: HOUGHTON, Raymond James   DOB: 9/1/62, Glasgow
FAPL Debut: Away v. Ipswich Town 15/8/92
Debut Goal: Home v. Norwich City 28/11/92
Eire International

Previous Club Details

Clubs	Signed	Fee	Apps Lge	FLC	FAC	Goals Lge	FLC	FAC
West Ham	7/89	–	0+1					
Fulham	7/82	–	129	12	4	16	2	3
Oxford Utd	9/85	£147,000	83	13	3	10	3	
Liverpool	10/87	£825,000	147+6	13	26+1	28	3	4
Aston Villa	7/92	£900,000						

FA Premier Lge Record

92/93			39	4	4	3		1

HOWELLS David — Tottenham Hotspur

Full Name: HOWELLS, David — DOB: 15/12/67, Guildford
FAPL Debut: Away v. Southampton 15/8/92
Debut Goal: Away v. Blackburn Rovers 7/11/92

Previous Club Details			Apps			Goals		
Clubs	Signed	Fee	Lge	FLC	FAC	Lge	FLC	FAC
Tottenham H	1/85	–	106+28	11+2	5+2	14	1	1
FA Premier Lge Record								
	92/93		16+2	0+1	2+1	1		

HOWEY Steve — Newcastle United

Full Name: HOWEY, Stephen — DOB: 26/10/71 Sunderland

Previous Club Details			Apps			Goals		
Clubs	Signed	Fee	Lge	FLC	FAC	Lge	FLC	FAC
Newcastle	12/89		57+17	6+2	3	3	1	

HOYLAND Jamie — Sheffield United

Full Name: HOYLAND, Jamie William — DOB: 23/1/66, Sheffield
FAPL Debut: Home v. Nottingham Forrest 24/10/92
Debut Goal: Home v. QPR 30/1/93

Previous Club Details			Apps			Goals		
Clubs	Signed	Fee	Lge	FFC	FAC	Lge	FLC	FAC
Man City	11/83	–	2	0+1				
Bury	7/86	–	169+3	14+1	6	35	5	
Sheffield Utd	7/90	£250,000	40+7	3+1	2	4	1	
FA Premier Lge Record								
	92/93		15+7		2			

HUGHES Mark — Manchester United

Full Name: HUGHES, Leslie Mark — DOB: 1/11/63, Wrexham
FAPL Debut: Away v. Sheffield United 15/8/92
Debut Goal: Away v. Sheffield United 15/8/92

Previous Club Details			Apps			Goals		
Clubs	Signed	Fee	Lge	FLC	FAC	Lge	FLC	FAC
Man Utd	11/80	–	85+4	5+1	10	37	4	4
Barcelona (Esp)	7/86	£2.5m						
Bayern Munich	10/87	Loan						
Man Utd	7/88	£1.5m	141+4	21	20+1	47	6	7
FA Premier Lge Record								
	92/93		41	3	2	15	1	

HUMPHRIES Mark   Leeds United
Name: HUMPHRIES, Mark   DOB: 23/12/71. Glasgow
Previous Club Details   *Apps*   *Goals*
Clubs	Signed Fee	Lge	FLC	FAC	Lge	FLC	FAC
Aberdeen	5/90						
Leeds Utd	8/93						

HUNT Paul   Swindon Town
Name: HUNT, Paul   DOB: 8/10/71 Swindon
Previous Club Details   *Apps*   *Goals*
Clubs	Signed Fee	Lge	FLC	FAC	Lge	FLC	FAC
Swindon Tn	7/89	5+6	0+3				

HURLOCK Terry   Southampton
Full Name: HURLOCK, Terence Alan   DOB: 27/9/58, Hackney
FAPL Debut: Home v. Tottenham H. 15/8/92   Debut Goal: –
Previous Club Details   *Apps*   *Goals*
Clubs	Signed Fee		Lge	FLC	FAC	Lge	FLC	FAC
Brentford	8/80	£6,000	220	17	17	18	2	4
Reading	2/86	£82,000	29	3	1			
Millwall	2/87	£95,000	103+1	7	5	8	2	
Rangers	8/90	£325,000						
Southampton	9/91	£400,000	27+2	4	5			
FA Premier Lge Record
| | 92/93 | | 30 | 3 | | | | |

HURST Lee   Coventry City
Full Name: HURST, Lee Jason   DOB: 21/9/70, Nuneaton
FAPL Debut: Home v. Middlesbrough 15/8/92
Debut Goal: Away v. Sheffield United 2/9/92
Previous Club Details   *Apps*   *Goals*
Clubs	Signed Fee	Lge	FLC	FAC	Lge	FLC	FAC
Coventry City	5/89 –	11+3	2+1	1+1			
FA Premier Lge Record
| | 92/93 | 35 | 1 | | 2 | | |

HUTCHISON Don   Liverpool
Full Name: HUTCHISON, Donald   DOB: 9/5/71, Gateshead
FAPL Debut: Away v. Aston Villa 19/9/92
Debut Goal: Home v. Sheffield Wednesday 3/10/92
Previous Club Details   *Apps*   *Goals*
Clubs	Signed Fee	Lge	FLC	FAC	Lge	FLC	FAC
Hartlepool Utd	3/90 –	19+5	1+1	2	3		
Liverpool	11/90 £175,000	0+3					
FA Premier Lge Record
| | 92/93 | 27+4 | 5 | 1+1 | 7 | 2 | |

HYDE Graham — Sheffield Wednesday

Full Name: HYDE, Graham DOB: 10/11/70, Doncaster
FAPL Debut: Away v. Everton 15/8/92
Debut Goal: Away v. Nottingham Forest 12/9/92

Previous Club Details

Clubs	Signed	Fee	Apps Lge	FLC	FAC	Goals Lge	FLC	FAC
Sheffield Wed	5/88	–	9+4	1	1+1			

FA Premier Lge Record

92/93			14+6	2+1	0+4	1		

IMPEY Andy — Queens Park Rangers

Full Name: IMPEY, Andrew Rodney DOB: 30/9/71, Hammersmith
FAPL Debut: Away v. Manchester City 17/8/92
Debut Goal: Away v. Coventry 26/8/92

Previous Club Details

Clubs	Signed	Fee	Apps Lge	FFC	FAC	Goals Lge	FLC	FAC
QPR	6/90	£35,000	13	0+1				

FA Premier Lge Record

92/93			39+1	3	0+1	2		

INCE Paul — Manchester United

Full Name: INCE, Paul Emerson Carlyle DOB: 21/10/67, Ilford
FAPL Debut: Away v. Sheffield United 15/8/92
Debut Goal: Home v. Manchester City 6/12/92

Previous Club Details

Clubs	Signed	Fee	Apps Lge	FLC	FAC	Goals Lge	FLC	FAC
West Ham	7/85	–	66+6	9	8+2	7	3	1
Man Utd	8/89	£1.250,000	87+3	15+1	6+1	6		2

FA Premier Lge Record

92/93			41	3	2	6		

IRELAND Simon — Blackburn Rovers

Name: IRELAND, Simon DOB:
FAPL Debut: Away v. Manchester City † 30/1/93 Debut Goal: –

Previous Club Details

Clubs	Signed	Fee	Apps Lge	FLC	FAC	Goals Lge	FLC	FAC
Huddersfield	7/90		10+9	1	0+1	1		
Wrexham	2/92	Loan	2+3					
Blackburn Rv	10/92	£200,000						

FA Premier Lge Record

92/93			0+1					

IRWIN Dennis — Manchester United

Full Name: IRWIN, Dennis Joseph DOB: 31/10/65, Cork
FAPL Debut: Away v. Sheffield United 15/8/92
Debut Goal: Home v. Ipswich 22/8/92

Clubs	Signed	Fee	Apps Lge	FLC	FAC	Goals Lge	FLC	FAC
Leeds Utd	10/83	–	72	5	3	1		
Oldham Ath	5/86	–	166+1	19	13	4	3	
Man Utd	6/90	£625,000	70+2	14+1	6	4		

FA Premier Lge Record

92/93			40	3	3	5		

JACKSON Matthew — Everton

Full Name: JACKSON, Matthew Alan   DOB: 19/10/71, Leeds
FAPL Debut: Home v. Sheffield Wednesday 15/8/92
Debut Goal: Away v. Crystal Palace 9/1/93

Clubs	Signed	Fee	Apps Lge	FLC	FAC	Goals Lge	FLC	FAC
Luton Town	7/90	–	7+2	2				
Preston N End	3/91	Loan	3+1					
Everton	10/91	£600,000	30		2	1		

FA Premier Lge Record

92/93			25+2	3	2	3		

JAMES David — Liverpool

Full Name: JAMES, David   DOB: 1/8/70, Welwyn Garden City
FAPL Debut: Away v. Nottingham Forest 16/8/92   Debut Goal: –

Clubs	Signed	Fee	Apps Lge	FLC	FAC	Goals Lge	FLC	FAC
Watford	7/88	–	89	6	2			
Liverpool	6/92	£1m						

FA Premier Lge Record

92/93			29	1				

JEMSON Nigel — Sheffield Wednesday

Full Name: JEMSON, Nigel Bradley   DOB: 10/8/69, Preston
FAPL Debut: Away v. Arsenal † 29/8/92   Debut Goal:

Clubs	Signed	Fee	Apps Lge	FLC	FAC	Goals Lge	FLC	FAC
Preston N End	6/87	–	28+4		2	8		1
Nottingham F	3/88	£150,000	45+2	9	3	13	4	3
Bolton Wnd	12/88	Loan	4+1					
Preston N End	3/89	Loan	6+3			2		
Sheffield Wed	9/91	£800,000	11+9	1+2	1	4		

FA Premier Lge Record

92/93			5+8	0+1	0+2			

JENKINSON Leigh
Coventry City

Full Name: JENKINSON, Leigh
DOB:
FAPL Debut: Home v. Arsenal 13/3/93
Debut Goal:

Previous Club Details			*Apps*			*Goals*	
Clubs	Signed	Fee	Lge	FLC	FAC	Lge	FLC	FAC
Hull City	3/93	£300,000						
Coventry City								

FA Premier Lge Record

| 92/93 | 2+3 |

JENSON John
Arsenal

Full Name: JENSON, John
DOB: 3/5/65
FAPL Debut: Home v. Norwich City 15/8/92
Debut Goal: –

Previous Club Details			*Apps*			*Goals*	
Clubs	Signed	Fee	Lge	FLC	FAC	Lge	FLC	FAC
Brondby (Den)								
Arsenal	8/92	£1.1m						

FA Premier Lge Record

| 92/93 | 29+3 | 3 | 4 |

JOBSON Richard
Oldham Athletic

Full Name: JOBSON, Richard Ian
DOB: 9/5/63, Holderness
FAPL Debut: Away v. Chelsea 15/8/92
Debut Goal: Away v. Manchester City 29/8/92

Previous Club Details			*Apps*			*Goals*	
Clubs	Signed	Fee	Lge	FLC	FAC	Lge	FLC	FAC
Watford	11/82	£22,000	26+2	2	0+1	4		
Hull City	2/85	£40,000	219+2	18	12	17		
Oldham Ath	9/90	£460,000	79+3	6	4	1	1	

FA Premier Lge Record

| 92/93 | 40 | 4 | 2 | 2 |

JOHNSEN Erland
Chelsea

Full Name: JOHNSEN, Erland
DOB: 5/4/67, Fredrikstad, Norway
FAPL Debut: Away v. Nottingham Forest 16/1/93
Debut Goal: –

Previous Club Details			*Apps*			*Goals*	
Clubs	Signed	Fee	Lge	FLC	FAC	Lge	FLC	FAC
Chelsea	11/89	£306,000	30+1		1			

FA Premier Lge Record

| 92/93 | 13 | 1 |

JOHNSON Andrew
Norwich City

Full Name: JOHNSON, Andrew James
DOB: 2/5/74, Bath
FAPL Debut: Home v. Manchester City † 20/2/93
Debut Goal: Away v. Middlesbrough 8/5/93

Clubs	Signed	Fee	Lge	FLC	FAC	Lge	FLC	FAC
			Apps			*Goals*		
Norwich City	3/92	–	2					

FA Premier Lge Record

92/93			1+1			1		

JOHNSON Gavin Ipswich Town

Full Name: JOHNSON, Gavin DOB: 10/10/70, Eye
FAPL Debut: Home v. Aston Villa 15/9/92
Debut Goal: Home v. Aston Villa 15/9/92

Previous Club Details

Clubs	Signed	Fee	Lge	FLC	FAC	Lge	FLC	FAC
			Apps			*Goals*		
Ipswich Town	2/89	–	45+14	1+1	5	5		1

FA Premier Lge Record

92/93	39+1	7	4	5	2		

JOHNSTON Mo Everton

Full Name: JOHNSTON, Maurice DOB: 30/4/63, Glasgow
FAPL Debut: Away v. Manchester United 19/8/92
Debut Goal: Away v. Manchester United 19/8/92

Previous Club Details

Clubs	Signed	Fee	Lge	FLC	FAC	Lge	FLC	FAC
			Apps			*Goals*		
Watford	11/83	£200,000	37+1	1	7	23		3
Celtic	10/84	£400,000						
Nantes (Fra)	6/87	£1m						
Rangers	7/89	£1.5m						
Everton	11/91	£1.5m	21	1	1	7		

FA Premier Lge Record

92/93	7+6	1+1	3		

JONES Lee Liverpool

Full Name: JONES, Lee DOB:

Previous Club Details

Clubs	Signed	Fee	Lge	FLC	FAC	Lge	FLC	FAC
			Apps			*Goals*		
Liverpool								

FA Premier Lge Record

92/93

JONES Rob Liverpool

Full Name: JONES, Robert Marc DOB: 5/11/71, Wrexham
FAPL Debut: Home v. Sheffield Utd 19/8/92 Debut Goal: –

Previous Club Details

Clubs	Signed	Fee	Lge	FLC	FAC	Lge	FLC	FAC
			Apps			*Goals*		
Crewe Alex	12/88		60+16	9	0+3	2		
Liverpool	10/91	£300,000	28		9			

FA Premier Lge Record
| | 92/93 | 30 | 2+1 | 2 |

JONES Ryan   Sheffield Wednesday

Full Name: JONES, Ryan   DOB: 23/7/73, Sheffield
FAPL Debut: Away v. Coventry City 3/3/93   Debut Goal:

Previous Club Details			*Apps*			*Goals*		
Clubs	Signed	Fee	Lge	FLC	FAC	Lge	FLC	FAC
Sheffield Wed	6/91							

FA Premier Lge Record
| | 92/93 | 9 |

JONES Steve   West Ham United

Full Name: JONES, Stephen Gary   DOB: 17/3/70, Cambridge

Previous Club Details			*Apps*			*Goals*		
Clubs	Signed	Fee	Lge	FLC	FAC	Lge	FLC	FAC
West Ham U	11/92	£22,500	4+2			2		

JONES Vinny   Wimbledon

Name: JONES, Vincent Peter   DOB: 5/1/65, Watford
FAPL Debut: Home v Oldham Ath. 15/8/92
Debut Goal: Away v Sheffield Wednesday 22/8/92

Previous Club Details			*Apps*			*Goals*		
Clubs	Signed	Fee	Lge	FLC	FAC	Lge	FLC	FAC
Non- League								
Wimbledon	11/86	£10,000	77	6+2	2+2	9		1
Leeds Utd	6/89	£650,000	44+2	2	1	5		
Sheffield Utd	9/90	£700,000	35	4	1	2		
Chelsea	8/91	£575,000	35	1	4	3		1
Wimbledon	9/92	£700,000						

FA Premier Lge Record
	92/93							
Chelsea		7			1			
Wimbledon		27	3	4	1	1		

JOSEPH Roger   Wimbledon

Name: JOSEPH, Roger Anthony   DOB: 24/12/65, Paddington
FAPL Debut: Away v Leeds United 15/8/92   Debut Goal:

Previous Club Details			*Apps*			*Goals*		
Clubs	Signed	Fee	Lge	FLC	FAC	Lge	FLC	FAC
Brentford	10/84		103+1	7	1	2		
Wimbledon	8/88	£150,000	108+6	12	5+1			

FA Premier Lge Record
| | 92/93 | 31+1 | 2+1 | 5 |

KANCHELSKIS Andrei   Manchester United

Full Name: KANCHELSKIS, Andrei   DOB: 23/1/69, Kirovograd, USSR
FAPL Debut: Away v. Sheffield United 15/8/93
Debut Goal: Home v. Leeds United 6/9/93

Previous Club Details

Clubs	Signed	Fee	Lge	FLC	FAC	Lge	FLC	FAC
			Apps			Goals		
Shakhtyor Donetsk								
Man Utd	3/91							

FA Premier Lge Record

	92/93	14+12	2+1	1		3		

KEANE Roy   Manchester United

Name: KEANE, Roy Maurice   DOB:10/8/71, Cork
FAPL Debut: Home v Liverpool 16/8/92
Debut Goal: Away v Leeds United 5/12/92
Eire International

Previous Club Details

Clubs	Signed	Fee	Lge	FLC	FAC	Lge	FLC	FAC
			Apps			Goals		
Cobh Ramblers								
Nottingham F	5/90	£10,000	74	12	14	16	5	2
Man Utd	7/93	£3.75m						

FA Premier Lge Record

Nottingham F	92/93	42	5	4	6	1	1

KEARTON Jason   Everton

Full Name: KEARTON, Jason   DOB: 9/7/69, Australia
FAPL Debut: Away v. QPR † 28/12/92   Debut Goal: –

Previous Club Details

Clubs	Signed	Fee	Lge	FLC	FAC	Lge	FLC	FAC
			Apps			Goals		
Everton	10/88							
Stoke City	8/91	Loan	16					
Blackpool	1/92	Loan	14					

FA Premier Lge Record

	92/93	2+3						

KEIZERWEERD Orpheo   Oldham Athletic

Full Name: KEIZERWERD, Orpheo   DOB: 21/11/68
FAPL Debut: Home v. Liverpool † 10/4/93   Debut Goal:

Previous Club Details

Clubs	Signed	Fee	Lge	FLC	FAC	Lge	FLC	FAC
			Apps			Goals		
Rodez, Fra								
Oldham Ath	3/93	Trial						

FA Premier Lge Record

	92/93	0+1						

KELLY Alan — Sheffield United

Name: KELLY, Alan
FAPL Debut: Home v Arsenal 19/9/92

DOB: 11/8/68, Preston
Debut Goal:

Previous Club Details			Apps			Goals		
Clubs	Signed	Fee	Lge	FLC	FAC	Lge	FLC	FAC
Preston NE	9/85		142	1	8			
Sheffield Utd	7/92	£150,000						

FA Premier Lge Record

	92/93		32+1	3	7			

KELLY David — Newcastle United

Full Name: KELLY, David

DOB: 25/11/65 Birmingham

Previous Club Details			Apps			Goals		
Clubs	Signed	Fee	Lge	FLC	FAC	Lge	FLC	FAC
Walsall	12/83		115+32	11+1	12+2	63	4	3
West Ham	8/88	£600,000	29+12	11+3	6	7	5	
Leicester	3/90	£300,000	63+3	6	1	22	1	
Newcastle	12/91	£250,000	70	4	5	35	2	1

KENNA Jeff — Southampton

Full Name: KENNA, Jeffrey Jude
FAPL Debut: Away v. QPR † 19/8/92
Debut Goal: Home v. Sheffield United 27/2/92

DOB: 27/8/70, Dublin

Previous Club Details			Apps			Goals		
Clubs	Signed	Fee	Lge	FLC	FAC	Lge	FLC	FAC
Southampton	4/89	–	15+1		3+1			

FA Premier Lge Record

	92/93		27+2		1	2		

KENNY Marc — Liverpool

Full Name: KENNY, Marc Vincent

DOB: 17/9/73, Dublin

Previous Club Details			Apps			Goals		
Clubs	Signed	Fee	Lge	FLC	FAC	Lge	FLC	FAC
Liverpool	9/90	–						

KENNY William — Everton

Full Name: KENNY, William
FAPL Debut: Home v. Manchester City 31/10/92
Debut Goal: Away v. Chelsea 11/3/93

DOB: 19/9/73, Liverpool

Previous Club Details			Apps			Goals		
Clubs	Signed	Fee	Lge	FLC	FAC	Lge	FLC	FAC
Everton	6/92	–						

FA Premier Lge Record

	92/93		16+1					

KEOWN Martin — Arsenal

Full Name: KEOWN, Martin Raymond DOB: 24/7/66, Oxford
FAPL Debut: Home v. Coventry City 17/10/92 Debut Goal: –

Previous Club Details			Apps			Goals		
Clubs	Signed	Fee	Lge	FLC	FAC	Lge	FLC	FAC
Arsenal	1/84	–	22		5			
Brighton &HA	2/85	Loan	21+2	2		1	1	
Aston Villa	6/86	£200,000	109+3	12+1	6	3		
Everton	6/89	£750,000	79+4	7		10		
Arsenal	2/93	£2m						

FA Premier Lge Record

Everton	92/93		13	4	2			
Arsenal			15+1					

KERR David — Manchester City

Full Name: KERR, David William DOB: 6/9/74, Dumfries
FAPL Debut: Home v. Crystal Palace † 5/5/93 Debut Goal: –

Previous Club Details			Apps			Goals		
Clubs	Signed	Fee	Lge	FLC	FAC	Lge	FLC	FAC
Man City	9/91							

FA Premier Lge Record

	92/93		0+1	

KERSLAKE David — Leeds United

Full Name: KERSLAKE, David DOB: 19/6/66
FAPL Debut: Home v. Manchester City 13/3/93 Debut Goal: –

Previous Club Details			Apps			Goals		
Clubs	Signed	Fee	Lge	FLC	FAC	Lge	FLC	FAC
QPR	6/83		38+20	6+2	2+2	6	4	
Swindon Town	11/89	£110,000	163+2	12	8	2		
Leeds Utd	3/93	£500,000						

FA Premier Lge Record

	92/93		8

KHARIN Dimitri — Chelsea

Full Name: KHARIN, Dimitri DOB: 16/8/68, Moscow
FAPL Debut: Away v. QPR 27/1/93 Debut Goal:

Previous Club Details			Apps			Goals		
Clubs	Signed	Fee	Lge	FLC	FAC	Lge	FLC	FAC
CSKA Moscow								
Chelsea	11/92	£200,000						

FA Premier Lge Record

	92/93		5

KILCLINE Brian — Newcastle United

Full Name: KILCLINE, Brian
DOB: 7/5/62 Nottingham

Previous Club Details			Apps			Goals		
Clubs	Signed	Fee	Lge	FLC	FAC	Lge	FLC	FAC
Notts County	5/80		156+2	16	10	9	1	2
Coventry City	6/84	£60,000	173	16+1	15	28	4	3
Oldham Ath	8/91	£400,000	8	2				
Newcastle Utd	2/92	£250,000	20+30	2+1	1+2			

KIMBLE Alan — Wimbledon

Name: KIMBLE, Alan
DOB: 6/8/66, Poole

Previous Club Details			Apps			Goals		
Clubs	Signed	Fee	Lge	FLC	FAC	Lge	FLC	FAC
Charlton Ath.	8/84		6					
Exeter City	8/85	Loan	1	1				
Cambridge Ud	8/86		295+4	23+1	29	29		1
Wimbledon	8/93	£175,000						

KING Phil — Sheffield Wednesday

Full Name: KING, Philip Geoffrey
DOB: 28/12/67, Bristol
FAPL Debut: Away v. Everton 15/8/92
Debut Goal: Home v. Southampton 12/4/93

Previous Club Details			Apps			Goals		
Clubs	Signed	Fee	Lge	FLC	FAC	Lge	FLC	FAC
Exeter City	1/85	–	24+3	1				
Torquay Utd	7/86	£3,00	24	2	1	3		
Swindon Town	2/87	£15,000	112+4	11	5	4		
Sheffield Wed	11/89	£400,000	106+1	13	8	1		
FA Premier Lge Record								
92/93			11+1	2	1	1		

KIWOMYA Chris — Ipswich Town

Full Name: KIWOMYA, Christopher Mark
DOB: 2/12/69, Huddersfield
FAPL Debut: Home v. Aston Villa 15/8/92
Debut Goal: Away v. Manchester United 22/8/92

Previous Club Details			Apps			Goals		
Clubs	Signed	Fee	Lge	FLC	FAC	Lge	FLC	FAC
Ipswich Town	3/87	–	112+23	6	8	32	1	1
FA Premier Lge Record								
92/93			38	7	3	10	6	1

KJELDBERG Jakob — Chelsea

Name: KJELDBERG, Jakob   DOB:

Previous Club Details			Apps			Goals		
Clubs	Signed	Fee	Lge	FLC	FAC	Lge	FLC	FAC
Silkeborg, Den								
Chelsea	8/93	£400,000						

LAKE Paul — Manchester City

Full Name: LAKE, Paul Andrew   DOB: 2/10/68, Denton
FAPL Debut: Home v. QPR 17/8/92   Debut Goal: –

Previous Club Details			Apps			Goals		
Clubs	Signed	Fee	Lge	FFC	FAC	Lge	FLC	FAC
Man City	5/87	–	104+4	10	9	27	1	2
FA Premier Lge Record								
92/93			2					

LEE David — Chelsea

Full Name: LEE, David John   DOB: 26/11/69, Kingswood
FAPL Debut: Away v. Aston Villa † 2/9/92
Debut Goal: Home v. Manchester United 19/12/92

Previous Club Details			Apps			Goals		
Clubs	Signed	Fee	Lge	FLC	FAC	Lge	FLC	FAC
Chelsea	6/88	–	53+19	6+1	1+3	6	1	
Reading	1/92	Loan	5			5		
Plymouth Arg	3/92	Loan	9			1		
FA Premier Lge Record								
92/93			23+2	6	1	2		

LEE Dave — Southampton

Full Name: LEE, David   DOB: 5/11/67, Blackburn

Previous Club Details			Apps			Goals		
Clubs	Signed	Fee	Lge	FLC	FAC	Lge	FLC	FAC
Bury	8/86	–	203+5	15	6	35	1	
Southampton	8/91	£350,000	11+8		0+1			
FA Premier Lge Record								
92/93			0+1					

LEE Robert — Newcastle United

Full Name: LEE, Robert   DOB:

Previous Club Details			Apps			Goals		
Clubs	Signed	Fee	Lge	FLC	FAC	Lge	FLC	FAC
Charlton Ath	7/83		274+24	16+3	14	58	1	2
Newcastle	9/92	£700,000	36	3	4	10	1	2

LE SAUX Graeme · Blackburn Rovers

Full Name: LE SAUX, Graeme Pierre DOB: 17/10/68, Jersey
FAPL Debut: Home v. Ipswich Town † 17/10/92 Debut Goal: –

Previous Club Details			*Apps*			*Goals*		
Clubs	Signed	Fee	Lge	FLC	FAC	Lge	FLC	FAC
Chelsea	12/87	–	67+9	6+3	6+1	8	1	
Blackburn Rv	3/93	Swap						
FA Premier Lge Record								
Chelsea	92/93		10+4	1+3	1			
Blackburn Rv			9					

LE TISSIER Matthew · Southampton

Full Name: LE TISSIER, Matthew Paul DOB: 14/10/68, Guernsey
FAPL Debut: Home v. Tottenham Hotspur 15/8/92
Debut Goal: Away v. QPR 19/8/92

Previous Club Details			*Apps*			*Goals*		
Clubs	Signed	Fee	Lge	FLC	FAC	Lge	FLC	FAC
Southampton	10/86	–	143+30	20+6	15+1	60	11	5
FA Premier Lge Record								
	92/93		40	3	1	15	2	1

LIMPAR Anders · Arsenal

Full Name: LIMPAR, Anders DOB: 24/8/65, Sweden
FAPL Debut: Home v. Norwich 15/8/92
Debut Goal: Away v. Liverpool 23/8/92

Previous Club Details			*Apps*			*Goals*		
Clubs	Signed	Fee	Lge	FLC	FAC	Lge	FLC	FAC
Arsenal	7/90	£1m	55+8	3	5	16		2
FA Premier Lge Record								
	92/93		12+11	4	2	2		

LING Martin · Swindon Town

Full Name: LING, Martin DOB: 15/7/66 West Ham

Previous Club Details			*Apps*			*Goals*		
Clubs	Signed	Fee	Lge	FLC	FAC	Lge	FLC	FAC
Exeter City	1/84		109+8	8	4	14		
Swindon Town	7/86	£25,000	2	1+1				
Southend Utd	10/86	£15,000	126+12	8	7	31	2	1
Mansfield Tn	1/91	Loan	3					
Swindon Town	3/91	Loan	0+1					
Swindon Town	7/91	£15,000	60+4	3	4	5	1	

LINIGHAN Andy · Arsenal

Full Name: LINIGHAN, Andrew DOB: 18/6/62, Hartlepool
FAPL Debut: Away v. Sheffield United † 19/9/92
Debut Goal: Away v. Oldham Athletic 20/2/93

Previous Club Details			*Apps*			*Goals*		
Clubs	Signed	Fee	Lge	FLC	FAC	Lge	FLC	FAC
Hartlepool Utd	9/80	–	110	7+1	8	4	1	
Leeds Utd	5/84	£200,000	66	6	2	3	1	
Oldham Ath	1/86	£65,000	87	8	3	6	2	
Norwich City	3/88	£350,000	86	6	10	8		
Arsenal	6/90	£1.25m	22+5	1+1	3+1			
FA Premier Lge Record								
	92/93		19+2	4	7	2	1	1

LINIGHAN David — Ipswich Town

Full Name: LINIGHAN, David   DOB: 9/1/65, Hartlepool
FAPL Debut: Home v. Aston Villa 15/8/92
Debut Goal: Away v. Southampton 13/4/93

Previous Club Details			*Apps*			*Goals*		
Clubs	Signed	Fee	Lge	FLC	FAC	Lge	FLC	FAC
Hartlepool Utd	3/82	–	84+7	3+1	4	5	1	
Derby County	8/86							
Shrewsbury Tn	12/86	£30,000	65	5	3	2		
Ipswich Town	6/88	£300,000	162+1	9	9	8		
FA Premier Lge Record								
	92/93		42	7	3	1		

LITTLEJOHN Adrian — Sheffield United

Full Name: LITTLEJOHN, Adrian Slyvester
DOB: 26/9/70, Wolverhampton
FAPL Debut: Away v. QPR † 22/8/93
Debut Goal: Home v. Liverpool 12/9/92

Previous Club Details			*Apps*			*Goals*		
Clubs	Signed	Fee	Lge	FLC	FAC	Lge	FLC	FAC
Walsall	5/89	–	26+18	2+1	1	1		
Sheffield Utd	8/91	–	5+2					
FA Premier Lge Record								
	92/93		18+9	3	3+2	8		1

LIVINGSTONE Steve — Chelsea

Full Name: LIVINGSTONE, Stephen   DOB: 8/9/68, Middlesbrough
FAPL Debut: Away v. Everton † 3/3/93   Debut Goal.

Previous Club Details			*Apps*			*Goals*		
Clubs	Signed	Fee	Lge	FLC	FAC	Lge	FLC	FAC
Coventry City	7/86	–	17+14	8+2		5	10	
Blackburn Rv	1/91	£450,000	24+4	1		10		
Chelsea	3/93	Swap						
FA Premier Lge Record								
Blackburn Rv	92/93		1+1	1	1			1
Chelsea			0+1					

LUKIC John   Leeds United

Full Name: LUKIC, Jovan   DOB: 11/12/60, Chesterfield
FAPL Debut: Home v. Wimbledon 15/8/92   Debut Goal: –

Previous Club Details			*Apps*			*Goals*		
Clubs	Signed	Fee	Lge	FLC	FAC	Lge	FLC	FAC
Leeds Utd	12/78	–	146	7	9			
Arsenal	7/83	£75,000	223	32	21			
Leeds Utd	6/90	£1m	80	11	7			
FA Premier Lge Record								
	92/93		39	3	3			

LYDERSON Pål   Arsenal

Full Name: LYDERSON, Pål   DOB: 10/9/65, Norway
FAPL Debut: Away v. Tottenham H. 12/11/92 Debut Goal: –

Previous Club Details			*Apps*			*Goals*		
Clubs	Signed	Fee	Lge	FLC	FAC	Lge	FLC	FAC
Arsenal	9/91	£500,000	5+2					
FA Premier Lge Record								
	92/93		7+1	1				

McALLISTER Brian   Wimbledon

Full Name: McALLISTER, Brian   DOB: 30/11/70, Glasgow
FAPL Debut: Away v. Sheffield Utd 25/8/92   Debut Goal:

Previous Club Details			*Apps*			*Goals*		
Clubs	Signed	Fee	Lge	FLC	FAC	Lge	FLC	FAC
Wimbledon	2/89	–	10+3					
Plymouth Arg	12/90	Loan	7+1					
Wimbledon								
FA Premier Lge Record								
	92/93		26+1	2	3			

McALLSTER Gary   Leeds United

Full Name: McALLISTER, Gary   DOB: 25/12/64, Motherwell
FAPL Debut: Home v. Wimbledon 15/8/92
Debut Goal: Home v. Liverpool 29/8/92

Previous Club Details			*Apps*			*Goals*		
Clubs	Signed	Fee	Lge	FLC	FAC	Lge	FLC	FAC
Leicester City	8/85	£125,000	199+2	14+1	5	46	3	2
Leeds Utd	6/90	£1m	79+1	11	7	7	2	1
FA Premier Lge Record								
	92/93		32	3	4	5	1	2

McCLAIR Brian   Manchester United

Full Name: McCLAIR, Brian John   DOB: 8/12/63, Bellshill
FAPL Debut: Away v. Sheffield United 15/8/92
Debut Goal: Away v. Everton 12/9/92

Previous Club Details			Apps			Goals		
Clubs	Signed	Fee	Lge	FLC	FAC	Lge	FLC	FAC
Man Utd	7/87	£850,000	190+3	28	24	70	14	11

FA Premier Lge Record					
92/93	41(1)	3	3	9	

McDONALD Alan   Queens Park Rangers

Full Name: McDONALD, Alan   DOB: 12/10/63, Belfast
FAPL Debut: Away v. Manchester City 17/8/92   Debut Goal: –

Previous Club Details			Apps			Goals		
Clubs	Signed	Fee	Lge	FLC	FAC	Lge	FLC	FAC
QPR	8/81	–	242+5	28	22	8	2	1
Charlton Ath	3/83	Loan	9					

FA Premier Lge Record				
92/93	39	3	2	

McDONALD David   Tottenham Hotspur

Full Name: McDONALD, David Hugh   DOB: 2/1/71, Dublin
FAPL Debut: Away v. Liverpool 8/5/92   Debut Goal: –

Previous Club Details			Apps			Goals		
Clubs	Signed	Fee	Lge	FLC	FAC	Lge	FLC	FAC
Tottenham H	7/88	–						
Gillingham	9/90	Loan	10					
Brentford	8/92	Loan						
Bradford City	9/92	Loan	7					
Reading	3/93	Loan	11					

FA Premier Lge Record		
92/93	2	

McDONALD Neil   Oldham Athletic

Full Name: McDONALD, Neil Raymond   DOB: 2/11/65, Wallsend
FAPL Debut: Home v. Aston Villa † 24/10/92   Debut Goal:

Previous Club Details			Apps			Goals		
Clubs	Signed	Fee	Lge	FLC	FAC	Lge	FLC	FAC
Newcastle Utd	2/83	–	163+17	12	10+1	24	3	1
Everton	8/88	£525,000	76+14	7	17	4	3	
Oldham Ath	10/91	£500,000	14+3	2		1		

FA Premier Lge Record		
92/93	2+2	1

McDONALD Paul   Southampton

Name: McDONALD, Paul   DOB: 20/04/68, Motherwell

Previous Club Details			Apps			Goals		
Clubs	Signed	Fee	Lge	FLC	FAC	Lge	FLC	FAC
Hamilton Acc								
Southampton	8/93	£150,000 (jt)						

McGEE Paul — Wimbledon

Full Name: McGEE, Paul DOB: 17/5/68, Dublin
FAPL Debut: Away v. Middlesbrough 21/11/92 Debut Goal: –

Previous Club Details			*Apps*			*Goals*		
Clubs	Signed	Fee	Lge	FLC	FAC	Lge	FLC	FAC
Colchester U	2/849	£35,000	3					
Wimbledon	3/89	£120,000	53+4	1+1	5	9	1	

FA Premier Lge Record

92/93		1+2		

McGOLDRICK Eddie — Arsenal

Full Name: McGOLDRICK, Edward John Paul DOB:30/4/65, Islington
FAPL Debut: Home v. Blackburn Rovers 15/8/92
Debut Goal: Away v. Oldham Athletic 19/8/92

Previous Club Details			*Apps*			*Goals*		
Clubs	Signed	Fee	Lge	FLC	FAC	Lge	FLC	FAC
N'hampton T	8/86	£10,000	97+10	9	6+1	9		1
Crystal Palace	1/89	£200,000	97+8	13+1	4	3		
Arsenal	07/93	£1m						

FA Premier Lge Record

Crystal Palace 92/93		42		8

McGOWAN Gavin — Arsenal

Full Name: McGOWAN, Gavin DOB: 16/1/76, Blackheath
FAPL Debut: Away v. Sheffield Wed. 6/5/93 Debut Goal:

Previous Club Details			*Apps*			*Goals*		
Clubs	Signed	Fee	Lge	FLC	FAC	Lge	FLC	FAC
Arsenal								

FA Premier Lge Record

92/93		0+2	

McGRATH Lloyd — Coventry City

Full Name: McGRATH, Lloyd Anthony DOB: 24/2/65, Birmingham
FAPL Debut: Away v. Wimbledon † 22/8/92 Debut Goal: –

Previous Club Details			*Apps*			*Goals*		
Clubs	Signed	Fee	Lge	FLC	FAC	Lge	FLC	FAC
Coventry City	12/82		170+8	19	15	4	1	

FA Premier Lge Record

92/93		20+5	2	1

McGRATH Paul — Aston Villa

Full Name: McGRATH, Paul DOB: 4/12/69, Ealing
FAPL Debut: Home v. Ipswich Town 15/8/92
Debut Goal: Home v. Nottingham Forest 12/12/92

Previous Club Details			Apps			Goals		
Clubs	Signed	Fee	Lge	FLC	FAC	Lge	FLC	FAC
Man Utd	4/82	£30,000	159+4	13	15+2	12	2	2
Aston Villa	7/89	£400,000	111	9	12	2		
FA Premier Lge Record								
	92/93		42	4	4	4		1

McLAREN Ross   Swindon Town
Name: McLAREN, Ross   DOB: 14/4/62 Edinburgh

Previous Club Details			Apps			Goals		
Clubs	Signed	Fee	Lge	FLC	FAC	Lge	FLC	FAC
Rangers								
Shrewsbury Tn	8/80		158+3	11	7+1	18	3	1
Derby County	7/85	£67,000	113+9	13	9	4	1	
Swindon Town	8/88	£165,000	182	19	11	9	2	

McMAHON Steve   Manchester City
Full Name: McMAHON, Stephen   DOB: 20/8/61, Liverpool
FAPL Debut: Home v. QPR 17/8/92
Debut Goal: Home v. Norwich 26/8/92

Previous Club Details			Apps			Goals		
Clubs	Signed	Fee	Lge	FLC	FAC	Lge	FLC	FAC
Everton	8/79		99+1	11	9	11	3	
Aston Villa	5/83	£175,000	74+1	9	3	7		
Liverpool	9/85	£375,000	202+2	27	30	28	13	7
Man City	12/91	£900,000	18		1			
FA Premier Lge Record								
	92/93		24+3	2	2	1		

McMANAMAN Steve   Liverpool
Full Name: McMANAMAN, Steven   DOB: 11/2/72, Bootle
FAPL Debut: Away v. Nottingham Forest † 16/8/92
Debut Goal: Home v. Wimbledon 26/9/92

Previous Club Details			Apps			Goals		
Clubs	Signed	Fee	Lge	FLC	FAC	Lge	FLC	FAC
Liverpool	2/90	–	26+6	5	8+1	5	3	3
FA Premier Lge Record								
	92/93		27+4	5	1	4	2	

MABBUTT Gary   Tottenham Hotspur
Full Name: MABBUTT, Gary Vincent   DOB: 23/9/61, Bristol
FAPL Debut: Away v. Wimbledon 25/10/92
Debut Goal: Home v. Nottingham Forest 28/12/92

Previous Club Details			Apps			Goals		
Clubs	Signed	Fee	Lge	FLC	FAC	Lge	FLC	FAC
Bristol Rv	1/79	–	122+9	10	5+1	10	1	1
Tottenham H	8/82	£105,000	326+13	49+2	28+2	25	2	4
FA Premier Lge Record								
	92/93		29	2	5	2		

MADDISON Neil   Southampton

Full Name: MADDISON, Neil Stanley   DOB: 2/10/69, Darlington
FAPL Debut: Home v. Middlesbrough 29/8/92
Debut Goal: Home v. Arsenal 5/12/92

Previous Club Details			Apps			Goals		
Clubs	Signed	Fee	Lge	FLC	FAC	Lge	FLC	FAC
Southampton	4/88	–	8+9	0+2	0+3	2		
FA Premier Lge Record								
	92/93		33+4	1	1	4		

MADDIX Danny   Queens Park Rangers

Full Name: MADDIX, Daniel Shawn   DOB: 11/10/67, Ashford, Kent
FAPL Debut: Away v. Southampton † 12/9/92 Debut Goal: –

Previous Club Details			Apps			Goals		
Clubs	Signed	Fee	Lge	FLC	FAC	Lge	FLC	FAC
Tottenham H	7/85	–						
Southend U	10/86	Loan	2					
QPR	7/87	–	113+12	14	13	6	2	1
FA Premier Lge Record								
	92/93		9+5	1	1			

MAKEL Lee   Blackburn Rovers

Full Name: MAKEL, Lee   DOB: 11/1/73, Sunderland
FAPL Debut: Home v. Middlesbrough 20/3/93 Debut Goal: –

Previous Club Details			Apps			Goals		
Clubs	Signed	Fee	Lge	FLC	FAC	Lge	FLC	FAC
Newcastle Utd	2/91	–	6+6	1		1		
Blackburn Rv	6/92	£160,000						
FA Premier Lge Record								
	92/93		1	0+2				

MARGETSON Martyn   Manchester City

Full Name: MARGETSON, Martyn Walter   DOB: 8/9/71, Neath
FAPL Debut: Home v. Everton 8/5/93   Debut Goal: –

Previous Club Details			Apps			Goals		
Clubs	Signed	Fee	Lge	FLC	FAC	Lge	FLC	FAC
Man City	7/90	–	0+5	0+1				
FA Premier Lge Record								
	92/93		1					

MARKER Nicky   Blackburn Rovers

Name: MARKER, Nicky   DOB: 03/06/65, Budleigh Salterton
FAPL Debut: Home v. Oldham Athletic † 26/09/92   Debut Goal:

Previous Club Details

Clubs	Signed Fee	Lge	FLC	FAC	Lge	FLC	FAC
		Apps			Goals		
Exeter City	5/83	196+6	11	8	3	1	
Plymouth Arg	11/87	201+1	15	9	13	3	1
Blackburn Rv	9/92 £250,000 (+ exch)						

FA Premier Lge Record

	92/93	12+3		3			

MARSH Mike   Liverpool

Full Name: MARSH, Michael Andrew   DOB: 21/7/69, Liverpool
FAPL Debut: Home v. Arsenal † 23/8/92
Debut Goal: Home v. Crystal Palace 28/11/92

Previous Clubs details

Clubs	Signed Fee	Lge	FLC	FAC	Lge	FLC	FAC
		Apps			Goals		
Liverpool	8/87 –	20+19	4+1	4+2			

FA Premier Lge Record

	92/93	22+6	6	2	1	3	

MARSHALL Ian   Ipswich Town

Full Name: MARSHALL, Ian Paul   DOB: 20/3/66, Liverpool
FAPL Debut: Away v. Chelsea 15/8/92
Debut Goal: Home v. Ipswich Town 19/9/92

Previous Clubs details

Clubs	Signed Fee	Lge	FLC	FAC	Lge	FLC	FAC
		App			Goals		
Everton	3/84 –	9+6	1+1	–		1	
Oldham Ath	3/88 £100,000	139+4	14	13	34		3
Ipswich Town	8/93 £750,000						

FA Premier Lge Record

Oldham Ath	92/93	26+1	3	1	2		

MARSHALL Scott   Arsenal

Full Name: MARSHALL, Scott Roderick   DOB: 1/5/73, Edinburgh
FAPL Debut: Away v. Sheffield Wed. 6/5/93   Debut Goal: –

Previous Clubs details

Clubs	Signed Fee	Lge	FLC	FAC	Lge	FLC	FAC
		App			Goals		
Arsenal	3/91 –						

FA Premier Lge Record

	92/93	2					

MARTIN Alvin   West Ham United

Full Name: MARTIN, Alvin   DOB: 29/7/58, Liverpool

Previous Clubs details			*App*			*Goals*		
Clubs	Signed Fee		Lge	FLC	FAC	Lge	FLC	FAC
West Ham U	8/74		422+2	66	34	25	6	

MASKELL Craig   Swindon Town

Name: MASKELL, Craig   DOB: 10/4/68 Aldershot

Previous Club Details			*Apps*			*Goals*		
Clubs	Signed Fee		Lge	FLC	FAC	Lge	FLC	FAC
Southampton	4/86		2+4			1		
Huddersfield Tn	5/88	£20,000	86+1	6	8	43	4	3
Reading	8/90	£250,000	60+12	2	5+1	27		
Swindon Town	7/92	Exchange	32+1	2	1	19	1	

MASON Paul   Ipswich Town

Name: MASON, Paul   DOB: 03/9/63, Liverpool

Previous Club Details			*Apps*			*Goals*		
Clubs	Signed Fee		Lge	FLC	FAC	Lge	FLC	FAC
Aberdeen								
Ipswich Town	8/93	£400,000						

MATTHEW Damian   Chelsea

Full Name: MATTHEW, Damian   DOB: 23/9/70, Islington

FAPL Debut: Home v. Oldham Athletic 15/8/92   Debut Goal: –

Previous Clubs details			*App*			*Goals*		
Clubs	Signed Fee		Lge	FLC	FAC	Lge	FLC	FAC
Chelsea	6/89	–	10+7	5				
Luton Town	9/92	Loan	3+2					
FA Premier Lge Record								
	92/93		3+1					

MAY David   Blackburn Rovers

Full Name: MAY, David   DOB: 24/6/70, Oldham

FAPL Debut: Away v. Crystal Palace 15/8/92

Debut Goal: Away v. Everton 3/3/93

Previous Clubs details			*App*			*Goals*		
Clubs	Signed Fee		Lge	FLC	FAC	Lge	FLC	FAC
Blackburn Rv	6/88	–	49	3	3	1		
FA Premier Lge Record								
	92/93		34	5+1	5	1	1	

MEAKER Michael   Queens Park Rangers

Full Name: MEAKER, Michael John   DOB: 18/8/71, Greenford

FAPL Debut: Home v. Norwich 6/3/93   Debut Goal: –

Previous Clubs details   App   Goals

Clubs	Signed	Fee	Lge	FLC	FAC	Lge	FLC	FAC
QPR	12/89		0+9					
Plymouth Arg	11/91	Loan	4					

FA Premier Lge Record

92/93			3					

MEGSON Gary   Norwich

Full Name: MEGSON, Gary John   DOB: 2/5/59, Manchester
FAPL Debut: Away v. Arsenal 15/8/92
Debut Goal: Away v. Manchester City 26/8/92

Previous Clubs details   App   Goals

Clubs	Signed	Fee	Lge	FLC	FAC	Lge	FLC	FAC
Plymouth Arg	5/77	–	78	9	5	10		
Everton	12/79	£250,000	20+2		3	2		1
Sheffield Wed	8/81	£130,000	123	13	12	13	2	5
Nottingham F	8/84	£175,000						
Newcastle Utd	11/84	£130,000	21+3	1+1	2	1		1
Sheffield Wed	12/85	£60,000	107+3	10	15	12		1
Man City	1/89	£250,000	78+4	5	7+1	2		

FA Premier Lge Record

92/93			20+3		2	1		

MERSON Paul   Arsenal

Full Name: MERSON, Paul Charles   DOB: 20/3/68, Harlesden
FAPL Debut: Home v. Norwich 15/8/92
Debut Goal: Home v. Sheffield Wednesday 29/8/92

Previous Clubs details   App   Goals

Clubs	Signed	Fee	Lge	FLC	FAC	Lge	FLC	FAC
Arsenal	11/85	–	139+28	13+2	13+2	49	5	3
Brentford	1/87	Loan	6+1					

FA Premier Lge Record

92/93			32+1	9	8	6	1	1

MIKLOSKO Ludec   West Ham United

Full Name: MIKLOSKO, Ludec   DOB: 9/12/61 Protesov, Czech

Previous Club Details   Apps   Goals

Clubs	Signed	Fee	Lge	FLC	FAC	Lge	FLC	FAC
Banik Ostrava								
West Ham	2/90	£300,000	146	10	12			

MIKE Adrian   Manchester City

Full Name: MIKE, Adrian Roosevelt   DOB: 16/11/73, Manchester
FAPL Debut: Home v. Middlesbrough † 12/9/92   Debut Goal: –

MILLER Alan   Arsenal
Full Name: MILLER, Alan John   DOB: 29/3/70, Epping
FAPL Debut: Away v. Leeds Utd † 21/11/92   Debut Goal: –

Previous Clubs details

Clubs	Signed	Fee	App Lge	FLC	FAC	Goals Lge	FLC	FAC
Arsenal	5/88							
Plymouth Arg	11/88	Loan	13		2			
West Brom Alb	8/91	Loan	3					
Birmingham C	12/91	Loan	15					

FA Premier Lge Record

92/93			3+1					

MILLER Paul   Wimbledon
Full Name: MILLER, Paul Anthony   DOB: 31/1/68, Woking
FAPL Debut: Away v. Leeds Utd 15/8/92
Debut Goal: Home v. Aston Villa 3/10/92

Previous Clubs details

Clubs	Signed	Fee	App Lge	FLC	FAC	Goals Lge	FLC	FAC
Wimbledon	8/87	–	54+7	2+2	2	9		
Newport Cnty	10/87	Loan	6			2		
Bristol City	1/90	Loan	0+3					
Wimbledon								

FA Premier Lge Record

92/93			11+8	1+1	1	1		

MILLIGAN Mike   Oldham Athletic
Full Name: MILLIGAN, Michael Joseph   DOB: 20/2/67, Manchester
FAPL Debut: Away v. Chelsea 15/8/92   Debut Goal: –

Previous Clubs details

Clubs	Signed	Fee	App Lge	FLC	FAC	Goals Lge	FLC	FAC
Oldham Ath	2/85	–	161+1	18+1	12	17	1	1
Everton	8/90	£1m	16+1	0+1	1	1		
Oldham Ath	7/91	£600,000	36	4		3	1	

FA Premier Lge Record

92/93			42	4	2	3		

MILTON Simon — Ipswich Town

Full Name: MILTON, Simon Charles DOB: 23/8/63, Fulham
FAPL Debut: Home v. Aston Villa † 15/8/92
Debut Goal: Away v. Blackburn Rovers 13/4/93

Previous Clubs details			App			Goals		
Clubs	Signed	Fee	Lge	FLC	FAC	Lge	FLC	FAC
Ipswich Town	7/87	£5,500	131+18	8+2	8	35	1	1
Exeter City	11/87	Loan	2			3		
Torquay Utd	3/88	Loan	4			1		
FA Premier Lge Record								
92/93			7+5			2		

MIMMS Bobby — Blackburn Rovers

Full Name: MIMMS, Robert Andrew DOB: 12/10/63, York
FAPL Debut: Away v. Crystal Palace 15/8/93 Debut Goal:

Previous Clubs details			App			Goals		
Clubs	Signed	Fee	Lge	FLC	FAC	Lge	FLC	FAC
Halifax Town	8/81	–						
Rotherham Utd	11/81	£15,000	83	7	3			
Everton	6/85	£150,000	29	2	2			
Notts County	3/86	Loan	2					
Sunderland	12/86	Loan	4					
Blackburn Rv	1/87	Loan	6					
Man City	9/87	Loan	3					
Tottenham H	2/88	£325,000	37	5	2			
Aberdeen	2/90	Loan						
Blackburn Rv	12/90	£250,000	67	2	4			
FA Premier Lge Record								
92/93			42	7	5			

MITCHELL Paul — West Ham United

Name: MITCHELL, Paul DOB: 20/10/71, Bournemouth

Previous Club Details			Apps			Goals		
Clubs	Signed	Fee	Lge	FLC	FAC	Lge	FLC	FAC
Bournemouth	8/89		6+6					
West Ham	8/93	£40,000						

MOLBY Jan — Liverpool

Full Name: MOLBY, Jan DOB: 4/7/63, Jutland, Denmark
FAPL Debut: Home v. Arsenal 23/8/92
Debut Goal: Away v. Ipswich 25/8/92

Previous Clubs details			App			Goals		
Clubs	Signed	Fee	Lge	FLC	FAC	Lge	FLC	FAC
Liverpool	8/84	£575,000	164+19	20+3	24+4	37	8	4
FA Premier Lge Record								
92/93			8+2	1		3		

MONCUR John — Swindon Town

Name: MONCUR, John DOB: 22/9/66 Stepney

Previous Club Details			*Apps*			*Goals*		
Clubs	Signed	Fee	Lge	FLC	FAC	Lge	FLC	FAC
Tottenham H	8/84		10+11	1+2		1		
Doncaster Rv	9/86	Loan	4					
Cambridge Utd	3/87	Loan	3+1					
Portsmouth	3/89	Loan	7					
Brentford	10/89	Loan	5			1		
Ipswich Town	10/91	Loan	5+1					
Nottingham F	2/92	Loan						
Swindon Town	3/92	£80,000	11+5	1		1		

MONKOU Ken — Southampton

Full Name: MONKOU, Kenneth John DOB: 29/11/64, Necare, Surinam

FAPL Debut: Home v. Manchester United 24/8/92

Debut Goal: Home v. Sheffield Wednesday 28/12/92

Previous Clubs details			*App*			*Goals*		
Clubs	Signed	Fee	Lge	FLC	FAC	Lge	FLC	FAC
Chelsea	3/89	£100,000	92+2	12	3	2		
Southampton	8/92	£750,000						
FA Premier Lge Record								
		92/93	33	3	1	1		

MOODY Paul — Southampton

Full Name: MOODY, Paul DOB: 13/6/67, Portsmouth

FAPL Debut: Home v. Wimbledon 17/10/92 Debut Goal: –

Previous Clubs details			*App*			*Goals*		
Clubs	Signed	Fee	Lge	FLC	FAC	Lge	FLC	FAC
Southampton	7/91	£50,000	2+2		0+1			
Reading	12/92	Loan						
FA Premier Lge Record								
		92/93	2+1					

MOORE Kevin — Southampton

Full Name: MOORE, Thomas Kevin DOB: 29/4/58, Grimsby

FAPL Debut: Home v. QPR 19/8/92

Debut Goal: Home v. Sheffield United 27/2/93

Previous Clubs details			*App*			*Goals*		
Clubs	Signed	Fee	Lge	FLC	FAC	Lge	FLC	FAC
Grimsby Town	7/76	–	397+3	41	25	28	3	3
Oldham Ath	2/87	£100,000	13			1		
Southampton	7/87	£125,000	112+4	15	12	8		
Bristol Rovers	1/92	Loan	7			1		
Bristol Rovers	10/92	Loan						

92/93			18	1		2		

MOORE Neil   Everton
Full Name: MOORE, Neil   DOB: 21/9/72, Liverpool
FAPL Debut: Away v. Manhester City † 8/5/93   Debut Goal: –

Previous Clubs details			*App*			*Goals*		
Clubs	Signed	Fee	Lge	FLC	FAC	Lge	FLC	FAC
Everton	6/91	–						

FA Premier Lge Record

92/93			0+1					

MORAN Kevin   Blackburn Rovers
Full Name: MORAN, Kevin Bernard   DOB: 29/4/56, Dublin
FAPL Debut: Away v. Crystal Palace 15/8/92   Debut Goal: –

Previous Clubs details			*App*			*Goals*		
Clubs	Signed	Fee	Lge	FLC	FAC	Lge	FLC	FAC
Man Utd	2/78	–	228+3	24+1	18	21	2	1
Gijon (Fra)	8/88	–						
Blackburn Rv	1/90	–	88+4	5	4	5		

FA Premier Lge Record

92/93								

MORAN Paul   Tottenham Hotspur
Full Name: MORAN, Paul   DOB: 22/5/68, Enfield
FAPL Debut: Away v. Norwich City † 26/12/92   Debut Goal: –

Previous Clubs details			*App*			*Goals*		
Clubs	Signed	Fee	Lge	FLC	FAC	Lge	FLC	FAC
Tottenham H	7/85	–	14+3	1+5	3+1	2		
Portsmouth	1/89	Loan	3					
Leicester City	11/89	Loan	10			2		
Newcastle Utd	2/91	Loan	1					
Southend Utd	3/91	Loan	1					
Cambridge	9/92	Loan						

FA Premier Lge Record

92/93			0+3					

MORLEY Trevor   West Ham United
Full Name: MORLEY, Trevor   DOB: 20/3/62 Nottingham

Previous Club Details			*Apps*			*Goals*		
Clubs	Signed	Fee	Lge	FLC	FAC	Lge	FLC	FAC
Derby County								
Non League								
Northampton	6/85	£20,000	107	10	6	39	4	2
Man City	1/88	£175,000	69+3	7	1	18	3	
West Ham	12/89	Exchange	130+12	7	11+3	44	2	7

MORGAN Steve
Coventry City

Full Name: MORGAN, Steve
DOB: 19/9/68, Manchester

Previous Clubs details

Clubs	Signed	Fee	App Lge	FLC	FAC	Goals Lge	FLC	FAC
Blackpool	8/86		135+9	13	16	10	2	1
Plymouth Arg	7/90	£115,000	85	5	3	5		
Coventry City	7/93	£110,000						

MORRISON Andy
Blackburn Rovers

Name: MORRISON, Andy
DOB: 30/7/70, Inverness

Previous Club Details

Clubs	Signed	Fee	Apps Lge	FLC	FAC	Goals Lge	FLC	FAC
Plymouth Arg	7/88		105+8	9+1	6	6		
Blackburn Rv	8/93	£150,000						

MORROW Steve
Arsenal

Full Name: MORROW, Stephen Joseph
DOB: 2/7/70, Bangor, N.I.
FAPL Debut: Home v. Oldham Athletic 26/8/92 Debut Goal:

Previous Clubs details

Clubs	Signed	Fee	App Lge	FLC	FAC	Goals Lge	FLC	FAC
Arsenal	5/88	–	0+2					
Reading	1/91	Loan	10					
Watford	8/91	Loan	7+1					
Reading	10/91	Loan	3					
Barnet	3/92	Loan	1					

FA Premier Lge Record

92/93			13+3	4+1	2+2		1	

MYERS Andy
Chelsea

Full Name: MYERS, Andrew John
DOB: 3/11/73, Hounslow
FAPL Debut: Away v. Wimbledon 28/12/92 Debut Goal: –

Previous Clubs details

Clubs	Signed	Fee	App Lge	FLC	FAC	Goals Lge	FLC	FAC
Chelsea	6/91	–	9+5	0+1	2	1		

FA Premier Lge Record

92/93			3	1				

NDLOVU Peter
Coventry City

Full Name: NDLOVU, Peter
DOB: 25/2/73, Bulawayo
FAPL Debut: Away v. Tottenham Hotspur † 19/8/92
Debut Goal: Away v. Sheffield Wednesday 2/9/92

Previous Clubs details

Clubs	Signed	Fee	App Lge	FLC	FAC	Goals Lge	FLC	FAC
Coventry City	7/91	£10,000	9+14	2		2		

FA Premier Lge Record

92/93			27+5	1	1	7	1	

NEILSON Alan   Newcastle United

Full Name: NIELSON, Alan   DOB: 26/9/72 Weyburg, Germany
Previous Club Details

Clubs	Signed	Fee	Apps Lge	FLC	FAC	Goals Lge	FLC	FAC
Newcastle	2/91		20+5	3		1		

NETHERCOTT Stuart   Tottenham Hotspur

Full Name: NETHERCOTT, Stuart   DOB: 21/3/73, Ilford
FAPL Debut: Home v. Norwich City † 9/4/93   Debut Goal: –
Previous Clubs details

Clubs	Signed	Fee	App Lge	FLC	FAC	Goals Lge	FLC	FAC
Tottenham H	7/91	–						
Maidstone Utd	9/91	Loan	13			1		
Barnet	2/92	Loan	3					

FA Premier Lge Record

92/93			3+2					

NEWELL Mike   Blackburn Rovers

Full Name: NEWELL, Michael Colin   DOB: 27/1/65, Liverpool
FAPL Debut: Away v. Crystal Palace 15/8/92
Debut Goal: Home v. Manchester City 22/8/92
Previous Clubs details

Clubs	Signed	Fee	App Lge	FLC	FAC	Goals Lge	FLC	FAC
Crewe Alex	9/83	–	3					
Wigan Ath	10/83	–	64+8	6	8	25	1	6
Luton Town	1/86	–	62+1		5	18		1
Leicester City	9/87	£350,000	81	9	2	21	5	
Everton	6/89	£1.1m	48+20	7+3	6+2	15	4	
Blackburn Rv	11/91	£1.1m						

FA Premier Lge Record

92/93			40	6+1	5	13	5	3

NEWHOUSE Aiden   Wimbledon

Full Name: NEWHOUSE, Aiden Robert   DOB: 23/5/72, Wallasey
FAPL Debut: Home v. Aston Villa † 3/10/92   Debut Goal:
Previous Clubs details

Clubs	Signed	Fee	App Lge	FLC	FAC	Goals Lge	FLC	FAC
Chester City	7/89	–	29+15	5+1	0+2	6		
Wimbledon	2/90	£100,000	7+15	0+1	2	2		

FA Premier Lge Record

92/93			0+1	1		1		

NEWMAN Rob   Norwich City

Full Name: NEWMAN, Robert Nigel   DOB: 13/12/63, Bradford on Avon
FAPL Debut: Away v. Arsenal 15/8/92
Debut Goal: Home v. Sheffield Wednesday 19/9/92

Previous Clubs details			*App*			*Goals*		
Clubs	Signed	Fee	Lge	FLC	FAC	Lge	FLC	FAC
Bristol City	10/81	–	382+12	29+1	27	52	2	2
Norwich City	7/91	£600,000	41	5	6	7	1	1
FA Premier Lge Record								
	92/93		16+2	3		2		

NEWSOME Jon   Leeds United

Full Name: NEWSOME, Jonathan   DOB: 6/9/70, Sheffield
FAPL Debut: Home v. Wimbledon 15/8/92   Debut Goal: –

Previous Clubs details			*App*			*Goals*		
Clubs	Signed	Fee	Lge	FLC	FAC	Lge	FLC	FAC
Sheffield Wed	7/81	–	6+1	3				
Leeds Utd	6/91	£150,000	7+3			2		
FA Premier Lge Record								
	92/93		30+7	2	0+1			

NEWTON Eddie   Chelsea

Full Name: NEWTON, Edward John Ikem
DOB: 13/12/71, Hammersmith
FAPL Debut: Away v. Norwich City † 19/8/92
Debut Goal: Home v. Sheffield Wednesday 22/8/92

Previous Clubs details			*App*			*Goals*		
Clubs	Signed	Fee	Lge	FLC	FAC	Lge	FLC	FAC
Chelsea	5/90	–	0+1			1		
Cardiff City	1/92	Loan	16			4		
FA Premier Lge Record								
	92/93		32+2	6	1	5	1	

NICOL Steve   Liverpool

Full Name: NICOL, Stephen   DOB: 1/12/61, Irvine
FAPL Debut: Away v. Nottingham Forest 16/8/92   Debut Goal: –

Previous Clubs details			*App*			*Goals*		
Clubs	Signed	Fee	Lge	FLC	FAC	Lge	FLC	FAC
Liverpool	10/81	£300,000	265+11	22	45	35	4	3
FA Premier Lge Record								
	92/93		32	4	1			

NIJHOLT Luc   Swindon Town

Name: NIJHOLT, Luc   DOB: 29/07/61, Zaandam

Previous Club Details			*Apps*			*Goals*		
Clubs	Signed	Fee	Lge	FLC	FAC	Lge	FLC	FAC
Motherwell								
Swindon Town	8/93	£175,000						

NILSSON Roland — Sheffield Wednesday

Full Name: NILSSON, Nils Lennart Roland
DOB: 27/11/63, Helsingborg, Sweden
FAPL Debut: Away v. Everton 15/8/92
Debut Goal: Away v. Leeds United 12/12/92

Previous Clubs details			*App*			*Goals*		
Clubs	Signed	Fee	Lge	FLC	FAC	Lge	FLC	FAC
Sheffield Wed	11/89	£375,000	81	5	4	1		
FA Premier Lge Record								
	92/93		32	5	8	1	1	

OGRIZOVIC Steve — Coventry City

Full Name: OGRIZOVIC, Steven
DOB: 12/9/57, Mansfield
FAPL Debut: Home v. Middlesbrough 15/8/93   Debut Goal: –

Previous Clubs details			*App*			*Goals*		
Clubs	Signed	Fee	Lge	FLC	FAC	Lge	FLC	FAC
Chesterfield	7/77	–	16	2				
Liverpool	11/77	£70,000	4					
Shrewsbury Tn	8/82	£70,000	84	7	5			
Coventry City	6/84	£72,000	316	32	19	1		
FA Premier Lge Record								
	92/93		33	2	1			

O'BRIEN Liam — Newcastle United

Full Name: O'Brien, Liam
DOB: 5/9/64 Dublin

Previous Club Details			*Apps*			*Goals*		
Clubs	Signed	Fee	Lge	FLC	FAC	Lge	FLC	FAC
Shamrock Rv								
Man Utd	10/86	£60,000	16+15	1+2	0+2	2		
Newcastle Utd	11/88	£300,000	127+18 9	12+2	19	1	1	1

O'LEARY David — Leeds United

Full Name: O'LEARY, David Anthony
DOB: 2/5/58, Stoke Newington
FAPL Debut: Away v. Wimbledon † 5/9/92   Debut Goal:

Previous Clubs details			*App*			*Goals*		
Clubs	Signed	Fee	Lge	FLC	FAC	Lge	FLC	FAC
Arsenal	7/75	–	517+30	66+2	65	11	2	3
Leeds Utd	6/93							
FA Premier Lge Record								
Arsenal	92/93		6+5	2	1+3			

OLNEY Ian — Oldham Athletic

Full Name: OLNEY, Ian Douglas
DOB: 17/12/69, Luton
FAPL Debut: Away v. Arsenal † 26/8/92
Debut Goal: Home v. Leeds United 1/9/92

Previous Clubs details			*App*			*Goals*		
Clubs	Signed	Fee	Lge	FLC	FAC	Lge	FLC	FAC
Aston Villa	7/88	–	52+26	17+2	8+1	16	4	2
Oldham Ath	5/92	£700,000						

FA Premier Lge Record

92/93			32+2	3	1	12		1

PALLISTER Gary — Manchester United

Full Name: PALLISTER, Gary Andrew   DOB: 30/6/65, Ramsgate
FAPL Debut: Away v. Sheffield Utd 15/8/92   Debut Goal: –

Previous Clubs details			*App*			*Goals*		
Clubs	Signed	Fee	Lge	FLC	FAC	Lge	FLC	FAC
Middlesbrough	11/84	–	156	10	10	5		1
Darlington	10/85	Loan	7					
Man Utd	8/89	£2.3m	108+3	20	14	4		

FA Premier Lge Record

92/93			42	3	3	1		

PALMER Carlton — Sheffield Wednesday

Full Name: PALMER, Carlton Lloyd   DOB: 5/12/65, Rowley Regis
FAPL Debut: Away v. Everton 15/8/92
Debut Goal: Home v. Oldham 17/10/92

Previous Clubs details			*App*			*Goals*		
Clubs	Signed	Fee	Lge	FLC	FAC	Lge	FLC	FAC
West Brom Alb	12/84	–	114+7	7+1	4	4	1	
Sheffield Wed	2/89	£750,000	134	15	8	8		

FA Premier Lge Record

92/93			33+1	8	6+1	1	1	

PALMER Roger — Oldham Athletic

Full Name: PALMER, Roger Neil   DOB: 30/1/59, Manchester
FAPL Debut: Away v. Chelsea 15/8/92   Debut Goal: –

Previous Clubs details			*App*			*Goals*		
Clubs	Signed	Fee	Lge	FLC	FAC	Lge	FLC	FAC
Man City	1/77	–	22+9	3+3		9	1	
Oldham Ath	11/80	£70,000	413+28	34+2	19+4	141	10	5

FA Premier Lge Record

92/93			5+12	0+1				

PALMER Steve — Ipswich Town

Full Name: PALMER, Stephen Leonard   DOB: 31/3/68, Brighton
FAPL Debut: Away v. Nottingham Forest 31/10/92   Debut Goal: –

Previous Clubs details			*App*			*Goals*		
Clubs	Signed	Fee	Lge	FLC	FAC	Lge	FLC	FAC
Ipswich Town	8/89	–	32+14	2	6	1		

PARKER Garry
Aston Villa

Full Name: PARKER, Garry Stuart DOB: 7/9/65, Oxford
FAPL Debut: Away v. Ipswich Town 15/8/92
Debut Goal: Away v. Sheffield United 29/8/92

Previous Clubs details

Clubs	Signed	Fee	App Lge	FLC	FAC	Goals Lge	FLC	FAC
Luton Town	5/83	–	31+11	1+3	6+2	3	1	
Hull City	2/86	£72,000	82+2	5	4	8		
Nottingham F	3/88	£260,000	99+4	22+1	16	17	4	5
Aston Villa	11/91	£650,000	25		5			1

FA Premier Lge Record

92/93			37	5	4	9		

PARKER Paul
Manchester United

Full Name: PARKER, Paul Andrew DOB: 4/4/64, West Ham
FAPL Debut: Home v. Liverpool 18/10/92
Debut Goal: Home v. Tottenham Hotspur 9/1/93

Previous Clubs details

Clubs	Signed	Fee	App Lge	FLC	FAC	Goals Lge	FLC	FAC
Fulham	4/82	–	140+13	16	11	2	1	
QPR	6/87	£300,000	121+4	14	16	1		
Man Utd	8/91	£2m	24+2	6	3			

FA Premier Lge Record

92/93			31	2	3	1		

PARLOUR Ray
Arsenal

Full Name: PARLOUR, Raymond DOB: 7/3/73, Romford
FAPL Debut: Home v. Sheffield Wednesday 29/8/92
Debut Goal: Home v. Sheffield Wednesday 29/8/92

Previous Clubs details

Clubs	Signed	Fee	App Lge	FLC	FAC	Goals Lge	FLC	FAC
Arsenal	3/91	–	2+4			1		

FA Premier Lge Record

92/93			16+5	3+1	4	1	1	

PEACOCK Darren
Queens Park Rangers

Full Name: PEACOCK, Darren DOB: 3/2/68, Bristol
FAPL Debut: Away v. Manchester City 17/8/92
Debut Goal: Home v. Coventry 20/2/93

Previous Clubs details

Clubs	Signed	Fee	App Lge	FLC	FAC	Goals Lge	FLC	FAC
Newport County	2/86	–	24+4	2	1			

| Hereford Utd | 3/89 | – | 56+7 | 6 | 6 | 5 | | | 1 |
| QPR | 12/90 | £200,000 | 58 | 4 | 1 | 1 | | | |

FA Premier Lge Record

| | 92/93 | | 35+3 | | | 2 | | | |

PEACOCK Gavin Chelsea

Full Name: PEACOCK, Gavin   DOB: 18/11/67 Welling, Kent

Previous Club Details			*Apps*			*Goals*		
Clubs	Signed	Fee	Lge	FLC	FAC	Lge	FLC	FAC
QPR	11/84		7+10		0+1	1		
Gillingham	10/87	£40,000	69+1	4	2	11		
Bournemouth	8/89	£250,000	56	6	2	8		
Newcastle Utd	11/90	£150,000	102+4	6	6	35	5	2
Chelsea	8/93	£1.25m						

PEARCE Andy Sheffield Wednesday

Full Name: PEARCE, Andrew John   DOB: 20/4/66, Bradford on Avon
FAPL Debut: Home v. Middlesbrough 15/8/92
Debut Goal: Home v. Crystal Palace 3/10/92

Previous Clubs details			*App*			*Goals*		
Clubs	Signed	Fee	Lge	FLC	FAC	Lge	FLC	FAC
Coventry City	5/90	£15,000	47	4	2	3		
Sheffield Wed	8/93	£500,000						

FA Premier Lge Record

| Coventry City | 92/93 | | 21+3 | 2 | 1 | 1 | | |

PEARCE Ian Chelsea

Full Name: PEARCE, Ian   DOB: 7/5/74 Bury St. Edmonds
FAPL Debut: Home v. Liverpool † 9/5/92   Debut Goal:

Previous Clubs details			*App*			*Goals*		
Clubs	Signed	Fee	Lge	FLC	FAC	Lge	FLC	FAC
Chelsea	8/91		0+3					

FA Premier Lge Record

| | 92/93 | | 0+1 | | | | | |

PEARSON Nigel Sheffield Wednesday

Full Name: PEARSON, Nigel Graham   DOB: 21/8/63, Nottingham
FAPL Debut: Away v. Everton 15/8/92
Debut Goal: Away v. Everton 15/8/92

Previous Clubs details			*App*			*Goals*		
Clubs	Signed	Fee	Lge	FLC	FAC	Lge	FLC	FAC
Shrewsbry Tn	11/81	£5,000	153	19	6	5		
Sheffield Wed	10/87	£250,000	159	14	9	13	5	1

FA Premier Lge Record

| | 92/93 | | 13+3 | 3+2 | 2 | 1 | | |

PEMBERTON John — Sheffield United

Full Name: PEMBERTON, John Matthew DOB: 18/11/64, Oldham
FAPL Debut: Away v. Norwich City 21/11/92 Debut Goal: –

Previous Clubs details

Clubs	Signed	Fee	App Lge	FLC	FAC	Goals Lge	FLC	FAC
Rochdale	9/84	–	1					
Crewe Alex	3/85	–	116+5	7	3	1	1	
Crystal Palace	3/88	£80,000	76+2	6+1	8	2		
Sheffield Utd	7/90	£300,000	40+1	3				

FA Premier Lge Record

92/93			19		4			

PENRICE Gary — Queens Park Rangers

Full Name: PENRICE, Gary Kenneth DOB: 23/3/64, Bristol
FAPL Debut: Away v. Coventry † 26/8/92
Debut Goal: Home v. Middlesbrough 19/8/92

Previous Clubs details

Clubs	Signed	Fee	App Lge	FLC	FAC	Goals Lge	FLC	FAC
Bristol Rv	11/84	–	186+2	11	11	53	3	7
Watford	11/89	£500,000	41+2		4	17		
Aston Villa	3/91	£1m	14+6			1		
QPR	10/91	£625,000	13+6	1	10+1	3	1	

FA Premier Lge Record

92/93			10+4	2+1	1	6		1

PETTERSON Andy — Ipswich Town

Full Name: PETTERSON, Andy DOB:
FAPL Debut: Home v. Nottingham Forest 8/5/93 Debut Goal:

Previous Club Details

Clubs	Signed	Fee	Apps Lge	FLC	FAC	Goals Lge	FLC	FAC
Ipswich Town								

FA Premier Lge Record

92/93			1					

PEYTON Gerry — West Ham United

Full Name: PEYTON, Gerald Joseph DOB: 20/5/56, Birmingham
FAPL Debut: Home v. Sheffield Wed. † 30/1/93 Debut Goal: –

Previous Clubs details

Clubs	Signed	Fee	App Lge	FLC	FAC	Goals Lge	FLC	FAC
Burnley	5/75	–	30	1	1			
Fulham	12/76	£40,000	345	26	20			
Southend Utd	9/83	Loan	10					
Bournemouth	7/86	–	202	15	13			
Everton	7/91	£80,000						
Bolton Wnd	2/92	Loan	1					

Brentford	9/92	Loan	14
Chelsea		Loan	
Brentford			5
West Ham Utd			
FA Premier Lge Record			
Chelsea	92/93		0+1

PHELAN Mike   Manchester United

Full Name: PHELAN, Michael Christopher   DOB: 24/9/62, Nelson
FAPL Debut: Away v. Sheffield Utd † 15/8/92 Debut Goal: –

Previous Clubs details			*App*			*Goals*		
Clubs	Signed	Fee	Lge	FLC	FAC	Lge	FLC	FAC
Burnley	7/80	–	166+2	16	16	9	2	
Norwich Cty	7/85	£60,000	155+1	14	11	9		1
Man United	6/89	£750,000	82+7	12+2	8	2		
FA Premier Lge Record								
	92/93		5+6		2			1

PHELAN Terry   Manchester City

Full Name: PHELAN, Terence   DOB: 16/3/67, Manchester
FAPL Debut: Home v. Norwich City 26/8/92
Debut Goal: Away v. Chelsea 9/1/93

Previous Clubs details			*App*			*Goals*		
Clubs	Signed	Fee	Lge	FLC	FAC	Lge	FLC	FAC
Leeds Utd	8/84	–	12+2	3				
Swansea City	7/86	–	45	4	5			
Wimbledon	7/87	£100,000	156+4	13+2	11	1		2
Man City	8/92	£2.5m						
FA Premier Lge Record								
	92/93		37	3	5			1

PHILLIPS David   Norwich City

Full Name: PHILLIPS, David Owen   DOB: 29/7/63, Wegberg
FAPL Debut: Away v. Arsenal 15/8/92
Debut Goal: Away v. Arsenal 15/8/92

Previous Clubs details			*App*			*Goals*		
Clubs	Signed	Fee	Lge	FLC	FAC	Lge	FLC	FAC
Plymouth Arg	8/81	–	65+8	2+1	12+1	15		
Man City	8/84	£65,000	81	8	5	13		
Coventry City	6/86	£150,000	93+7	8	9	8		1
Norwich City	6/89	£525,000	110	10	12	9		1
FA Premier Lge Record								
	92/93		42	2	2	9		

PIECHNIK Torben   Liverpool

Full Name: PIECHNIK, Torben   DOB:
FAPL Debut: Away v. Aston Villa 19/9/92   Debut Goal:

Previous Club Details

			Apps			*Goals*		
Clubs	Signed	Fee	Lge	FLC	FAC	Lge	FLC	FAC
FC Copenhagen								
Liverpool	9/92	£500,000						

FA Premier Lge Record

92/93			15+1	5	2			

POINTON Neil   Oldham Athletic

Full Name: POINTON, Neil Geoffrey   DOB: 28/11/64, Warsop, Vale
FAPL Debut: Home v. Nottingham Forest 22/8/92
Debut Goal: Home v. Middlesbrough 28/11/92

Previous Clubs details

			App			*Goals*		
Clubs	Signed	Fee	Lge	FLC	FAC	Lge	FLC	FAC
Scunthorpe Utd	8/82	–	159	9	13	2	1	
Everton	11/85	£75,000	95+7	6+2	16+2	5		
Man City	7/90	£600,000	74	8	4	2		
Oldham								

FA Premier Lge Record

92/93			34	4		3		

POLSTON John   Norwich City

Full Name: POLSTON, John David   DOB: 10/6/68, Walthamstow
FAPL Debut: Away v. Arsenal 15/8/92
Debut Goal: Home v. Aston Villa 24/3/93

Previous Clubs details

			App			*Goals*		
Clubs	Signed	Fee	Lge	FLC	FAC	Lge	FLC	FAC
Tottenham H	7/85	–	17+7	3+1		1		
Norwich City	7/90	£250,000	43+3	0+1	9+1	5		

FA Premier Lge Record

92/93			34	2		1		

POTTS Steve   West Ham United

Full Name: POTTS, Steve   DOB: 7/5/67, Hartford, USA

Previous Club Details

			Apps			*Goals*		
Clubs	Signed	Fee	Lge	FLC	FAC	Lge	FLC	FAC
West Ham	7/83		185+10	20+1	23	1		

POWELL Lee   Southampton

Full Name: POWELL, Lee   DOB: 2/6/73, Caerleon
FAPL Debut: Home v. Wimbledon † 17/10/92   Debut Goal: –

Previous Clubs details

Clubs	Signed	Fee	App Lge	FLC	FAC	Goals Lge	FLC	FAC
Southampton	5/91	–	1+3					

FA Premier Lge Record

92/93			0+2					

POWER Lee — Norwich City

Full Name: POWER, Lee Michael — DOB: 30/6/72, Lewisham
FAPL Debut: Home v. Everton † 22/8/92
Debut Goal: Away v. Crystal Palace 29/8/92

Previous Clubs details

Clubs	Signed	Fee	App Lge	FLC	FAC	Goals Lge	FLC	FAC
Norwich City	7/90	–	15+6	1		4		
Charlton Ath	12/92	Loan	5					

FA Premier Lge Record

92/93			11+7	0+1		6		

PRESSMAN Kevin — Sheffield Wednesday

Full Name: PRESSMAN, Kevin Paul — DOB: 6/11/67, Fareham
FAPL Debut: Home v. Southampton 12/4/92 — Debut Goal: –

Previous Clubs details

Clubs	Signed	Fee	App Lge	FLC	FAC	Goals Lge	FLC	FAC
Sheffield Wed	3/92	–	59	6				
Stoke City	3/92	Loan	4					

FA Premier Lge Record

92/93			3	2				

PRIOR Spencer — Norwich City

Name: PRIOR, Spencer — DOB: 22/04/71, Hockley

Previous Club Details

Clubs	Signed	Fee	Apps Lge	FLC	FAC	Goals Lge	FLC	FAC
Southend Utd	5/89		135	9	5	3		
Norwich City	8/93	£200,000						

QUIGLEY Mike — Manchester City

Full Name: QUIGLEY, Michael Anthony — DOB: 2/10/70, Manchester
FAPL Debut: Away v. Norwich City † 20/2/93 — Debut Goal: –

Previous Clubs details

Clubs	Signed	Fee	App Lge	FLC	FAC	Goals Lge	FLC	FAC
Man City	7/89	–	0+5					

FA Premier Lge Record

92/93			1+4					

QUINN Niall　　　　　　　　　　　　　　　　　Manchester City

Full Name:　QUINN, Niall John　　　　DOB: 6/10/66, Dublin
FAPL Debut:　Home v. QPR 17/8/92
Debut Goal:　Home v. Oldham Athletic 29/8/92

Previous Clubs details

Clubs	Signed	Fee	App			Goals		
			Lge	FLC	FAC	Lge	FLC	FAC
Arsenal	11/83	–	59+8	14+2	8+2	14	4	2
Man City	3/90	£800,000	82	7	3	36	2	1
FA Premier Lge Record								
	92/93		39	3	5	9	1	1

QUINN Mick　　　　　　　　　　　　　　　　　Coventry City

Full Name:　QUINN, Mick　　　　　　DOB: 2/5/62, Liverpool
FAPL Debut:　Home v. Manchester City 21/11/92
Debut Goal:　Home v. Manchester City 21/11/92

Previous Clubs details

Clubs	Signed	Fee	App			Goals		
			Lge	FLC	FAC	Lge	FLC	FAC
Derby County								
Wigan Ath	9/79		56+13	5	3	19	1	1
Stockport C	7/82		62+1	5	2	39	2	
Oldham Ath	1/84	£50,000	78+2	4	2	34	2	1
Portsmouth	3/86		115+6	7	7	54	6	7
Newcastle U	6/89	£680,000	110+5	7+2	7	59		4
Coventry C	11/92	£250,000						
FA Premier Lge Record								
	92/93		26		1	17		

RADOSAVIJEVIC Redray　　　　　　　　　　　　　Everton

Full Name:　RADOSAVIJEVIC, Pedray　DOB:
FAPL Debut:　Away v. Leeds United 26/9/92
Debut Goal:　Away v. Middlesbrough 10/4/93

Previous Clubs details

Clubs	Signed	Fee	App			Goals		
			Lge	FLC	FAC	Lge	FLC	FAC
St. Louis, USA								
Everton	9/92	£100,000						
FA Premier Lge Record								
	92/93		13+11	1	1	3		

READY Karl　　　　　　　　　　　　Queens Park Rangers

Full Name:　READY, Karl　　　　　　DOB: 14/8/72, Neath
FAPL Debut:　Home v. Coventry 20/2/93　Debut Goal: –

Previous Clubs details

Clubs	Signed	Fee	App			Goals		
			Lge	FLC	FAC	Lge	FLC	FAC
QPR	8/90	–	1	0+1				
FA Premier Lge Record								
	92/93		2+1					

REDKNAPP Jamie — Liverpool

Full Name: REDKNAPP, Jamie Frank   DOB: 25/6/73, Barton on Sea
FAPL Debut: Away v. Leeds United 29/8/92
Debut Goal: H.v Chelsea 5/9/92

Previous Clubs details			*App*			*Goals*		
Clubs	Signed	Fee	Lge	FLC	FAC	Lge	FLC	FAC
Bournemouth	6/90	–	6+7	3	3			
Liverpool	1/91	£350,000	5+1		2	1		
FA Premier Lge Record								
	92/93		27+2	6	1	2	1	

REDMOND Steve — Oldham Athletic

Full Name: REDMOND, Stephen   DOB: 2/11/67, Liverpool
FAPL Debut: Away v. Chelsea 15/8/92   Debut Goal:

Previous Clubs details			*App*			*Goals*		
Clubs	Signed	Fee	Lge	FLC	FAC	Lge	FLC	FAC
Man City	12/84	–	231+15	24	17	6		
Oldham Ath								
FA Premier Lge Record								
	92/93		28+3	4	0+1			

REID Peter — Manchester City

Full Name: REID, Peter   DOB: 20/6/56, Huyton
FAPL Debut: Away v. Wimbledon 1/9/92   Debut Goal: –

Previous Clubs details			*App*			*Goals*		
Clubs	Signed	Fee	Lge	FLC	FAC	Lge	FLC	FAC
Bolton Wand	5/74	–	222+3	18+1	17	23	1	1
Everton	12/82	£60,000	155+4	23+2	35	8	1	3
QPR	2/89	–	29	2+1		1		
Man City	12/89	–	75+4	2	5		1	1
FA Premier Lge Record								
	92/93		14+6	1+1	2			

RENNIE David — Coventry City

Full Name: RENNIE, David   DOB:
FAPL Debut: Home v. Arsenal 13/3/93   Debut Goal:

Previous Clubs details			*App*			*Goals*		
Clubs	Signed	Fee	Lge	FLC	FAC	Lge	FLC	FAC
Leicester	5/82		21	2		1		
Leeds Utd	1/86	£50,000	95+6	7	7	5		1
Bristol City	7/89	£175,000	103+3	8	9	8		
Birmingham	2/92	£120,000	32+3	1		4		
Coventry City	3/93	Swop						
FA Premier Lge Record								
	92/93		4					

RICHARDSON Kevin   Aston Villa

Full Name: RICHARDSON, Kevin   DOB: 4/12/62, Newcastle
FAPL Debut: Away v. Ipswich Town 15/8/92
Debut Goal: Home v. Chelsea 2/9/92

Previous Clubs details

Clubs	Signed Fee	App Lge	FLC	FAC	Goals Lge	FLC	FAC
Everton	12/80 –	95+14	10+3	13	16	3	1
Watford	9/86 £225,000	39	3	7	2		
Arsenal	8/87 £200,000	88+8	13+3	9	5	2	1
Real Sociedad	6/90 £750,000						
Aston Villa	8/91 £450,000	42	2	5	6		

FA Premier Lge Record

92/93		42	5	4	2	1	

RIDEOUT Paul   Everton

Full Name: RIDEOUT, Paul D.   DOB: 14/8/64, Bournemouth
FAPL Debut: Home v. Sheffield Wednesday 15/8/92
Debut Goal: Away v. Nottingham Forest 7/11/92

Previous Clubs details

Clubs	Signed Fee	App Lge	FLC	FAC	Goals Lge	FLC	FAC
Swindon Town	8/81	90+5			38		
Aston Villa	6/83	50+4			19		
Southampton	7/88	68+7			19		
Bari (Ita)							
Rangers							
Everton							

FA Premier Lge Record

92/93		17+7	4	1	3	2	

RIPLEY Stuart   Blackburn Rovers

Full Name: RIPLEY, Stuart Edward   DOB: 20/11/67, Middlesbrough
FAPL Debut: Away v. Crystal Palace 15/8/92
Debut Goal: Away v. Crystal Palace 15/8/92

Previous Clubs details

Clubs	Signed Fee	App Lge	FLC	FAC	Goals Lge	FLC	FAC
Middlesbrough	11/85	210+39	21+2	17+1	3	1	1
Bolton Wand	2/86 Loan	5					
Blackburn Rv							

FA Premier Lge Record

92/93		38+2	6	4	7	2	

RITCHIE Andy   Oldham Athletic

Full Name: RITCHIE, Andrew Timothy   DOB: 28/11/60, Manchester
FAPL Debut: Home v. Manchester City † 26/1/93
Debut Goal: Away v. Middlesbrough 23/3/93

Clubs	Signed Fee	App Lge	FLC	FAC	Goals Lge	FLC	FAC
Man Utd	12/77 –	26+7	3+2	3+1	13		
Brighton & HA	10/80 £500,000	82+7	3+1	9	23	1	2
Leeds Utd	3/83 £150,000	127+9	11	9	40	3	1
Oldham Ath	8/87 £50,000	139+11	15	6	67	17	3

FA Premier Lge Record

92/93		10+2			3		

ROBERTS Tony   Queens Park Rangers

Full Name: ROBERTS, Anthony Mark   DOB: 4/8/69, Holyhead
FAPL Debut: Home v. Southampton 19/8/92   Debut Goal: –

Previous Clubs details

Clubs	Signed Fee	App Lge	FLC	FAC	Goals Lge	FLC	FAC
QPR	7/87 –	19	3				

FA Premier Lge Record

92/93		28	2	2			

ROBINS Mark   Norwich City

Full Name: ROBINS, Mark Gordon   DOB: 22/12/69, Ashton-U-Lyne
FAPL Debut: Away v. Arsenal 15/8/92
Debut Goal: Away v. Arsenal 15/8/92

Previous Clubs details

Clubs	Signed Fee	App Lge	FLC	FAC	Goals Lge	FLC	FAC
Man Utd	12/86 –	19+29	0+7	4+4	11	2	3
Norwich City	8/92 £800,000						

FA Premier Lge Record

92/93		34+3	2+1		15	1	

ROBINSON Mark   Newcastle United

Full Name: ROBINSON, Mark   DOB: 21/11/68 Manchester

Previous Club Details

Clubs	Signed Fee	Apps Lge	FLC	FAC	Goals Lge	FLC	FAC
WBA	1/87	2	0+1				
Barnsley		118+19	5+2	4+1	5		
Newcastle Utd	3/93 £450,000	2+10					

ROBSON Bryan   Manchester United

Full Name: ROBSON, Bryan   DOB: 11/1/57, Witton Gilbert
FAPL Debut: Away v. Middlesbrough † 3/10/92
Debut Goal: Away v. Wimbledon 8/5/93

Previous Clubs details

Clubs	Signed Fee	App Lge	FLC	FAC	Goals Lge	FLC	FAC
West Brom Alb	8/74 –	194+4	17+1	10+2	39	2	3
Man Utd	10/81 £1.5m	311+5	44+1	32	72	5	9

ROBSON Mark   West Ham United

Full Name: ROBSON, Mark   DOB: 22/5/69, Stratford, London

Previous Clubs details

Clubs	Signed	Fee	App Lge	FLC	FAC	Goals Lge	FLC	FAC
Exeter City	10/86		26		2	7		
Tottenham	7/87		3+5					
Reading	3/88	Loan	5+2					
Watford	10/89	Loan	1					
Plymouth A	12/89	Loan	7					
Exeter City	1/92	Loan	7+1			1		
West Ham U	8/92		41+3	2	2	8		

ROBSON Stewart   Coventry City

Full Name: ROBSON, Stewart Ian   DOB: 6/11/64, Billericay

FAPL Debut: Home v. Middlesbrough 15/8/92 Debut Goal: –

Previous Clubs details

Clubs	Signed	Fee	App Lge	FLC	FAC	Goals Lge	FLC	FAC
Arsenal	11/81	–	150+1	20	13	16	3	1
West Ham	1/87	£700,000	68+1	8	6	4	1	1
Coventry City	3/91	–	40+1	2	1	3		

FA Premier Lge Record

92/93   14+1

ROCASTLE David   Leeds United

Full Name: ROCASTLE, David Carlyle   DOB: 2/5/67, Lewisham

FAPL Debut: Away v. Ipswich Town 3.10.92

Debut Goal: Home v. Manchester City 13/3/93

Previous Clubs details

Clubs	Signed	Fee	App Lge	FLC	FAC	Goals Lge	FLC	FAC
Arsenal	12/84	–	204+14	32+1	18+2	24	6	4
Leeds United	7/92	£2m						

FA Premier Lge Record

92/93   11+7   0+2   0+3   1

ROGERS Paul   Sheffield United

Full Name: ROGERS, Paul Anthony   DOB: 21/3/65, Portsmouth

FAPL Debut: Away v. Tottenham Hotspur 2/9/92

Debut Goal: Home v. Tottenham Hotspur 2/3/93

Previous Clubs details

Clubs	Signed	Fee	App Lge	FLC	FAC	Goals Lge	FLC	FAC
Sheffield Utd	1/92	£35,000	13					

FA Premier Lge Record

92/93   26+1   4   3   3   1

ROSENTHAL Ronny — Liverpool

Full Name: ROSENTHAL, Ronny DOB: 4/10/63, Haifa, Israel
FAPL Debut: Away v. Nottingham Forest † 16/8/92
Debut Goal: Away v. Aston Villa 19/9/92

Previous Clubs details

Clubs	Signed Fee	App Lge	FLC	FAC	Goals Lge	FLC	FAC
Liverpool	3/90 £1m	16+28	0+6	4+2	15		

FA Premier Lge Record

	92/93	16+11	2+1	1+1	6	1	

ROWLAND Keith — West Ham United

Name: ROWLAND, Keith DOB: 1/9/71, Portadown
FAPL Debut: Away v Norwich City † 16/1/9 Debut Goal: –

Previous Club Details

Clubs	Signed Fee	Apps Lge	FLC	FAC	Goals Lge	FLC	FAC
Bournemouth	10/89	65+6	5	8	2		
Coventry City	1/93 Loan						
West Ham	8/93 £110,000						

FA Premier Lge Record

Coventry City	92/93	0+2					

RUDDOCK Neil — Liverpool

Full Name: RUDDOCK, Neil DOB: 9/5/68, Wandsworth
FAPL Debut: Away v. Southampton 15/8/92
Debut Goal: Home v. Liverpool 31/10/92

Previous Clubs details

Clubs	Signed Fee	App Lge	FLC	FAC	Goals Lge	FLC	FAC
Millwall	3/86 –						
Tottenham H	4/86 £50,000	7+2		1+1			1
Millwall	6/88 £300,000	0+2	2		1	3	
Southampton	2/89 £250,000	100+7	14+1	10	9	1	3
Tottenham H	5/92 £750,000						
Liverpool	7/93 £2.5m						

FA Premier Lge Record

Tottenham H	92/93	38	4	5	3		

RUSH Ian — Liverpool

Full Name: RUSH, Ian James DOB: 20/10/61, St Asaph
FAPL Debut: Away v. Nottingham Forest 16/8/92
Debut Goal: Away v. Manchester United 18/10/92

Previous Clubs details

Clubs	Signed Fee	App Lge	FLC	FAC	Goals Lge	FLC	FAC
Chester City	7/79 –	33+1		5	14		3
Liverpool	4/80 £300,000	224	47	31+1	139	25	19
Juventus (Ita)	6/87 £3.8m						

Liverpool	8/88	£2.2m	105+10	13	20+2	45	9	15
FA Premier Lge Record								
92/93			31+1	4	1	14	1	1

SAMWAYS Vinny   Tottenham Hotspur

Full Name: SAMWAYS, Vincent   DOB: 27/10/67, Bethnal Green
FAPL Debut: Away v. Southampton 15/8/92   Debut Goal:

Previous Clubs details			*App*			*Goals*		
Clubs	Signed	Fee	Lge	FLC	FAC	Lge	FLC	FAC
Tottenham H	10/85	–	92+28	18+4	7+1	8	3	
FA Premier Lge Record								
92/93			34	3	5		1	2

SANCHEZ Lawrie   Wimbledon

Full Name: SANCHEZ, Lawrence Philip   DOB: 22/10/59, Lambeth
FAPL Debut: Away v. Leeds United 15/8/93
Debut Goal: Home v. Arsenal 5/9/93

Previous Clubs details			*App*			*Goals*		
Clubs	Signed	Fee	Lge	FLC	FAC	Lge	FLC	FAC
Reading	9/76	–	249+13	20+1	14		1	
Wimbledon	12/84	£29,000	216+12	17	18+1		2	
FA Premier Lge Record								
92/93			23+4	1	3	4		

SAUNDERS Dean   Aston Villa

Full Name: SAUNDERS, Dean Nicholas   DOB: 21/6/64, Swansea
FAPL Debut: Home v. Nottingham Forest 16/8/92
Debut Goal: Home v. Chelsea 5/9/92

Previous Clubs details			*App*			*Goals*		
Clubs	Signed	Fee	Lge	FLC	FAC	Lge	FLC	FAC
Swansea City	6/82	–	42+7	2+1	1	12		
Cardiff City	3/85	Loan	3+1					
Brighton & HA	8/85	–	66+6	4	7	20		5
Oxford Utd	3/87	£60,000	57+2	9+1	2	22	8	2
Derby Cnty	10/88	£1m	106	12	4	42	1	
Liverpool	7/91	£2.9m	36	5	8	10	2	2
Aston Villa	9/92	£2.3m						
FA Premier Lge Record								
Liverpool	92/93		6			1		
Aston Villa			35	5	4	13	2	2

SCALES John   Wimbledon

Full Name: SCALES, John Robert   DOB: 4/6/66, Harrogate
FAPL Debut: Away v. Leeds United 15/8/92
Debut Goal: Home v. Middlesbrough 9/3/93

Previous Clubs details			App			Goals		
Clubs	Signed	Fee	Lge	FLC	FAC	Lge	FLC	FAC
Bristol Rvrs	7/85	–	68+4	3	6	2		
Wimbledon	7/87	£70,000	163+5	11+1	11+1	10		
FA Premier Lge Record								
	92/93		32	2	5	1		

SCHMEICHEL Peter Manchester United

Full Name: SCHMEICHEL, Peter Boleslaw DOB: 18/11/68, Denmark
FAPL Debut: Away v. Sheffield Utd 15/8/92 Debut Goal:

Previous Clubs details			App			Goals		
Clubs	Signed	Fee	Lge	FLC	FAC	Lge	FLC	FAC
Man Utd	8/91	£550,000	40	6	3			
FA Premier Lge Record								
	92/93		42					

SCOTT Andy Sheffield United

Name: SCOTT, Andy DOB: 2/8/72, Epsom
FAPL Debut: Away v Sheffield Wednesday † 21/4/93
Debut Goal: Home v Chelsea 8/5/93

Previous Club Details			Apps			Goals		
Clubs	Signed	Fee	Lge	FLC	FAC	Lge	FLC	FAC
Non-League								
Sheffield Utd	11/92	£50,000						
FA Premier Lge Record								
	92/93		1+1					

SCOTT Kevin Newcastle United

Full Name: SCOTT, Kevin DOB: 17/12/66 Easington

Previous Club Details			Apps			Goals		
Clubs	Signed	Fee	Lge	FLC	FAC	Lge	FLC	FAC
Newcastle Utd	12/84		209	16	7+1	8		1

SEALEY Les Manchester United

Full Name: SEALEY, Les DOB: 29/9/57, Bethnal Grn

Previous Clubs details			App			Goals		
Clubs	Signed	Fee	Lge	FLC	FAC	Lge	FLC	FAC
Coventry City	3/76		156	11	9			
Luton Town	8/83	£100,000	207	21	28			
Man Utd	12/89	Loan						
Man Utd	3/90	Loan	2		1			
Man Utd	6/90		31	8	3			
Aston Villa	7/91		18		4			
Coventry City	3/92	Loan	2					
Birmingham C	10/92	Loan	12					
Man Utd	1/93							

SEAMAN David   Arsenal

Full Name: SEAMAN, David Andrew   DOB: 19/9/63, Rotherham
FAPL Debut: Home v. Norwich 15/8/92   Debut Goal: –

Previous Clubs details

Clubs	Signed	Fee	App Lge	FLC	FAC	Goals Lge	FLC	FAC
Leeds Utd	9/81	–						
Peterboro Utd	8/82	£4,000	91	10	5			
Birmingham C	10/84	£100,000	75	4	5			
QPR	8/86	£225,000	141	13	17			
Arsenal	5/90	£1.3m	80	7	9			

FA Premier Lge Record

92/93			39	9	8			

SEDGLEY Steve   Tottenham Hotspur

Full Name: SEDGLEY, Stephen Philip   DOB: 26/5/68, Enfield
FAPL Debut: Home v. Crystal Palace 22/8/92
Debut Goal: Home v. Crystal Palace 22/8/92

Previous Clubs details

Clubs	Signed	Fee	App Lge	FLC	FAC	Goals Lge	FLC	FAC
Coventry City	5/86	–	81+3	9	2+2	3	2	
Tottenham H	7/89	£750,000	85+15	13+1	7+2		1	

FA Premier Lge Record

92/93			20+2	3	2	3		1

SEGERS Hans   Wimbledon

Full Name: SEGERS, Johannes   DOB: 30/10/61, Eindhoven
FAPL Debut: Away v. Leeds United 15/8/92   Debut Goal: –

Previous Clubs details

Clubs	Signed	Fee	App Lge	FLC	FAC	Goals Lge	FLC	FAC
Nottingham F	8/84	£50,000	58	4	5			
Stoke City	2/87	Loan	1					
Sheffield Utd	11/87	Loan	10					
Dunfermline	3/88	Loan						
Wimbledon	9/88	£180,000	149	13	10			

FA Premier Lge Record

92/93			41	4	5			

SELLARS Scott   Newcastle United

Full Name: SELLARS, Scott   DOB: 27/11/65, Sheffield
FAPL Debut: Away v. Southampton † 19/9/92   Debut Goal: –

Previous Clubs details

Clubs	Signed	Fee	App Lge	FLC	FAC	Goals Lge	FLC	FAC
Leeds Utd	7/83	–	72+2	4	4	12	1	
Blackburn Rv	7/86	£20,000	194+8	12	11	35	3	1
Leeds Utd	7/92	£800,000						

| Newcastle Utd | 3/93 | £700,000 | 13 | | 2 | | |

FA Premier Lge Record

Leeds Utd	92/93		6+1	1+1			

SELLEY Ian   Arsenal

Full Name: SELLEY, Ian   DOB: 14/6/74, Chertsey
FAPL Debut: Home v. Blackburn Rovers 12/9/92 Debut Goal:

Previous Clubs details			App			Goals		
Clubs	Signed	Fee	Lge	FLC	FAC	Lge	FLC	FAC
Arsenal	5/92	–						

FA Premier Lge Record

	92/93		9	1	3			

SHARPE Graeme   Oldham Athletic

Full Name: SHARPE, Graeme Marshall   DOB: 16/10/60, Glasgow
FAPL Debut: Away v. Chelsea 15/8/92
Debut Goal: Home v. Crystal Palace 19/8/92

Previous Clubs details			App			Goals		
Clubs	Signed	Fee	Lge	FLC	FAC	Lge	FLC	FAC
Everton	4/80	£125,000	306+16	46+2	52+2	110	15	20
Oldham Ath	7/91	£500,000	42	4	2	12	2	1

FA Premier Lge Record

	92/93		20+1	4	1+1	7		

SHARP Kevin   Leeds United

Full Name: SHARP, Kevin   DOB:
FAPL Debut: Away v. Crystal Palace 17/4/93 Debut Goal:

Previous Clubs details			App			Goals		
Clubs	Signed	Fee	Lge	FLC	FAC	Lge	FLC	FAC
Auxerre (Fra)		£120,000						

FA Premier Lge Record

	92/93		4					

SHARPE Lee   Manchester United

Full Name: SHARPE, Lee Stuart   DOB: 27/5/71, Halesowen
FAPL Debut: Away v. Aston Villa 7/11/92
Debut Goal: Home v. Coventry City 28/12/92

Previous Clubs details			App			Goals		
Clubs	Signed	Fee	Lge	FLC	FAC	Lge	FLC	FAC
Torquay Utd	5/88	–	9+5			3		
Man Utd	5/88	£185,000	60+17	11+4	8+2	3	7	

FA Premier Lge Record

	92/93		27		3	1		

SHEARER Alan Blackburn Rovers

Full Name: SHEARER, Alan DOB: 31/8/70, Newcastle
FAPL Debut: Away v. Crystal Palace 15/8/92
Debut Goal: Away v. Crystal Palace 15/8/92

Previous Clubs details

Clubs	Signed	Fee	Lge	FLC	FAC	Lge	FLC	FAC
						Goals		
Southampton	4/88	–	105+13	16+2	11+3	23	11	4
Blackburn Rv	7/92	£3.3m						

FA Premier Lge Record

92/93			21	5		16	6	

SHEEDY Kevin Newcastle United

Full Name: SHEEDY, Kevin DOB: 21/10/59 Buith Wells

Previous Club Details

Clubs	Signed	Fee	Lge	FLC	FAC	Lge	FLC	FAC
			Apps			*Goals*		
Hereford Utd	10/76		47+4	2+1	2	4		1
Liverpool	7/78	£80,000	1+2	2			2	
Everton	8/82	£100,000	263+11	31+1	38	67	7	15
Newcastle Utd	2/92		36+2	4	2+1	3		1

SHERIDAN Tony Coventry City

Full Name: SHERIDAN, Anthony Joseph DOB: 21/10/74, Dublin
FAPL Debut: Away v. Leeds Utd 31/10/92 Debut Goal:

Previous Clubs details

Clubs	Signed	Fee	Lge	FLC	FAC	Lge	FLC	FAC
			App			*Goals*		
Coventry City	10/91	–						

FA Premier Lge Record

92/93			1					

SHERIDAN John Sheffield Wednesday

Full Name: SHERIDAN, John Joseph DOB: 1/10/64, Manchester
FAPL Debut: Home v. Blackburn Rovers 31/10/92
Debut Goal: Home v. Manchester United 26/12/92

Previous Clubs details

Clubs	Signed	Fee	Lge	FLC	FAC	Lge	FLC	FAC
			App			*Goals*		
Leeds Utd	3/82	–	225+5	14	11+1	47	3	5
Nottingham F	7/89	£650,000	1					
Sheffield Wed	11/89	£500,000	96+1	11	7	18	1	2

FA Premier Lge Record

92/93			25	7	8	3	2	1

SHERINGHAM Teddy Tottenham Hotspur

Full Name: SHERINGHAM, Edward Paul DOB: 2/4/66, Walthamstow
FAPL Debut: Home v. Liverpool 16/8/92
Debut Goal: Home v. Liverpool 16/8/92

Previous Clubs details			App			Goals		
Clubs	Signed	Fee	Lge	FLC	FAC	Lge	FLC	FAC
Millwall	1/84		205+15	16+1	12	94	8	4
Aldershot	2/85	Loan	4+1					
Nottingham F	7/91	£2m	39	10	4	13	5	2
Tottenham H	8/92	£2.1m						
FA Premier Lge Record								
Nottingham F	92/93		3			1		
Tottenham H			38	4	5	21	3	4

SHERON Mike — Manchester City

Full Name: SHERON, Michael Nigel   DOB: 11/1/72, Liverpool
FAPL Debut: Home v. QPR † 17/8/92
Debut Goal: Home v. Southampton 24/10/92

Previous Clubs details			App			Goals		
Clubs	Signed	Fee	Lge	FLC	FAC	Lge	FLC	FAC
Man City	7/90	–	20+9	2+2	0+1	6	1	
Bury	3/91	Loan	1+4			1		
FA Premier Lge Record								
	92/93		33+5	2	5	11		3

SHERWOOD Tim — Blackburn Rovers

Full Name: SHERWOOD, Timothy Alan   DOB: 2/2/69, St Albans
FAPL Debut: Away v. Crystal Palace 15/8/92
Debut Goal: Home v. Norwich City 3/10/92

Previous Clubs details			App			Goals		
Clubs	Signed	Fee	Lge	FLC	FAC	Lge	FLC	FAC
Watford	2/87	–	23+7	4+1	9	2		
Norwich City	7/87	£175,000	66+5	7	4	10	1	
Blackburn Rv	2/92	£500,000	7+4					
FA Premier Lge Record								
	92/93		38+1	6	4(1)	3		

SHIPPERLEY Neil — Chelsea

Full Name: SHIPPERLEY, Neil   DOB: 30/10/74 Chatham
FAPL Debut: Away v. Southampton 10/4/93
Debut Goal: Home v. Wimbledon 12/4/93

Previous Clubs details			App			Goals		
Clubs	Signed	Fee	Lge	FLC	FAC	Lge	FLC	FAC
Chelsea								
FA Premier Lge Record								
	92/93		2+1			1		

SHIRTLIFF Peter — Sheffield Wednesday

Full Name: SHIRTLIFF, Peter Andrew   DOB: 6/2/61, Hoyland

FAPL Debut: Away v. Crystal Palace 25/8/92   Debut Goal: –

Previous Clubs details			*App*			*Goals*		
Clubs	Signed	Fee	Lge	FLC	FAC	Lge	FLC	FAC
Sheffield Wed	10/78	–	188	17+1	17+1	4		1
Charlton Ath	7/86	£125,000	102+1	10	5	7		
Sheffield Wed	7/89	£500,000	84	13	6	4	1	2
FA Premier Lge Record								
	92/93		20	5	3			

SHUTT Carl   Leeds United

Full Name: SHUTT, Carl Steven   DOB: 10/10/61, Sheffield
FAPL Debut: Away v. Southampton † 19/8/92   Debut Goal: –

Previous Clubs details			*App*			*Goals*		
Clubs	Signed	Fee	Lge	FLC	FAC	Lge	FLC	FAC
Sheffield Wed	5/85	–	36+4	3	4+1	16	1	4
Bristol City	10/87	£55,000	39+7	5+2	7+1	10	4	4
Leeds Utd	3/89	£50,000	40+25	5+2	6	17	1	
FA Premier Lge Record								
	92/93		6+9	1	4		1	1

SIMPSON Fitzroy   Manchester City

Full Name: SIMPSON, Fitzroy   DOB: 26/2/70, Bradford on Avon
FAPL Debut: Home v. QPR 17/8/92
Debut Goal: Home v. Nottingham Forest 3/10/92

Previous Clubs details			*App*			*Goals*		
Clubs	Signed	Fee	Lge	FLC	FAC	Lge	FLC	FAC
Swindon Tn	7/88	–	78+26	9+1	2+1	9	1	
Man City	3/92	£500,000	9+2					
FA Premier Lge Record								
	92/93		27+2	3	5	1		

SINCLAIR Frank   Chelsea

Full Name: SINCLAIR, Frank Mohammed   DOB: 3/12/71, Lambeth
FAPL Debut: Away v. Manchester City 20/9/92   Debut Goal: –

Previous Clubs details			*App*			*Goals*		
Clubs	Signed	Fee	Lge	FLC	FAC	Lge	FLC	FAC
Chelsea	5/90	–	12		1			
West Brom	12/91	Loan	6			1		
FA Premier Lge Record								
	92/93		32	6	1	1		

SINTON Andy   Sheffield Wednesday

Full Name: SINTON, Andrew   DOB: 19/3/66, Newcastle
FAPL Debut: Away v. Manchester City 17/8/92
Debut Goal: Away v. Manchester City 17/8/92

Previous Clubs details			*App*			*Goals*		
Clubs	Signed	Fee	Lge	FLC	FAC	Lge	FLC	FAC
Cambridge Utd	4/83	–	90+3	6	3	13	1	
Brentford	12/85	£25,000	149	8	11	28	3	1
QPR	3/89	£350,000	124	10	11	15		2
Sheffield Wed	8/93	£2.75m						

FA Premier Lge Record

92/93	36	4	2	7

SKINNER Justin — Wimbledon

Full Name: SKINNER, Justin James   DOB: 17/9/72, Dorking
FAPL Debut: Away v. Liverpool 26/9/92   Debut Goal:

Previous Clubs details			*App*			*Goals*		
Clubs	Signed	Fee	Lge	FLC	FAC	Lge	FLC	FAC
Wimbledon	7/91	–						

FA Premier Lge Record

92/93	1

SMALL Bryan — Aston Villa

Full Name: SMALL, Bryan   DOB: 15/11/71, Birmingham
FAPL Debut: Home v. Blackburn Rv. † 19/10/92   Debut Goal: –

Previous Clubs details			*App*			*Goals*		
Clubs	Signed	Fee	Lge	FLC	FAC	Lge	FLC	FAC
Aston Villa	7/90	–	8		2+1			

FA Premier Lge Record

92/93	10+4	1

SMALL Mike — West Ham United

Full Name: SMALL, Mike   DOB: 2/3/62 Birmingham
FAPL Debut: Debut Goal:

Previous Club Details			*Apps*			*Goals*		
Clubs	Signed	Fee	Lge	FLC	FAC	Lge	FLC	FAC
Luton Town			0+3					
(PAOK, Standard Liege, FC Twente, Go Ahead Eagles)								
Brighton	8/90	£50,000	39	2	3	15	1	2
West Ham	8/91	£400,000	42+7	4+1	4	13	4	

SMITH Alan — Arsenal

Full Name: SMITH, Alan Martin   DOB: 21/11/62, Bromsgrove
FAPL Debut: Home v. Norwich 15/8/92
Debut Goal: Away v. Nottingham Forest 17/10/92

Previous Clubs details			*App*			*Goals*		
Clubs	Signed	Fee	Lge	FLC	FAC	Lge	FLC	FAC
Leicester City	6/82	£22,000	190+10	8+1	4	76	4	4
Arsenal	5/87	£800,000	177+12	22+1	16	77	12	4

FA Premier Lge Record

92/93	27+4	7	5+2	3	2	1

SMITH David   Norwich City
Full Name: SMITH, David Christopher   DOB: 26/12/70, Liverpool
FAPL Debut: Home v. Blackburn Rovers 28/2/93   Debut Goal: –

Previous Clubs details			*App*			*Goals*		
Clubs	Signed	Fee	Lge	FLC	FAC	Lge	FLC	FAC
Norwich City	7/89	–	3+2		2			

FA Premier Lge Record

92/93	5+1

SMITH Jason   Coventry City
Name: SMITH, Jason   DOB:

Previous Club Details			*Apps*			*Goals*		
Clubs	Signed	Fee	Lge	FLC	FAC	Lge	FLC	FAC
Coventry City	8/93							

SNODIN Ian   Everton
Full Name: SNODIN, Ian   DOB: 15/8/63, Rotherham
FAPL Debut: Home v. Coventry City † 17/10/92   Debut Goal: –

Previous Clubs details			*App*			*Goals*		
Clubs	Signed	Fee	Lge	FLC	FAC	Lge	FLC	FAC
Doncaster Rv	8/80	–	181+7	9	11+1	25	1	1
Leeds Utd	5/85	£200,000	51	3	1	6	2	
Everton	1/87	£840,000	93+3	15+1	22	2	1	2

FA Premier Lge Record

92/93	19+1	2	2	1

SOUTHALL Neville   Everton
Full Name: SOUTHALL, Neville   DOB: 16/9/78, Llandudno
FAPL Debut: Home v. Sheffield Wed. 15/8/92   Debut Goal: –

Previous Clubs details			*App*			*Goals*		
Clubs	Signed	Fee	Lge	FLC	FAC	Lge	FLC	FAC
Bury	6/80	£6,000	39					
Everton	7/81	£150,000	371	48	55			
Port Vale	1/83	Loan	9					

FA Premier Lge Record

92/93	40	6	1

SPACKMAN Nigel   Chelsea
Full Name: SPACKMAN, Nigel   DOB:
FAPL Debut: Home v. Norwich City 12/9/92   Debut Goal:

Previous Clubs details			*App*			*Goals*		
Clubs	Signed	Fee	Lge	FLC	FAC	Lge	FLC	FAC
Bournemouth	5/80		118+1	4	7	10		

Chelsea	6/83	139+2	21+1	6	12	
Liverpool	2/87	39+2	1	6		1
QPR	2/89	27+2	2		1	1
Rangers	11/89					
Chelsea						

FA Premier Lge Record
92/93

SPEED Gary   Leeds United
Full Name: SPEED, Gary Andrew   DOB: 8/9/69, Hawarden
FAPL Debut: Home v. Wimbledon 15/8/92
Debut Goal: Away v. Aston Villa 19/8/92

Previous Clubs details			*App*			*Goals*		
Clubs	Signed	Fee	Lge	FLC	FAC	Lge	FLC	FAC
Leeds Utd	6/88	–	89+16	11+1	7	6		

FA Premier Lge Record

| 92/93 | | | 39 | 3 | 4 | 7 | 1 | 3 |

SPENCER John   Chelsea
Full Name: SPENCER, John   DOB:
FAPL Debut: Away v. Norwich City † 19/8/92
Debut Goal: Home v. Manchester City 9/1/93

Previous Clubs details			*App*			*Goals*		
Clubs	Signed	Fee	Lge	FLC	FAC	Lge	FLC	FAC
Rangers								
Chelsea	8/92	£450,000						

FA Premier Lge Record

| 92/93 | | | 13+10 | 0+2 | 0+1 | 7 | | |

SPINK Nigel   Aston Villa
Full Name: SPINK, Nigel Philip   DOB: 8/8/58, Chelmsford
FAPL Debut: Away v. Ipswich Town 15/8/92   Debut Goal: –

Previous Clubs details			*App*			*Goals*		
Clubs	Signed	Fee	Lge	FLC	FAC	Lge	FLC	FAC
Aston Villa	1/77	£4,000	306	39	24			

FA Premier Lge Record

| 92/93 | | | 25 | 5 | 3 | | | |

SRNICK Pavel   Newcastle United
Full Name: SRNICK, Pavel   DOB: 10/3/68 Ostrava, Czech

Previous Club Details			*Apps*			*Goals*		
Clubs	Signed	Fee	Lge	FLC	FAC	Lge	FLC	FAC
Banik Ostrava								
Newcastle Utd	1/91	£350,000	52	2	5			

STAUNTON Steve   Aston Villa

Full Name: STAUNTON, Stephen   DOB: 19/1/69, Drogheda
FAPL Debut: Away v. Ipswich Town 15/8/92
Debut Goal: Home v. Crystal Palace 5/9/92

Previous Clubs details			App			Goals		
Clubs	Signed	Fee	Lge	FLC	FAC	Lge	FLC	FAC
Liverpool	9/86	£20,000	55+10	6+2	14+2		4	1
Bradford City	11/87	Loan	7+1	2				
Aston Villa	8/91	£1.1m	37	2	4	4		
FA Premier Lge Record								
92/93			42	5	4	2		

STEJSKAL Jan   Queens Park Rangers

Full Name: STEJSKAL, Jan   DOB: 15/1/62, Czechoslovakia
FAPL Debut: Away v. Manchester City 17/8/92   Debut Goal: –

Previous Clubs details			App			Goals		
Clubs	Signed	Fee	Lge	FLC	FAC	Lge	FLC	FAC
QPR	10/90	£600,000	67	4	2			
FA Premier Lge Record								
92/93			14+1					

STERLAND Mel   Leeds United

Full Name: STERLAND, Melvyn   DOB: 1/10/61, Sheffield
FAPL Debut: Away v. Blackburn Rovers 26/12/92   Debut Goal: –

Previous Clubs details			App			Goals		
Clubs	Signed	Fee	Lge	FLC	FAC	Lge	FLC	FAC
Sheffield Wed	10/79	–	271+8	30	34+1	37	7	5
Rangers	3/89	£800,000						
Leeds Utd	7/849	£600,000	108+3	13	8	16	1	1
FA Premier Lge Record								
92/93			3		2			

STEWART Paul   Liverpool

Full Name: STEWART, Paul Andrew   DOB: 7/10/64, Manchester
FAPL Debut: Away v. Nottingham Forest 16/8/92
Debut Goal: Home v. Sheffield United 19/8/92

Previous Clubs details			App			Goals		
Clubs	Signed	Fee	Lge	FLC	FAC	Lge	FLC	FAC
Blackpool	10/81	–	188+3	11	7	56	3	2
Man City	3/87	£200,000	51	6	4	27	2	1
Tottenham H	6/88	£1.7m	126+23		9	28	7	2
Liverpool								
FA Premier Lge Record								
92/93			21+3	3	1	1		

STEWART Simon — Sheffield Wednesday

Full Name: STEWART, Simon DOB: 1/11/73, Leeds
FAPL Debut: Away v. Ipswich Town 10/3/93 Debut Goal: –

Previous Clubs details

Clubs	Signed	Fee	App			Goals		
			Lge	FLC	FAC	Lge	FLC	FAC
Sheffield Wed	6/92 –							

FA Premier Lge Record

	App			Goals		
92/93	6	0+1				

STIMSON Mark — Newcastle United

Full Name: STIMSON, Mark DOB: 27/12/67 Plaistow, London

Previous Club Details

Clubs	Signed	Apps			Goals		
		Fee	Lge	FLC	FAC	Lge	FLC	FAC
Tottenham H	7/85		1+1					
Leyton Orient	3/88	Loan	10					
Gillingham	1/89	Loan	18					
Newcastle Utd	6/89	£150,000	82+6	5	7	2		1

STOCKWELL Mike — Ipswich Town

Full Name: STOCKWELL, Michael Thomas DOB: 14/2/65, Chelmsford
FAPL Debut: Home v. Aston Villa 15/8/92
Debut Goal: Home v. Wimbledon 12/8/92

Previous Clubs details

Clubs	Signed	Fee	App			Goals		
			Lge	FLC	FAC	Lge	FLC	FAC
Ipswich Town	12/82	–	205+14	15+2	10+3	15	2	

FA Premier Lge Record

	App			Goals		
92/93	38+1	5+1	3	4		

STRACHAN Gordon — Leeds United

Full Name: STRACHAN, Gordon David DOB: 9/2/57, Edinburgh
FAPL Debut: Home v. Wimbledon † 15/8/92
Debut Goal: Away v. QPR 24/10/92

Previous Clubs details

Clubs	Signed	Fee	App			Goals		
			Lge	FLC	FAC	Lge	FLC	FAC
Man Utd	8/84	£500,000	155+5	12+1	22	33	1	2
Leeds Utd								

FA Premier Lge Record

	App			Goals		
92/93	25+6	3	4	4	1	

STRANDLI Frank — Leeds United

Full Name: STRANDLI, Frank DOB:
FAPL Debut: Home v. Middlesbrough † 30/1/93
Debut Goal: Home v. Middlesbrough † 30/1/93

STUART Graham — Chelsea

Full Name: STUART, Graham Charles   DOB: 24/10/70, Tooting
FAPL Debut: Home v. Oldham Athletic 15/8/92
Debut Goal: Away v. Norwich City 19/8/92

Previous Clubs details			App			Goals		
Clubs	Signed	Fee	Lge	FLC	FAC	Lge	FLC	FAC
Chelsea	6/89	–	39+9	5	4+1	5	1	1
FA Premier Lge Record								
92/93			31+8	6	1	9	1	

SULLIVAN Neil — Wimbledon

Full Name: SULLIVAN, Neil   DOB: 24/2/70, Sutton
FAPL Debut: Away v. Southampton 17/10/92   Debut Goal: –

Previous Clubs details			App			Goals		
Clubs	Signed	Fee	Lge	FLC	FAC	Lge	FLC	FAC
Wimbledon	7/88	–	2					
Crystal Palace	5/92	Loan	1					
FA Premier Lge Record								
92/93			1					

SUMMERBEE Nicky — Swindon Town

Name: SUMMERBEE, Nicky   DOB: 26/8/71, Altrincham

Previous Club Details			Apps			Goals		
Clubs	Signed	Fee	Lge	FLC	FAC	Lge	FL	
Swindon Tn	7/89		53+21	6+1	1+3	2	1	

SUTCH Daryl — Norwich City

Full Name: SUTCH, Daryl   DOB: 11/9/71, Beccles
FAPL Debut: Away v. Crystal Palace † 29/8/92
Debut Goal: Home v. Middlesbrough 31/10/92

Previous Clubs details			App			Goals		
Clubs	Signed	Fee	Lge	FLC	FAC	Lge	FLC	FAC
Norwich City	7/90	–	7+6	0+1	0+1	1		
FA Premier Lge Record								
92/93			14+8	3		2		

SUTTON Chris — Norwich City

Full Name: SUTTON, Christopher Roy DOB: 10/3/73, Nottingham
FAPL Debut: Away v. Arsenal 15/8/92
Debut Goal: Home v. QPR 17/10/92

Previous Clubs details

Clubs	Signed	Fee	App Lge	FLC	FAC	Goals Lge	FLC	FAC
Norwich City	7/91	–	16+7	2	6	2		3

FA Premier Lge Record

92/93			32+6	3	2	8		2

TALBOYS Steven — Wimbledon

Full Name: TALBOYS, Steven John DOB: 18/9/66, Bristol
FAPL Debut: Away v. Norwich City 5/12/92 Debut Goal:

Previous Club Details

Clubs	Signed	Fee	Apps Lge	FLC	FAC	Goals Lge	FLC	FAC
Wimbledon	9/92	£10,000						

FA Premier Lge Record

92/93			3+4	0+1	0+1			

TANNER Nicky — Liverpool

Full Name: TANNER, Nicholas DOB: 24/5/65, Kingswood, Bristol
FAPL Debut: Away v. Nottingham Forest 16/8/92 Debut Goal: –

Previous Club Details

Clubs	Signed	Fee	Apps Lge	FLC	FAC	Goals Lge	FLC	FAC
Bristol Rv	6/85	–	104+3	5	10	5		
Liverpool	7/88	£20,000	34+3	5	2			
Norwich City	3/90	Loan	6					
Swindon	9/90	Loan	7					

FA Premier Lge Record

92/93			2+2	2+1				

TAYLOR Shaun — Swindon Town

Name: TAYLOR, Shaun DOB: 20/2/63, Bideford

Previous Club Details

Clubs	Signed	Fee	Apps Lge	FLC	FAC	Goals Lge	FLC	FAC
Exeter City	12/86		200	12	9	17		
Swindon Town	7/91	£200,000	88	9	4	14	2	

TEALE Shaun — Aston Villa

Full Name: TEALE, Shaun DOB: 10/3/64, Southport
FAPL Debut: Away v. Ipswich Town 15/8/92
Debut Goal: Home v. Middlesbrough 17/1/93

Previous Club Details

Clubs	Signed	Fee	Apps Lge	FLC	FAC	Goals Lge	FLC	FAC
Bournemouth	1/89	£50,000	99+1	8	5	4		1

			Apps			Goals		
Aston Villa	7/91	£300,000	42	2	5		1	
FA Premier Lge Record								
92/93			39	4	4	1	1	

THOMAS Michael   Liverpool
Full Name: THOMAS, Michael   DOB: 24/8/67, Lambeth
FAPL Debut: Home v. Southampton † 1/9/92
Debut Goal: Home v. Norwich City 25/10/92

Previous Club Details			*Apps*			*Goals*		
Clubs	Signed	Fee	Lge	FLC	FAC	Lge	FLC	FAC
Arsenal	12/84	–	149+14	22+2	14+3	24	5	
Portsmouth	12/86	Loan	3					
Liverpool	12/91	£1.5m	16+1		5	3		2
FA Premier Lge Record								
92/93			6+2	1	2	1		

THOMAS Mitchell   West Ham United
Full Name: THOMAS, Mitchell   DOB:2/10/64 Luton

Previous Club Details			*Apps*			*Goals*		
Clubs	Signed	Fee	Lge	FLC	FAC	Lge	FLC	FAC
Luton Town	8/82	106+1	5	18		1		
Tottenham H	7/86	£233,000	136+21	28+1	12	6	1	1
West Ham	8/91	£500,000	37+1	5	4	3		

THOMPSON Alan   Newcastle United
Full Name: THOMPSON, Alan   DOB: 22/12/73, Newcastle

Previous Club Details			*Apps*			*Goals*		
Clubs	Signed	Fee	Lge	FLC	FAC	Lge	FLC	FAC
Newcastle Utd	3/91		13+3					

THOMPSON Gary   Queens Park Rangers
Full Name: THOMPSON, Gary Lindsay   DOB: 7/10/59, Birmingham
FAPL Debut: Away v. Manchester City † 17/8/92   Debut Goal: –

Previous Club Details			*Apps*			*Goals*		
Clubs	Signed	Fee	Lge	FLC	FAC	Lge	FLC	FAC
Coventry City	6/77	–	127+7	12+1	11	38	7	4
West Brom Alb	2/83	£225,000	91	9	5	39	5	1
Sheffield Wed	3/85	£450,000	35+1	2+1	5	7	1	1
Aston Villa	6/86	£450,000	56+4	6	4	17	2	
Watford	12/88	£325,000	24+10	0+1	7+1	8		
Crystal Palace	3/90	£200,000	17+3	0+1		3	1	
QPR	8/91	£125,000	10+5	3		1	3	
FA Premier Lge Record								
92/93			0+4					

THOMPSON Neil Ipswich Town

THOMPSON Neil   **Ipswich Town**
Full Name: THOMPSON, Neil   DOB: 2/10/63, Beverley
FAPL Debut: Home v. Aston Villa 15/8/92
Debut Goal: Away v. Oldham 19/9/92

Previous Club Details			*Apps*			*Goals*		
Clubs	Signed	Fee	Lge	FLC	FAC	Lge	FLC	FAC
Hull City	11/91	–	29+2					
Scarborough	8/83	–	87	8	4	15	1	
Ipswich Town	6/89	£100,000	122+6	4+1	8	15		
FA Premier Lge Record								
	92/93		31	7	4	3	1	1

THORSTVEDT Erik Tottenham Hotspur

THORSTVEDT Erik   **Tottenham Hotspur**
Full Name: THORSTVEDT, Erik   DOB: 28/10/62, Stavanger, Norway
FAPL Debut: Home v. Coventry City † 19/8/92   Debut Goal:

Previous Club Details			*Apps*			*Goals*		
Clubs	Signed	Fee	Lge	FLC	FAC	Lge	FLC	FAC
Tottenham H	12/88	£400,000	113	18	8			
FA Premier Lge Record								
	92/93		25+2	2	5			

TINKLER Mark Leeds United

TINKLER Mark   **Leeds United**
Full Name: TINKLER, Mark Roland   DOB: 24/10/74, Bishop Auckland
FAPL Debut: Away v. Sheffield United 6/4/93   Debut Goal: –

Previous Club Details			*Apps*			*Goals*		
Clubs	Signed	Fee	Lge	FLC	FAC	Lge	FLC	FAC
Leeds Utd	11/91	–						
FA Premier Lge Record								
	92/93		5+2					

TOLSON Neil Oldham Athletic

TOLSON Neil   **Oldham Athletic**
Full Name: TOLSON, Neil   DOB: 25/10/73, Wordsley
FAPL Debut: Away v. Chelsea † 15/8/92   Debut Goal: –

Previous Club Details			*Apps*			*Goals*		
Clubs	Signed	Fee	Lge	FLC	FAC	Lge	FLC	FAC
Walsall	12/91	–	3+6		0+1	1		1
Oldham Ath	3/92	£150,000						
FA Premier Lge Record								
	92/93		0+3					

TOWNSEND Andy Aston Villa

TOWNSEND Andy   **Aston Villa**
Full Name: TOWNSEND, Andrew David   DOB: 23/7/63, Maidstone
FAPL Debut: Home v. Oldham Athletic 15/8/92
Debut Goal: Home v. Norwich 12/9/92

Previous Club Details			Apps			Goals		
Clubs	Signed	Fee	Lge	FLC	FAC	Lge	FLC	FAC
Southampton	1/85	£35,000	77+6	7+1	2+3	5		
Norwich City	8/88	£300,000	66+5	3+1	10	8		2
Chelsea	7/90	£1.2m	67	11	6	8	4	
Aston Villa	7/93	£2.1m						
FA Premier Lge Record								
Chelsea	92/93		41	6	1	4	3	

TRACEY Simon   Sheffield United

Full Name: TRACEY, Simon Peter   DOB: 9/12/67, Woolwich
FAPL Debut: Home v. Manchester United 15/8/92   Debut Goal: –

Previous Club Details			Apps			Goals		
Clubs	Signed	Fee	Lge	FLC	FAC	Lge	FLC	FAC
Wimbledon	2/86	–	1					
Sheffield Utd	10/88	£7,500	113	4	10			
FA Premier Lge Record								
	92/93		10	1				

TURNER Andrew   Tottenham Hotspur

Full Name: TURNER, Andrew Peter   DOB: 23/3/75, Woolwich
FAPL Debut: Away v. Southampton 15/8/92
Debut Goal: Home v. Everton 5/9/92

Previous Club Details			Apps			Goals		
Clubs	Signed	Fee	Lge	FLC	FAC	Lge	FLC	FAC
Tottenham H	4/92	–						
FA Premier Lge Record								
	92/93		7+11	1+2	0+1	3	1	

TUTTLE David   Sheffield United

Full Name: TUTTLE, David Philip   DOB: 6/2/72, Reading
FAPL Debut: Home v. Crystal Palace 22/8/92   Debut Goal: –

Previous Club Details			Apps			Goals		
Clubs	Signed	Fee	Lge	FLC	FAC	Lge	FLC	FAC
Tottenham H	2/90	–	6+2	1+1				
Peterborough	1/93	Loan	7					
Sheffield Utd	8/93	£350,000						
FA Premier Lge Record								
Tottenham H	92/93		4+1	2				

UNSWORTH David   Everton

Full Name: UNSWORTH, David   DOB: 16/10/73, Chorley
FAPL Debut: Home v. Liverpool 7/12/92   Debut Goal: –

Previous Club Details			Apps			Goals		
Clubs	Signed	Fee	Lge	FLC	FAC	Lge	FLC	FAC
Everton	5/92	–	1+1			1		

	92/93	3	1+1

VAN DEN HAUWE Pat — Tottenham Hotspur

Full Name: VAN DEN HAUWE, Patrick William Roger
DOB: 16/12/60, Dendermonde, Belgium
FAPL Debut: Home v. Sheffield United 2/9/92   Debut Goal:

Previous Club Details			Apps			Goals		
Clubs	Signed	Fee	Lge	FLC	FAC	Lge	FLC	FAC
Birmingham C	8/78	–	119+4	12	5	1		
Everton	9/84	£100,000	134+1	20	30	2		1
Tottenham H	8/89	£575,000	97+1	14	8		1	

FA Premier Lge Record

	92/93	13+5	2

VENISON Barry — Newcastle United

Full Name: VENISON, Barry   DOB: 16/8/64, Consett

Previous Club Details			Apps			Goals		
Clubs	Signed	Fee	Lge	FLC	FAC	Lge	FLC	FAC
Sunderland	1/82		169+4	21	7+1	2		
Liverpool	7/86	£200,000	103+7	14+3	16+5	1		
Newcastle Utd	7/92	£250,000	44	4	4			

VIVEASH Adrian — Swindon Town

Name: VIVEASH, Adrian   DOB: 30/9/69, Swindon

Previous Club Details			Apps			Goals	
Clubs	Signed	Fee	Lge	FLC	FAC	Lge	FL
Swindon Town	7/88		37+3	5+1	0+1	1	

VONK Michel — Manchester City

Full Name: VONK, Michel Christian   DOB: 28/10/68, Netherlands
FAPL Debut: Home v. QPR 17/8/92   Debut Goal: Home v. Oldham 29/8/92

Previous Club Details			Apps			Goals		
Clubs	Signed	Fee	Lge	FLC	FAC	Lge	FLC	FAC
Man City	3/92	£500,000	8+1					

FA Premier Lge Record

	92/93	26		3+1	3	1

WADDLE Chris — Sheffield Wednesday

Full Name: WADDLE, Christopher Roland   DOB: 14/12/60, Felling
FAPL Debut: Away v. Everton 15/8/92
Debut Goal: Home v. Everton 6/2/93

Previous Club Details			Apps			Goals		
Clubs	Signed	Fee	Lge	FLC	FAC	Lge	FLC	FAC
Newcastle Utd	7/80	£1,000	169+1	8	12	46	2	4
Tottenham H	6/85	£590,000	137+1	21	14	33	4	5

	Marseile (Fra)	7/89	£4.25m						
	Sheffield Wed	6/92	£1m						

FA Premier Lge Record

92/93			32+1	9	8	1		2	

WALKER Des   Sheffield Wednesday

Name: WALKER, Desmond Sinclair   DOB:26/11/65, Hackney

Previous Club Details			*Apps*			*Goals*		
Clubs	Signed	Fee	Lge	FLC	FAC	Lge	FLC	FAC
Nottingham F	11/83		259+5			1		
Sampdoria, Ita								
Sheffield Wed	8/93	£2.75m						

WALKER Ian   Tottenham Hotspur

Full Name: WALKER, Ian Michael   DOB: 31/10/71, Watford
FAPL Debut: Away v. Southampton 15/8/92   Debut Goal: –

Previous Club Details			*Apps*			*Goals*		
Clubs	Signed	Fee	Lge	FLC	FAC	Lge	FLC	FAC
Tottenham H	12/89	–	19	1				
Oxford Utd	9/90	Loan	2	1				
Millwall	3/93	Loan						

FA Premier Lge Record

92/93			17	2					

WALLACE Danny   Manchester United

Full Name: WALACE, David Lloyd   DOB: 21/1/64, Greenwich
FAPL Debut: Away v. Tottenham H. 19/9/92   Debut Goal: –

Previous Club Details			*Apps*			*Goals*		
Clubs	Signed	Fee	Lge	FLC	FAC	Lge	FLC	FAC
Southampton	1/82	–	240+15	36	21+1	64	6	4
Man Utd	9/89	£1.2m	39+9	3+3	6+2	6	2	2

FA Premier Lge Record

92/93			0+2	1	1		1		

WALLACE Ray   Leeds United

Full Name: WALLACE, Raymond George   DOB: 2/10/69, Greenwich
FAPL Debut: Home v. Ipswich Town 27/2/93   Debut Goal: –

Previous Club Details			*Apps*			*Goals*		
Clubs	Signed	Fee	Lge	FLC	FAC	Lge	FLC	FAC
Southampton	4/88	–	33+2	8	2			
Leeds Untied	5/91	£100,000						
Swansea City	3/92	Loan	2					

FA Premier Lge Record

92/93			5+1						

WALLACE Rod — Leeds United

Full Name: WALLACE, Rodney Seymour   DOB: 2/10/69, Greenwich
FAPL Debut: Home v. Wimbledon 15/8/92
Debut Goal: Home v. Tottenham Hotspur 25/8/92

Previous Club Details

			Apps			Goals		
Clubs	Signed	Fee	Lge	FLC	FAC	Lge	FLC	FAC
Southampton	4/88	–	111+17	18+1	10	44	6	3
Leeds Untied	5/91	£1.6m	34	3	1	11	2	

FA Premier Lge Record

92/93			31+1			7		

WALTERS Mark — Liverpool

Full Name: WALTERS, Mark Everton   DOB: 2/6/64, Birmingham
FAPL Debut: Away v. Nottingham Forest 16/8/92
Debut Goal: Home v. Sheffield United 19/8/92

Previous Club Details

			Apps			Goals		
Clubs	Signed	Fee	Lge	FLC	FAC	Lge	FLC	FAC
Aston Villa	5/82	–	168+13	21+2	11+1	39	6	1
Rangers	12/87	£500,000						
Liverpool	8/91	£1.25m	18+7	4	2+1	3	2	

FA Premier Lge Record

92/93			26+8	5	1	11	2	

WARD Mark — Everton

Full Name: WARD, Mark William   DOB: 10/10/62, Huyton
FAPL Debut: Home v. Sheffield Wednesday 15/8/92
Debut Goal: Away v. Coventry City 7/3/93

Previous Club Details

			Apps			Goals		
Clubs	Signed	Fee	Lge	FLC	FAC	Lge	FLC	FAC
Everton	9/80	–						
Northwich V	8/81	–						
Oldham Ath	7/83	£10,000	84	5	3	12		
West Ham	8/85	£250,000	163+2	20+1	17	12	2	
Man City	12/89	£1m	54	3	6	14		
Everton	8/91	£1.1m	37	2	2	4		

FA Premier Lge Record

92/93			19			1		

WARD Mitch — Sheffield United

Full Name: WARD, Mitchum David   DOB: 19/6/71, Sheffield
FAPL Debut: Home v. Southampton † 3/10/92   Debut Goal: –

Previous Club Details

			Apps			Goals		
Clubs	Signed	Fee	Lge	FLC	FAC	Lge	FLC	FAC
Sheffield Utd	7/89	–	7+3	0+1	1			
Crewe Alex	11/90	Loan	4		1		1	

WARHURST Paul — Sheffield Wednesday

Full Name: WARHURST, Paul DOB: 26/9/69, Stockport
FAPL Debut: Away v. Everton 15/8/92
Debut Goal: Away v. Nottingham Forest 12/9/92

			Apps			*Goals*		
Clubs	Signed	Fee	Lge	FLC	FAC	Lge	FLC	FAC
Man City	6/88	–						
Oldham Ath	10/88	£10,000	60+7	8	5+4	2		
Sheffield Wed	7/91	£750,000	31+2	2	1			

FA Premier Lge Record

92/93	25+4	7	6+1	6	4	5

WARK John — Ipswich Town

Full Name: WARK, John DOB: 4/8/57, Glasgow
FAPL Debut: Home v. Aston Villa 15/8/92
Debut Goal: Home v. Tottanham Hotspur 30/8/92

			Apps			*Goals*		
Clubs	Signed	Fee	Lge	FLC	FAC	Lge	FLC	FAC
Ipswich Town	8/74	–	295+1	4+1	36+1	94	12	10
Liverpool	3/84	£450,000	64+6	6+4	11+2	28	3	6
Ipswich Town	1/88	£100,000	87+2	4	3	23		
Middlesbro	8/90	£50,000	31+1	5	2	3		
Ipswich Town	8/91	–	36+1	1	5	3		

FA Premier Lge Record

92/93	36+1	6+1	4	6		1

WARZYCHA Robert — Everton

Full Name: WARZYCHA, Robert DOB: 20/8/63, Wielun, Poland
FAPL Debut: Home v. Sheffield Wednesday † 15/8/92
Debut Goal: Away v. Manchester United 19/8/92

			Apps			*Goals*		
Clubs	Signed	Fee	Lge	FLC	FAC	Lge	FLC	FAC
Everton	3/91	£300,000	33+12	1+1	1+1	5		

FA Premier Lge Record

92/93	15+5	3+1	2	1		1

WATSON Dave — Everton

Full Name: WATSON, David DOB: 20/11/61, Liverpool
FAPL Debut: Home v. Sheffield Wednesday 15/8/92
Debut Goal: Away v. Middlesbrough 10/4/93

Previous Club Details			Apps			Goals		
Clubs	Signed	Fee	Lge	FLC	FAC	Lge	FLC	FAC
Liverpool	5/79	–						
Norwich City	11/80	£100,000	212	21	18	11	3	1
Everton	8/86	£900,000	199+1	23	30	16	2	3
FA Premier Lge Record								
	92/93		40	6	2	1		1

WATSON Gordon — Sheffield Wednesday

Full Name: WATSON, Gordon William George   DOB: 20/3/71, Sidcup
FAPL Debut: Away v. Everton † 15/8/92
Debut Goal: Away v. Oldham Athletic 7/4/93

Previous Club Details			Apps			Goals		
Clubs	Signed	Fee	Lge	FLC	FAC	Lge	FLC	FAC
Charton Ath	4/89	–	20+11	2	0+1	7	1	
Sheffield Wed	2/91	£250,000	5+4	1	1			
FA Premier Lge Record								
	92/93		4+7	1+2	1	1	3	

WATSON Kevin — Tottenham Hotspur

Full Name: WATSON, Kevin Edward   DOB: 3/1/74, Hackney
FAPL Debut: Away v. Sheffield Wednesday † 27/9/92
Debut Goal: Away v. Manchester City 28/11/92

Previous Club Details			Apps			Goals		
Clubs	Signed	Fee	Lge	FLC	FAC	Lge	FLC	FAC
Tottenham H	5/92	–						
FA Premier Lge Record								
	92/93		4+1	1+1	0+1	1	1	

WATSON Steve — Newcastle United

Full Name: WATSON, Stephen   DOB: 1/4/74 North Shields

Previous Club Details			Apps			Goals		
Clubs	Signed	Fee	Lge	FLC	FAC	Lge	FLC	FAC
Newcastle Utd	7/90		46+8		5	1		

WATTS Julian — Sheffield Wednesday

Full Name: WATTS, Julian   DOB: 17/3/71, Sheffield
FAPL Debut: Away v. Liverpool † 3/3/93   Debut Goal: –

Previous Club Details			Apps			Goals		
Clubs	Signed	Fee	Lge	FLC	FAC	Lge	FLC	FAC
Rotherham Utd	7/90		17+3	1	4	1		
Sheffield Wed	3/92	£80,000						
Shrewsbury Tn	12/92	Loan	9					
FA Premier Lge Record								
	92/93		2+1					

WEBSTER Simon — West Ham United

Full Name: WEBSTER, Simon   DOB: 20/1/64, Earl Shilton

Previous Club Details

Clubs	Signed	Fee	Apps Lge	FLC	FAC	Goals Lge	FLC	FAC
Tottenham H	12/81		2+1					
Exeter City	11/83	Loan	26					
Huddersfield	2/85		118	7	7	4		
Sheffield Utd	3/88	£35,000	26+11	5	5+1	3		
Charlton Ath	9/90		130	7	6	7		
West Ham Utd	7/93	£525,000						

WEGERLE Roy — Coventry City

Full Name: WEGERLE, Roy Connon DOB: 19/3/64, Johannesburg, S.A.
FAPL Debut: Away v. Coventry City † 29/8/92
Debut Goal: Home v. Norwich City 3/10/92

Previous Club Details

Clubs	Signed	Fee	Apps Lge	FLC	FAC	Goals Lge	FLC	FAC
Tampa Bay								
Chelsea	6/86	£100,000	15+8		1+1	3		1
Swindon Town	3/88	loan	7			1		
Luton Town	7/88	£75,000	39+6	10	1	10	8	
QPR	12/89	£1m	71+4	5	11	29	1	1
Blackburn Rv	3/92	£1.2m	9+3			2		
Coventry City	3/93	£1m						

FA Premier Lge Record

Blackburn Rv	92/93		11+11	3+3	4+1	4	4	2
Coventry City			5+1					

WETHERALL David — Leeds United

Full Name: WETHERALL, David   DOB: 14/3/71, Sheffield
FAPL Debut: Away v. Southampton 19/9/92
Debut Goal: Home v. Chelsea 24/3/93

Previous Club Details

Clubs	Signed	Fee	Apps Lge	FLC	FAC	Goals Lge	FLC	FAC
Sheffield Wed	7/89	–						
Leeds United	7/91	£125,000	0+1					

FA Premier Lge Record

	92/93		13	2	4	1		

WHELAN Phil — Ipswich Town

Full Name: WHELAN, Philip James   DOB: 7/8/72, Stockport
FAPL Debut: Home v. Aston Villa 15/8/92 Debut Goal: –

Previous Club Details

Clubs	Signed	Fee	Apps Lge	FLC	FAC	Goals Lge	FLC	FAC
Ipswich Town	7/90	–	8			2		

WHELAN Noel   Leeds United

Full Name: WHELAN, Noel   DOB:

FAPL Debut: Away v. Sheffield Wednesday 4/5/93   Debut Goal:

Previous Club Details		*Apps*			*Goals*		
Clubs	Signed Fee	Lge	FLC	FAC	Lge	FLC	FAC
Leeds Utd							

FA Premier Lge Record

	92/93	1					

WHELAN Ronnie   Liverpool

Full Name: WHELAN, Ronald   DOB: 25/9/1, Dublin

FAPL Debut: Away v. Nottingham Forest 16/8/92

Debut Goal: Away v. Leeds United 29/8/92

Previous Club Details		*Apps*			*Goals*		
Clubs	Signed Fee	Lge	FLC	FAC	Lge	FLC	FAC
Liverpool	10/79 –	311+11	46+4	41+1	45	14	7

FA Premier Lge Record

	92/93	17			1		

WHITBREAD Adrian   Swindon Town

Name: WHITBREAD, Adrian   DOB: 22/10/71, Epping

Previous Club Details		*Apps*			*Goals*		
Clubs	Signed Fee	Lge	FLC	FAC	Lge	FLC	FAC
Leyton Orient	11/89	125	10+1	11	2		1
Swindon Town	8/93 £500,000						

WHITE David   Manchester City

Full Name: WHITE, David   DOB: 30/10/67, Manchester

FAPL Debut: Home v. QPR 17/8/92

Debut Goal: Home v. QPR 17/8/92

Previous Club Details		*Apps*			*Goals*		
Clubs	Signed Fee	Lge	FLC	FAC	Lge	FLC	FAC
Man City	10/85 –	215+12	17+2	17	64	9	1

FA Premier Lge Record

	92/93	42	3	5	16		3

WHITE Devon   Queens Park Rangers

Full Name: WHITE, Devon   DOB: 2/3/64, Nottingham

FAPL Debut: Home v. Chelsea † 27/1/93

Debut Goal: Away v. Ipswich 9/2/93

Clubs	Signed	Fee	Apps Lge	FLC	FAC	Goals Lge	FLC	FAC
Lincoln City	12/84		21+8			4		
Bristol Rv	8/87		190+12	9	10	54	2	3
Cambridge Utd	3/92	£100,000	14+7			4		
QPR	1/93	£100,000						

FA Premier Lge Record

92/93			3+4			2		

WHITE Steve   Swindon Town
Name: WHITE, Steve   DOB: 2/1/59, Chipping Sodbury

Previous Club Details

Clubs	Signed	Fee	Apps Lge	FLC	FAC	Goals Lge	FL
Bristol Rovers	7/77		46+4	2	3	20	1	3
Luton Town	12/79	£200,000	63+9	3+1	2+1	25	1
Charlton Ath	7/82	£150,000	29			12	
Lincoln City	1/83	Loan	2+1				
Luton Town	3/83	Loan					
Bristol Rv	8/83		89+12	8	7+1	24	2	2
Swindon Tn	2/86		198+40	20+6	9+2	83	11	2

WHITEHOUSE Dane   Sheffield United
Full Name: WHITEHOUSE, Dane Lee   DOB: 14/10/70, Sheffield
FAPL Debut: Home v. Liverpool 12/9/92
Debut Goal: Home v. Arsenal 19/9/92

Previous Club Details

Clubs	Signed	Fee	Apps Lge	FLC	FAC	Goals Lge	FLC	FAC
Sheffield Utd	7/89	–	37+18	3	6+3	8	1	

FA Premier Lge Record

92/93			14	1	3	5	1	

WHITTINGHAM Guy   Aston Villa
Name: WHITTINGHAM, Guy   DOB: 10/11/64, Evesham

Previous Club Details

Clubs	Signed	Fee	Apps Lge	FLC	FAC	Goals Lge	FLC	FAC
Portsmouth	6/89		149+11	7+2	7+3	88	3	10
Aston Villa	7/93	£1.2m						

WHITTON Steve   Ipswich Town
Full Name: WHITTON, Stephen Paul   DOB: 4/12/60, East Ham
FAPL Debut: v. Chelsea † 17/10/92   Debut Goal: v. Chelsea † 17/10/92

Previous Club Details

Clubs	Signed	Fee	Apps Lge	FLC	FAC	Goals Lge	FLC	FAC
Coventry City	9/78	–	64+10	3+2	3	21	2	2
West Ham	7/83	£175,000	35+4	6	1	6	2	

			Apps			Goals		
Birmingham C	1/86	Loan	8			2		
Birmingham C	8/86	£60,000	94+1	7+1	5	28	4	
Sheffield Wed	3/89	£275,000	22+10	3	0+1	4	4	
Ipswich Town	1/91	£120,000	53	2	5	11		1
FA Premier Lge Record								
	92/93		20+4	4	4	3	1	1

WHYTE Chris — Leeds United

Full Name: WHYTE, Christopher Anderson   DOB: 2/9/61, Islington
FAPL Debut: Home v. Wimbledon 15/8/92
Debut Goal: Home v. Sheffield United 17/10/92

Previous Club Details			Apps			Goals		
Clubs	Signed	Fee	Lge	FLC	FAC	Lge	FLC	FAC
Arsenal	9/79	–	86+4	5	3+1	8	2	
Crystal Palace	8/84	Loan	13	4				
Los Angeles	7/86							
West Brom Alb	8/88	–	83+1	5	5	27	2	
Leeds United	6/90	£400,000	79	12	5	4	1	
FA Premier Lge Record								
	92/93		34	2+1	3	1		

WIDDRINGTON Chris — Southampton

Full Name: WIDDRINGTON, Christopher   DOB: 1/10/71, Newcastle
FAPL Debut: Away v. Crystal Palace 26/9/92   Debut Goal: –

Previous Club Details			Apps			Goals		
Clubs	Signed	Fee	Lge	FLC	FAC	Lge	FLC	FAC
Southampton	5/90	–	2+1					
Wigan Ath	9/91	Loan	5+1	2				
FA Premier Lge Record								
	92/93		11+1	0+1				

WILCOX Jason — Blackburn Rovers

Full Name: WILCOX, Jason Malcolm   DOB: 15/3/71, Farnworth
FAPL Debut: Home v. Arsenal 18/8/92
Debut Goal: Away v. Middlesborough 5/12/92

Previous Club Details			Apps			Goals		
Clubs	Signed	Fee	Lge	FLC	FAC	Lge	FLC	FAC
Blackburn Rv	6/89	–	49+8	2		4		
FA Premier Lge Record								
	92/93		31+2	5+1	5	4		

WILKINS Ray — Queens Park Rangers

Full Name: WILKINS, Raymond Colin   DOB: 14/9/56, Hillingdon
FAPL Debut: Away v. Manchester City 17/8/92
Debut Goal: Home v. Tottenham Hotspur 3/10/92

Previous Club Details			Apps			Goals		
Clubs	Signed	Fee	Lge	FLC	FAC	Lge	FLC	FAC
Chelsea	10/73	–	176+3	6+1	11+1	30	2	2
Man Utd	8/79	£25,000	158+2	14+1	10	7	1	1
A.C Milan (Ita)	7/84	£1.5m						
Paris S-G (Fra)	7/87							
Rangers	11/87	£250,000						
QPR	11/89	–	7+1	5	10	4		2
FA Premier Lge Record								
	92/93		27	4	1	2		

WILLIAMS Geraint   Ipswich Town
Full Name: WILLIAMS, Geraint   DOB: 5/7/62, Treorchy
FAPL Debut: Home v. Aston Villa 15/8/92   Debut Goal:

Previous Club Details			Apps			Goals		
Clubs	Signed	Fee	Lge	FLC	FAC	Lge	FLC	FAC
Bristol Rovers	1/80		138+3	14	9+2	8		2
Derby City	3/85	£40,000	276+1	26+3	17	9	1	
Ipswich Town	7/92	£650,000						
FA Premier Lge Record								
	92/93		37	4+1	4			

WILLIAMS John   Coventry City
Full Name: WILLIAMS, John   DOB: 11/5/68 Birmingham
FAPL Debut: Home v. Middlesbrough 15/8/92
Debut Goal: Home v. Middlesbrough 15/8/92

Previous Club Details			Apps			Goals		
Clubs	Signed	Fee	Lge	FLC	FAC	Lge	FLC	FAC
Swansea City	8/91	£5,000	36+3	2+1	3	11		
Coventry City	7/92	£250,000						
FA Premier Lge Record								
	92/93		38+3	2	1	8		

WILLIAMS Mike   Sheffield Wednesday
Full Name: WILLIAMS, Michael Anthony   DOB: 21/11/69, Bradford
FAPL Debut: Home v. Southampton † 12/4/93   Debut Goal: –

Previous Club Details			Apps			Goals		
Clubs	Signed	Fee	Lge	FLC	FAC	Lge	FLC	FAC
Sheffield Wed	2/91	–						
Halifax	12/92	Loan						
FA Premier Lge Record								
	92/93		2+1					

WILSON Clive   Queens Park Rangers
Full Name: WILSON, Clive   DOB: 13/11/61, Manchester
FAPL Debut: Away v. Manchester City 17/8/92

Debut Goal: Home v. Manchester City 6/8/92

Previous Club Details

Clubs	Signed	Fee	Apps Lge	FLC	FAC	Goals Lge	FLC	FAC
Man City	12/79	–	107+2	10	2	9	2	
Chester City	9/82	Loan	21			2		
Chelsea	5/87	£250,000	68+13	3+3	4	5		
QPR	7/90	£450,000	51+2	6	2	4		

FA Premier Lge Record

92/93			41	3	2	3		

WINTERBURN Nigel   Arsenal
Full Name: WINTERBURN, Nigel   DOB: 11/12/63, Nuneaton
FAPL Debut: Home v. Norwich 15/8/92
Debut Goal: Home v. Oldham 26/8/92

Previous Club Details

Clubs	Signed	Fee	Apps Lge	FLC	FAC	Goals Lge	FLC	FAC
Birmingham C	8/81	–						
Wimbledon	8/83	–	164+1	13	12	8		
Arsenal	5/87	£407,000	169+1	19	17	4	2	

FA Premier Lge Record

92/93			29	7	8	1	1	

WISE Dennis   Chelsea
Full Name: WISE, Dennis Frank   DOB: 16/12/66, Kensington
FAPL Debut: Home v. Blackburn Rovers 26/8/92
Debut Goal: Away v. Aston Villa 2/9/92

Previous Club Details

Clubs	Signed	Fee	Apps Lge	FLC	FAC	Goals Lge	FLC	FAC
Wimbledon	3/85	–	127+8	14	11	26		3
Chelsea	7/90	£1.6m	70+1	9	5	21	3	2

FA Premier Lge Record

92/93			27	5		3	1	

WIRMOLA Jonas   Sheffield United
Name: WIRMOLA, Jonas   DOB:

Previous Club Details

Clubs	Signed	Fee	Apps Lge	FLC	FAC	Goals Lge	FLC	FAC
Sparvagens, Swe								
Sheffield Utd	8/93	£50,000						

WOOD Steve   Southampton
Full Name: WOOD, Stephen Alan   DOB: 2/2/63, Bracknell
FAPL Debut: Home v. Tottenham H. 15/8/92   Debut Goal: –

WOODS Chris   Sheffield Wednesday

Full Name: WOODS, Christopher Charles Eric DOB: 14/11/59, Boston
FAPL Debut: Away v. Everton 15/8/92   Debut Goal: –

Previous Club Details			Apps			Goals		
Clubs	Signed	Fee	Lge	FLC	FAC	Lge	FLC	FAC
Nottingham F	12/76	–		7				
QPR	7/79	£250,000	63	8	1			
Norwich City	3/81	£225,000	216	26	19			
Rangers	6/86	£600,000						
Sheffield Wed	8/91	£1.2m	41	4	2			
FA Premier Lge Record								
92/93			39	7	8			

WOODTHORPE Colin   Norwich City

Full Name: WOODTHORPE, Colin John DOB: 13/1/69, Ellesmere Port
FAPL Debut: Away v. Manchester City † 26/8/92   Debut Goal: –

Previous Club Details			Apps			Goals		
Clubs	Signed	Fee	Lge	FLC	FAC	Lge	FLC	FAC
Chester City	9/86	–	154+1	10	8+1	6		
Norwich City	7/90	£175,000	13+3	0+2	4	1		
FA Premier Lge Record								
92/93			5+2					

WORTHINGTON Nigel   Sheffield Wednesday

Full Name: WORTHINGTON, Nigel   DOB: 4/11/61, Ballymena
FAPL Debut: Away v. Everton 15/8/92
Debut Goal: Home v. Norwich City 10/1/93

Previous Club Details			Apps			Goals		
Clubs	Signed	Fee	Lge	FLC	FAC	Lge	FLC	FAC
Notts County	7/81	£100,000	62+5	11	4	4		
Sheffield Wed	2/84	£125,000	264+3	31	20	10		
FA Premier Lge Record								
92/93			40	7	8	1	1	

WRIGHT Alan   Blackburn Rovers

Full Name: WRIGHT, Alan Geoffrey   DOB: 28/9/71, Ashton-U-Lyne
FAPL Debut: Away v. Crystal Palace 15/8/92 Debut Goal:

Previous Club Details			Apps			Goals		
Clubs	Signed	Fee	Lge	FLC	FAC	Lge	FLC	FAC
Blackpool	4/89	–	91+7	10+2	8			
Blackburn Rv	10.91	£400,000	32+1		2	1		
FA Premier Lge Record								
	92/93		24	6	3			

WRIGHT Ian   Arsenal

Full Name: WRIGHT, Ian Edward   DOB: 3/11/63, Woolwich
FAPL Debut: Home v. Norwich † 15/8/92
Debut Goal: Away v. Liverpool 23/8/92

Previous Club Details			Apps			Goals		
Clubs	Signed	Fee	Lge	FLC	FAC	Lge	FLC	FAC
Crystal Palace	8/85	–	206+19	19	9+2	90	9	3
Arsenal	9/91	£2.5m	30	3		24	2	
FA Premier Lge Record								
	92/93		30+1	8	7	15	5	10

WRIGHT Mark   Liverpool

Full Name: WRIGHT, Mark   DOB: 1/8/63, Dorchester on Thames
FAPL Debut: Away v. Nottingham Forest 16/8/92
Debut Goal: Home v. Southampton 1/9/92

Previous Club Details			Apps			Goals		
Clubs	Signed	Fee	Lge	FLC	FAC	Lge	FLC	FAC
Oxford United	8/80	–		1				
Southampton	3/82	£80,000	170	25	17	7	2	1
Derby County	8/87	£760,000	144	12	6	10		
Liverpool	7/91	£2.2m	21	1	9			
FA Premier Lge Record								
	92/93		32+1	2+2		2		

WRIGHT Tommy   Newcastle United

Full Name: WRIGHT, Tommy   DOB:29/8/63, Belfast

Previous Club Details			Apps			Goals		
Clubs	Signed	Fee	Lge	FLC	FAC	Lge	FLC	FAC
Linfield								
Newcastle Utd	3/88	£30,000	70	6	4			
Hull City	2/91	Loan	6					

YALLOP Frank   Ipswich Town

Full Name: YALLOP, Frank Walter   DOB: 4/4/64, Watford
FAPL Debut: Away v. QPR † 5/9/92
Debut Goal: Home v. Tottenham Hotspur 27/1/93

Previous Club Details			Apps			Goals		
Clubs	Signed	Fee	Lge	FLC	FAC	Lge	FLC	FAC
Ipswich Town	1/82	–	238+17	18+1	12+2	4	1	

FA Premier Lge Record

	92/93		5+1	2	1+1	2		

YORKE Dwight
Aston Villa

Full Name: YORKE, Dwight **DOB:** 3/11/71, Tobago, West Indies
FAPL Debut: Home v. Leeds United 19/8/92
Debut Goal: Home v. Crystal Palace 5/9/92

Previous Club Details			Apps			Goals		
Clubs	Signed	Fee	Lge	FLC	FAC	Lge	FLC	FAC
Aston Villa	11/89	£120,000	35+17	3	7	13		5

FA Premier Lge Record

	92/93		22+5	2+2	4	6		1

YOUDS Eddie
Ipswich Town

Full Name: YOUDS, Edward Paul **DOB:** 3/5/70, Liverpool
FAPL Debut: Home v. Aston Villa † 15/8/92 **Debut Goal:** –

Previous Club Details			Apps			Goals		
Clubs	Signed	Fee	Lge	FLC	FAC	Lge	FLC	FAC
Everton	6/88	–	5+3	0+1				
Cardiff City	12/89	Loan	0+1		0+1			
Wrexham	2/90	Loan	20			2		
Ipswich Town	11/91	£250,000	1					

FA Premier Lge Record

	92/93		10+6	1+2	0+1			

The A-Z of Ex-FA Premier League Players 1992-93

Player	Apps	Goals
ALLON, Joseph Ball		
Chelsea	27+1	9
ANDERSON, Vivien		
Sheffield Wednesday	23+2	3
BILLING, Peter Graham		
Coventry	3	
BLACK, Kingsley		
Nottingham Forest	19+3	5
BLAKE, Mark Anthony		
Aston Villa	0+1	
BOWRY, Robert		
Crystal Palace	6+5	1
CARRUTHERS, Martin George		
Aston Villa	0+1	
CHANNING, Justin		
Queens Park Rangers	2	1
CHAPMAN, Lee		
Leeds United	36+4	14
CHETTLE, Stephen		
Nottingham Forest	30	
COLEMAN, Christopher		
Crystal Palace	31+7	5
COLLETT, Andrews Alfred		
Middlesbrough	0+2	
COTTERILL, Stephen John		
Wimbledon	4+3	3
CROSBY, Gary		
Nottingham Forest	20+2	1
CROSSLEY, Mark Geoffrey		
Nottingham Forest	37	0

Player	Apps	Goals
DAY, Mervyn Richard		
Leeds United	2	
FLEMING, Terence Maurice		
Coventry City	8+1	
GEMMILL, Scot		
Nottingham Forest	33	1
GORDON, Dan		
Middlesborough	31+1	
GREENMAN, Chris		
Coventry City	1+1	
GYNN, Michael		
Coventry City	18+3	2
HENDRIE, John Grattan		
Crystal Palace	6+4	
HILL, Keith		
Blackburn Rovers	0+1	
HOHAN, Nicholas		
Middlesbrough	17	2
HUMPHREY, John		
Crystal Palace	28+4	
INGEBRIGHTSEN, Kare		
Manchester City	2+5	
IRONSIDE, Ian		
Middlesbrough	11+1	
JENKINS, Iain		
Everton	1	
KAMARA, Christopher		
Sheffield United	6+2	
Middlesbrough	3+2	

Player	Apps	Goals	Player	Apps	Goals
KEELEY, John Henry Oldham Athletic	1		**OSBORN, Simon Edward** Crystal Palace	27+4	2
KERR, Dylan Leeds United	3+2	2	**PARKINSON, Gary Anthony** Middlesbrough	2	
KOZMA, Istvan Liverpool	0+1		**PATES, Colin George** Arsenal	2+5	
LAW, Brian Nottingham Forest	32		**PEAKE, Andrew Michael** Middlesbrough	33	
LEE, Dave Southampton	0+1		**PEARCE, Stuart** Nottingham Forest	23	2
McAVENNIE, Frank Aston Villa	0+3		**PEARS, Stephen** Middlesbrough	26	
McKINNON, Raymond Nottingham Forest	5+1	1	**PENNYFATHER, Glen** Ipswich Town	2+2	
McLEARY, Alan Wimbledon	4		**PEYTON, Gerald Joseph** Chelsea	0+1	
MARRIOTT, Andrew Nottingham Forest	5		**PHILLIPS, James Neil** Middlesbrough	42	
MARTYN, Anthony Nigel Crystal Palace	42		**POLLOCK, Jamie** Middlesbrough	15+5	1
MIDDLETON, Craig Coventry City	1		**PRICE, Chris** Blackburn Rovers	2+4	
MINETT, Jason Norwich City	0+1		**PROCTOR, Mark Gerard** Middlesbrough	5+5	
MOORE, Alan Middlesbrough	0+2		**RANSON, Ray** Manchester City	17	1
MORTIMER, Paul Henry Crystal Palace	1		**REGIS, Cyrille** Aston Villa	7+6	1
MOULDEN, Paul Oldham Athletic	1+3		**RODGER, Simon Lee** Crystal Palace	22+1	2
MUSTOE, Robin Middlesbrough	22+1	1	**ROSARIO, Robert Michael** Coventry City Nottingham Forest	28 10	4 1
NAYIM, Mohamed Ali Amar Tottenham Hotspur	15+3	3	**SALAKO, John Akin** Crystal Palace	12+1	
ORLYGSSON, Thorvaldur Nottingam Forest	15+5	1			

Player	Apps	Goals	Player	Apps	Goals
SANSOM, Kenneth Graham			**WOAN, Ian Simon**		
Coventry City	21		Nottingham Forest	27+1	3
Everton	6+1	1	**YOUNG, Eric**		
SINNOTT, Lee			Crystal Palace	38	6
Crystal Palace	18+1				
SLAVEN, Bernard Joseph					
Middlesbrough	14+5	4			
SMITH, David					
Coventry City	6				
SOUTHGATE, Gareth					
Crystal Palace	33	3			
SPEEDIE, David					
Southampton	11				
STONE, Steven Brian					
Nottingham Forest	10+1	1			
THOMAS, Geoffrey Robert					
Crystal Palace	28+1	2			
THORN, Andrew Charles					
Crystal Palace	34	1			
TILER, Carl					
Nottingham Forest	37				
VARADI, Imre					
Leeds United	2+2	1			
WEBB, Neil John					
Manchester United	0+1	1			
Nottingham Forest	10				
WILKINSON, Paul					
Middlesbrough	41	15			
WILLIAMS, Paul					
Sheffield Wednesday	7	1			
Crystal Palace	15+3				
WILLIAMS, Paul					
Coventry City	1+1				
WILSON, Danny					
Sheffield Wednesday	21+5	2			

Diary 1993-94

Month	Date	Competition	Round
August	18 & 25	Coca-Cola Cup	1st Round, 1st Leg & 2nd Leg
September	14/15	C1, C2, C3	1st Round, 1st Leg
	22	Coca-Cola Cup	2nd Round, 1st Leg
	28/29	C1, C2, C3	1st Round, 2nd Leg
October	06	Coca-Cola Cup	2nd Round, 2nd Leg
	19/20	C1, C2, C3	2nd Round, 1st Leg
	27	Coca-Cola Cup	3rd Round
November	02/03	C1, C2, C3	2nd Round, 2nd Leg
	13	FA Challenge Cup	1st Round Proper
	24	Champions' League	Series one matches
	23/24	C3	3rd Round, 1st Leg
December	01	Coca-Cola Cup	4th Round
	04	FA Challenge Cup	2nd Round Proper
	08	Champions' League	Series two matches
	07/08	C3	3rd Round, 2nd Leg
January	08	FA Challenge Cup	3rd Round Proper
	12	Coca-Cola Cup	5th Round
	29	FA Challenge Cup	4th Round Proper
February	13/16	Coca-Cola Cup	Semi-Final, 1st Leg
	19	FA Challenge Cup	5th Round Proper
	23/27	Coca-Cola Cup	Semi-Final, 2nd Leg
March	02	Champions' League	Series three matches
	01/02	C2, C3	Quarter-Finals, 1st Leg
	12	FA Challenge Cup	6th Round Proper
	16	Champions' League	Series four matches
	15/16	C2, C3	Quarter-Finals, 2nd Leg
	27	Coca-Cola Cup	Final
	30	Champions' League	Series five matches
	29/30	C2, C3	Semi-Finals, 1st Leg
April	10	FA Challenge Cup	Semi-Final
	13	Champions' League	Series six matches
	12/13	C2, C3	Semi-Finals, 2nd Leg
	27	C1	Semi-Finals †
	26/28	C3	Final, 1st Leg
May	04	C2	Final
	14	FA Challenge Cup	Final
	11	C3	Final, 2nd Leg
	18	C1	Final

† Champions' Cup Semi-Finals played as single tie on grounds of the clubs finishing top of their respective Champions' League groups.